LITTLE DID THEY KNOW . . .

Nathan put his arms around Anna. "I never want to lose you, my love."

"You'll never lose me, Nathan." Anna pressed her mouth against his. "I love you. I'll never stop loving you."

Her hands went around his neck and their bodies molded to each other. Nathan lifted her up and carried her to the bed. The smell of night-blooming jasmine wafted through the room and the warm night breeze rustled the curtains against the balcony doors.

"I want you so much," he whispered, his mouth seeking hers. His hands touched her in ways he had never done before, and her soft moans of pleasure drove him wild. She opened herself to him and he gave himself to her completely.

"Nathan," she whispered, digging her nails into his back, "I can't wait any longer."

Their bodies moved together in a dance of passion. "My God, Anna," Nathan whispered, his arms encircling her, "I could die a happy man right now."

SWEET MEDICINE'S PROPHECY
by Karen A. Bale

#1: SUNDANCER'S PASSION (2790, $3.95)
Stalking Horse was the strongest and most desirable of the tribe, and Sun Dancer surrounded him with her spell-binding radiance. But the innocence of their love gave way to passion—and passion, to betrayal. Would their relationship ever survive the ultimate sin?

#2: LITTLE FLOWER'S DESIRE (2791, $3.95)
Taken captive by savage Crows, Little Flower fell in love with the enemy, handsome brave Young Eagle. Though their hearts spoke what they could not say, they could only dream of what could never be. . . .

#3: WINTER'S LOVE SONG (2792, $3.95)
The dark, willowy Anaeva had always desired just one man: the half-breed Trenton Hawkins. But Trenton belonged to two worlds—and was torn between two women. She had never failed on the fields of war; now she was determined to win on the battleground of love!

#4: SAVAGE FURY (2793, $3.95)
Aeneva's rage knew no bounds when her handsome mate Trent commanded her to tend their tepee as he rode into danger. But under cover of night, she stole away to be with Trent and share whatever perils fate dealt them.

#5: SUN DANCER'S LEGACY (2804, $3.95)
Aeneva's and Trenton's adopted daughter Anna becomes the light of their lives. As she grows into womanhood, she falls in love with blond Steven Randall. Together they discover the secrets of their passion, the bitterness of betrayal—and fight to fulfill the prophecy that is Anna's birthright.

#6: CHEYENNE SURRENDER (2789, $3.95)
Anna and Nathan were too much in love to notice when the dark, brooding stranger stole Anna's sacred Cheyenne medicine pouch. But when the stranger forces Anna to ride away with him, Nathan doesn't know which he needs more—the sacred medicine to stop his burning cholera or Anna.

Available wherever paperbacks are sold, or order direct from the Publisher. Send cover price plus 50¢ per copy for mailing and handling to Zebra Books, Dept. 2789, 475 Park Avenue South, New York, N.Y. 10016. Residents of New York, New Jersey and Pennsylvania must include sales tax. DO NOT SEND CASH.

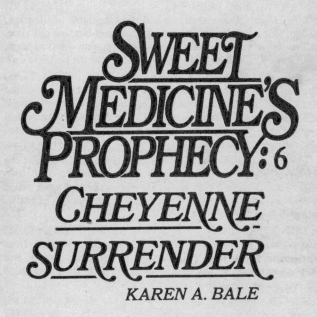

SWEET MEDICINE'S PROPHECY: 6
CHEYENNE SURRENDER

KAREN A. BALE

ZEBRA BOOKS
KENSINGTON PUBLISHING CORP.

*For my brother, Michael.
I'm proud of you—
the first step is always the hardest.*

Chapter I

The cool morning breeze blew through the large oaks, the leaves and branches brushing against each other, making a rustling sound. Nathan looked at the scaffoldings that stood side by side on the hill, and the bodies of his mother, Aeneva, a full-blooded Cheyenne, and his father, Trenton, who had been half Arapaho and had been reared with the Cheyenne. For almost ten years they had lived what could be termed a civilized life in Arizona, but had both remained Indians at heart, and Nathan couldn't put them under the ground now that they were dead. He knew he had to say farewell to them the Cheyenne way.

He tested the scaffoldings, then brought some of his parents' personal possessions to place beside them. When his father and mother walked the Hanging Road on their way to Seyan, he wanted them to have their favorite things. It was impossible, he had heard as a boy, for a person to live in Seyan for all eternity without his own favorite possessions. As he hung his father's knife on the scaffolding, he felt tears flood his eyes. His father had taught him so much, had given him so much, had loved him so much. He was not prepared to go on without his guidance. He continued the solemn act of putting his father's prized possessions all around the scaffolding until he was finished. Then he turned to his mother. Aeneva. The word meant "winter" in Cheyenne. Her parents had named her Aeneva because she had been born during a horrible snowstorm and yet she had seemed to blossom. Aeneva was not really his mother by blood but, as she had once told him, if she had borne him herself, she could not have loved him more. Nathan cradled the precious things in his arms and rested his head against the wood of the scaffolding. Aeneva had been more than a mother to him—she had been a friend, a wise one, one who had always seemed to know the right answers. He had been able to talk to her about anything and know that she would still love him.

He wiped his face with the sleeve of his shirt and began hanging Aeneva's possessions on the scaffolding. His hands trembled and he shook his head. "I cannot," he said sadly, sitting down under one of the shady oaks. "I cannot say good-bye to you and father." He rested his head on his knees, trying to figure out how his life had become so complicated in so short a time. If only he'd never left for California all those years ago, perhaps things would be different today. "Help me, Aeneva. Help me to think clearly. I need your guidance, mother." It still made no sense to him that his parents were dead. It wasn't like the old days; this was the 1870s. There were new medicines now. He should have been able to help them.

Nathan let his thoughts take him back. It was time to go over the events in his mind. Perhaps then he would know if he could have done something differently.

Trenton and Aeneva had loved each other since they were children, but events had conspired to keep them apart. Trenton married when he was still only a boy, and the result of that union was Nathan. When Nathan's mother died, Trenton went back to the Cheyenne to find

Aeneva. They were still in love, and they lived for a while in peace until their camp was raided by Comancheros and Aeneva was taken to Mexico to be sold. Her owner took her as his mistress, and they had a child together, a son named Roberto. Trenton eventually found Aeneva and took her home. They left Cheyenne country with their two sons, Nathan, age six, and the baby, Roberto, and headed west, settling in Arizona. They both loved the country, and built a good life for themselves and their boys.

Ten years passed, and they were on their way to visit California when they encountered a wagon train and a cholera epidemic. Aeneva could not leave the people to die, so she stayed to help them, while Trenton put the boys on a stage to California. Aeneva saved an eight-year-old girl, Anna, and her father, Patrick O'Leary.

The boys made it to San Francisco and immediately got into trouble. Roberto ran away, and before Nathan could stop him he had made his way into a cockfight. There was a fight, and an older man tried to hurt Roberto. Nathan, defending his brother, was shot and knifed; Roberto was murdered and thrown into the bay. Nathan was rescued and looked after by a Chinese gentleman named Chin, who helped him regain his physical and emotional strength. He wrote to his parents, but when there was no reply he assumed that they blamed him for Roberto's death. He felt he had nothing to live for—except revenge.

Ten more years passed. Nathan became quite wealthy, mining gold for many years. While seeking revenge on the man who had killed Roberto, Nathan met Anna O'Leary who, at first unknown to him, had been reared by his father and Aeneva. They fell in love.

Before they married, Nathan wanted to go home and make peace with his parents. He felt he must go alone, so he persuaded Anna to stay in San Francisco. Nathan enjoyed his time with his parents and the three of them

9

spent days getting to know each other again. It was as if he had never been gone. But their joy wasn't to last for long. While his parents were visiting neighbors, they were exposed to a deadly fever which would kill them both within weeks. There was nothing Nathan could do but watch them grow weaker. He had hated it. He had almost wished that someone had murdered them; revenge was easier to deal with than fate.

Aeneva had called out many times for Roberto, and then realized that he wasn't there. She had held onto Nathan's hand and told him what a good son he had been. He had cried and, as always, she had wiped away the tears. Both of his parents had begged him not to send for Anna; neither of them wanted her to see them suffer. So he had acquiesced and had taken care of them himself.

He smiled as he thought of his father. Trenton had tried to play cards when he had the strength, and he smiled when he beat Nathan. He also told Nathan that he was prouder of him than he could possibly know. Nathan nodded his head and began to cry. He had cried a lot during that two weeks, but it was over now.

He stood up and finished hanging Aeneva's possessions on the scaffolding, then climbed to the top to make sure her body was wrapped snugly in the buffalo robe her grandmother had made for her when she was a girl. Nathan opened her hand, poured some dirt into it, then closed it into a fist. "I will miss you, my mother. You gave me guidance, wisdom, strength, and love. If ever I have a child I hope that I can show him the kind of love you have shown me." He kissed Aeneva on the cheek and covered her face with the robe, making sure it was securely fastened to the scaffolding. He climbed down and walked to his father, reaching down to pick up more dirt. He opened his father's hand and poured in the dirt, closing it into a fist as he had Aeneva's. "I will miss you, father. It does not seem possible that you are gone, but at

10

least I know that you and Aeneva will live happily in Seyan with your parents and grandparents. And you will see Roberto. Tell him I am sorry. I never meant for anything to happen to him." Nathan rested his head on his father's chest for a moment, then looked at his face once more. "Thank you for all that you have given me, father. I hope that you can be proud of me. I love you. *Nesta-va-hose-voomatse*. I will see you again." Nathan fastened Trenton's robe securely around his face and body and climbed down from the scaffolding.

He stood on the ground below and looked up past the scaffoldings, to the great expanse of sky beyond. He slowly lifted his arms. "Oh, Great Father, please let these two people have a safe journey on the Hanging Road, the road where all footprints point the same way. Grant them peace in their new life, for they surely deserve it. Please look favorably upon them, as I'm sure you have their parents and grandparents. They are bringing dirt from the earth to prove they have lived their life here, and they are bringing their prized possessions. Help them to find what they could not find here on earth—true peace. And please, Great Father, help them to find my brother Roberto. They all deserve to be happy." Nathan looked at the scaffoldings once more, then turned to walk down the hill, his mind too occupied to notice the dim outline of the stranger in the rocks above, who watched and studied Nathan as a hawk watches it prey.

Nathan watched Anna as she walked down the hill from the burial ground. It had been over a month since his parents' death and he still hadn't come to grips with his loss. As Anna got closer, he could see the tears that streaked her face. Her deep blue eyes were angry, and a strand of her long dark hair blew across her face.

"You should have sent for me, Nathan," she said

angrily. She continued on past him, stomping through the low, prickly sage as though it were nothing more than delicate wildflowers, swinging her arms in long, defiant arcs.

Nathan got up and followed her, reaching out to grab her arm. "Would you wait a minute?"

Anna yanked her arm free. "No, I won't wait. Why should I? You didn't wait for me!" Anna continued on and Nathan let her go.

He watched as she strode down the hill into the valley. Her dark hair swirled around her shoulders and he could imagine the scowl that covered her lovely face. Of course, he didn't blame her at all for being angry. He knew how he would have felt had the situation been reversed.

Nathan started on down the hill but stopped suddenly. A strange feeling had come over him. He turned around and looked back up the hill, shielding his eyes against the sun. Was there something in the rocks? He couldn't see. He shook his head. It was probably his imagination, or possibly it was a mountain cat. He was jumpy these days; he couldn't seem to calm down. He walked to the tree where his horse was tethered and found Anna sitting on the ground, chewing a long stalk of wild grass.

"What were you looking at up there?"

"Nothing."

"Nothing? Nathan, I know you better than that."

"As I said, it was nothing. Probably a mountain cat."

"I like those cats. If it hadn't been for one of those mountain cats, you and I might never have gotten together. Remember?"

Nathan nodded. How could he forget? Anna had run away into the hills the night she'd learned that Nathan was Trenton's son—and therefore, almost like a brother to her. He and everyone else had searched for her. He'd found her at night, in a tree, scared to death by an

12

enormous mountain lion. They'd spent the night in a cave and had made love. It was a night Nathan would never forget.

"I see you do remember," Anna said with a knowing smile.

"Of course I remember." Nathan squinted his eyes. "It's strange, Anna."

"What?"

"That you and I fell in love. It doesn't seem—right, somehow."

"What's the matter with you, Nathan? Are you saying you don't want to marry me?"

"Anna, I'm serious. According to our Indian ways, I'm your older brother."

"No, you're not. We're not related by blood. We weren't even raised in the same house at the same time! Your parents felt sorry for me and they raised me, but that doesn't make me your sister. Nathan, what's the matter with you?"

Nathan shook his head. "I don't know, Anna. I still can't believe they're dead."

Anna moved closer to Nathan. "I know. I feel the same way. They were more family to me than my real father ever was. And how they loved you, Nathan!"

"I think I disappointed them. I let Roberto get killed and then I fell in love with you. It doesn't make sense, somehow."

"Let it go, Nathan. Roberto's been dead for ten years. Your parents never blamed you for that. And as for us, I know they were happy we fell in love. They loved us both very much."

Nathan got up. "I don't know, Anna. I just don't know." Nathan untied his horse and swung up. "I'm going to ride for a bit. I'll see you back at the ranch a little later."

Nathan was gone before Anna could say a word. She

watched as he rode away, and fear started to creep up on her. Had she lost not only Trenton and Aeneva, but Nathan as well? She untied her horse and started walking, leading the animal. She turned and looked back into the rocks, wondering if Nathan had been imagining things. Maybe he was overtired. Maybe it had all been too much for him. She continued walking. She, too, had not yet been able to accept the fact that Trenton and Aeneva were dead.

Anna's real mother had died when Anna was young, and her father was a drunk who had taken her from town to town, then left her with Aeneva and Trenton. She had not heard from him since. She had spent only ten years with Trenton and Aeneva, but they had made all the difference in her life. She had loved them more than she thought it possible to love anyone. She could imagine what Nathan was going through.

Anna swung up on her horse and rode, digging her knees into her mount, feeling the wind against her face, and the freedom that only riding could give her. She smiled as she imagined Aeneva as a young girl, studying to be a warrior, proud, tall, beautiful, yet every bit as deadly as many of the boys. And the only boy who was not afraid of her was Trenton. Anna imagined their love to have been like no other. She wondered if she and Nathan would ever share a love like that. She slowed her horse as she saw a rider rapidly approaching. It was Jake from the ranch.

"What is it, Jake?"

"It's Mr. Nathan. He's gone loco. He says he's going to burn the house down."

Anna kicked her mount and headed toward the ranch, riding as hard as she could. As they rode into the courtyard, she jumped off the horse before he stopped, and ran up the steps to the ranch house. The front door was wide open. Nathan was in the living room, throwing things around like a wild man.

"Nathan!" She ran to him, taking a picture out of his hand. "What's the matter with you?"

Nathan backed up, his eyes searching wildly around the room. "It's my fault. Everything is my fault. I just want to get rid of everything. I want to burn it. I want everything out of here!"

"Well I don't. Please, sit down, Nathan." Anna's voice echoed through the room. "Trenton and Aeneva wouldn't want you to act this way. This isn't like you."

"What is like me? I don't know anymore. For sixteen years I was Nathan Hawkins; for the next ten years I was Steven Randall. For the past few months I don't know who I've been. All I know is that I can't deal with this any longer. I've got to get away. I've got to get away, Anna." Nathan sank down against the wall, his head hanging loosely.

Anna knelt down next to him and felt his head; he was burning up. His eyes were glazed and he wasn't making sense. "Nathan, can you remember anything about the fever that Trenton and Aeneva had?"

"I don't know," Nathan mumbled softly, closing his eyes.

"I'll be right back."

Anna ran out on the steps and found Jake waiting for her. "Is he all right, Miss Anna?"

"I don't know, Jake. Can you tell me anything about the sickness that Trenton and Aeneva had? Anything, Jake?"

"They was both real delirious and ran real high fevers. Mr. Nathan couldn't hardly get them to drink or eat anything."

"I need your help, Jake. I think Nathan has the same fever that killed his parents."

"No," Jake replied sadly, rumpling the old hat he held between his hands.

"I want you to see if you can get the doctor to come on out here, and on your way home from town I want you to stop by Clare's, Mrs. Richardson's, and tell her about Nathan and tell her that I need her help. Also, before you go, bring in some buckets of water and have two of the men carry Nathan up to his room." Anna headed back into the house. "Thank you, Jake."

While two ranch hands carried Nathan upstairs, Anna tried to mix one of Aeneva's medicines. Aeneva had been a healer and Anna had watched her many times, but she had never fully understood how to mix all the different herbs and roots and plants together. Now, she wished she had paid more attention. Anna looked through all of Aeneva's containers and baskets, but she couldn't find the mixture she was looking for. It was the medicine she saved for the worst sicknesses, a mixture she had brought from the Cheyenne. "Of course!" Anna muttered to herself. The medicine was in a pouch that Aeneva either wore or kept with her always. She ran upstairs to check on Nathan. He was asleep. She asked one of the ranch hands to stay close and make sure he didn't leave his room. She quickly mounted her horse and rode out to the hill where the scaffoldings had been erected. She knew that was where Nathan had put Aeneva's medicine pouch.

She rode quickly up the hill, dismounted, and looked all around the scaffolding, but she couldn't find the pouch. She carefully climbed to the top, taking a deep breath as she got close to Aeneva's body. "Forgive me, Aeneva, but I know that you, of all people, will understand that I need this medicine to make your son well. You must help me." Anna searched the robe but the pouch was nowhere to be found. Was it possible that it was hanging from another part of the scaffolding? As she leaned over, she froze, unable to move.

"Is this what you're looking for?"

Anna stared at the stranger below her, dressed all in black, his face partially covered by a black hat. "That doesn't belong to you!" Anna's initial fear fled when she realized this man had defiled Aeneva's burial site. She climbed down the scaffolding and held out her hand. "Please give it back; it doesn't belong to you."

"And does it belong to you?" His voice was rich and deep but it held a note of—what? Contempt, perhaps?

"No, but it belongs to my mother."

"So why were you trying to take it?"

"Because I need it."

"You are beautiful, Anna," the stranger responded.

"How did you know my name? Who are you?"

"That's not important right now, but apparently this is." He held out the pouch. "What will you give me for it?"

"Nothing. I won't give you anything for it. It belongs to my family."

"It also belongs to *my* family."

Anna looked at the man again. He was tall, his skin and hair were dark, and his eyes were almost black. The hat made him appear older than he really was. Anna stepped forward and stared at the handsome young face in front of her. The man was Mexican; there was no doubt about it, but there was also no doubt that he was part Indian. He had the chiseled features of many of the Cheyenne she had known. More than that, he had the kind of beauty that only a very few men possess and can still be called handsome. *This was Aeneva's son. This was Roberto.* "It's you, isn't it?" she whispered. "You're not dead." Before she could stop herself, Anna threw her arms around the young man and hugged him fiercely. "You are what Nathan needs to make him well."

"I will make him well?"

"He has always blamed himself for your death. He has agonized over it."

17

"What about this?" He held up Aeneva's pouch.

"That is the medicine that will make him well, but once he recognizes you—"

"I'll sell you the medicine."

"Are you crazy? You're his brother. Don't you want to help him?"

"Why should I want to help him? He never helped me. I notice that he made it out of that stinking place just fine."

Anna shook her head. "I don't understand why you hate Nathan, but I don't have time to stand around and argue with you. If you don't give me that pouch I'll find another way to make him well." Anna reached for the reins but Roberto grabbed her arm.

"I'll sell you the medicine for a price. Surely, no price is too much to make your beloved well."

"What is your price?"

Roberto smiled, revealing straight white teeth and a beautiful yet malevolent smile. "You."

"What?"

"You are my price. Marry me and I will give you the medicine that will save my brother's life."

Anna backed away, scowling. "The Roberto I heard about would never ask such a price. He would willingly give anything to his brother to save his life. And before you tell me that Nathan left you in Chinatown, try to recall who got you both in trouble in the first place. It was you, Roberto. Nathan only tried to protect you, but you nearly managed to get both of you killed. You cannot possibly be Aeneva's son. No son of hers would act with such hatred toward his own brother." Anna grabbed the reins of the horse. "I will find another way to make Nathan well." She mounted her horse, but Roberto held onto the reins.

"I think you'll change your mind when you see how quickly he slips away from you. I'll be here every day at noon for the next three days. If by the third day you have not come, I'll take the medicine and you'll never hear from me or see me again." He let go of the reins. "You will also never see your beloved Nathan again."

Anna pulled her horse away and rode as fast as she could, not daring to look back at the evil man who held Nathan's life in his hands.

Anna laid the cool cloth on Nathan's head, watching as he tossed and turned on the bed. His fever had risen and he was nearly out of his mind with pain. The doctor had ridden out with Jake. He examined Nathan and was sure that Nathan had the same fever that had killed Trenton and Aeneva. Nothing could be done except to try to get him to drink fluids and keep him as comfortable as possible. If he made it through the first week, the doctor said, there was a good chance he would live. Anna rested her head on Nathan's chest, listening to his rapid heartbeat and his raspy breathing. She didn't know what she would do if Nathan died. She felt a hand on her head. It was Clare.

"Here, I want you to have some of this soup. We don't need you to get sick too. I'll look after Nathan."

Anna smiled and took Clare's hand. They had built a tenuous friendship out of love for the same man. "Thank you, Clare. You've been such a help."

"I want him to make it too, Anna. I've always loved him, you know."

"I know."

"Do you?"

"Yes," Anna said, "I'd feel the same way if something were ever to happen to Garrett. I love him with all my heart."

"But you love Nathan more."

"Yes." She looked at Nathan. "I don't think I can go

on if something happens to him, Clare."

"Don't talk like that. Nathan's as strong as a bull. And don't I know it?" She stopped, realizing that she was bringing up a delicate part of her past, but when her eyes met Anna's there was no anger there. "Sorry. I didn't mean anything by it."

"It's all right. I know you and Nathan share a past. I'm a little more grown-up now than I was a year ago."

"We all are, darling."

Nathan flailed around on the bed, striking his hand against the nightstand. "Oh, God, he's cut himself! You'd better get some of that salve your mother used to use," Clare said, trying to calm Nathan down.

Anna rummaged through the containers she had brought up to Nathan's room and found the salve. She opened the top and crinkled her nose. "God, this stuff stinks. My father used to say that this was really only bear grease mixed in with cow manure." She held firmly onto Nathan's hand, wiping off the blood and applying the salve.

"There, he's quieted down," Clare said. "But, Anna, he's burning up again. If we can't break this fever—"

"I know." Anna put the salve back and leaned against the wall. She closed her eyes and an image of a third scaffolding came into her mind. "Clare, I have to ask you a question."

Clare walked over to Anna with the soup. "You take a few spoonfuls of soup and I'll answer anything."

Anna complied until the bowl was empty. "Clare, something strange has happened."

"What? What is it?"

"Roberto, Nathan's little brother, is alive."

"I'm not sure I heard you right."

"You heard me right." Anna paced around the room, clenching and unclenching her hands as she related her meeting with Roberto to Clare. "What should I do?"

20

"He doesn't sound like any brother of Nathan's. He sounds like a scoundrel."

"But he has the medicine that could save Nathan's life."

"Wait a minute. Don't you think Aeneva would have used this medicine on herself and Trenton? It didn't save them, Anna."

"I know. I thought about that. It has to be mixed with other things and then brewed. If she was too sick, she couldn't have done that for herself or Trenton."

"Couldn't she have told someone else?"

"Look at Nathan. He just started acting this way this morning. God only knows what he'll be like in a week. I don't think Aeneva had a chance to use the medicine."

"Is there any way we could sneak up on this man and take the medicine from him?"

"No. The only way is to do what he says."

"But why would he want to marry you? He doesn't even know you."

"I think he holds Nathan responsible for what happened to him in San Francisco. He doesn't realize that Nathan almost died, too. I don't know, Clare. The only thing I know for sure is that the medicine works. I've seen it. Aeneva used it on me and my father when we were dying from cholera. It might be Nathan's only chance. I'll do anything to save him."

"Including marrying his brother?"

Anna shrugged her shoulders. "If I marry him, it doesn't mean I have to live with him. Surely, a judge will understand the circumstances once Nathan is well."

"I know a judge who might help us out. Just do what the man wants you to do for now and then when Nathan gets well you can explain everything to him."

"I'm going out there now, Clare."

"Are you crazy? It's the middle of the night. There's no telling what's out there."

21

"I don't care. I know he's in those rocks somewhere and I'm going to find him. I need that medicine, Clare."

Clare took Anna's arm. "Be careful, Anna. I don't want you to get hurt."

"I won't get hurt. You just take care of Nathan until I get back."

Anna sat up on the rocks that overlooked Trenton's and Aeneva's burial site. The moon was in its quarter so the night was barely lit. She wasn't afraid. Perhaps it was because she felt guarded by Trenton and Aeneva. She knew Roberto would find her if she waited long enough. She heard him jump to the rock behind her but she didn't move.

"So, you decided to take me up on my offer?"

"Yes, but I want to get some things straight first. I want to know why you want to marry me."

"That's my business."

"It's my business if I agree to marry you."

"You want my brother to get well. I want you. It's simple."

"No it's not. You don't even know me. You blame Nathan for what happened in San Francisco, don't you, 'Berto?"

"Don't call me that! Don't ever call me that!"

Anna nodded to herself. That had been Nathan's nickname for Roberto when they were children. "You think that if you marry me it will destroy Nathan? You don't know your brother very well, Roberto. He's much stronger than that. He can live without me."

"And I say he can't."

"Even if you do marry me it won't change a thing."

"It will change everything, Anna."

"I won't live with you. I will still stay with Nathan."

"You will live with one man even though you are

22

legally married to another?"

"If I have to do that I will. I love Nathan more than you could ever know."

"Well then, these are my terms: you marry me and I give you the medicine. If Nathan gets well, you will leave him and go away with me. If he doesn't get well, I will have the marriage annulled."

"What do you mean, go away with you?"

"You don't think I'm going to let you stay with him, do you?"

"I won't leave him."

"You'll have to, if you want to save his life, Anna. You do want to save his life, don't you?"

"Of course I want to save his life, but I can do it without your ridiculous marriage agreement. I will find a way to save Nathan without your help."

"What will you do, Anna, call upon the Great Father to save my beloved brother? Do you think he will actually hear you?"

Anna looked at Roberto in the dim light of the moon. He didn't resemble Aeneva at all. She slapped him as hard as she could. "I hate you! I'm glad Aeneva didn't live to see what kind of man you have become." She started toward her horse, but Roberto pulled her back. "You know nothing about me, Anna."

"I know all I need to know about you. You have the ability to save your own brother and you won't do it."

"You have the ability to save him also, Anna. All you have to do is marry me. Nathan could be dying right now. You could be wasting precious time."

Anna hesitated. "All right. I'll marry you. But I will not promise you anything."

"You must promise to go away with me."

"I will promise nothing. I don't even know that you will give me the medicine. How can I trust you?"

Roberto reached into his shirt and pulled out the

pouch. "If I ride with you to the ranch and help you with Nathan, will you leave with me when he is better?"

"How can you help me?"

"I told you, you know nothing about me. I learned many things in the time I was gone. One of them was healing. I think my mother would have liked that."

"Yes, she would have." Anna walked to her horse, patting his shoulder. "All right, Roberto, I will marry you if Nathan gets well. I don't know why you are doing this, but I don't have the time to find out. But understand one thing—you will have me, but you will never have my love. Never."

"Agreed."

Anna mounted her horse and headed down the hill toward the valley and the ranch house. She rode as quickly as she could, thinking only of Nathan and praying that Aeneva's medicine would help him. She tried not to think of Roberto or the way he followed her in the night. She tried to concentrate on Nathan. She knew that in her heart any life with Roberto couldn't compare with the misery she would experience knowing that Nathan was dead and she had done nothing to help him.

She reached the ranch house ahead of Roberto and waited for him at the top of the porch. She was silent as she led him into Aeneva's kitchen. She took down one of Aeneva's large pots, filled it with water, and hung it on the hook over the fire. Then she turned to Roberto, her hand outstretched. "May I have the pouch?"

Roberto took the pouch from around his neck and handed it to Anna. "You will need something else." He took another pouch from around his neck and sprinkled some of the contents into the pot.

Anna eyed him suspiciously. "How do I know that you didn't pour in some poison?"

"You don't know. You have to trust me."

Anna shook some of the contents of Aeneva's pouch into the pot and shook her head in frustration. "I should have paid closer attention. I don't know how to do this."

Roberto took the pouch from Anna. "I will mix the medicines. Where are her other baskets?"

"I took most of them upstairs."

"What did you plan to do with them?"

"I don't know. I suppose I thought if I threw them all together maybe they would make Nathan well."

"It doesn't work that way. Hurry, bring me all the medicines." Roberto looked around his mother's kitchen as he stirred some of the roots and herbs into the pot. It was just as he had remembered it—warm and loving. He remembered watching her make remedies for ailing neighbors, and always, Trenton would try to talk her out of it. "I am a healer," she would say. "Healers must heal." Roberto felt a vague sense of sadness as he thought of his mother and Trenton, but he wouldn't let those feelings stop him now. He had too much to accomplish.

Anna quickly returned, carrying numerous baskets and containers. Roberto looked through each one, taking a pinch of this or a dash of that. He seemed to know exactly what he was doing. He looked up at Anna as he stirred the mixture. "Don't worry, I won't poison your beloved. It will be so much more satisfying to see him suffer when I take you away with me."

"I don't believe you. I think you still love your brother but for some reason you are afraid to show it."

"If I ever loved my brother, that love died the day I was thrown into the bay."

"Roberto, surely you must see—" Anna's voice was cut off by Nathan's blood-curdling scream. She ran up the stairs, followed closely by Roberto. Anna pushed open Nathan's door. He was standing in a corner of the room, looking wild and frenzied. "Nathan," Anna said softly, walking slowly into the room. Clare was standing

25

paralyzed on the other side of the room. "It's all right, Nathan. It's Anna."

Nathan stared at her, his eyes searching frantically for an answer. "What?"

"It's Anna. Please let me help you, Nathan." Anna moved closer to Nathan, but he pushed past her, heading for the door. "Roberto, stop him!"

Roberto blocked the doorway. "Go back to your bed, Nathan." His words were slow and deliberate and the menace was obvious.

"Who are you?"

"That's not important. It is important that you go back to bed. You have to get well." He put his arms around Nathan and led him back to the bed. "Come on, you'll feel better when you lie down." Nathan's legs collapsed and Roberto held onto him, picking him up and leading him to the bed. "It's all right. You'll be all right."

Nathan sat on the edge of the bed. Sweat poured down his face and his breathing was labored. He reached his hand out to his brother. "Roberto? Is that you?" He strained to look, but he couldn't see anything. He reached out his hand again. "'Berto? I'm sorry, 'Berto. God, I'm so sorry."

Roberto crouched by the bed, helping Nathan to lie back down. "It's all right, Nate. Just lie down and rest. Everything will be all right."

"'Berto?"

"What, Nate?"

"Are ma and pa all right?"

For the first time, Roberto looked over at Anna. "Yes, they're fine. You rest now."

"I'm glad you're here, 'Berto. God, I hate it when you run away from me. . . ." Nathan drifted off to sleep.

Anna rinsed a cloth in the bedside bowl and wiped Nathan's face. She sat on the bed and stared at him. His golden-blond hair was wet and matted against his face, his normally dark skin had a deathlike pallor to it, and his eyes, those incredibly serene sky-blue eyes, wore a look of complete madness. She leaned down and kissed his cheek. "I love you, Nathan. Do you hear me? I love you." Anna felt her tears mix with the sweat on Nathan's face.

"Let me do that, honey." Clare took the cloth from Anna. "Why don't you and Roberto finish your conversation." Clare flashed Roberto an angry look as he walked past her.

Anna and Roberto went back to the kitchen. Anna poured herself a small glass of whiskey and sat down. Her hands were shaking as she lifted the glass to her mouth.

"You shouldn't be drinking that. You should be drinking tea."

Anna flashed Roberto an angry look and downed the fiery liquid, trying not to cough as it went down. "I don't need you to tell me what to drink." She tapped her glass against the table, trying to think what she should do next. "He's going to die, isn't he?"

Roberto didn't turn away from the pot. "I don't know. We'll have to see."

"You don't care anyway. I'm sure you'd like to see him dead."

"You're wrong about that, Anna. I don't want to see my brother dead."

"But you want to see him suffer. God, I hate you."

Roberto finally turned. His black eyes burned into Anna. "Hate me all you want, but it won't get Nathan well. If you want to help, stop drinking that stuff and come over here."

Anna slammed the glass down on the table and walked to the fire. "What?"

"Find me something to use as a strainer."

Anna rummaged through the shelves and found the piece of cloth Aeneva had always used to strain her

27

mixtures. "This is what your mother used."

"Good. Now get me the strainings. We'll use those on his chest."

Anna did as Roberto ordered. He seemed to know what he was doing, and in some strange way, she believed that he was trying to save Nathan's life, even if it was for the wrong reason. She held the cloth over the pot as Roberto used a cup to pour. He took the cloth from her and wrapped it up in a kitchen cloth. "Is there honey?"

"Yes. Why do you need honey?"

"It makes it go down easier."

Anna reached up into a cupboard and brought down a jar of rich, brown honey. "Shall I put some in the cup?"

"Yes, two or three spoonfuls. Also, add some of that whiskey you were drinking."

"You just told me I shouldn't drink whiskey. Now you're putting it in Nathan's tea?"

"It will help him to sleep." Roberto poured tea into the cup and mixed it with a spoon. "Carry the tea." He picked up the warm pack of herbs and led the way up the stairs to Nathan's room. He glanced at Clare as he sat on the bed next to Nathan. He unbuttoned Nathan's shirt and took it from his brother's almost lifeless body. He placed the warm pack on his chest and covered him with a blanket. "Nate, can you hear me?" He patted Nathan's cheeks with his hands. "Wake up, Nate. I want you to drink something."

Nathan moved around but he didn't open his eyes. "Come on, Nathan. You have to drink this." Roberto sat behind Nathan, trying to prop him up.

Nathan started to move. He opened his eyes and looked around the room. "'Berto?"

"I'm right beside you, Nate. I've got some tea for you to drink."

"I don't want tea, 'Berto. I want to talk to you."

"We can talk as soon as you drink this. Come on."

Roberto held the cup to Nathan's lips as Nathan sipped the liquid.

"It's good. It tastes like mother's tea."

Roberto looked at Anna. "Yes, it does. Drink it up now."

Nathan greedily drank up the tea. "Where are they? Where are mother and father?"

"They're safe, Nate. Don't worry." He laid Nathan gently on the bed. "You try to rest now."

"Don't run away again, 'Berto."

"I won't, Nate. I'll be here when you wake up."

Nathan closed his eyes. Anna walked over to him and put her hand on his head. She bent down and kissed him on the cheek. Then she tiptoed out of the room and down the stairs to the kitchen, waiting for Roberto to follow.

"What?" Roberto came up behind her. "I know you probably have something to say."

"How can you pretend to be so kind to him when you don't really care? You are a monster. Why don't you just kill him now?"

"I never said I wanted to kill him."

"What do you want then, Roberto? Is this all for revenge?"

Roberto ignored Anna, draining the rest of the tea from the large pot into a smaller pot. He hung the smaller pot on the arm over the fire. "We should try to get him to drink this every few hours. Hopefully, it will help sweat out some of the fever." He turned to Anna. "I'll sleep in the barn. If you need something, send for me." He turned and walked out of the kitchen without another word.

Anna watched Roberto as he left the room; she had no inclination to stop him and persuade him to stay in the house. As far as she was concerned, he was nothing but trouble. She shook her head in disgust. She filled a pot with water and set it on the fire, then pulled a chair over to the counter and reached up to get two china cups. She smiled as she rubbed her fingers over the smooth pink flowers. Trenton had bought the set for Aeneva when he was in St. Louis. Aeneva had been totally delighted. The fine china cups and saucers had appealed to her Indian sense of delicate beauty.

"Are you all right?" Clare walked into the kitchen.

"Yes, I was just going to make us some tea. These were Aeneva's favorite cups." She stepped down from the chair and put the cups and saucers on the table. She poured some of Aeneva's favorite tea leaves into the pot to brew. "Do you want some cake? Jake's wife sent it over." Anna sliced it and put the slices on a plate. She did as much as she could to keep herself from thinking.

"Where is he?"

Anna looked up from the table. "He's sleeping in the barn."

"Perfect place for him, if you ask me." Clare grabbed the bottle of whiskey from the table and poured some into her teacup. "For medicinal purposes only." She held her cup up to Anna and downed the contents. The whiskey didn't seem to bother her at all. "You aren't really going to marry that monster, are you?"

"What choice do I have?"

"If Nathan gets well, all you have to do is tell him you've changed your mind."

"I've thought about that, Clare, but things aren't that simple with Roberto. I'm afraid to cross him. If I don't hold up my end of the bargain, he might do something to hurt Nathan."

Clare shook her head. "I can't believe they're brothers. My God, the man is crazy. He's also a very good actor."

"What do you mean?"

"The way he was talking to Nathan, you'd think he really cared for him."

"I think he does."

"Oh, come on, Anna."

"I do. I don't think he was pretending."

"Then why does he want to hurt him?"

"I don't know the answer to that. If I did, maybe some of this would make sense."

"Anna, you can't go away with him. It would destroy Nathan."

"I don't have a choice, Clare. And maybe if I get to know him a little better I can find out why he wants to hurt Nathan so badly."

"I think you're letting yourself and Nathan in for a lot of hurt. Nothing good can come of this."

"If Nathan gets well, it will be worth it. Clare, I want you to look after Nathan when I'm gone."

"You really have gone loco. You do remember that Nathan and I were to be married last year, don't you? You also know that I still love him?"

"I know that. No one else is better qualified to take care of him."

"What am I supposed to tell him? That you've run off with his little brother, that you don't really love his brother but you did it to save his life? This is crazy!"

"You don't have to tell him anything. I'll tell him when he's well."

"I don't envy you, Anna. It's going to break his heart."

"I'm not leaving forever, Clare. Roberto may think he's gaining a wife, but he'll soon realize what a mistake he's made. I will always love Nathan and nothing will ever change that."

"What do you have in mind?"

"I'm going to make sure Roberto regrets the day he ever tried to hurt his brother. One way or another, I'll find a way to bring those two back together."

"I hope that's possible, honey."

"Anything is possible, Clare. I learned that a long time ago from Trenton and Aeneva." She thought of Ladro and Aeneva, and she thought of all the time Aeneva had spent away from Trenton, but still they had finally found their way back to each other. That was the way it would be with her and Nathan. She had to find a way back to him. Life without Nathan would be unbearable.

Chapter II

Roberto lay in the darkness, his arms folded under his head. He stretched out on the hay in the loft and thought about his plan. Once Nathan was well, he would take Anna and they would go away. At first he thought they'd go to Mexico, to the town where his father had lived with his mother. Perhaps there he could finally find a new life for himself. He would have enough money to make a good life in Mexico, and he would have a beautiful wife, one with dark skin and hair, just like him. She wouldn't be like his brother—fair-haired with light eyes. He had seen enough people like that to last him a lifetime. But he knew he couldn't go to Mexico. He had to go back to New Orleans. There was too much unfinished business there.

He turned onto his side. He knew what he was doing was wrong, but he couldn't help himself. Too many years had passed between him and Nathan and they were too different. They had always been different. Nathan had always been the fair-haired boy, while he was the illegitimate son of the man who had kidnapped his mother. Trenton tried to treat him the way he treated Nathan, but it was never the same. And it never would be the same. If there was one thing he had learned being on his own, it was that people with skin of a different color

33

were treated differently. It was something he would never forget, and something he would always resent.

Caroline had taught him that lesson well. He had loved her with his heart and soul, he had told her everything about himself, and she had made him believe she loved him. They made plans to run away together, but her father found out and Caroline accused Roberto of raping her. Her father hadn't called the law; he had handled the situation himself. He had Roberto stripped to the waist and lashed to a pole in plain view of everyone on the plantation. Then he brought Caroline outside. He wanted a public confession from Roberto, but Roberto had said nothing. He had looked into Caroline's placid blue eyes, seeking the love they had known together and hoping for some reassurance, but she only turned her back on him and walked away. Her father beat Roberto with a birch branch every time he asked him to confess, and every time Roberto refused to answer, he got beaten again. By the time Mr. Thornston was through with him, his back was ripped to pieces. Mr. Thornston had had his men throw him in the nearby swamp. But Roberto still managed to survive. He was found by a Negro family and they took him in and cared for him. He stayed with them for more than six months, until he felt strong enough to leave. But he decided on that day that he would pay back every white person for everything they had ever done to him, and that included his brother.

It took Roberto six more months to work his way out west to Arizona. During that time, he had gambled, he'd shot and killed three men, and he'd slept with numerous women, all of them white. The most satisfaction he'd ever gotten in his young life was making love to those rich white women and then taking their money and their jewels. He knew that women were immediately attracted to him; he'd found that out at the age of fourteen, on a steamer ship, when a woman twice his age had seduced

34

him. He also knew that using his looks was a quick way to make money.

When he'd arrived in Arizona, it wasn't difficult finding out about his parents and Nathan. It was amazing how much people would say for the right price. Especially Clare. She had proved to be extremely helpful. He wouldn't have known about Anna if Clare hadn't told him about her. Now Clare would have to make sure Nathan believed that Anna had left on her own. His brother would be in pain, but Clare would be there to console him.

He closed his eyes tightly as he recalled Nathan as he had looked that night. He did look as if he were dying. He wanted to hurt Nathan, but he didn't want him to die. In spite of himself, he was touched by Nathan's attempts to reach out for him. But he wouldn't be fooled by such displays of affection ever again.

He thought of Anna. Life with her wouldn't be easy, but it would be worth it. Once he took her to Louisiana and showed her around, Caroline Thornston would be devastated. And so would Nathan.

Roberto finally felt his body relax. Soon Nathan would be well and Roberto would take what was his, as well as Anna, and he would set his plan in motion. Revenge would be sweet.

A week had passed, and Anna felt as if she would drop. She had been up most nights making sure Nathan drank the tea and was comfortable. She had known Nathan only as a strong, dependable man. It was very difficult for her to see him so helpless. He looked like a little boy, and she was afraid to leave him. She couldn't face the idea that he might die; she refused to believe that was a possibility anymore.

By the middle of the second week, Nathan began to ask

for things. He would wake up and ask for water or some tea, or he would ask to see Roberto. Roberto would sit with Nathan and talk to him as though nothing was wrong, and Anna hated him for that. But Clare had been a real comfort through it all, and Anna knew she had been wrong about Clare. She had turned out to be a good friend to both her and Nathan.

Anna was dozing in the chair next to Nathan's bed when she felt a hand on hers. She opened her eyes. Nathan was staring at her, a strange look in his eyes.

She sat forward in the chair. "Nathan, are you all right?"

"They're dead, aren't they? Mother and father are dead?"

Anna took his hand. "Yes. It's been about six weeks now since it happened. Do you understand what happened to you?"

Nathan looked around the room and down at the bed. "I guess I've been sick."

"You almost died, Nathan. I almost lost you." Anna sat on the bed, putting her head on Nathan's chest. "I don't know what I would have done if I'd lost you."

Nathan's arm went around Anna. "It's all right, Anna. I won't be leaving you for a long time now. Nothing will separate us."

Anna closed her eyes tightly, trying to stop the tears that formed. "I do love you, Nathan. I love you with all my heart."

"I know that. I'm sorry you had to go through this."

Anna wiped her face. "It doesn't matter now that you're well." She brushed the hair from his eyes. "Are you hungry?"

"I could manage some soup, I think. Anna, I didn't dream about 'Berto, did I? He is here, isn't he?"

"Yes, he's here."

"Where is he? I'd like to talk to him."

"He took Clare home. She's been here most of the time, helping me out. I told her to go home and get some rest."

"He's alive. I can't believe it. I just wish mother and father could have seen him."

Anna suppressed an angry look. "Yes, it is too bad." She stood up. "I'm going to get you some soup. Is there anything else?"

Nathan held out his arms. "Come here again." Anna lay on the bed next to him and he held her tightly. "God, it feels so good to hold you in my arms. My mind was crazy. I had a dream that I lost you again."

Anna buried her face in Nathan's chest. "No matter what happens, I will always love you, Nathan. Nothing will ever change that."

"You sound awfully serious."

"You almost died. That tends to make me serious."

"I'm sorry." Nathan kissed Anna's head. "We have plans to make, you know."

"What plans?"

"What plans? Have you forgotten already that we were planning to be married?"

Anna sat up and gazed lovingly into Nathan's eyes. "I haven't forgotten."

"I was thinking maybe we should wait before we move to California. I'd like to stay here for a while. I don't want to sell this place."

"I don't blame you."

"So you wouldn't mind living here?"

"Why would I mind? This was my home too, remember?"

"We could do all the things pa wanted to do, and Roberto could live with us. What do you think?"

"If that's what you want."

"What's wrong?"

"Nothing's wrong. I'm just tired."

"Why don't you get some sleep? I'll be fine until 'Berto comes back. We'll talk more later." He took Anna's face in his hands and kissed her cheek. "I do love you, Kathleen Anna O'Leary."

Anna couldn't contain a smile. "I love you too, Nathan Hawkins." She stood up and walked to the door, glancing back at Nathan as she walked out. She decided right then that there was no way she would ever go away with Roberto. She didn't owe him anything. She would stay with Nathan and together they would find a way to deal with Roberto.

"When do you plan to leave?" Clare handed Roberto a snifter of brandy. She sat down on the couch next to him.

"As soon as possible."

"When is that?"

"Maybe tomorrow. Nathan seems to be coming along just fine."

"What do you plan to do with Anna? You don't really love her, do you?"

"Of course I don't love her, but I need her. She will serve a purpose."

"What purpose is that—hurting your brother?"

Roberto swirled the brandy around in the snifter and smiled, a devastatingly beautiful smile. "You are clever, Clare. I can see why poor Anna has been taken in by you. You should be an actress."

"You should talk. You played your scenes well with Nathan."

"I played at nothing. I truly wanted him to live."

"Only so you could exact your revenge." Clare sipped her brandy. "You are a strange one."

"And you aren't? You know that Nathan doesn't love you, you know he will always love Anna, yet you're

38

willing to lie to him and deceive him in order to keep him."

"Once he realizes that Anna is out of his life for good, he will gladly come to me."

"He didn't go to you last time. He went searching for Anna until he found her."

"Ah, but she was kidnapped that time," Clare said. "He felt sorry for her. This time she will have left on her own. It would injure his pride to follow a woman who didn't want him. I know Nathan."

"We'll see. I happen to think he won't give Anna up. He loves her too deeply."

"You act as if you want them to be together."

"I admire any two people who can love each other so much that they will sacrifice anything for each other," Roberto said.

"You admire Anna for loving Nathan, and yet you're still taking her with you?"

"It doesn't mean I can't admire her." Roberto sipped his brandy and looked around Clare's lavish sitting room. "If I were smart, I'd stay here and marry you. It would certainly simplify things."

Clare smiled. She reached out and ran her fingers along the smooth skin of Roberto's face. "You certainly are a handsome devil. You've got a lot of your mother in you."

"That's not what Anna says."

"Oh, Anna is too good to be true. No one is that pure."

"I think you like her, Clare, just as I do."

Clare shrugged her shoulders. "Maybe I do, but that doesn't mean I'm going to let her have Nathan. He belongs to me."

Roberto smiled again. "Yeah, you two were something, all right."

"What are you talking about?"

"I saw you both behind your father's barn when you were about fourteen years old. You two were rolling in the hay and making sounds and I couldn't get enough. I would've stayed there all day watching if I hadn't heard your father coming."

"You heard my father coming and you didn't warn us?"

"I figured you could handle it. Besides, I enjoyed watching. You'll never know what you did for me that day, Clare."

Clare playfully hit Roberto on the shoulder. "You were all of eight years old then."

"I know, but when I saw your bare breasts and those long white legs of yours, I thought I would die."

Clare lowered her eyes in mock embarrassment, but she actually enjoyed Roberto's story. In fact, she found him quite attractive. "I bet you've had your share of ladies along the way, haven't you?"

"I've done all right."

"You've also been hurt. Is that the reason you want to marry Anna? Do you want to prove something to someone?"

"Maybe." Roberto stood up, putting the glass on the round wooden table by the couch. "Look, Clare, I just need for you to keep my brother occupied until I can get Anna out of here."

"Where are you going?"

"Maybe Mexico, maybe somewhere in the south. I don't know right now."

Clare stood up. "You're lying, boy; you know exactly where you're taking Anna." She put her arms around Roberto's neck. "But I don't care, as long as she's out of Nathan's life." She pressed her mouth to Roberto's until she felt him respond. "You know, if I didn't want Nathan so much, I think I might go for his younger brother."

Roberto laughed, gently pushing Clare away from him. "I think you'd be too much for me to handle, Clare. But thanks anyway."

"Will I hear from you?"

"I'll be in touch." Roberto walked out into the darkness. It seemed to him that he was always in the darkness, always alone. He had lied to Clare. Once he and Anna left Arizona, no one would hear from them again.

Nathan stood up in the creek, shaking off the water. He was beginning to feel almost alive again. He still felt extremely weak, but he knew he would get stronger every day. He got out of the water and slipped on his pants. He looked up at the outlines of the scaffoldings on the hill. "I wish I had been able to help you, as you helped me with your medicine. But I promise you one thing, I will never let anything happen to Anna or Roberto. I will take care of them both as long as I live." He smiled to himself. He liked the feeling of having his parents close. He knew it was something that most people wouldn't understand. It was something only an Indian could understand.

He was standing by the old oak when he saw Anna ride up, practically jumping off her horse. "What do you think you're doing, Nathan Hawkins?"

"What does it look like I'm doing?"

Anna looked at Nathan. He was tall and lean, but after his illness he looked almost too thin. "You shouldn't be out here. I can't believe Jake let you ride out here by yourself."

"I'm a big boy, Anna." He moved closer to Anna. "Or don't you know that yet?"

"Stop it! This isn't funny. You almost died. You might still be sick. I couldn't stand it if—"

Nathan put his hand over Anna's mouth. He pulled her

41

into the circle of his arms. "Nothing is going to happen to me, I told you that. The Great Spirit is looking after me." He touched his lips lightly to Anna's. "I have missed you."

Anna pulled away from Nathan's grasp. "I've missed you, too, but you need to rest. Nathan, you could still come down with that fever again. Please listen to me. Go back to the ranch and rest."

"I can rest here." He pulled Anna to the trunk of the oak and sat down. "With my head in your lap." He lay down, nestling his head in Anna's lap. "I feel more peaceful now."

"What do you mean?" Anna ran her hand through Nathan's blond hair.

"Maybe that fever helped me to get rid of some of the guilt I've been carrying around about 'Berto for so long. And I know now that there was nothing I could do to help mother and father."

"I'm glad. There is no reason for you to feel guilty about anything. You did your best for Roberto, just as you did for your parents."

"I can't wait to talk with 'Berto. I want to find out where he's been and what he's been doing all this time. It's still hard to believe he's alive." He looked up at Anna, his blue eyes once again clear and bright. "Thank you for everything you did for me. I'm not sure I would've made it without you."

Anna kissed his forehead. "As I recall, you did the same thing for me when you got me off that horrid slave ship. You even managed to stay with me until I got the opium out of my system. You must love me."

"I do." Nathan pulled Anna's head down to his. His mouth touched hers lightly, caressingly. "I feel stronger already."

"What am I going to do with you?"

"Marry me, I hope, and have my children."

Anna's eyes filled with tears. "Nathan, I have to talk to you. I need your help."

Nathan sat up. "What is it?"

"It's Roberto. He—" Anna wasn't able to finish her sentence because Roberto rode up to where they were sitting.

"I thought you two would be here." He swung his right leg over the saddle and jumped down, his bright smile disguising his true feelings for Nathan. "This was always your favorite place to go, Nate. As I recall, you and Clare used to—"

"That's enough, 'Berto. I don't think Anna wants to hear about the old days with Clare."

Anna threw Roberto an angry look and stood up. "Come on, Nathan, I think you should get back now. I don't want you to tire yourself out."

Nathan smiled and stood up. "See how lucky I am, 'Berto, to have this beautiful woman care so much about me?"

"Yes, I'd say you're very lucky, big brother." He walked toward Nathan. "I'd like to talk to you, Nate. It's been a while."

"It sure has." Nathan reached out and grabbed his brother in a tight hug. "I'm so glad you're here."

"So am I."

"Why don't you go back to the ranch, Anna. I'd like to talk to 'Berto for awhile."

"No!"

"What's the matter with you? I haven't seen my brother in almost eleven years."

"I realize that, Nathan, but I don't want you to get sick again. You two can talk back at the ranch." Anna took Nathan's hand. "Please, for me."

Nathan shrugged his shoulders. "I guess we better

43

head on back. You've never seen her when she gets really mad."

"No, and I hope I don't."

The three mounted their horses, Nathan riding in the middle. He seemed as happy and careless as a young boy. "We do need to talk, 'Berto."

"I know."

"I mean we need to talk about what mother and father left. You get half of everything, you know."

Roberto seemed genuinely surprised. "What do you mean? They left us some money?"

"Not a lot, but enough to help each one of us out."

"What do you mean each one of us?"

"You were never written out of their will, 'Berto. I think they always hoped you'd come back."

Roberto slowed his horse to a walk. "Your father left money to me in his will?"

"What do you mean, my father? He was your father too. He was as much your father as Aeneva was my mother. What in hell's the matter with you?"

"I don't know. I just didn't expect this."

"Well, you get half of this ranch, half of some property they own in California, and half of all the money they left. You won't be rich but you'll be pretty well off."

"Surprised, Roberto?" Anna couldn't keep the contempt from her voice.

Roberto ignored Anna. "Maybe we could talk later, Nate. I need some time to think."

"Why don't you just come back to the ranch with us? We can talk there. We both need to sort out some things. Hell, I still can't get over the fact that you're all grown up and as tall as I am."

"Taller," Roberto couldn't resist the jibe.

"We'll see. But I bet I can still beat you at arm wrestling."

"I was only eleven years old when you last saw me. I've changed a lot since then. I wouldn't count on anything if I were you, Nate."

Anna touched Nathan's arm. "Nathan, please."

Nathan nodded his head. "I'll talk to you later, little brother. By the way, I'm glad you're home."

Roberto watched Nathan and Anna as they rode off and, for the first time, he had conflicting feelings. It was hard for him to believe that his mother and Trenton had not forgotten about him, and what was even more incredible to him, Nathan seemed so genuinely eager to share everything with him. It didn't make sense, or at least it didn't make sense to a young man who had been through as much as he had in the last eleven years. His life with his mother, Trenton and Nathan had seemed like a lifetime ago, and something that hadn't seemed entirely real. The only thought on his mind for the longest time was survival. He knew nothing else. And when he had finally found a place where he felt somewhat accepted and loved, he had been almost totally destroyed. He would never forgive Caroline or her father for that, and he would never forgive Nathan for not trying to find him. In spite of his slight misgivings, he decided, his plan would remain the same—he would take Anna away from Nathan and make him suffer as he had suffered. Suffering seemed to be the only feeling with which he was completely intimate, and suffering was what he would give to others who tried to get close to him.

Anna lay on her bed, trying to think of a way to tell Nathan about Roberto. He was so happy to see his brother; she didn't want to destroy that happiness. But she would not, could not, go away with Roberto. She despised him more and more every day.

A knock on her door woke her from her reverie. "Who is it?"

Roberto opened the door and stepped inside the room. "Clare wants to see you."

Anna sat up on the bed. "Why would Clare send you to get me?"

"She's sick. I think she might have what Nathan had."

"Oh, God." Anna stood up. "Do you have the medicine?"

"Yes, I have everything we need."

"Let me tell Nathan where we're going."

"No, he's sleeping. He needs the rest."

Anna grabbed a piece of paper from her desk and quickly wrote a note. She walked down the hall and opened the door. Nathan was sleeping soundly. She left the note on the table next to the bed. She bent down and kissed his cheek. "I love you," she said softly. She walked back into the hall and followed Roberto down the stairs and out of the house. The horses were ready and Roberto had a saddlebag thrown over his.

They rode in silence to Clare's, neither one wishing to speak to the other. Anna's only concern at the moment was Clare, and making sure that she was well. It took more than an hour to reach Clare's. Anna quickly dismounted and ran up the stairs to the ornate house. She banged on the door, but she didn't wait for Celestina, the maid, to answer. She walked inside. "Clare? Clare, where are you?"

"I'm in here, Anna," Clare's voice came from the study.

Anna hurried into the study to find Clare standing by the fireplace, a strange man standing next to her. "I'm sorry. I didn't mean to interrupt anything, but Roberto told me you were ill."

"I'm not ill, Anna." Clare looked past Anna to

Roberto, who quietly shut the door.

"What is it? What's the matter?" Anna quickly turned around to look at Roberto. "Who is this man?"

"He's a friend of Clare's."

"This is Judge Wilkins. He has been kind enough to do me a favor."

Anna looked from Clare to Roberto. "And what favor is that, Clare?"

"I think you'd better ask him."

Roberto stepped forward. "It's time, Anna. Judge Wilkins is going to marry us."

"No!" Anna moved away from Roberto and back toward the door. "You can't make me do this."

"I can and I will. I kept my promise. Now it's your turn to do the same."

"Never! I'll never marry you."

Roberto's eyes hardened. "Clare, Judge, would you mind leaving us alone for a few minutes?" Roberto closed the door when they left. "You don't have a choice, Anna. Either you marry me or I will kill Nathan."

"You wouldn't do that. I saw the way you took care of him. You still love him."

"You're wrong. I don't love him. I don't love anyone. I don't know how to love anymore." His black eyes seared into Anna's. "I'm not playing games with you, Anna. Either you marry me right now or I'll ride back to the ranch and I'll give Nathan a nice cup of hot tea with enough poison in it to kill ten men."

Anna covered her face with her hands. "I can't believe this."

"You knew this would happen. Did you think I would forget about our bargain?"

"This can't be happening. Roberto, please. Nathan and I finally have a chance at happiness together. Don't take that away from us. Please."

Roberto grabbed Anna's shoulders. "Don't you understand that I don't care about Nathan's happiness? I want him to suffer as I have suffered for so many years. I hate him. I hate him for who he is and what he stands for. It would be easy for me to kill him."

Anna looked into Roberto's dark eyes and saw the hatred in them. She knew he meant what he said. "All right, I'll marry you."

"Willingly?"

Anna nodded her head. "Will you at least let me leave a note for Nathan?"

"No, I think Clare can take care of Nathan from now on."

"How long have you known Clare?"

"Since I was a boy, remember? When I came back here to check up on Nathan and my family, I also found out that Clare was widowed and still very much in love with Nathan. She told me how much he loved you."

"So you've been planning this for some time?"

"It wasn't quite the way I had planned, but when Nathan got sick it seemed to work in my favor. The end result is still the same—you become my wife."

Anna crossed her arms in front of her, taking measured breaths. She felt like a trapped animal that knows it's about to be shot. She also felt something else—hatred. She hated Roberto and Clare for what they had done, and somehow, some way, she would find a way to repay them. She turned to face Roberto, and her eyes were as full of hatred as his had been. "I want you to remember something, Roberto. I, too, am half Cheyenne. I don't forget easily when people have wronged me. I don't care how long it takes; I will find a way to get back at you and Clare for what you have done today. Don't ever make the mistake of trusting me, Roberto." Her eyes burned as she spoke.

"Fair enough. Now, shall I call the judge and our witness back inside?"

Anna nodded silently. She barely heard the brief ceremony that the judge performed and fairly mumbled an "I do" to make it legal. There was no ring, no kiss, no love involved in this ceremony. When it was over, Clare paid the judge and walked him to the door. Roberto grabbed Anna's hand.

"I don't have a ring for you, but I want you to wear something to prove that you are married to me."

"Why not a rope tied around my neck?"

Roberto ignored Anna's sarcastic remark and spoke to Clare when she returned. She ran out of the room, returning in a short while. She handed something to Roberto. It was a ring. He held it up and looked at it. It was a gold band with small sapphire chips in it. "This will do." He took Anna's hand. She yanked it away.

"You don't actually expect me to wear that thing, do you? You two make a wonderful pair—Nathan's ex-mistress and his brother conspiring to tear his world apart."

"I never meant to hurt you, Anna."

"Save it for someone who cares, Clare." Anna took the ring from Roberto and threw it across the room. "I will never wear anything of hers." She started toward the door and stopped. "I want you to remember one thing, Clare—when you are making love to Nathan, he will always be thinking of me. Always. No matter what you try to do to make him forget, he will never forget me. And I hope that drives you crazy." She stomped out of the room.

Roberto tipped his hat to Clare as he walked by her. "Good luck, Clare. You're going to need it.

"We're both going to need it, honey," Clare mumbled as she watched Roberto and Anna leave. Deep inside, in

49

that small, honest part of her heart, she knew that Anna was right. She knew that no matter what she did to make Nathan forget Anna, he never would forget her. All she could hope for was time, time to make him fall in love with her, but she knew that that would never happen. Just as she knew Anna would never fall in love with Roberto, she knew that Nathan would never fall in love with her. She had made a bargain with the devil and she would somehow have to make the best of it.

Richard Thornston stood on his bedroom balcony, whiskey in hand, and looked out over the grounds of his estate. He owned more than three hundred acres of prime Louisiana farm land. He raised cotton and tobacco, but since the end of the war and that damned Emancipation Proclamation, he found it increasingly difficult to find good slaves. Slave. He wasn't even supposed to use the word anymore, and that went against everything he believed in. The South wouldn't have grown as strong and powerful as it had if they hadn't had slave labor to help them. But then that damned liberal, Abe Lincoln, had to come along and free the whole damned bunch of them. Of course, true Southerners knew that just because the government said they were free, didn't actually make the slaves free. The vast majority of them were uneducated and unable to find work elsewhere, so most of them stayed and worked on the plantations and farms. But he could see a definite change in them. They weren't as frightened as they had been before. Now, they knew they could leave whenever they wanted to. Damn Abe Lincoln, Thornston thought. It's a good thing someone had shot him. He had ruined everything.

But Richard Thornston had been lucky. His estate had been one of the few to survive the war intact. He had willingly sheltered Confederate soldiers in return for their protection. It had also worked out nicely that he was one of the biggest gun-runners and black-marketeers in the South. He was able to obtain goods that few other people had been able to get. He quickly became a favorite of the Confederate Army. Richard Thornston, unlike most of his friends and neighbors, came out of the war a wealthy man. When the war was over, he was able to buy up land around him at a low price. Actually, he liked to think he stole it. He drank his fine Southern whiskey, feeling rather self-satisfied. All in all, things had gone well for him. There had been only one chink in his plan.

The love of his life was his daughter, Caroline. He had made big plans for her. She would marry a wealthy, influential Southerner and live on an estate much like Rolling Oaks, the Thornston estate, and that would enable him to have even more power. Since he'd lost his wife, he'd never had much of an interest in remarrying. His only interest lay in his daughter and in her future. Whenever he needed a woman, he took a week and went into New Orleans to satisfy his needs. But he would never bring a woman into his home to compete with Caroline's affections.

Caroline had grown up to be a beautiful young woman, but she was extremely shy. It was very difficult for her to talk to other people. Parties didn't appeal to her, and much to Thornston's chagrin, money didn't seem to matter to her either. She spent a great deal of her time with the Negroes, helping them if they were ailing, and teaching the little ones how to read. No matter how many times he had warned her to stay away from the Negro shacks, Caroline was determined to be with those people. His only solution was to send her away to boarding school.

Thornston clenched his jaw, remembering. He had

thought he had found a way out of the trouble with Caroline when he had sent her away. But then there was the boy. The boy had saved his life when he got washed overboard in a storm, and Thornston had taken a liking to him. Although he was dark-skinned, he was extremely good-looking and very bright. Thornston had decided to take him home.

Roberto had had a tough life, but he made no excuses. Thornston admired that. He was also surprised to find that Roberto knew how to read. The boy had real promise. Thornston had him cleaned up and bought him clothes. He gave him a room and he taught him as much as he could about the business. Roberto was very bright, and before long he was helping Thornston run the estate. Although Thornston had an intense dislike for those with dark skin, there was something about Roberto that he liked. Perhaps it was that he was so tough and had had to make his own way in the world, much as Thornston had had to do. He grew more fond of the boy every day.

By the time summer came, Roberto was firmly ensconced at Rolling Oaks. He worked harder than anyone else on the estate, including Thornston himself. He made sure the workers did their fair share, but he also talked Thornston into providing them with better living conditions and better food. He helped the overseer, and at the end of the day he would go over the books with Thornston. Then they would sit in the library and Roberto would read out loud to Thornston. Roberto had become the son that Thornston had never had. So it came as a real blow when Thornston saw that Caroline and Roberto were attracted to each other. He was willing to help Roberto get a good start in life, willing even to let him live in his house, but he would not tolerate the dark-skinned boy spending any time with his darling Caroline.

When Caroline came home from boarding school that

summer, she was in the full bloom of her youth. She had long, golden hair and deep blue eyes. She was small and very delicate and her father treated her like a porcelain doll, something to be looked at and admired but never to be touched.

Roberto and Caroline became instant friends. There was no attraction between them at first, other than that of two people who genuinely liked and cared about each other. But Thornston had seen that their feelings for each other were growing day by day. Again he sent Caroline off to boarding school, thinking that it would break any tie she had to Roberto. He did this for the next two years, allowing Caroline to come home only on holidays. When she did come home he made sure that she spent time with young men whom he felt were suitable for her. By the time Caroline was seventeen, she had finished boarding school and wanted to come home.

Roberto was nineteen by this time, and very much a man. He had assumed many of the responsibilities at Rolling Oaks, but he was always careful to remember his place. It was during this time that Richard Thornston suffered a stroke. It incapacitated him for months, and Roberto virtually ran the estate. It was also during this time that Roberto and Caroline realized how much they loved each other. Without Thornston's interference, they were free to be together whenever possible, and soon they were spending the nights together. As Thornston began to improve, he was able to see the way Roberto and Caroline looked at each other. What he had feared most had happened—his daughter had fallen in love with someone beneath her social status. As much as he liked Roberto, he could never allow the boy to marry his daughter.

Thornston clenched his left hand. The doctor said he would never regain full function of the arm. But the doctor didn't know about his medicine, the kind of medicine that made men powerful beyond their dreams.

He thought back to the day he searched Caroline's room. When he found her diary and read it; he wanted to kill Roberto. Not only was his daughter in love with the boy, but they had slept together many times, and she was sure she was pregnant. They had made plans to run away to Mexico and get married—plans that Thornston would thwart.

He confronted Roberto and the boy didn't lie; he said he was in love with Caroline. He begged Thornston to let them be married. He swore that he would love her and take care of her for the rest of his life. Thornston was moved by the boy's plea; and he knew that no other man would love his daughter as Roberto did. But there was the matter of his skin color. He had worked too long and too hard to have his daughter marry a half-breed. No matter how he felt about the boy, he could never accept him as his son-in-law.

He knew the only way to separate the two was to publicly humiliate Roberto and make him confess to raping his daughter, something he knew Roberto would never do. At first it had been a painful thing to do, to have the boy beaten in front of everyone on the estate, but then he enjoyed it. He enjoyed the kind of exhilaration he got by humiliating and hurting Roberto. When he was finished, he had his men throw the boy in the swamp, knowing full well that he would die in there. Roberto had been eliminated from their lives. Or so he hoped.

Caroline had grown increasingly difficult since Roberto had been gone, even going so far as to argue with her father in front of the servants. He had had to put her in her place; she had to know who was boss.

Thornston remembered the look on Roberto's face when they took him away; it was a look he would never forget. Roberto's eyes were filled with fear, a sense of betrayal, and intense hatred.

Nathan sat in the large living room, his feet propped on the table. He tried to concentrate on his father's papers, but he could not. He kept thinking about Roberto. There was something strange about him. His eyes. His eyes were not the doors to his soul. They were cold and unfeeling, and Nathan wondered what his brother had been through to make him look so hard. He stood up and stretched, still feeling weak. He wished that Anna and Roberto would get back from Clare's. He worried about Anna; he didn't like it when she was away from him. He couldn't help her if he wasn't with her.

Nathan shook his head. "What's the matter with you?" He asked himself. He walked over to the large window that overlooked the courtyard and the mountains beyond. He had a feeling that something was wrong, and it wasn't just Clare. When he was small, Aeneva had always teased him about his being more Indian than most of the Indians she knew. He had always had "gut feelings" about things and he'd almost always been right. Just like the night, almost eleven years ago, when Roberto had wandered away from him in Chinatown and gone into that cockfight. He knew then that something bad was going to happen, as surely as he knew it now. He reached for his hat on the rack and headed toward the door. Halfway down the stairs of the porch, his legs buckled. "Damn it!" He sat down on the stairs, wiping the beads of sweat from his face. He was still too weak to make the ride all the way to Clare's. He would have to send Jake.

He forced himself to stop, to take a deep breath. He looked out on the mountains that his parents had grown to love so much. If something was wrong, he would find the strength to deal with it, just as his parents and grandparents had always done. He closed his eyes and a face came into his mind. It was a woman's face. An Indian. She was tall and straight and she had the face of a princess. She was also strong. Nathan recognized Sun Dancer, Aeneva's grandmother, the great Healer of the Cheyenne tribe. Nathan remembered when Sun Dancer had taken care of him when he was a small boy. His father had gone to look for Aeneva when she had been kidnapped by a band of Crows. Sun Dancer had taught him many things. He had fallen down a bank by the river and hit some rocks. He began to cry and Sun Dancer picked him up and washed his cuts. She told him: "Come, little one, you must be brave. You will have terrible hurts in your lifetime, and you must find the strength within yourself to face them. Do not count on anyone but yourself, for you, and only you, know the strength that lies within you." Nathan recalled those words as clearly as if he had heard them this very day. He opened his eyes and looked up at the sky. "Thank you, Sun Dancer. I will be strong." Nathan didn't move when he heard the sound of the carriage wheels coming into the yard. When Clare stepped out of the carriage, he knew that his suspicions were confirmed. He sat very still as Clare ran toward him.

"Nathan, something terrible has happened."

Nathan eyed Clare suspiciously. "You look well for someone who is supposed to be sick, Clare."

"I was never sick. Roberto used that to get Anna to my house."

"Why did he want to do that?"

Clare paced nervously in front of Nathan. "I don't know how to tell you."

"Just tell me, Clare."

"Anna and Roberto are married. They have run away together."

Nathan forced himself to remain motionless. "I don't believe you." He continued to gaze out at the mountains in the distance.

"Nathan, haven't you heard what I said? Your brother and your lover ran off together. They were married in my house this afternoon."

Nathan stood up, towering over Clare. "Now, why don't you tell me what really happened, Clare?"

"I just told you."

"No, you told me what you wanted me to hear."

"You can choose to believe what you want, Nathan, but Anna and Roberto are in love. It seems they have been planning this for quite some time."

Nathan bit his lower lip in an effort to control his temper. "Why were they married at your house, Clare? Anna didn't know you that well. She didn't even like you."

"That's not true. We became friends when you were sick. I helped her nurse you."

"Why would she have bothered to nurse me back to health if she was in love with my brother? You're lying, Clare."

"I have nothing to gain by lying to you, Nathan. I only want to see you happy. I tried to talk Anna out of leaving, but she said she loved Roberto."

"How were they married?"

"By a judge."

"And who brought the judge to your house?"

"Roberto did."

"Roberto hasn't been around here long enough to know any judges. Was the judge a friend of yours, Clare?"

"Yes, he was." Clare stood by the railing. "I didn't have a choice, Nathan. Roberto said he'd hurt you if I didn't do as he said."

"And Anna?"

Clare's expression changed from one of fear to one of anger. "I know you don't want to believe me, but Anna went on her own. Roberto, didn't force her. She even kissed him at the end of the ceremony."

Nathan studied Clare's face to see if she was lying, and he couldn't tell. She seemed to be telling him the truth, but what kind of truth was she telling him? Was he supposed to believe that Anna had been in love with his brother, had known he was alive, and had planned to run away with him? He couldn't believe it. "When did Anna and Roberto meet?"

"I'm not sure, but I think it was in San Francisco last year." Clare stopped, making sure her words cut. "She said something about some land she could get her hands on. I don't know if she was talking about Garrett's land or not but—"

"Were they lovers?"

"I don't know for sure—"

Nathan grabbed Clare's shoulders tightly. "Were they lovers, Clare?"

Clare lowered her head. "Yes."

"You're sure?"

"Yes. I walked in on them one night here in Anna's bedroom." She touched Nathan's arm. "I'm so sorry, Nathan. I didn't want to hurt you."

"You didn't hurt me, Clare." Nathan paced back and forth on the porch, trying to get things straight in his mind. Was it possible that Anna and Roberto had been lovers? No, it wasn't possible. The only time she had been away from him she was held captive by Franklin Driscoll.

"Are you all right, Nathan?"

Nathan ignored Clare. No, there was another time. He'd left her alone in San Francisco for more than three months while he came back to Arizona to be with his parents. But she wasn't alone. She had stayed with Larissa and Joe, and Larissa was Roberto's aunt. If he

58

came back to San Francisco, that was the place he'd go. God, he couldn't think now. "Would you leave me alone, Clare. I need to get some rest."

"I'm going to stay with you. You're not completely well yet. You've had quite a shock."

"I don't want you here."

"But you're still sick. I can't just leave you alone like this."

Nathan stared at Clare, his blue eyes narrowed. "I'm not sure what really happened, but I will find out. I know you, Clare, and I know how shrewd you can be. I also know Anna. She loves me, not Roberto. If you won't tell me the truth, I'll find the truth out myself."

"But I've told you the truth, Nathan. You just don't want to accept the fact that your darling Anna could love someone else. Have you forgotten about Garrett already?"

"Garrett is her friend. They've known each other since they were children."

"Like we have?" Clare moved next to Nathan, putting her hands on his chest. "Do you remember how close we've been? Do you remember the times you've made love to me, Nathan?"

"I remember. I also remember the times I've made love to Anna. No man will ever love her the way I do."

"Believe what you will, Nathan, but the truth is Roberto and Anna are husband and wife and there's nothing you can do to change that."

Nathan laughed derisively. "You really don't know me very well, do you, Clare? Did you actually think I would just accept your story? Well, obviously you and my brother haven't given me enough credit."

"What do you mean?"

"I will look for Anna all over the face of this earth if that's what it takes to find her."

"You'll never find her. Roberto didn't even tell me

where they were going."

"Why should he? He knows he can't trust you." Nathan started for the house.

"Nathan, wait. I'm sorry."

"I just want to know one thing, Clare. What did you hope to get out of this little deal with my brother?"

"I wanted you, as I've always wanted you. I love you, Nathan."

"You don't have the slightest idea what love means, Clare. I feel sorry for you."

"Don't you dare feel sorry for me, Nathan Hawkins! I don't need your pity."

Nathan ignored Clare and went inside, closing the door in her face. He went upstairs and lay down on the bed. He needed to rest and get his strength back. It would take every bit of knowledge and all of his strength to track down Roberto and Anna. But he would do it. He had no doubt of that.

Chapter III

Anna didn't move, although the stage bounced them around continually. She refused to look at Roberto. She thought about Nathan and what it would be like to be with him again. Every time the tears started to well up in her eyes she willed them back. She refused to let Roberto see her weakness. Somehow she would find her way back to Nathan.

They had been on a stage for three days now. She hated it. It was uncomfortable, hot, dirty, and terribly confining. She would much rather have ridden a horse. Roberto sat across from her, his black eyes constantly watching her. She refused to acknowledge his presence. They were the only two passengers aboard the coach, and she wished there were more.

"What are you thinking?"

Anna stared at Roberto. "I'm thinking about what a wonderful time I'm having."

Roberto smiled. "I can see why my brother loves you so much."

"How long are we supposed to pretend we're married?"

"We're not pretending anything. We are married."

"I thought you were smart, Roberto. I don't know

what it's going to take to get through to you that I hate you. I don't care if you take me away and lock me up somewhere for the rest of my life; my feelings for you will never change. I will always hate you."

"I don't expect your feelings to change."

"Then what do you expect?"

"I expect you to act as a wife would act toward her husband in public. I won't ask anything more of you."

"You have already asked too much of me, Roberto." For the first time, Anna couldn't control the tears. She quickly averted her eyes. She felt Roberto move to her side of the coach but she didn't look at him.

"Please look at me, Anna."

Anna refused to turn her head.

"Please." There was a note of despair in Roberto's voice.

Anna looked at him, wiping the tears from her face. "What? What could you possibly have to say to me?"

"I need your help."

"You need my help? Is this some kind of game?"

"No, I assure you it's no game. Anna, I never meant to hurt you. I hope you believe that."

"How can you expect me to believe anything you say?"

"I don't. I can only ask that you be patient for a while longer. Then I will tell you what this is all about."

"And what about my life with Nathan? Am I supposed to forget that I ever loved him?"

"I don't want to talk about Nathan right now."

"God, you are driving me crazy. I am supposed to be patient with you and you won't even tell me if I'll ever see Nathan again. You are asking far too much of me, Roberto." Anna leaned her head against the side of the coach and looked out at the endless desert. She remembered the first time she had seen Nathan, at a ball in San Francisco. They had danced and she was completely enchanted by him. She remembered how it had felt to dance so close to him, to be held in his arms, to feel his body against hers.

"Anna, wake up."

Anna opened her eyes. They were at another stage stop. Anna sighed. The bed would be saggy, the house dirty, and the food inedible. She had never realized before how much she loved her home. The owner of the stop opened the door of the coach and helped Anna down.

"How ya do, miss?"

"Mrs.," Roberto interjected.

"Oh, pardon me, ma'am. You look so young and all."

"That's all right," Anna replied in a friendly tone. "What is your name, sir?"

"My name's Bender."

"Is there someplace I can wash up, Mr. Bender?"

"Yes, ma'am, right over there's the pump. I'll have the missus bring you a towel."

"Thank you." Anna took off her hat and traveling jacket and stood by the pump. She lifted the handle and pumped until water came out. She put her face down by the water and drank greedily; then quickly washed off her face and hands. When she was finished, Mrs. Bender was standing near her with a towel.

"Here you go, ma'am."

"Thank you." As Anna dried her face and hands, she looked at the woman in front of her. She was probably around Anna's age, but because of the kind of life she had led, she looked at least ten years older. Her face was already lined and tired-looking, her hair pulled back in a bun from which thin strands fell in her face. Anna felt an immediate kinship with the woman. "My name is Anna. Can I help you with dinner, Mrs. Bender?"

"No, thank you, ma'am. Mr. Bender wouldn't take kindly to that."

"But I'd like to help. Please."

63

Mrs. Bender looked around at her husband, who was busy unharnassing the horses from the stagecoach. "Well, I suppose it would be all right. Only if you really want to."

"I'd love to." Anna followed Mrs. Bender inside the worn-down wooden house that served as their home as well as hotel for stagecoach passengers. The house was essentially one large, square room. On the south side of the room there were four beds separated by curtains. The walls were plain and unadorned. A long table dominated the middle of the room. The table had twelve roughhewn chairs around it, and it was set with blue tin plates and coffee mugs. There was a large pitcher of milk and a pot of coffee already on the table. There were also bread and butter. A pot-bellied stove stood in a corner of the room and Mrs. Bender walked to it.

"My husband bought me this stove in St. Louis," she said proudly. "It's my pride and joy."

"Yes, I can see why. It's very practical."

"It's my stove," the woman replied. "This don't belong to no one else."

"I understand." Anna touched the woman's hand. "What is your name?"

Mrs. Bender stirred the pot on the stove, then dried her hands on her soiled apron. "My name's Ellie. But my husband always calls me 'Mrs.'"

"I think Ellie is a lovely name. May I call you by your name?"

Ellie thought for a moment, then nodded to herself. "I don't suppose that would harm no one."

"Good. Now, what can I help you with?"

"Well, I've made us some rabbit stew and I've got a pie baking. It's apple."

"How about if I serve the stew and you can check on the pie?"

"I don't think my husband would take kindly to your

helping me, Mrs.—"

"Anna."

"My husband wouldn't like it, Anna."

"I want to help. Surely, he can't object to that." Anna took the large pot from Ellie's hands and walked to the table. She ladled stew into six of the plates. "I've counted six of us, including the drivers."

"There'll be two more."

"You have children?"

"My husband has two sons."

"Oh, I didn't see any children when we drove up."

"These boys is all grown up." Ellie looked toward the door. "I think you better let me have that pot."

The door burst open as Ellie walked toward Anna. Jarrod Bender strode toward his wife. "What the hell is the matter with you, woman?" He slapped his wife across the face with the back of his hand and took the pot from Anna's hands. "You should never let our guests do work. You are a good-for-nothing lazy woman."

Ellie Bender took the pot and quickly dished out the food. "I'm sorry, Jarrod. I didn't mean to."

"You never mean to. Lord, how did I wind up with such a stupid woman?" He turned toward Anna. "I'm sorry, Mrs. Hawkins. My wife seems to have lost her manners."

"Mr. Bender, I asked your wife if I could help her. She didn't want me to but I—"

"It doesn't matter, ma'am. My wife knows her place and she shouldn't ever step out of it."

"She works hard, Mr. Bender. She could use a little help."

Jarrod Bender's eyes blazed with anger. "Is that what she told you?" He moved toward his wife.

Anna stood between Ellie and Jarrod. "No, I offered to help. She never said a word to me." Anna put her hand on Jarrod Bender's arm. He brushed her away.

"I think you would do best to mind your own business, Mrs. Hawkins. Sticking your nose into other people's business can only get you into trouble."

"Is there a problem, Bender?" Roberto walked into the room.

"No, sir, we was just having a little discussion."

Roberto glanced at Anna. He knew she was angry. He could also see that Ellie Bender was scared to death. "I hope my wife didn't offend you. She tends to talk without thinking sometimes."

Anna tried to protest but Roberto grasped her arm tightly. His eyes dared her to contradict him. Anna pulled away from him and sat down at the table, ignoring everyone in the room. When Roberto sat down next to her, she glared at him and whispered, "How could you embarrass me like that?"

"Don't you see that that man is crazy? He'd like nothing better than to hurt someone real badly."

Anna glanced over at Jarrod Bender, who was taking a heavy drink from a liquor jug. "I only wanted to help his wife. I feel sorry for her."

"I feel sorry for her too, but sometimes it's best not to get involved."

Anna reached across the table and yanked a piece of bread from the loaf, not offering any to Roberto. The stagecoach drivers came inside and sat down. Jarrod Bender glared at his wife, who stood at the stove, looking more like a frightened doe than a grown woman. Anna tried to ignore the grunts of delight as Jarrod Bender stuffed his mouth with food. She couldn't believe she was in a place like this, with people like this, with a man who didn't care about her. She dabbed at the stew on her plate, but she didn't really care about eating. She kept looking up at Ellie Bender, and her heart went out to the woman.

The sound of horses and men's voices broke the

disturbing silence. The door flew open and in walked two young men, dirty, disheveled and obviously quite drunk. Anna looked at Ellie and saw the look of terror in her eyes. Ellie quickly added more stew to the plates on the table.

"Well, howdy folks. Sorry we's late for dinner."

"Where you boys been?" Jarrod Bender managed to ask between stuffing his mouth with stew and bread.

"We been real busy, pa." The younger of the two men brushed past Ellie, obviously making her uncomfortable. "Smells real good, Ellie. Just like always." The young man plopped down in the chair opposite Anna and, without taking off his hat or coat, began slurping up the stew.

"Howdy, folks." The other brother threw his hat across the room and hastily took off his coat. His hands were covered with dirt, but he grabbed a piece of bread without thinking about it.

"Mr. and Mrs. Hawkins, these here's my boys, Eli and Cain. Say hello to the folks, boys."

"We already did." Cain sat across from Anna, and for the first time he looked at her. "Well, now, ain't you a pretty little thing. Do you know about my name? Says in the Good Book that Cain rose up and killed his brother. He was not his brother's keeper. Did you know that?"

Anna glanced over at Roberto. "No, but my husband knows all about that passage from the Bible."

"Is that right?"

"No, I don't know anything about it," Roberto responded tersely.

"That's strange, I think you could have written that passage," Anna replied angrily, slamming her fork onto the plate.

"What are you all talking about?" Cain asked, gravy dripping down the side of his mouth.

"I think these two's having a fight." Eli spoke for the

first time.

Roberto looked over at Eli. Slowly, he laid down his fork and rested his hand by his hip, close to his gun. "I don't think it's any of your business."

Eli put his fork down. "Are you challenging me, mister?"

Roberto smiled. "Now why would I do that?"

Eli seemed genuinely confused. "Well, I dunno. I just thought you was aiming to get in a fight or something."

Roberto shook his head. "Like I told your father earlier this evening, my wife tends to speak a little out of turn sometimes. Can make a man edgy, if you know what I mean."

"I sure know what you mean," Jarrod Bender agreed. "Bring me some more of that stew, woman. Hurry up!"

Anna pushed back her chair in disgust and took her plate and cup to the washbucket. When she started to wash the dishes, Ellie quickly took them from her.

"Please, ma'am, I'll only suffer for it."

"I'm sorry, Ellie. I didn't mean to get you into trouble." Anna crossed the room and went outside, leaving behind the stale, filthy odor of the men. She walked out past the stable and looked around. There wasn't much out here except rocks, cactus and mountains. A woman like Ellie Bender could easily go mad in a place like this.

Anna walked toward a large boulder. She clambered up until she was on top, brought her knees to her chest and wrapped her arms around them. She had never felt so lonely in her life. She hated this place, hated the people who lived here. She just wanted to go home and be with Nathan.

"Come on, Ellie, let me help you." Cain's voice traveled easily in the evening silence. He followed Ellie as she came outside to get more water. He followed her around like a puppy, constantly touching her, never giving her a moment's peace.

"Leave me alone, Cain. If your father comes out here, he'll kill me."

"He won't do no such thing. I'd kill him before I'd let him hurt you." Cain took the heavy bucket from Ellie and walked to the pump. Ellie looked around her, making sure her husband wasn't anywhere around. When the bucket was full, Ellie reached for it, but Cain put it on the ground. He put his arms around Ellie and pulled her toward him. "You know how I feel about you, Ellie. Why do you always fight me so?"

"Because I'm married to your father." She reached for the bucket but Cain took her arm.

"I know you want me, Ellie. That old man in there can't please you like I can." He wrapped his arms around her and kissed her.

Ellie tried to pull away, but she only managed to move her face away. "Please, Cain, if you care for me, you'll leave me be. And don't say such terrible things ever again."

"What's so terrible about wanting a woman so much your loins ache?"

Ellie made a desperate sound, much like the sound a rabbit makes when it's caught in a trap. "Cain, leave me alone or I'll scream."

"No, I don't think you'll do that, 'cause if that old man comes out here, all I have to do is tell him you were making eyes at me and I had to push you away. Who do you think he's going to believe?"

Anna could see Ellie's shoulders slump as Cain pulled her toward the stable. "That's right, you just come in here with me. It won't take long and it'll feel so good."

"Cain, please let me go!"

Anna couldn't listen any longer. She slid off the rock and ran to the stables, clearing her throat. "Excuse me, Ellie. Are you in here? Your husband needs you inside now."

There was a rustle of hay and Ellie stood up, obviously embarrassed but grateful. She gave Anna a squeeze on the hand as she hurried by. "Thank you," she said softly.

Anna stood by the stable, waiting for Cain to emerge. He stomped out of the stall, pushing Anna aside as he did so. "Now what in hell did you do that for?"

"Do what?"

"Don't get smart with me, little lady. I've dealt with your kind before."

Cain stood in front of Anna. She could smell his dank breath and the heavy odor of a man who hadn't bathed in weeks. She felt sorry for Ellie. "I was only delivering a message from your father."

"You're lying. You wasn't even inside the house." Cain grabbed Anna's arm and dragged her back into the stall. "I guess one woman's as good as the next when you're in need." He pushed her down on the hay.

Anna rolled to one side and stood up, looking around for something to defend herself with. She couldn't see anything. She screamed as loudly as she could, but Cain covered her mouth with his hand and pulled her down on the hay, climbing atop her as he would a horse.

"You are a wild little thing, ain't you?" Cain sat astride Anna, while pinning her arms to the ground. "I think you might even be better than Ellie."

Anna managed to move her head. She let out another scream. Cain slapped her violently, stifling any sound. "I don't want to hear another sound out of you, or I'll snap that little neck of yours like it's a dry twig." He took his hand away from her mouth and smiled as Anna lay there silent. "Good girl. Now, let's see what we've got under here." Cain started to push up Anna's skirt, when the sound of a cocked pistol made him stop. The barrel of the pistol was right next to his face.

"Get up!" Roberto's voice was ominous in the darkness. Cain did as he was told. Roberto held onto Cain's jacket and pushed him back against the wall. "Didn't you get the idea that the lady didn't like you?"

"I was only playing, mister. 'Sides, she was cozying up to me."

"Is that right?" Roberto put the barrel of his gun at Cain's throat. "I don't like men who hurt women. I think they're cowards."

"Now, listen here, I ain't no coward."

"Then why not fight me?" Roberto let the hammer back on his gun and dropped it by Anna. "Let's see what you've got, Cain."

Cain came straight at Roberto, his head like a battering ram in Roberto's chest. He pushed him back against the railing. Roberto held onto Cain's shoulders and shoved him backward. He followed him across the small stall and before Cain could raise his head, Roberto hit him. His fist smashed into Cain's face two more times, sending Cain flying into the hay. He didn't move.

Roberto walked over to where Anna had crawled to a corner of the stall. He picked up his gun and pulled Anna to her feet, leading her out of the stall. He took her to the pump. "Are you all right?"

"I don't want to go back in there." Anna held her hand to her throbbing cheek and mouth, spitting out blood. She let Roberto wipe her face.

Roberto held the tin cup that hung from the pump underneath and filled it with water. "Here, drink some of this."

"I won't drink out of that cup." She shook her head adamantly. She held her hands under the pump as Roberto forced the water out. "God, here they come." The door of the house opened and Jarrod and Eli came out, as well as the two coach drivers.

"What's the problem here?" One of the drivers asked.

"I think you better ask him," Roberto answered,

71

pointing back to the stable. He looked over at Eli and Jarrod. "If he comes near my wife again, I'll kill him. Do you understand?"

"My boy wouldn't do nothing to harm no one. Was probably your wife that—"

Roberto grabbed Jarrod's shirt until he was practically choking him. "My wife is a lady, do you understand? She's not used to scum like you and your sons. If you value your life, stay the hell away from her."

Jarrod Bender nodded his head as he stumbled backward toward his son. "I won't forget this."

"Neither will I." Roberto guided Anna toward the house. "Go inside." He turned back to the two drivers. "Either you hitch up that coach right now, or I'll take two of the horses."

"You got no argument from me, Mr. Hawkins. I'm real sorry if anything happened to your wife." He turned to Jarrod. "This is the last time a stage will stop here if I have anything to say about it."

Roberto walked into the house. Ellie was wiping the blood from Anna's face with a cloth. He took the cloth from her hand and gently dabbed at the broken skin on Anna's cheek and mouth. His dark eyes were masked. "I'm sorry. I never meant for this to happen."

Anna lowered her eyes, trying to keep from crying. She started to take the cloth from Roberto but he brushed her hand away. "I'm so sorry." He put his arms around Anna and held her. "I didn't mean to hurt you."

Anna relaxed in the circle of Roberto's arms, knowing he was the only safe haven she had. "Take me home, Roberto. Please, take me home."

"I can't do that, Anna." He held the cloth up to her still-bleeding mouth, but she pulled away.

"Then you will continue to hurt me as long as you keep me away from Nathan." She sat down in one of the chairs, covering her face with her hands.

"I'll go check on the stagecoach." Roberto reached out to touch her shoulder as he walked by, but he pulled his hand back. He wasn't sure how to comfort someone. It was an emotion that had been stripped away from him, along with all of his other human emotions.

Anna felt a comforting hand on her shoulder. She took the cup of coffee that Ellie handed her. "Thank you."

"It's the least I could do. I'm sorry you got hurt, Anna. It was my fault."

"No, it wasn't your fault, Ellie. There's no reason for you to take that from Cain."

"I don't have a choice." She looked around her. "This here's all I got. It ain't much, but it's my home."

"But is this the way you want to be treated the rest of your life, Ellie?"

"Like I said, I don't have a choice."

"But you do. You can come with us."

"No, I couldn't do that, Anna. I wouldn't know how to live without Jarrod. I been with him since I was sixteen years old. He's done everything for me."

Anna forced herself to keep quiet. She could see that nothing would change the woman's mind. "Why don't you have any children, Ellie?"

"I can't have none. That's why Jarrod married me."

"He married you because you couldn't have children?"

"He said he didn't want no more after he had Eli and Cain."

"I can understand why," Anna replied dryly.

"They ain't always so bad. Sometimes they can be downright nice, especially when they ain't drinking."

"Do you mind if I ask you a question, Ellie?"

"Guess not."

"How old are you?"

"I'll be twenty-one years of age in the fall."

Anna couldn't believe it. Ellie was only a year older

73

than Anna, but she looked at least ten to fifteen years older. "I should be getting outside."

Ellie took Anna's hand in an awkward gesture. "I appreciate what you tried to do for me but I'm different from you. I ain't smart or pretty. This here's all I got."

Anna squeezed Ellie's hand. "Good luck, Ellie." She picked up her hat and jacket and walked outside. The drivers had almost finished hitching up the team. Jarrod and Cain stood by the stables, acting like young boys who'd been caught with their hands in the cookie jar. Anna couldn't see Roberto. Jarrod and Cain walked toward her. She tried to remain calm.

"My son here has something to say to you, ma'am."

Cain took off his hat and shuffled his feet. "I didn't mean no harm, ma'am. I was just looking for a little fun. Thought you was too."

Anna couldn't believe her ears. The man wasn't apologizing; he was making excuses. "I think you actually believe that, Cain," she said angrily.

"Believe what?" He stepped toward her. "That you wanted it?"

Anna tried to walk away, but Cain stepped in front of her. "I don't like women with big mouths. They tend to make me nervous."

"Get out of my way." She looked around. "If my husband sees you, you'll regret it."

Cain laughed. "I don't see your husband anywhere around. Looks like maybe he took off without you." Cain grabbed her arm.

"He wouldn't do that." Anna's eyes searched frantically for Roberto. Where was he? She saw Eli appear from behind the stable. He walked toward his father and brother.

"Everything's all taken care of." He looked at Anna. "She's all yours, Cain."

"Thank you, brother." Cain looked back at the drivers

of the coach. "I think you and pa better do something about them."

Jarrod Bender shook his head in disgust. "I sure hope she's worth it, Cain. I don't like killing men over a woman."

"I'll make her worth it, pa." He pulled Anna toward the house. Anna hit and kicked, but Cain didn't budge. Two gunshots exploded in the night, and Anna turned her head to see the two drivers from the coach drop to the ground. Cain pulled her into the house and slammed the door. Ellie was cleaning the table. "Get out of here, Ellie. I'd like some privacy."

"Cain, you can't do this."

"Don't you ever be telling me what I can and can't do, woman!" Cain shoved Ellie back against the table. He put his arm around Anna's waist and lifted her off the floor. He carried her behind one of the curtains that separated the large dining room, threw her on one of the beds and climbed on top of her. "I think you and I are gonna have a good time." He held her face with his hands and covered her mouth with wet, smelly kisses.

Anna couldn't force her head from his grasp. His weight had her pinioned to the bed, but she managed to get one arm free. She reached up to the crotch of his pants and squeezed as hard as she could. Cain yelled and rolled to the side, onto the floor. Anna stood up on the other side and ran toward the curtain.

"You weren't planning to go anywhere, were you, little lady?" Eli Bender was standing on the other side of the curtain.

"Thank you, brother. It looks like I got me one here who likes to fight. Nothing I like better than a good fight." He wrapped his fingers through Anna's long hair and pulled her back to the bed. This time Anna didn't resist. She knew she didn't have a chance. She closed her eyes and wished she were dead.

Ellie Bender stomped out of the house with a bucket in her hands. Jarrod stopped her at the door. "Where you going?"

"I can't listen to this. I'm going to get some more water." She brushed past Jarrod, slamming the door behind her. When she got outside she dropped the bucket and ran behind the stable. She had heard Eli tell his father he had killed Anna's husband behind the stable.

Ellie stumbled behind the stable in the darkness. She saw a body lying on the ground. She knelt next to Roberto, but she couldn't see well enough to tell if he was alive. She put her head to his chest. His heart was beating. She felt his face and slapped his cheeks. "Wake up, mister. You got to wake up." She lifted his head up in her arms and felt the matted blood on the back of his head. "Mister, please wake up." She slapped his face a few more times until she heard Roberto groan. She pulled him to a sitting position. "You got to listen, Mr. Hawkins. Cain has your wife. He's going to hurt her."

Roberto heard a voice through the haze but he couldn't see. "Who is that?"

"It's me, Ellie. You got to hurry. Cain has your wife in the house right now."

Roberto stumbled to his feet. He leaned against Ellie while he got his balance. He reached down for his gun. It was gone. "Can you get me a gun?"

"Follow me." Ellie led Roberto along the back of the barn and out into the yard by the stagecoach. "They shot the drivers."

Roberto reached down and felt for the men's guns. They were gone. He thought of the rifle that was always kept behind the seat on top of the stagecoach. He climbed onto the seat and reached behind it, then jumped down. "You'd better stay out here. I don't know what's going to happen in there."

"Just save your wife, mister. Do what you have to."

Roberto ran across the yard and stood at one side of the door. It was the only way in. He could hear the men laughing. He didn't hear Anna. It would be too dangerous if he just ran inside. They could kill Anna before he had a chance to do anything. He ran to Ellie. "I need your help."

"What do you want me to do?"

They walked to the front door. "I want you to scream for your husband. Make it sound real."

"I don't know if he'll come, mister."

"He'll come."

Ellie nodded. She stood back from the door and screamed as loudly as she could. Roberto smiled at her. It sounded real. Ellie fell to the ground and screamed again.

The door flew open and Eli and Jarrod came running out. Roberto hit Jarrod on the back of the head with the butt of the rifle. Jarrod went sprawling on the ground behind Eli. Eli stopped to look at his father, but it was too late. Roberto had the rifle aimed at Eli's head. "Don't move. Lie down on the ground with your hands over your head. Call your brother out here."

"I'll kill you for this, Ellie."

"Do what I said. Ellie, get his guns." Ellie quickly took Eli's guns and ran to Roberto. "Call him." Eli yelled for his brother.

Cain walked tentatively to the door, holding Anna in front of him. "What's the matter with you, Eli? What're you doing lying on the ground?"

"Look out, Cain! He's by the door."

Cain looked to the right of the door. Before he could react, the butt of the rifle smashed into his face and he fell backward into the house. Roberto pulled Anna outside. He checked to make sure Cain and Jarrod were still unconscious and told Ellie to keep Eli covered. Anna stumbled to her knees and he knelt down to lift her up. "Come on, Anna. Let's get you to the coach." Anna didn't respond. Roberto lifted her in his arms and started for the stagecoach. Ellie's voice stopped him.

"Eli, don't!"

Eli was standing, walking toward Ellie. She held one of his pistols in front of her. "You know you won't shoot me, Ellie. You couldn't."

"Don't come any closer, Eli."

Eli laughed and lunged forward, reaching for the gun. Ellie squeezed the trigger and the bullet hit Eli in the arm. He stopped and looked at Ellie. "How could you do this, Ellie? I never hurt you. I always treated you real good. Not like Cain and my pa."

"You always treated me like dirt, you and your whole family."

"But you never said anything. I thought you liked it."

"Jarrod used to beat me if I said anything, and you know it. Your father and your brother and you are no better than animals. You all had me believing that I deserved to be treated this way. I hate you all."

Eli reached out to Ellie. "Ellie, I didn't mean no harm. I always thought you was so pretty."

"But you never thought of asking me how I felt, did you, Eli? You just took what you wanted."

"Ellie—"

"No more, Eli. No more." Ellie squeezed the trigger three times. Eli fell to the ground without another sound. Ellie walked over to her husband. She stood over him, aiming the pistol at his head. "I hate you, Jarrod."

Roberto set Anna down by the stagecoach and came running back across the yard. He stood between Ellie and Jarrod. "Ellie, don't. They're not worth it."

"He don't deserve to live."

"Maybe not, but you can't just kill him in cold blood. That would make you the same as them. You're better than they are, Ellie."

Ellie's hand began to shake and she dropped the pistol.

Roberto gathered up the guns. "I want you to find me some rope. Bring it over to the coach."

Roberto dragged Jarrod and then Cain over to the stagecoach. He set each of them up against the two front wheels, on either side of the coach. When Ellie returned with the rope, he tied Jarrod and Cain securely to the wheels of the coach, gagging them with their bandanas. He dragged Eli's body over to the bodies of the drivers. He would have to bury them all in the morning. He lifted Anna off the ground and carried her into the house. Ellie followed close behind.

"Put her right here, mister. This bed's clean."

Roberto laid Anna on the first bed. "Can you get me something to clean her up?" Roberto removed Anna's ripped blouse and covered her up with a blanket.

Ellie hurried across the room and came back with a bowl of water and a clean cloth. "Here you go, mister."

Roberto sat next to Anna. He looked at her face, which was bruised and swollen. She was bleeding from the mouth and from her nose. He closed his eyes. He had never wanted to hurt her. She was completely innocent. He ran his hand across her face, pulling away the stray strands of dark hair. She looked like a child, an innocent, beautiful child.

Ellie took the cloth from Roberto's hand. "Why don't you let me do that? You've got yourself a nasty cut on your head. Go get yourself some coffee or, better yet, I got some real good homemade plum brandy in that jug by the cupboard. Why don't you get us both a glass? And here, put this on your head." Ellie handed Roberto another wet cloth from the bowl.

Roberto complied, pouring the drinks and coming back to Anna's bedside with a chair. "Why did you put up with these men, Ellie?"

"Your wife asked me the same thing. I dunno. Guess it seemed like the best thing to do at the time. I was young

79

and poor and I didn't have much. Jarrod paid my pa fifty dollars. At least I helped my family out."

"Why don't you come with us?"

"What would I do? I don't know no one. I ain't educated or smart. I can't even read."

"We'll help you."

"I dunno. This's been my home for a long time now. This's all I know."

"What about Jarrod and Cain? They're dangerous men."

"I don't know. I don't know what I'll do about them."

Roberto handed Ellie her brandy. "Why don't you drink this and go to sleep. I'll look after Anna now. We'll talk about what to do tomorrow."

Ellie stood up. "I'm sorry, mister. I hope they didn't hurt her real bad. I feel like it's my fault cause she tried to help me."

"It's not your fault, Ellie. Just get some rest. And thanks for your help tonight."

"It's the least I could do, mister."

Roberto propped his feet against the wall, sipping at the brandy and staring at Anna. He wondered, for the first time, if it had been the right thing to do to take Anna away from Nathan. If he wanted to make his brother suffer, perhaps he could have done it some other way. There was also another thought that plagued him—what if Nathan actually had done everything in his power to help him? After all, he did remember Nathan fighting the fat man, trying to save him, but he couldn't remember much after that. What he couldn't understand was why he had spent the last eleven years of his life just trying to survive, while Nathan had grown prosperous. It didn't seem fair.

"Nathan," Anna murmured.

Roberto put his feet on the floor and leaned toward the bed. "Anna?" He wrung the cloth out in the bowl and

80

placed it on Anna's forehead. "Can you hear me, Anna?"

Anna moved her head and slowly opened her eyes. She looked up at Roberto. "Where is Nathan?"

"He's not here."

Anna started to get up but the pain in her head stopped her. "What happened to my head?"

"Do you remember where you are?"

Anna looked around her, and suddenly her eyes were filled with fear. "Where are they?"

"They won't hurt you. Eli is dead and Cain and Jarrod are tied up."

Roberto put the cloth back on her forehead and took her hand in his. "Did they hurt you?"

Anna's eyes met Roberto's. She knew what he meant. "They beat me up a little, but they didn't really hurt me."

"Thank God," Roberto sighed. He lowered his head, running his fingers through his hair. "I wouldn't forgive myself if something happened to you."

"I almost think you mean that."

"I do mean it. You haven't done anything to me. I don't want to hurt you."

"But you don't mind using me?"

"I never said I was an honorable person, Anna. I wasn't brought up the way you and Nathan were brought up."

"But you were, 'Berto."

Roberto's dark eyes narrowed. "I was only with them for the first eleven years. The next part of my life wiped out anything they ever taught me."

"I don't believe that."

"Don't try to make me into something I'm not, Anna. I'm not my brother and I'm not Trenton."

"But you are like them, just as you are like Aeneva. She is in your blood, Roberto. Nothing can change that."

Roberto stood up suddenly, knocking over the chair behind him. "Why are you so intent on finding something in me that's not there?"

Anna took the cloth from her head and dropped it in the bowl. She propped herself up on her elbows. "I know you better than you know yourself, 'Berto. You are angry and you are hurt, and you feel as if your family abandoned you, so you want to make Nathan suffer just like you did. But what you don't understand is that Nathan already has suffered."

"I don't want to hear about my brother's pain. I don't want to hear about my brother at all." Roberto stomped away from the bed.

Anna lay back down on the bed. She was convinced, as never before, that Roberto would never hurt her. It was her job now to convince him that Nathan had not deserted him. She had to make Roberto realize how much Nathan had always loved him. Her head throbbed. She closed her eyes and thought of the time she was kept captive on the slave ship. It was a horrible experience, but it had somehow made her stronger. She felt as if she could endure anything after that.

"Anna?"

Anna opened her eyes. Roberto was standing by the bed, looking like a contrite little boy.

"I want you to know that I really am sorry for everything that's happened to you."

Anna held out her hand. Slowly, Roberto moved forward and took it. "Sit down." Roberto complied. "I won't keep badgering you about Nathan. I will go with you to wherever it is you have to go, but someday you will have to listen to me about Nathan. I want you to know about him. It will change your mind to know the truth."

"I already know the truth," Roberto responded quietly.

"You think you know the truth but you don't. You aren't ready to hear it yet, so I won't keep trying to make you listen. But I am going to say one thing, and I want you to listen to me. You are Aeneva's blood son and that is a true honor. She was a wonderful human being. She was everything I could ever hope to be. She loved you so much, Roberto."

"I thought you said she would be ashamed to see me now."

"I was angry then."

"You're not angry now?"

"I think I understand you a little bit better. At least I know you care for me."

Roberto cocked an eyebrow. "What makes you think that?"

"You saved my life twice tonight. If you didn't care for me, you could've let me die."

"I would've done it for anybody."

"I don't think so. Why is it so hard for you to show your true feelings, Roberto?"

Roberto finally let go of Anna's hand. "I had to learn to hide my true feelings in order to survive."

"What happened to you, 'Berto? What has cut you so deeply inside?"

"Maybe one day I'll tell you, but not now. Anyway, you should rest." Roberto touched Anna's face. "I should kill them for what they did to you."

Anna grabbed his hand and held onto it. "It's all right. I'll be all right."

"Will you?"

"Yes. Will you do me a favor?" Roberto nodded. "Will you stay with me until I fall asleep? I feel a little strange."

"I'll stay with you." Roberto reached over and rubbed her forehead. "Just relax and go to sleep. You don't have to worry about anything." Anna nodded her head and closed her eyes. She was asleep within minutes. Roberto watched her chest rise and fall and he was fascinated by the way her dark eyelashes were silhouetted against her cheeks. He had never watched a woman sleep before, not

83

even Caroline. Their meetings had always been so clandestine, so hurried, he had never had time to fully enjoy her femininity or her beauty. He leaned down and kissed Anna on the cheek, a gesture that was completely foreign to him but, nevertheless, one that felt good. For the first time in a very long time, he felt a tie to another human being. It was a feeling he was beginning to like.

Chapter IV

Nathan watched Garrett as he paced back and forth across the room. "So, what do you think?"

"What do I think? It's unbelievable!"

"Yeah, that's what I thought." Nathan shook his head as he went over the past three months. His parents had died, he had almost died, Roberto had miraculously reappeared, but only to marry Anna and take her away with him. Now, he was sitting in Garrett McReynolds's ranch house in California, trying to enlist his help in finding Anna. It was an odd situation, considering Garrett and Anna had grown up together and had almost gotten married. Nathan knew that Garrett was probably still in love with Anna; that was one of the reasons he wanted his help. He knew Garrett would stop at nothing to find her.

"You mean to tell me that not only did Roberto come back from the dead, but he married Anna and took her away with him?"

"That's about the size of it."

"What did Clare have to do with all of this?"

"She won't admit it, but I'm convinced she planned the whole thing with Roberto."

"Why?"

"God, I don't know. She says she still loves me."

"Yeah, I still love Anna, but that doesn't mean that when I find her I'm going to steal her away from you."

"I'm glad to hear it." Nathan stood up. "I can't quite figure it out myself. I've gone over it a hundred times."

"Did Roberto act strangely?"

"No, not really."

"But?"

Nathan shrugged his shoulders. "I don't know. I just sensed something really different about him."

"Like what?"

"I can't explain it. I just felt it."

"And Clare swears that Anna was in love with Roberto?"

"She says they met when Anna was in San Francisco."

Garrett shook his head. "There is no way that Anna could've been with Roberto here. When she wasn't with me, she was with you."

"I know. I thought about that. I thought maybe she met him when Driscoll kidnapped her and sold her to the slavers, but I don't think that's possible."

"I don't either. Clare is lying."

"Why are you so sure?"

"Because I know Anna. As much as I hate to admit it, she loved you. And she loved me too. Roberto never entered into the picture."

Nathan nodded. "I just needed to hear someone else say it."

"You didn't actually doubt it, did you?"

"I don't know, Garrett. My parents die suddenly, I get sick, and when I wake up, I find my brother, who has supposedly been dead for over ten years, suddenly alive. Then Anna disappears without a note or anything. I admit I've had my doubts."

"I think he kidnapped her."

"But why, Garrett? Why would my brother kidnap the

woman I love?"

"Only he can tell you that, Nathan. I'm just here to tell you what I know, and that is that Anna would never deceive you in any way. When she discovered how much she loved you, it practically killed her to tell me she couldn't marry me, but she did. She couldn't lie to me. She wouldn't lie to you."

"That's what makes this so damned strange. Roberto talked to me—hell, he even helped get me well. Now why would he do that if he was planning to kidnap Anna? Why wouldn't he have just taken her and gone when I was sick?"

"As I said, only he can answer that. So, what do we do now?"

"I've got to find them. I was hoping you'd help."

"Of course I'll help. Do you know where we're going?"

"I don't have any idea."

"What about your friend Chin? He knows a lot of people. Maybe he could find out if Roberto was ever in San Francisco, or maybe he could find out what really happened to him that night."

"He already told me that after it happened. All he knew was that Roberto was thrown into the bay."

"Maybe he knew more than he was telling you."

"Chin wouldn't lie to me."

"Maybe he would if he thought he was protecting you. Maybe he found out something worse about Roberto, something he thought you couldn't accept."

"What could be worse than telling me he was dead?" Nathan stood up. "Can you be ready to leave this week?"

"I can be ready to leave tomorrow."

"I'll be going into San Francisco. I need to talk to Joe and Chin. I'll be in touch."

"Take care, Nate."

Nathan nodded. It felt strange to have Garrett call him the name his father and brother used to call him. This man loved Anna, yet he was selfless enough to help him find her. He was a good friend. He held out his hand to Garrett and Garrett took it. Nathan shook his hand firmly. "Thanks, Garrett."

"What for?"

"I know this can't be easy for you."

"It's easy, all right. I want to make sure Anna gets home safely. And if I can't have her, maybe, somewhere along the way, I'll find some beautiful young woman who's just dying to fall in love with me."

Nathan smiled. "With your charm, how can you miss?"

"Nate?"

"What?"

"I want you to remember something real important."

"What's that?"

"Anna is a survivor. She's made it through a lot in her young lifetime; she'll make it through this."

Nathan nodded. "I know." Nathan grabbed his hat. "I'll be back here in two days."

"I'll be ready."

Joe, Larissa and Chin sat very still as Nathan told them the events of the past three months. It was an especially painful story for Joe and Larissa to hear because Trenton had been Joe's best friend and Larissa had once been in love with Trenton. Larissa was also Roberto's aunt; she was his father's sister.

"I can't believe this," Joe said solemnly. "My friends are dead and I wasn't even there to help them."

"There was nothing you could have done, Joe."

"But you made it. How?"

"Anna and Roberto mixed some of my mother's special medicines together and I guess it did the trick. I just wish I had been able to do the same thing for my parents."

"It was not meant to be." Chin spoke for the first time, his voice low and measured.

Nathan looked at the man who had saved his life so many years ago. "It doesn't make it any easier, Chin. I should have been able to do something."

"And I should have been able to do something about my sister when she was murdered by Driscoll, but I could not. We all do what we are capable of on this earth, boy. Do you not realize that by now?"

"Don't start, Chin. I'm not in the mood for your sage Chinese advice."

"Perhaps it would behoove you to close your mouth and open your mind, Nathan. One is never too old or too wise to heed the words of others."

Nathan rolled his eyes, looking much like an indignant child. "What do you have to say, Joe?"

"I say old Chin's right. You remind me so much of your father it scares me. You're just as stubborn, and twice as mean as he ever thought of being."

Nathan couldn't contain a smile. "I'll take that as a compliment."

"You damn well better. Now, tell us about Roberto. When did he show up?"

"All I know is that he came during the time when I was sick. Anna said he helped get me well." He shook his head in disgust. "Then he took Anna away with him."

"No, I don't believe it." Larissa finally spoke up. "That doesn't sound like the sweet boy I used to know."

"He's not the boy we used to know, Larissa. He's a man now, a man with a lot of hatred inside him."

"But why, Nathan? Why would he take Anna just to hurt you? He absolutely idolized you."

"I don't know, Larissa."

"Is it possible that Anna went willingly with him?"

Nathan's eyes softened. He could understand why

89

Larissa would want to think the best of her nephew. "You knew Anna. She stayed with you. Do you think she would have run off with someone she barely knew?"

"Maybe she did know him." She looked at the other men. "It's possible that she met him here."

Joe touched her hand. "Honey, you saw the look in that girl's eyes when she looked at Nate. There was no way she was in love with any other man. No way."

Larissa lowered her eyes. "I know. I was just hoping there was some good left in Roberto. He's just like Ladro, taking Aeneva away from Trenton."

"We don't know what happened to him to make him like this. If Chin hadn't taken care of Nate, there's no telling what he'd be like today."

"I just wish he would've talked to me. I could've helped him," Nathan said angrily.

"Perhaps he did not want your help." Chin's slanted eyes regarded Nathan. "Perhaps you were the enemy to him."

"The enemy? Why would I be the enemy? I'm his brother, for God's sake."

"You are not the brother he knew."

"So? He's not the brother I knew. That doesn't mean I regard him as my enemy."

"You are not listening to me, Nathan." Chin stood up and looked at the tall young man in front of him. "Perhaps your brother has been through something which none of us can understand, not even you. You do not know what he has endured, and perhaps he is not ready to tell you, or anyone, what has happened to him."

"I understand what you're saying, Chin, but what does that have to do with Anna? Why would Roberto take Anna? She hasn't done anything to him."

"Perhaps he doesn't want to hurt Anna. Perhaps he wants to hurt you."

Nathan walked back and forth across the room.

"Maybe he blames me for what happened to him. Maybe he thinks I should have done more to help him."

"You could not have done more. You know that to be the truth. You almost died trying to save your brother."

"But he doesn't know that, Chin."

"He saw you get shot and stabbed, Nathan. That is when he attacked Driscoll and Driscoll shot him. Driscoll's men dragged him away and threw his body into the bay."

"Or so you say." Nathan's eyes pierced Chin's. "Do you really know what happened to my brother, Chin? Were you just trying to save me from more hurt?"

Chin looked at the young man who stood in front of him, so tall and strong, with a face as honest and open as the sun. "I cannot lie to you."

"What do you mean, you can't lie to me? You did know Roberto was alive, didn't you, Chin?"

"Yes, I knew, but only after he was gone."

"Gone? Where did he go?"

"It was true that he was thrown into the bay."

"You knew that and you didn't help him?" Larissa asked.

"I did not know it until after it was too late."

"You knew what pain I was in. You knew I blamed myself for his death. Why didn't you tell me that he was alive?"

Chin sat down, looking very composed. "When I found out he was alive you were already working in the mines with Tong."

"But I would've gone to look for him. You must have known that."

"I knew that. That is why I made the decision not to tell you."

"It wasn't your decision to make, Chin."

"Perhaps not, but I had grown to love you by that time. I could see the hatred and bitterness inside you because of what Driscoll had done to you and your brother. I was afraid that if I told you the truth you would run after your brother and get yourself killed. I did not want to see you die."

Nathan looked at Chin and recalled the way this gentle man had taken him in and cared for him. He knew Chin well enough to know that he would never do anything to harm him. If he hadn't told him about Roberto, he must have had a good reason.

"As I recall," Joe interrupted, "you made me and Larissa lie to your parents. I had to keep from them for ten years the knowledge that you were alive. Do you know how it hurt me to do that to them? But I did it because you asked me not to tell them. You thought it was in their best interest not to know."

Nathan threw Joe an angry look. "Thank you for reminding me of my mistakes, Joe."

"That's what I'm here for, boy." Joe flashed a huge grin.

"Chin, I'm sorry. I didn't mean to accuse you of anything. I just need to know what happened to Roberto. If I know, maybe it will help me to figure out why he took Anna and where they went."

"I had friends trying to find out about your brother for a long time. Many of them knew about Driscoll and hated him. They wanted to help you. It was later discovered that your brother was taken out of the bay and put on a ship."

"What kind of ship?" Nathan asked anxiously.

"It was a trading ship. It sailed to many places in Mexico and along the southern coast of this country."

"Did it deal in illegal merchandise?"

"It actually was a ship that traded in goods such as hardware, clothing material, farm goods, and liquor. The ship was one of many that was in a fleet of the Thornston Shipping Company."

"What was so bad about it?"

"Your brother was taken on board and put to work."

"You mean as a cabin boy?"

"More like a slave. The captain of the ship used him as his own personal servant and the crew thought of him the same way. When they sailed into any port he was locked inside the hold. He was never allowed on land."

"For how long?" Nathan tried to compose himself.

"The last my friend heard, your brother had been aboard that ship for eight years."

"That's impossible. A person couldn't just live on a ship for eight years. He'd die."

"He almost did, several times. He contracted malaria and typhoid fever."

"My God." Larissa clutched Joe's arm.

"You said eight years, Chin. What happened to him after that?"

"All my friend knows is that he left the ship in Louisiana."

"How did he manage to get off?"

"He saved the life of the owner. The owner then freed your brother."

"What else?"

"That's all I know."

"Who was the owner?"

"Richard Thornston."

"Thornston Shipping Company. That's out of New Orleans, isn't it?" Joe asked.

Chin nodded. "My friend tells me that Richard Thornston is a very wealthy and influential man."

"So was Franklin Driscoll."

"Apparently, Thornston is much different from Driscoll. He is highly thought of around that area."

"Do you think it's possible that Roberto has been in New Orleans for the last couple of years?"

"Not only possible, but quite likely. If Thornston is

the kind of man my friend says he is, he probably helped your brother in some way. He will probably remember him."

"Then I need to go to New Orleans and talk to Richard Thornston."

"This is an amazing story," Joe said. He stood next to Nathan. "I'm not defending Roberto, Nate, but now I can understand why he'd be so bitter. But I still don't understand why his bitterness is aimed at you."

"Well, I'll just have to find that out." He went over to Chin and smiled. "Thank you, old friend. Like the rock, you have remained solid and unmovable. Thank you."

"It gives me great pleasure to be able to help you, Nathan. I am sorry that I could not tell you so many years ago."

"It's all right. I understand." He went to Larissa and took her hands in his. "I promise you, Larissa, that I will find Roberto and bring him home."

Larissa stood up and smiled. She placed her hands on Nathan's face. "You are so like your father, yet you have so much of Aeneva in you, so much good." She kissed him on the cheek.

"I've already lost my parents, and I don't intend to lose my brother and the woman I love. It may take a while, but the three of us will be back. I promise you all."

Roberto couldn't contain a smile as he watched Anna. She kept a straight face as she looked at the men around the table. "I see your twenty dollars and I raise it another ten." Her normally sweet face now wore an expression of tough indifference. As all the men around the table threw down their cards, it was just Anna and another man, a Cajun named LeBeau.

"As beautiful as you are, madam, I don't think that I believe you. I think that you are lying. So I see your bet and I call you."

Anna carefully fanned out her cards. "Straight flush, queen high." Her blue eyes pierced LeBeau's.

His eyes met hers, never varying, but he slowly began to smile. "You are clever." He fanned his cards out. "A straight flush, jack high. You have me beat by one card, madam. I take my hat off to you."

"Thank you." Anna nodded her head as she pulled the money in toward her. She looked up at Roberto. "I told you Trenton taught me how to gamble."

"So I see. What do you plan to do with your winnings?"

"I don't know." A sad look crossed her face. "I don't really have anyone to spend it on."

"What? A beautiful woman like you does not want to go out and buy clothes? Unbelievable!" LeBeau exclaimed.

Anna laughed. "As you've probably already noticed, women in the West don't really care too much for fashion."

"On the contrary, madam, if you are an indication of what women in the west look like, I think I must immediately jump ship and head that way."

"I bet you say that to every woman you meet, don't you, Mr. LeBeau?"

"Not all of them. Just the beautiful ones."

Roberto was quickly growing tired of the banter between Anna and LeBeau. "I think it's time we turned in, Anna. We have a big day tomorrow."

"You are getting off in New Orleans?"

"Yes. Have you ever been there, Mr. LeBeau?"

"LeBeau, please. I don't use my first name. Yes, I was born there. But I have left it many times."

"You are French?"

"Yes, my father was a French trapper. He came from France and traveled around this area, but he always came back here. He finally decided to stay here when he met my mother. She was a Spaniard, a beautiful woman who completely captured my father's heart. You remind me much of her."

"It's getting late, Anna," Roberto said impatiently.

"Why don't you go on ahead, 'Berto. I'm sure Mr. LeBeau would be happy to see me to our cabin."

"I would be most honored."

Roberto leaned down and whispered to Anna, "Can I speak to you for a minute? Alone."

"Will you please excuse us for a moment, Mr. LeBeau? I need to talk to my husband."

"But of course. I need to refill my glass anyway. May I bring you something?"

"No, thank you." Anna turned to Roberto. "What? Are you going to tell me I should conduct myself like your wife? If you'll recall, I'm not your wife."

Roberto sat down. "And if you'll recall, the last time I warned you about a man he tried to rape you."

Anna looked at Roberto. He was right, of course. The episode with the Benders hadn't been that long ago. She could still see the looks on their faces when Roberto and she had taken them to the sheriff. And Ellie, poor Ellie, had decided to stay at that stage stop. Anna hoped she'd be all right.

Anna had an intense desire to touch Roberto's face. He was so very handsome, yet so very sad. She wanted to help him, but she didn't know how. "What do you want from me, Roberto? I've made this trip willingly. I said I would help you, and I don't even know what I'm helping you with. Why do you begrudge me a conversation with such a nice man?"

"Because I've seen men like him before. He's smooth and he wants nothing more than to take you to his cabin and to his bed."

"You don't think very highly of me, do you?"

Roberto leaned forward. His dark eyes narrowed. "I think you are an incredible woman, Anna. I am envious that you love Nathan so much."

"You don't have to be envious. You could have a love of your own, 'Berto. There is probably some woman in this world who is waiting to love you with all of her heart."

"There's no such woman for me." Roberto stood up, ending their moment of intimacy. "Are you coming or not?"

"No, I think I'll wait for LeBeau to come back. I like him," Anna responded flippantly, instantly angry with herself for acting so childish.

"Do as you wish, but don't expect me to run to your rescue."

"I never asked you to rescue me before. If you hadn't taken me in the first place, I would never have been put in a position to be harmed." Anna regretted her words. She could see that she had hurt Roberto, for in spite of his immense show of toughness, she now knew that there was a gentleness inside. She had already seen it on more than one occasion. She reached out for Roberto's hand, but he stepped backward. "Roberto, I'm sorry. I say silly things when I'm angry."

"It doesn't matter." He looked up. LeBeau was walking toward the table, carrying two glasses. "Here comes your friend. Enjoy yourself."

Anna watched Roberto walk off. He was a graceful man and one who commanded attention in a room. His dark good looks were extremely appealing, but there was something else about him that made people look. Perhaps it was the air of danger that accompanied him.

"Everything is all right?"

Anna looked up at LeBeau. He was not a tall man, not like Roberto or Nathan, but he had a stocky build and he held himself as if he were ten feet tall. He had nondescript brown hair and a long, thin moustache. His face was wide and his jaw strong. He was not what you would term a handsome man, but he was good-looking just the same. And he had the strangest eyes, eyes that changed colors whenever he moved, as if he didn't want you to guess what he was thinking. Unlike Roberto, she liked him. "Yes, everything is all right."

"I brought this for you." He set a glass down by Anna. "It is champagne. I hope you like it."

"Thank you." Anna sipped at the bubbly wine. She liked the taste of it much better than whiskey. She looked at LeBeau's expensive clothes and the large diamond ring he wore on his right hand, and assumed he was a man of some means. "What exactly do you do, Mr. LeBeau?"

"First of all, my name is LeBeau. I know it is strange, but that is what I am called."

"All right."

"I own some properties in New Orleans and I own some land and a home in the country. Perhaps you could come for a visit."

"I would have to ask my husband." Anna sipped at the wine. "You never answered my question, LeBeau. What do you do for a living?"

LeBeau smiled. "Apparently, you women from the West are not taught that it is impolite to inquire as to a man's profession, especially when he has already given you an answer."

"I don't know about the women in the West, but I know that I was taught that if you want to find out something, you ask. And if you don't find out what you want to know, then you ask again."

"Touché." LeBeau raised his glass to Anna and took a drink. "I like your tenacity, madam."

"Anna."

"Anna. It is a beautiful name."

"Thank you. Are you going to answer my question, or

do I have to keep being impolite?"

"No, I will answer your question. Basically, I make my living doing what I did on the boat this evening. I gamble and then I invest the money. I have bought many properties in New Orleans, the most profitable being an establishment where gentlemen of great wealth may go and choose a woman to their liking. Do you understand?"

"You mean a whorehouse?"

LeBeau laughed loudly. "You are impudent. I like that very much in a woman. You would do very well in my establishment. You could make a lot of money."

"Have you forgotten that I am a married woman, LeBeau? I thank you for the compliment anyway."

"You aren't offended by what I say?"

"Why should I be offended?"

LeBeau shrugged. "Most women pretend to be offended if you look at them even a little bit, when in reality they like being looked at. You, on the other hand, admit that you like men, yet you are faithful to your husband. I find that particularly fascinating."

"Why?"

"Because you do not love your husband."

Anna was stunned. How could LeBeau possibly know that?

"You are wondering how I know this?" LeBeau leaned forward, his eyes piercing Anna's. "When a woman loves a man she looks at him a certain way. She makes love to him with her eyes. She yearns for him. Although your eyes are very beautiful, you do not have that look in them when you look at your husband."

Anna felt the stem of the champagne glass with her fingers. She thought of Nathan. She remembered the way Aeneva described Trenton the first time she had seen him, and that was the way she felt about Nathan—hair the color of corn and eyes the color of the sky.

"You now have that look."

"What?" Anna looked at LeBeau.

"You now have that look of which I was speaking. You are in love with another man, are you not?"

Anna rested her chin in her hand. "You are a strange man, LeBeau. I'm not sure what to think of you."

"You may think what you want, but you must answer my question. I answered your question."

"Yes, I am in love with another man. This is a marriage of convenience."

"You do not strike me as the kind of woman who would marry a man she did not love."

"I didn't have a choice."

"Your parents forced you into the marriage?"

"My parents are dead."

"Then what is it? Why would a woman like you marry a man she did not love?"

"It is getting late, LeBeau. Would you walk me to my cabin?" Anna stood up, beginning to feel uneasy. Maybe Roberto was right about LeBeau. Maybe he wanted nothing more than to take her to his bed.

"I will walk you to your cabin, Anna." LeBeau put his hand on Anna's elbow, guiding her out of the large dining hall and onto the outer deck. "What do you think of the South? Do you like it?"

"I haven't had a chance to see it yet to know if I like it." Anna leaned out over the railing and breathed in the sweet air. She longed for the outdoors. "Do you have horses, LeBeau?"

"Yes."

"Perhaps my husband and I will visit you then."

"You ride?"

"Yes, I ride." Anna smiled to herself, thinking of the times she had raced across the land, her hair blowing in the wind, her body moving in rhythm to the galloping horse. "I'd better get in. Roberto will be worried."

"Whatever you say." LeBeau walked Anna to her cabin. "It has been a very entertaining evening, Anna. I hope we will meet again."

"Won't I see you tomorrow?"

"I will be leaving early. Where are you and your husband staying?"

"I don't know. I don't think he knows anyone in the city."

"Then I must give you my card." He reached into the pocket of his brocade vest and handed Anna a card. "If you need me for anything, anything at all, please call on me at this address. I will be at your service." He took Anna's hand and kissed it softly. "It has been my pleasure to speak with you this evening, Anna. I wish you well."

"And you also, LeBeau. Thank you." Anna watched LeBeau as he walked away, thinking what a strange person he was. She put his card in her purse and opened the door of the cabin. Roberto was sitting at the small table, drinking a steaming cup of coffee. She thought how incongruous it looked to see a man drinking a cup of coffee instead of liquor.

She shut the door and walked inside. Since they had traveled together, Roberto had made sure that she was as comfortable as possible. He also made sure to stay as far away from her as possible, even to the point of sleeping on the floor next to the bunk in the cabin. Anna walked up to him. "Are you all right?"

"Why wouldn't I be?"

She sat down at the table, taking the coffee from him and sipping at its rich, warm flavor. She handed the cup back to him. "You don't drink." It was a statement, not a question.

"I've seen what happens to men who drink. It makes them crazy and out of control, and later they use it as an excuse. I don't ever want to be out of control, and I don't want to make excuses. If I make mistakes, I'll make them on my own."

"I'm sorry if I offended you this evening. I didn't mean to."

"You don't have to apologize. You're right. You wouldn't be here if it weren't for me, and the Benders wouldn't have hurt you if you hadn't been with me."

"That's over and done with. There's no use going over it now."

"Why do you make things so easy for me? If I were you, I'd hate me."

"But I'm not you, 'Berto. I'm me. We come from two different backgrounds. I don't know what's happened to make you so bitter, but it must have been something horrible."

"How do you know anything happened to me at all?"

"Because I've seen a gentle side of you. You are not as cold and callous as you would like to seem."

"You don't know me, Anna. You don't know what I'm capable of."

"I know exactly what you're capable of." She leaned forward and covered his hand with hers. "The night the Benders attacked me, you helped me. You cleaned my wounds and you stayed with me until I fell asleep. You have a lot of gentleness inside you, but you're afraid to let it show. You don't want to get hurt again."

"Tell me about Nathan." Again Roberto had changed the subject from himself, but this time Anna didn't mind. She thought it was a good sign that Roberto wanted to know about his brother. "Nathan is one of the finest people I have ever known. He is loving and kind and he's very funny. I love being with him. He makes me feel as if anything is possible. I love him, 'Berto. I love him with all my heart."

Roberto nodded his head. "I know. What happened that night, Anna? I need to know."

102

Anna knew what night Roberto was talking about. "What do you remember?"

Roberto shrugged his shoulders. "Not much. Just that I ran away from Nathan and ran into some shop."

"You wanted to see a cockfight. Nathan tried to dissuade you, but as usual you got your own way. It was very crowded inside and you managed to move away from Nathan. Men were betting heavily on the birds and it started to get wild. You accidentally fell into the pit while the two champions were fighting, and one of the birds killed the other. A man named Franklin Driscoll had bet a lot of money on the bird who got killed, and he went crazy. He started beating up on you. Nathan interfered and the man fought with him; then he knifed him." Roberto looked up in surprise.

"He stabbed Nathan?"

"Yes, and then he started to beat you. Nathan had a knife in his boot and tried to throw it, but Driscoll pulled a gun and held it to your head. Nathan was forced to drop the knife, and Driscoll shot him. Then he shot you."

Roberto stood up. "I don't remember any of this. Are you sure Nathan didn't make this up?"

"I know Nathan. He wouldn't lie about something like this. Besides, there was another witness."

"Who?"

"A Chinaman named Chin. He watched the whole thing. He managed to get Nathan out of there, but Driscoll had you thrown into the bay. Chin had people search for you, but they didn't find your body. Chin assumed you were dead."

Roberto nodded his head. "Of course they wouldn't find my body. I had already been taken out of the water by then." He was talking more to himself than to Anna. "What happened to Nathan after that?"

"Chin took care of him until he got well, and then he went into the hills and mined for gold."

"Why didn't he go home?"

"He didn't think your parents wanted him. He thought they blamed him for your death."

"I don't understand."

"He wrote two letters to your parents, but for some reason they never got them. He assumed that they didn't want to see him. So he worked in the mine and, with Chin's help, he became educated. He had a plan. He wanted to get even with Driscoll for what he had done, but in order to do that he had to have enough money to pass himself off as a rich man. He worked in the mine for almost ten years until he hit it big. He came back into the city and passed himself off as Steven Randall. He got to know Driscoll's daughter, and she fell in love with him. He got close to Driscoll."

"Did he marry Driscoll's daughter?"

"No, he fell in love with another woman."

"You."

"Yes, I had been living with Trenton and Aeneva for ten years and they wanted me to go to San Francisco to visit your Aunt Larissa and Joe. When I got there we went to a party and I saw Nathan. I fell in love with him the first time I looked at him."

"You only knew him as Steven Randall, but what about your name? Didn't he know who you were?"

"My name is O'Leary. He had no idea who I was, and we didn't talk much about my family."

"What happened to Driscoll?"

"Nathan found out who I was and decided to break it off with me. He didn't think it was right that we fall in love. But Trenton got attacked by a mountain lion and we were called home. It was there that I found out he was really Nathan. I was shocked and angry, but we worked it out. We decided to go to California and get married. But Driscoll had me kidnapped and taken to California." Anna stopped for the first time, looking acutely uncomfortable. "Driscoll gave me opium and he sold me to a slaver who was going to sell me in China."

"My God, Anna. I didn't realize you two had been through so much."

Anna lowered her head. "It was a horrible experience. The captain of the ship made sure I stayed addicted to opium, and then he used me for his own pleasure." Her hands began to shake. This was the first time she had talked about the incident with anyone besides Nathan. "When Nathan finally got me off the ship, I was a mess. I was addicted to opium, and I wanted it more than I wanted him. I even left him and went to Chinatown, to an opium den. It's so humiliating to think that I could have done something like that."

"I'm sorry." Roberto stood behind her, his hands on her shoulders. "You don't have to talk about it if you don't want to."

"It's good for me to talk about it. I need to realize that it wasn't my fault."

"How did you quit the opium?"

"Nathan locked me in a room at Larissa's and Joe's and gave me this Chinese tea that made me incredibly sick. By the time I had vomited and sweated most of the opium out of my system, I didn't want it anymore."

"And Driscoll?"

"Chin gave him to Nathan as a present."

Roberto smiled for the first time. "I like this Chin, and I don't even know him."

"Nathan put Driscoll on a ship to China, where he was to be sold as a slave."

"Yes, a fitting ending." Roberto continued to pace around the room. "I still don't understand why Nathan just didn't go home. He must have known that mother and father would have forgiven him anything."

"He didn't know that for sure. He agonized over your death, and he blamed himself for not taking better care of you. He was sure that Trenton and Aeneva would blame him, and he couldn't live with that."

"So he stayed away from them all that time. He was serving penance."

"Yes, I think so. He stayed by himself. He worked and read. The only thing that drove him was his need to avenge your death and make sure that Driscoll suffered as you had."

"This doesn't make sense." Roberto took his hat from the chair and walked to the door. "I need to think. Thank you for telling me everything, Anna. I know it wasn't easy."

"It was easier than I thought. I'm beginning to trust you, 'Berto. Perhaps someday you'll feel you can trust me enough to tell me why you feel Nathan deserves to be punished."

Roberto listened, but said nothing. Anna watched him as he walked out the door. She wondered if she had gotten through to him, but she could only hope. She wanted desperately to be with Nathan again, but she also wanted to help Roberto with whatever was eating away at him and, she hoped, reunite him with his brother.

LeBeau sat in the carriage, looking at Anna and Roberto as they walked down the platform of the boat. "I want them followed everywhere they go," he said to the man who stood outside the carriage. "I want to know everything about them, especially him. I want to know what he's doing here and if he's ever been here before. Don't come back until you have the information I want."

"*Oui*, Monsieur LeBeau."

LeBeau handed the man some money and continued to watch Anna and Roberto. He was totally fascinated by Anna; more than that, he wanted her. But he also wanted to find out about Roberto. There was something about the man that he recognized. Perhaps it was just that he understood what it was like to be a loner.

LeBeau's carriage traveled through the bustling city, past the Negro women who balanced flat baskets on their heads, and the peddlers pushing their carts. To someone who had never seen the city it would be an exciting sight, but LeBeau, who had grown up here, could no longer see the excitement or the beauty. The carriage left the city and went into the country, traveling along the narrow rutted road that wound through the perfectly arched grove of oak trees that led to the plantation gates. LeBeau sat upright as the carriage pulled through the gates of Rolling Oaks. He smiled to himself. This was what he had always wanted. If he played his cards right, he would have Caroline Thornston and Rolling Oaks, as well as most of Richard Thornston's money.

The carriage stopped in front of the impressive white columns of the estate. LeBeau stepped out of the carriage and walked up the steps, lifting the brass knocker as he stood at the door. He looked out over the grounds as he waited.

"Good morning, Samuel," LeBeau said, handing the butler his hat and gloves. He followed the man through the enormous entryway into the dining room. "Please help yourself to breakfast, sir," Samuel said as he pointed to the large sideboard. "Miss Caroline and Mr. Thornston will be down momentarily."

"Thank you, Samuel." LeBeau picked up a china plate and filled it with rolls, eggs, ham, and fat sausages. He set his plate on the table and poured himself a cup of coffee from the large silver pot, adding three cubes of sugar. He sat down at one end of the long table, imagining what it would be like to live in a place like this. He could easily be married to Caroline Thornston. While she was not a raving beauty, she had a delicate loveliness that many men might admire. She was small and quite fragile, but she had a lovely smile. He could never stay faithful to a wife like Caroline, however; she did not excite him. He was more attracted to women like Anna. Still, a marriage to Caroline Thornston could prove quite profitable.

"Good morning, LeBeau." Richard Thornston's deep voice never ceased to surprise LeBeau.

LeBeau stood up, extending his hand. "How are you, Richard?"

"I am well. And you?"

"Well, thank you."

"Sit down; finish your breakfast. Your trip was fruitful, I trust?"

"Not as much as we had hoped. I would like to discuss the details of it with you later."

"Yes, after breakfast." Thornston turned as Caroline walked into the room, dressed in a soft green dress that complimented her tiny figure.

"It is good to see you, LeBeau."

LeBeau walked to Caroline and took her hand, kissing it softly. "You look wonderful, Caroline. I don't think I have ever seen you look so beautiful."

Caroline blushed slightly. "Thank you."

"You have been well, I hope."

"Very well."

"So, LeBeau, did you meet anyone new on your travels?" Richard asked.

"As a matter of fact, I met a nice couple on the boat. They are new here in our city. I was thinking that it would be a good idea to invite them to a party. What do you think, Caroline?"

"We haven't entertained in a long time, father. We could have a party here."

"Whatever you want, my dear," Thornston replied

off-handedly. The last thing he wanted was a party. He would have to talk Caroline out of it. "So, LeBeau, what do you think of my lovely daughter? She gets prettier every day, doesn't she?"

"Indeed." LeBeau surveyed Caroline. "She is like a delicate flower of the South, only she doesn't wilt in the heat."

"That's enough, you two. LeBeau, there's a big party at the Meades's later this month. Would you be interested in accompanying me?"

LeBeau was pleased. If Caroline wanted to be seen in public with him, it was a good sign. "I'd be honored, Caroline."

"Perhaps we could invite the couple you spoke of. It would be a good way to introduce them to people around here."

"Yes, I'll speak to them. I'm sure they'd enjoy that."

"Are they young?"

"Yes, the wife is not much older than you. She's very friendly. I think you and she would get along well."

"I'd like to meet someone my own age for a change. It gets so tiresome staying on the estate all the time."

"Then I will make sure to arrange something." LeBeau looked at Thornston. "Are you finished with breakfast, Richard? I have some business matters to attend to this morning."

Thornston stood up. "Finish your breakfast, dear. I'll walk LeBeau out."

LeBeau walked to Caroline. "May I see you later this week? Perhaps we could go for a ride in the carriage."

Caroline looked at her father, her face suddenly going white. "I don't know about that, LeBeau. It's been so long since I've been out."

"Well then, I'll just come here for a visit. We can take a walk around the grounds."

"I'd like that very much, LeBeau."

LeBeau and Thornston walked out of the house and stood on the wide stone steps. "Did you learn anything?" Richard asked.

"I've followed every lead you've given me. The man has virtually disappeared."

"How could he just disappear?"

"He could be dead, Richard."

"But there would be evidence of that somewhere."

"Not necessarily. He could have gone back to Mexico."

"What if he comes back, LeBeau? If he finds out—" Thornston stopped himself. "Well, I don't know what he'll do."

"I've done everything I can, Richard. I went to San Francisco and talked to everyone I could find who was on the ship with him when he was a cabin boy. Nobody knew anything about his background."

"I don't like it. I just know he'll be back."

"I have to admit that what you did to the boy was brutal, Richard."

"I didn't ask for your opinion, LeBeau. If you entertain any idea of marrying my daughter, if would be in your best interest to do as I say."

LeBeau was not used to being ordered around by anyone, not even Richard Thornston. "I think you should be careful, Richard. There are not many men who would marry a young woman, however lovely she may be, who is in Caroline's situation. I think she would be considered, how do you say, damaged goods?"

"How dare you." Thornston moved close to LeBeau. "Don't you ever say anything about my daughter. You're not good enough to be in the same room with her."

"Then why is it you want me to marry her?" LeBeau looked Thornston in the eye. "I would be getting a good deal if I married your daughter, Richard, but we both know that she, too, would be getting a good deal. I am a man of some means, and I am becoming quite influential in this city. And if you're going to bring up the whorehouse, I think I can soothe your nerves by telling you that just about every respectable man in this city, including you, has visited it."

Beads of sweat broke out on Thornston's face. "Don't you try to blackmail me, you son of a bitch. I'll give you more trouble than you can deal with."

"I don't think so, Richard. You wouldn't want your dear Caroline to find out the truth about you. Oh yes, I could tell her lots of things about her dear, loving father."

"What do you want, LeBeau?"

"You know what I want. I want to marry your daughter, and I want enough money to last me for the rest of my life."

"And?"

"I think that's enough for now."

"Let's understand each other, LeBeau. I don't trust you. In fact, the thought of my daughter marrying you makes me sick."

"But you won't object."

"No, I won't object. She seems happy enough with you, and she'll finally have a father for her son. But if you ever hurt her, even a little bit, I swear I'll kill you, LeBeau."

"I think you should look to yourself, Richard. If anyone has hurt the girl, it is you. You have put that girl through hell." LeBeau pulled on his gloves and put on his hat. He walked down the steps and stopped at the carriage door. "If I were you, Richard, I'd look behind me from now on. If I were that boy, I'd find a way to come back here and kill you."

Thornston watched LeBeau as he drove away. He wiped the sweat from his brow. He knew LeBeau was right. He knew Roberto, and he knew how he worked. He never gave up at anything. If he was still alive, he would come back.

Thornston wondered what the boy would do when he did.

Chapter V

Nathan and Garrett had been riding for weeks. They had traveled by stagecoach to Arizona and picked up horses at Nathan's ranch. From there, they had ridden along the Colorado River and into New Mexico, along the Rio Grande and the Pecos River, and finally they crossed the New Mexico border into Texas. They were tired and bone-weary, but a special bond had grown between them. A year before, they had started out as enemies, fighting for the love of the same woman, and now they had become friends, bound by that love.

"If I never ride another mile, or see another horse, or taste another piece of jerky, I'll die a happy man."

"Or taste any more trail dust."

Garrett laughed. "Who would've ever thought we'd be riding together? Strange world."

"Yeah." Nathan thought about Roberto and how close they had been when they were younger. They'd fought, but they would've done anything for each other. What had happened to make Roberto hate him so much?

"Are you thinking about Anna?"

"I was thinking about 'Berto. I still can't figure any of this out."

"You'll drive yourself crazy trying. Just wait till we get

113

there and ask him yourself."

"I keep hoping he doesn't hurt Anna in any way. It would make it real hard for me to forgive him if he hurt her."

"I don't think he'll hurt her. Besides, we all know how tough she can be."

"That's what scares me. I'm afraid she'll fight him and get hurt. She's been through a lot, Garrett."

"I know, Nate, but I think she'll be fine. Besides, she's got to know that you'll be coming after her, you and your trusty sidekick, that is."

Nathan laughed and shook his head. "I can see why you were such a good friend to Anna. I understand why she didn't want to let you go."

"It's hard to give something like that up, but we all have to grow up. Anyway, I'm ready to find myself a woman. One who's gorgeous, rich and totally in love with me."

"You might have to wait a long time for a woman like that." Nathan laughed again as Garrett cussed under his breath.

They rode all day, every day, resting only when the sun went down. They camped in the desert, in the hills, along rivers, wherever there was a good spot. By the time they reached eastern Texas, they had been riding for almost two months. They were worn out, and they decided to rest for a few days in a town just west of the Louisiana border.

Onion Creek was a small, dusty town that catered mostly to cowboys, travelers and prostitutes. It was so named because one of the first inhabitants found that the only thing that would grow in the soil was onions. The name had stuck. Onion Creek had one restaurant that was located in the hotel, a general store that carried everything from flour and sugar to French perfume, a blacksmith, a doctor, who also served as dentist and barber, a sheriff, and one saloon, called the Three Sisters. Garrett and Nathan tied up at the saloon and went inside. It would've been just like any other saloon west of the Mississippi, except for one big difference—this saloon had been opened by three sisters, all young, all smart, and all very pretty. The two younger sisters had quickly grown tired of the business and had gone back to the east coast to marry, but the oldest sister still ran the saloon.

Garrett and Nathan were mightily surprised when they went inside. They expected a dirty, dingy place, full of old wooden tables that had been marked up by bored drunks; tired, sad-looking women; and beat-up, over-the-hill cowboys. Instead, the inside was brightly lit. Gaily colored lamps hung from the ceiling. Shiny, unmarked wooden tables were set all around the room. A long wooden bar dominated the room; it was fully as long as one entire side of the saloon. A large mirror hung behind it, reflecting everything that went on in the room. There were stacks of glasses, with every kind of bottle of liquor that a person could imagine, lined in neat rows on the counter in front of the glasses. A piano stood against another wall, and above it hung a painting of three women—one a redhead, one a blonde, the third a brunette. On the opposite side of the room from the bar, there was a staircase that led upstairs to rooms, one assumed, for use with the saloon girls. The place was filled with men and women, and the real surprise was that everyone seemed so clean.

"I'll be damned," Garrett said gleefully. His eyes lit up like a little boy's. "Who would've ever thought."

"Not me. This place belongs in San Francisco, not in Texas."

"They probably make more money here than they would in San Francisco."

"I assume they're the three sisters." Nathan nodded to the painting above the piano.

115

"I wonder if they're real."

Nathan poked Garrett in the side with his elbow. "Of course they're real. Why would they have a painting of them if they weren't real?"

They wandered over to the bar, both of them still in slight shock at the sight of the rather elegant saloon.

"How do you do, gentlemen." The bartender was dressed in a pristine white shirt with a black bow-tie, a black vest, and black pants. He had very little hair, and a dark, graying moustache. He had the kind of face a person would see on their favorite uncle. He set up two shot glasses and filled them with whiskey. "The first ones are on the house."

"Much obliged," Garrett replied, downing the whiskey with a flick of his wrist.

"Thank you." Nathan picked up the glass. "This is quite a place you have here. I've never seen anything like it in these parts."

"You never will, either. Miss Molly, she believes in running a first-class place. She doesn't allow any trouble in here." He nodded toward the saloon girls. "If you're interested in a girl, you ask her, you just don't take her. If she's interested in you, she'll take you upstairs. Prices are different for different girls."

"Who are the sisters?" Garrett asked, placing a dollar coin on the counter for a refill.

"They came from the East somewhere. No one knows for sure. They came out here with their parents to build a ranch and raise cattle. Their parents were killed by the Comanche and the sisters were left on their own. They had some money, so the oldest one, Miss Molly, decided to go into business. It started out small at first, but you can see how well it's done. It's driven the other saloons out of business."

"Is there a place in town where we could get a room and a bath?"

"And a decent meal?" Garrett added.

"The hotel isn't bad, but it's not great. Sometimes Miss Molly rents out rooms here, but she's pretty choosey about the people she rents to. Where you gents from?"

"San Francisco and Arizona. We're on our way to New Orleans."

The bartender eyed the two young men who stood before him. They were dirty and dusty, but they had a clean, wholesome look. "We have a cook here. I'll order you up some food if you like. Go find yourselves a table and I'll talk to Miss Molly."

"Thank you kindly." Garrett laughed. "I think we hit the jackpot, my friend."

"I just want a bath and a clean bed."

"I wouldn't mind one of these women."

They found a table in the corner and watched the people in the room. The piano player played a lively tune and some of the men and women were dancing. There was one table of cardplayers, and the rest of the men just seemed to be passing the time enjoying the company.

Garrett leaned forward. "I've never seen anything like this. These people all seem so happy."

"Wouldn't you be happy if you lived around these parts and this was the only place you could go?"

"Yeah, I guess I would be, at that." Garrett's eyes widened. "Holy Mother of God, look at that!"

Nathan turned to look where Garrett was staring. Coming toward them, followed closely by the bartender, was one of the most striking women either man had ever seen. She was very tall, with golden blond hair, much the same color as Nathan's. Her hair was pulled straight back at her neck and braided down her back. She wore tight brown pants made of leather, and a silk blouse that did nothing to hide her ample breasts. When she got to the table, they could see that her eyes were almost black, a

117

stunning contrast to her light hair.

"Hello, gentlemen. My name is Molly O'Brien." She held out her hand.

Nathan and Garrett stumbled to their feet to shake hands with the striking woman who stood before them.

"My name is Nathan Hawkins."

"I'm Garrett McReynolds. Pleased to meet you, ma'am."

"Nice to meet both of you. Please, sit down." Molly pulled out a chair and sat. "It's okay, Duke. You can go on back to the bar now. Thank you."

"Whatever you say, Miss Molly."

Molly fixed the two young men with her incredible black eyes. "I'm a pretty good judge of character. I haven't been wrong yet. I'll rent you two a room for as long as you like if you abide by my rules."

"Sounds fair to me," Garrett replied impatiently.

"You haven't heard my rules yet. You aren't allowed to take women up to your room unless they work here in the saloon, and no women allowed during the day. No excessive drunkenness, or you'll be asked to leave or, if the need arises, you'll be thrown out. It's a dollar a day, each, a week payable in advance if you plan to stay that long. We serve all meals here. We have one bathtub, so if you want a bath you have to let us know so we can heat up the water."

"I'd like a bath." Nathan said.

"All right. What do you boys plan to do while you're here?"

"Just rest up, that's all," Nathan replied.

"And maybe get to know a few people." Garrett stared at the woman across the table from him. It had been so long since he'd been with a woman, he couldn't even remember what it was like.

"Well, I guess that's all for now. I run the place. So what I say goes. Do you understand?"

Nathan nodded. He handed over seven dollars. "This is for both of us for three days. If we decide to stay longer, we'll let you know."

"Fair enough." Molly stood up. "Nice meeting you boys. Enjoy your stay here."

Garrett and Nathan watched her as she walked away, both transfixed by the way she walked.

"I never knew a woman could look so good in a pair of men's pants."

"Neither did I. She's very impressive."

"Impressive? Is that all you have to say? Hell, she's just about the most beautiful thing I've ever seen." Garrett tilted his head to one side. "Next to Anna, of course."

"Of course."

Duke brought them each a plate. "Hope you boys like your steaks cooked raw. Miss Molly said to give each of you a cold glass of beer."

"Thanks, Duke." Garrett looked at the thick steak and the fried potatoes. "I think I'm dreaming, Nate, because this can't be real."

"It's real all right, and you'd better eat it before it gets cold."

The two men ate as if they hadn't eaten in over a month. When they were finished, Duke showed them their room.

"Miss Molly says to tell you that your bath will be ready in about a half hour. The tub is out back of the kitchen. It's easier to carry the hot water there."

"I don't care where it is, Duke, just as long as I can wash this dirt off me."

"If you'll leave your clothes outside the tub, I'll see that they get washed tomorrow."

"Thank you." Garrett walked around the room. It had a brass bed, a wood clothes closet, a small table with a mirror, and a nightstand with a pitcher and bowl. Garrett stood in front of the bed, looking quite obviously perturbed.

"What's the matter with you?"

"I've never slept in the same bed with a man before. It's gonna seem kind of strange."

"We can flip for it if you like."

"Hell no, I'm not taking any chances. I'd rather sleep on half a bed than none at all. I'll somehow get used to you as my bed partner."

"It won't be a picnic for me either, you know. You're not exactly what I had in mind to keep myself warm."

"I'll go down and bring up the saddlebags. You do have a change of clothes, don't you?"

"Yes, I have a change of clothes."

"Good, I'd hate for you to embarrass me in front of that pretty Miss Molly."

Nathan picked up a pillow from the bed and threw it in Garrett's face. "Get out of here." He heard Garrett laugh as he left the room. He sat down on the edge of the bed and attempted to get his boots off his swollen feet. When he finally succeeded, he picked each foot up and rubbed it. He looked at the nice, clean bedspread and stood up, taking off his holster, shirt and pants until he had nothing on but his longjohns. He lay on the bed, his hands under his head, and stared up at the ceiling. Anna would have loved a room like this; he remembered how she had liked his room at the hotel in San Francisco. He was scared suddenly; he couldn't remember her voice, and he had just a vague picture in his mind of what she looked like. How could he forget her so soon? He tried to recall how she'd looked the first night he had ever seen her, when they had danced together, and her face came back just as clearly as if she were standing in front of him. Her large blue eyes stared up at him with open innocence and her dark hair fell loosely around her shoulders. He could never forget her face.

The door opened and Garrett walked in, tossing the saddlebags on the floor. "Your bath is ready. Duke said you can go down this hall and out the door. The stairs lead down to the tub."

Nathan slipped on his pants and grabbed his saddlebag. "I hope you don't mind waiting for a while, because I'm going to take my time."

Garrett smiled, lifting the bottle of whiskey he held in his hand. "I don't mind. I think I'll just lie here and dream about Miss Molly."

"That's all it'll be is a dream."

Garrett took off his holster and hung it over the bedpost. He unbuttoned his shirt and took it off, rubbing his neck and shoulders. "I'm so goddamned tired I could sleep for a week," he mumbled to himself, taking a swig from the whiskey bottle. He did have to admit to himself, though, that if they had to stop somewhere for a time, this was the place to stop. He walked to the window and lifted the lace curtain, looking out on the town. No lights shone. He assumed this was the only place open in town. There was a knock on the door. Garrett put the bottle on the nightstand and walked to the door. Molly O'Brien was standing outside when he opened the door.

"Miss O'Brien."

"May I come in, Mr. McReynolds?"

Garrett stood to one side as Molly came in. He watched her as she walked, the tight-fitting pants practically molding themselves to her buttocks and thighs. This wasn't what he needed to see right now. He closed the door. "What can I do for you?"

"You and your friend look like honest men."

Garrett walked to the table and picked up the bottle. He took another swig. "We could be thieving murderers for all you know."

"I don't think so. I've had my share of those, and you and your friend are not murderers."

Garrett didn't know what she wanted, but he wanted her out. She was making him uncomfortable. It had been too long since he'd had a woman, and having her in his room alone wasn't helping matters any. "What do you want, Miss O'Brien?"

"Molly."

"What do you want, Molly?"

"I need your help."

"You need my help? You don't look like you need anyone's help. You look like you can take care of yourself just fine."

"Have you ever heard of the Strickland Gang?"

"No, can't say as I have."

"They roam around Texas and Mexico and occasionally wander into Louisiana. They're river rats—thieves and murderers."

"What about them?"

"They were here about a year ago. Wandered into the place pretty as you please and tried to take it over. They wound up killing five men and taking my sisters captive."

"Where were you?"

"I had a friend who had just had a baby. She used to work here and I was real fond of her. I stayed with her for a few weeks to help her and her husband. When I came back to town I found out what was happening from one of the men in town. This gang of eight men had virtually taken this town hostage."

"What about your sheriff?"

"Our sheriff is a worthless drunk."

"What did you do?"

"I devised a plan. I sent a note to the leader, Jeremiah Strickland. I told him I'd give him ten thousand dollars in cash if he'd meet with me alone."

"Did he?"

"Yes, he came alone. We met in the middle of town where his brothers could watch."

"Did you give him the money?"

"Hell no. I took him captive. I knew that was the only way I could get my sisters back alive."

"You took him captive?"

"It wasn't all that hard, Mr. McReynolds. I am a woman, after all."

"So I've noticed."

"I told him I wanted to talk to him alone, inside somewhere. We went to my house on the edge of town. It was easy enough. A few of his brothers followed, thinking they were protecting him. We went to my bedroom and undressed, and when we got into bed, I pulled a knife from underneath my pillow. I knocked him out with the butt of the knife and then I hog-tied him but good."

"I like you more and more, Molly. What happened then?"

"I put him by the upstairs window so he could yell down to his brothers. I made him tell them to let my sisters go or I'd kill him. It was that simple."

"Didn't his gang try to break into your house?"

"I told him if I heard one noise, one sound, I'd blow his head off with his own gun. I shot one of them in the foot just to get my point across."

"Did they let your sisters go?"

"Strickland told them not to let them go, but I think they felt useless without him. That's what I was counting on. They let my sisters go, but I held onto Strickland until they rode out of town. When I was cutting him loose, he reached for the knife. We struggled and I cut him pretty badly in the face. I imagine he's pretty scarred from that. He swore he'd make me pay for it if it was the last thing he ever did."

"And now he's coming back here."

"That's what I hear, and I don't have enough men to help me. At least, I don't have enough men who are good with a gun."

"What do you want Nathan and me to do?"

"I want you to stay until they show up. I need to have someone I can trust besides Duke. I have a feeling that this time it won't be so easy getting Strickland out of here."

"Why don't you leave, go somewhere for a while?"

"Because this is my home, and I'll be damned if some no-good two-bit killer is going to run me off."

"Even if it costs you your life?"

"Even if it costs me my life."

Garrett moved closer to Molly. "Are your sisters as stubborn as you?"

"Pa always said I had a stubborn streak a mile long. I suppose he was right."

"Do you have a man in your life, Molly?"

"No man, just this business and my house."

"Why isn't a beautiful woman like you married?"

"Marriage never much appealed to me. I never liked the way it makes women seem like they're in bondage. I don't want that. I'd rather be independent."

"And alone."

"If that's the way it has to be."

"It doesn't have to be that way." Garrett reached back and picked up the braid from her back. "You have beautiful hair."

Molly jerked her head away. "If you plan to stay, I think we should get something straight. I'll pay you and your friend for your help, but I'm not included in the bargain."

"I wasn't planning on paying for you." Garrett's voice was low. He stepped closer to Molly, so close he could see the tiny freckles that dotted her nose. "I'll talk to Nathan and let you know. In the meantime, I'd like you to think about something." Garrett cupped his hand around the back of Molly's head and pulled her close to him. He kissed her lightly and then stepped back, picking up his bottle of whiskey. "For a woman who is so independent, you sure are afraid of men."

"Don't you dare judge me. You don't know anything about me."

"And you don't know anything about me, yet something in you decided to trust me. I won't take advantage of you and I won't hurt you, Molly."

"All men hurt women. I see it every day in this business."

"Then why are you in this business?"

"Because we had to survive somehow."

"You seem like a smart woman. Couldn't you have done something else?"

"Like what? Get married and live on some farm so I could raise babies and work myself to death? No, thank you. I'd rather have the life I have right now."

"What about your friend, the one who had the baby? Wasn't there a part of you that envied her?"

Molly's dark eyes narrowed. "You can't change the way you are. Things are the way they are for a reason."

"What's the matter, Molly? Maybe I can help you."

For one brief moment, Molly looked as if she might talk to Garrett, but not for long. Her protective wall went up quickly. "The only way you can help me is if you and your friend stay."

"Like I said, I'll let you know." Garrett watched Molly as she walked out the door, brushing past Nathan as he came in.

"Excuse me." Nathan looked at Molly as she left the room. "What's the matter with her?"

"Nothing a good roll in the sack wouldn't cure."

"That doesn't sound like you, Garrett. What's the matter? Did she turn you down?"

"No, as a matter of fact. She came here to ask us for our help. Seems a gang is on its way here and the leader has a score to settle with our Miss Molly."

Nathan walked over to the night table and picked up the bottle of whiskey, taking a small swig. "And you would just love to show her what a hero you are, and stay here and fight off the gang single-handed."

Garrett grabbed the bottle from Nathan's hand. "Get your own damned bottle and leave me alone."

"She really got to you, didn't she?" When Garrett wouldn't answer, Nathan softened. "Listen, I'm the guy who made a complete fool of himself over Anna, remember?"

"Yeah, I do remember." Garrett grinned broadly. "There's something about her. I don't think she's as tough as she tries to act."

"If you want to stay, we'll stay."

"I can't ask you to do that, Nate. You've got to find Anna, and I promised to help you."

"I'll find Anna, don't worry about that. But I think it's time I helped you out. You can use it. You're a mess."

"Thanks."

"How about if we stay here for a few weeks and see what we can do? If this gang doesn't show up, then we'll head on south. How does that sound?"

"I'd appreciate it. I think she could use the help." Garrett picked up the bottle and his saddlebag and headed for the door. "Did you leave me any bathwater?"

"I left you plenty of bath water. It's just not real clean."

"Great. Of all the people I had to pick to travel with," Garrett mumbled as he walked out the door. He walked down the hall, distracted by the sound of a woman's laughter. "Probably having a high old time in there," he grumbled enviously. He walked down the back stairs to the large wooden tub and felt the water. It was still warm.

"I took some of the other water out and put some more hot water in, sir." Duke came out of the kitchen with another pail of steaming water.

126

"Thanks, Duke. You didn't have to do that."

"Miss Molly said to treat you real good."

"She did, did she?" Garrett smiled to himself, throwing his saddlebag on the railing by the tub. There was a slight chill in the air but not much. It was almost summer, and the nights would soon be warm. He dropped his pants and took off his longjohns, stepping into the warm, steaming water. He leaned his head back against the side of the tub and stretched out as much as he could. He closed his eyes. "Oh, God, I think I've died and gone to heaven."

"Doesn't take much to please you, does it?"

Garrett loved the sound of Molly's voice. He opened his eyes. "Did you forget something?"

"Only this." She threw a towel at him. He caught it before it hit the water.

"Why, that was real considerate of you."

"I like to take care of my customers."

"How many customers do you have, Molly?"

"What do you mean?"

"How many personal customers do you have?" Garrett couldn't see her face in the darkness, but he could sense her growing anger. "I assume you have your own paying customers."

"You are a real bastard."

"I was just asking a question. You do run a whorehouse, don't you?"

"It's not a whorehouse. We run a saloon and hotel, and if some of the men and women want to be together then why not? It's better than being in some stinking, rotten place that rats wouldn't even live in."

"How would you know about places like that?"

"I don't accept paying customers, Mr. McReynolds." Molly quickly changed the subject. "If you'd like to pick one of the girls out to be with tonight, I'd be glad to send her to your room later."

127

"I'm twenty-one years old and I've never yet had to pay a woman to make love to me, Miss Molly."

"So you think that makes you pretty special, don't you?"

"I didn't say that. I just don't need you sending women to my room. If I want a woman, I'll get her myself." Garrett submerged himself under the water, scrubbing his face and hair. When he came up, Molly was still standing there, her hands on her hips.

"Is there something else you want?"

"I thought you might want this." She threw a large bar of soap into the tub, where it plopped with a loud thunk.

"Can't a man take a bath in peace around here?"

For the first time Molly smiled. She walked over to the tub and leaned on the side. "I do believe I make you uncomfortable, Mr. McReynolds."

Garrett moved to the edge of the tub, splashing water on Molly. "Not as uncomfortable as I make you, I'll wager."

"Would you like to go for a ride tomorrow? Maybe have a picnic. I know a real pretty place with lots of trees."

"You don't have to do this, you know."

"Do what?"

"Be nice to me so I'll stay."

"You don't give me much credit, do you?"

"On the contrary, I give you a lot of credit. I think you're a real smart woman."

"Then will you come with me tomorrow or not?"

"I'd be much obliged."

"Good. You can pick me up at my house. It's on the edge of town. It has rose bushes in the front."

"I would've never figured you for the kind of woman who liked roses."

"You don't know me very well, Mr. McReynolds."

"I hope tomorrow will change that."

Garrett watched Molly's outline as she walked into the kitchen. He splashed the water and gave a loud whoop. Things were beginning to look up. He couldn't wait for tomorrow.

Molly stood behind the long counter of the bar, counting out the evening's money.

"Why don't you go home, Miss Molly? I can take care of that for you. You don't take care of yourself." Duke had to admit to himself that Molly had always been his favorite of the three sisters. Molly was like a mother to the other two; in fact, she'd spoiled them. She worked hard and she always was the first one in the saloon in the morning and the last one to leave at night. He had taken her under his wing years before, when they decided to buy the saloon. He had been in the business a long time and he had guided her along. He wasn't sure if he approved of three young women running a saloon by themselves, but he understood that they had to survive somehow, and they didn't have any relatives. All they had was one another. It had been Molly's idea to make the saloon something classy, something that would attract more than just trail hands. Duke had liked the idea, and he had helped her order many of the furnishings from shops in St. Louis. He had grown to respect Molly for the way she looked after her two sisters and the way she treated people. She was fair and honest. You couldn't ask more of a person. "Please go, Miss Molly. I'm beginning to think you don't trust me."

"I'm sorry, Duke. I just don't want to go home tonight."

"Are you all right? If you're afraid, I'll go home with you. Better yet, why don't you stay here. You can have my room. I'll sleep in the kitchen."

Molly kissed Duke on the cheek. "I don't know what

129

I'd do without you, Duke. You've been like a father to me ever since my parents died."

"And that's why I want you to listen to me. You've got to find something else for yourself besides this place. It's not healthy for a young woman like you to spend all her time in a place like this. You need something else in your life."

"You mean a man."

"What's wrong with a good man? You deserve to be taken care of a little."

"I think we've had this conversation before, Duke, and it always winds up the same way."

"What do you think of that young man who came in here tonight? The tall one."

"They were both tall, Duke."

"You know whick one I mean. The one who couldn't take his eyes off you."

"He's nice enough."

"You are a stubborn woman. Just go on home and let me earn my money."

"All right, Duke. I'll see you in the morning." Molly started out the back door and stopped. "I just remembered. I won't be in until the afternoon tomorrow. I made some plans."

Duke smiled. "It's about time."

Molly picked up her jacket and headed out the kitchen door. Her house was on the edge of town and the town was not very long. She enjoyed her walks at night. It was quiet. She always felt this was her time.

A pack of coyotes yipped wildly in the hills and Molly smiled to herself. She loved the sound of the animals. It somehow made her feel closer to the land. She breathed deeply. The fresh night air filled her lungs. This was not her favorite place. In fact, if she'd been able to support herself and her sisters elsewhere, she would have done so. But she was trying to realize her father's dream—

making a new life in the great open West, with no restrictions or boundaries. She wanted to realize her father's dream—but at what personal cost?

She unlatched the gate to her yard and walked up the steps of the wooden porch. One thing she did love about this place was her house. It was the kind of house she had always dreamed of having. When its previous owners had decided to sell and move back to the east coast, she had bought the house.

She unlocked the door and stepped inside, reached to the table by the door and found the matchbox, struck a match and held it to the wick of the lamp. She thought about making herself something to eat, but she was too tired. She picked up the lamp and went upstairs to her bedroom. She had started to unbutton her blouse when she thought she heard a noise. She listened carefully, pulled her pistol out of its holster, and walked to the door and waited. There was nothing. She laid the pistol on the dresser and continued to undress. When she opened the door of the clothes cupboard, something moved. She turned toward the dresser to reach for her pistol, but a hand came over hers.

"Well, we was wondering when you'd be getting home, Miss Molly."

Molly recognized Jeremiah Strickland's voice immediately. She would never forget it. There was a sinking feeling in the pit of her stomach. No one would come looking for her. She had told Duke she wouldn't be in until the afternoon, and Garrett wouldn't come until noon. Jeremiah Strickland was going to kill her.

"What's the matter? You're awfully quiet for a woman with such a big mouth." Strickland took Molly's hand and wrenched it behind her back. "I told you I'd be back. I don't think you believed me."

"What do you want, Strickland?"

Strickland held one arm around Molly's throat and the

other held her arm behind her back. "I haven't quite decided what I want yet. But you'll be the first to know when I do decide." Strickland dragged Molly over to the bed and threw her down. "Don't waste your time looking under your pillow. I already got your knife. I don't make the same mistake twice."

"What a shame," Molly said dryly, trying to force the fear from her voice.

"I don't think you're going to be quite so sassy when I'm done with you." Strickland moved closer to the bed. "Boys, come on in here." Strickland stood by the side of the bed, waiting until three of his men came into the room. "Hand me that lamp." He held the lamp up to his face. "Can you see well enough?" He leaned forward. "Can you see the scars you left on my face?" He sat down on the bed and took Molly's hand, running it over the scars on his face. "I used to be a handsome man until you did this to me. I've thought and thought what I'd do if I ever came back here again. I've tried to imagine what might hurt you as much as you hurt me. Nothing came to mind until I thought about what meant the most to you. I know you love your sisters, but I heard they moved away. I could scar you up the way you scarred me, but you're a woman who don't seem overly concerned with her appearance. And then it came to me. What does she care most about? That saloon and this house."

"No!"

"I knew that's what would get to you." Strickland sat on the bed, forcing Molly down, his hand at her throat. "You see, Miss Molly, I'm not the monster I'm made out to be. I could've come here and hurt you real bad, but instead I'm just going to try to make you understand that you have to pay when you hurt someone."

"Please, Strickland. It's all I have."

"And this face is all I have, you bitch!" Strickland squeezed his hand around Molly's throat. "I don't like you much."

"The feeling's mutual."

"But I do respect the fact that you're a woman on your own and you haven't relied on a man for help. I like that. And because I respect that, I'm not going to ruin your looks. You're going to need them to get started again."

"I'd rather you cut me, Strickland."

"Jesus, woman, I think you mean that."

"I do."

"Well, then, you just told me what I needed to know. You care more about that place and this house than you do yourself. I feel kinda sorry for you."

"Don't you dare feel sorry for me! The last thing in the world I need is pity from someone like you."

"Don't worry, lady, I don't feel *that* sorry for you." Strickland got up from the bed and walked to the window. He lifted the curtain and looked down the street into town. "How many people you got staying in that place of yours?"

Molly sat up, rubbing her neck. "There are ten rooms upstairs and they're all full. Why?"

"Well, it'll be a real shame if that place catches on fire and all them people are caught inside."

"You can't do that, Strickland." Molly stood up and walked to the window. "If you set that place on fire it would turn into a death trap."

"Well, that's just too bad, isn't it? You should've thought of that when you cut me up."

"Strickland, listen. I've got money. I'll give it all to you."

"I don't give a damn about your money. Hell, if I need money, all I have to do is rob someone. There's nothing you can offer me, lady, that'll make me change my mind." Strickland looked out the window again. "Johnny, come here." A man with a rifle in his hands walked to the window. "I want you and the boys to go

133

ahead with the plan. There are ten rooms upstairs, so that means there are ten to twenty people in there. Just in case any of them is up, be quiet. Then you all hurry back here as quickly as you can."

"Okay, Jeremiah. Will you be all right here with her?"

"I can handle her. But make sure Harry stays up here with me."

"All right."

"Make sure the back stairs go up first."

"Strickland, please."

Strickland grabbed Molly's arm and pulled her to the window. "Don't waste your breath, Miss Molly. Just sit here and relax and enjoy the show."

Nathan tossed in his sleep. He was dreaming that a prairie fire had swept through the Cheyenne camp and burned everything in its wake. He saw Anna trying to get out of the camp, but the fire had completely engulfed her and she couldn't get out. He heard her frantic cries, but he couldn't get to her. He tried to run through the flames but the heat was too intense. He was losing her. "Anna!" he screamed, trying to reach through the flames. "Anna!"

"Nate, wake up! Jesus, wake up."

Nathan opened his eyes and sat up, looking around the strange room. "Garrett?"

"I'm right here."

"I had a dream about a fire and Anna was caught in it. I couldn't get to her." He looked around the room. "I smell smoke, Garrett."

"You're still asleep. There's no fire here."

Nathan jumped up and ran to the door. He carefully opened it and smoke filtered through into the room. He slammed the door shut. "There's a fire, Garrett." He quickly pulled on his pants and boots and grabbed his shirt and holster.

"Jesus Christ!" Garrett quickly got dressed and grabbed everything, including the saddlebags. "Can we get out through the hall?"

"I think the back stairs and the downstairs are on fire. We're going to have to go through the window."

"What about the people who are asleep? We've got to wake them up, Nate."

"Let's make it quick."

Both men covered their faces as they ran down the hall banging on doors. Nathan saw that the fire was rapidly spreading up the back stairs, and he and Garrett tried to get everyone to jump out of their windows. When they were satisfied that they had awakened everyone, they went into the nearest room and climbed out the window, jumping to the ground below. They stood out in front with all the other people who had gathered and watched helplessly as the fire engulfed the entire place. Within minutes, the whole building was up in flames and falling to the ground.

"Jesus." Garrett shook his head. "Good thing you had a dream about a fire or we'd all be inside there right now."

Nathan watched the orange-red flames and wondered how he had come to dream about the fire. He wondered if he had smelled the smoke and then dreamed the dream or—he wondered if Aeneva had helped to wake him up. Perhaps she put the dream in his mind. Whatever had happened, he was grateful.

"I wonder where Molly is," Garrett said anxiously, looking around.

"Does she live here?"

"No, she has a house on the outside of town. I should probably tell her." He looked around again. "Maybe I should have Duke tell her."

"I don't see him anywhere around."

"Jesus, you don't suppose he was still in there, do you?"

"Maybe he lives somewhere else."

Garrett ran up to one of the girls from the saloon. "Have you seen Duke?"

"No, I haven't seen him."

"Does he live here, in the saloon?"

"Yes, he has a room on the bottom floor."

Garrett shook his head. He had known by the way Duke had looked at Molly that he had cared for her as a father cared for a daughter, and Molly had felt a real affection for Duke. In one night, this woman had lost not only her livelihood, but probably the only person beside her sisters that she truly cared about.

"He's not around?"

Garrett shook his head. "He had a room on the bottom floor. From what you said, it sounds like the fire started on the bottom. I think he was still inside."

"Maybe you'd better go out to her house."

"Why don't you come with me? I could use your support."

"I guess there's nothing we can do here." Nathan took his saddlebag from Garrett. The horses were standing in the middle of the street, untied by one of the first people out of the saloon. They took their horses and hitched them farther up the street. "Which way?"

"She said on the edge of town."

"There are two edges of town."

"Let's try this way. I don't remember seeing a house the other way."

They walked in silence, occasionally turning around to look at the flames that lit the sky. Each was absorbed in his own thoughts. Nathan was thinking about Anna and Garrett was thinking about how this would affect Molly, when something stopped them both. There were some men standing outside what they assumed to be

136

Molly's house.

Nathan grabbed Garrett's arm and pulled him to the side of the road. "Who the hell are they?"

"Maybe they're some of the townsfolk coming to tell Molly about the fire."

"Then why aren't there any lights on?" Nathan peered out from the stand of trees they were in. "Molly said that gang was on its way. Maybe that's them."

Garrett looked back over his shoulder at the fire. "And maybe they started the fire to distract people."

"That doesn't make sense. They must've known someone would tell her about it. I think we'd better find a way in there and make sure she's all right."

"Got any ideas?"

"We're going to have to try to get in from the back. There's no telling how many of them are in the house."

"Then we'll have to find out from one of them." Garrett took his holster from his shoulder and fastened it around his hips. He took out his gun and made sure it was loaded. "Ready when you are."

They moved quietly along the stand of trees that led to Molly's house. Men's voices were easy to detect from the front of the house, as well as from the inside. There was no window on the ground floor in the back, but there was a window on the second floor.

"That's our only way in."

"I'll go," Garrett said anxiously. "Besides, we all know how much stronger you are than I am. You shouldn't have any problem holding me on your shoulders."

"Right," Nathan mumbled, getting down into a crouch so Garrett could step on his back. Nathan slowly stood up until Garrett was able to touch the window. "Can you reach it?"

"I'm right here, but the damned thing's locked."

"Is the room empty?"

"I can't see anyone moving around."

"Can you break the glass without making too much noise?"

"I guess I'll have to." Garrett took out his gun and wrapped his bandana around the butt. He tapped lightly against the lock area of the window. Nothing happened. "Holy Jesus, wouldn't you think we'd get a break? We are the good guys, you know."

"Just shut up and try again," Nathan grumbled, trying to balance Garrett's six foot, one inch frame on his shoulders.

Garrett peered into the room again, making sure there was no movement. He held the barrel of the gun and tapped the butt firmly against the glass. This time it cracked. He tapped once more and a portion of the glass broke. Garrett reached carefully through the jagged edges and unlocked the window, pushed it up, climbed inside, and walked quietly across the room. The door was shut, but he could hear voices. He put his ear against the door, carefully turned the knob, and peered out. There was a narrow hallway and at the other end there was another room that he assumed was Molly's. The staircase was on that side of the hallway. He could hear a man's voice coming from Molly's room, but he couldn't hear what he was saying. There were more voices coming from downstairs. He shut the door, went back to the window, and leaned out. "Molly's room is at the other end of the hallway by the stairs. I can hear at least one man in her room and more downstairs."

"The leader is probably with her. If you get him, maybe the others will take off."

"We can't count on that. We need some kind of distraction of our own. Come on, Nate, you're part Indian, can't you think of something?"

Nathan remembered the countless stories he'd heard about his father rescuing Aeneva or Stalking Horse rescuing Sun Dancer. "Give me fifteen minutes. Then go

138

in after Molly."

"What if your plan doesn't work?"

"Then you can die a hero." Nathan was gone.

"Goddamn him," Garrett mumbled to himself. He stood by the bedroom door and waited.

Nathan stayed under the cover of trees as he ran back to town. It seemed that all the townspeople were out to see the fire and make sure that it didn't spread to any of the adjoining buildings. Buckets of water were being handed down a long human line to keep the other buildings wet and to contain the fire to the sidewalk. Nathan looked for Duke but couldn't see him. He saw some of the girls who worked in the Three Sisters and went up to them. "I need your help." He explained the situation and the girls agreed to help. The girls also rounded up five men to go with them. Nathan told them all to make sure they had guns. "You girls will go in the front, pretending to tell Molly about the fire. When the men stop you, do what you have to do to get close to them and try to get their guns. Most importantly, keep them quiet. Hit them over the head if you have to."

"Don't worry, mister, we can handle it," one of the girls replied.

Nathan turned to the men. "While the girls are in the front, I want three of you to back the girls up. Try to get inside. Be careful. Strickland has men inside. Then I need one of you"—Nathan pointed to the strongest-looking man—"to help the two of us get in the second-story window. Then you go around the front. Once we're all inside, we'll just hope we can overtake them and get Molly in time. Let's go."

While the three women ran up the middle of the road, the men ran through the trees, taking care to be as quiet as possible. When they reached the back of the house, the large man immediately braced himself against the side of the house and helped Nathan and the other man up to the second story. Nathan was the first one up.

"Howdy," he whispered to Garrett.

"It's about time. So, what's the plan?" Garrett stared past Nathan to the man who followed him into the room. "Who is that?"

"A friend."

"He's our distraction?"

Nathan put his hand on the door. "Three of Molly's girls are in front. They'll do what they have to. There are also four men to back them up." He opened the door and peered out into the hallway.

"There's more than one of them in the room."

Garrett came to the door and listened. He could hear two men's voices distinctly. "If we go down there and surprise them, even if we get one of them, the other one can still kill Molly."

"Not if we get one of them out of the room."

"And just how are we supposed to do that? No, don't tell me—a distraction."

"Funny. What if I go downstairs and see if I can get one of them? I'll get him to call out to one of the men in the room."

"Why you?"

"I'm part Indian, remember?"

"What in hell are we doing in here?" The man behind them asked.

"Sorry, we're just trying to think of a plan."

"Well, do you have one?"

"We think there are two men in the room with Molly."

"Then let's go get 'em!"

"We can't do that. They could kill Molly before we get to her."

"So, what's the plan?"

Garrett looked at Nathan and couldn't contain a smile. "Well, I thought I'd go downstairs and try to get one of them to call up to one of them in the room. Then we can

140

get him out of there and go for the one who's with Molly."

"Sorry, mister, but I think you're wasting your time."

Nathan walked up to the man. "What's your name?"

"My name is Ethan, but my friends call me 'Slim.'"

"Well, Slim, do you have something else in mind?"

"Why go to all that trouble? We're in here. Why not try to get 'em to come in here?"

Garrett walked forward. "I like your way of thinking, Slim. Go on."

"Well, we'll just make some kind of noise, something to get their attention. One of 'em has to see what it is."

Nathan nodded his head. "Sounds good to me. Let's get behind the door. Since it was your idea, Slim, why don't you do the honors?"

Slim smiled slightly and walked over to the night table. He pushed over the pitcher and bowl, then quickly ran behind the door with the other two.

It wasn't long before there were footsteps in the hallway leading to the room. "Is that you, Buck? You know I don't much like those games of yours. The last time you tried to scare me like this you almost lost your hand." The man walked to the door, slowly opening it. "I swear to God, Buck, if you're in there I'm gonna fix it so you'll never love a woman again." The door opened and a head slowly came around, peering into the darkness of the room. "I know you're in here, Buck. Come on out and face the music."

Slim was on the man in an instant, pulling him from the door to the wall, his arm up against the man's throat so he couldn't speak. He placed his revolver at his nose. "Who else is in there with Miss Molly?"

The man looked at the man in front of him and the other two men behind him. He didn't think he had much of a chance of coming out of the room alive if he lied. Loyalty was fine if your life wasn't in jeopardy. "It's

141

Strickland. He's the only one in there with her."

"How many others in the house?" Garrett stood on the other side of the man, while Nathan watched the hallway.

"Three downstairs, three out front."

"Are you sure?" Slim pushed the barrel of his gun into the man's nose.

"Yeah, I'm sure. I ride with those men all the time."

"What's Strickland got planned for Molly?"

"He wanted her to watch while he burned her place down. Then he was planning to burn the house."

"Has he hurt her?" Garrett edged closer to the man.

"No, he hasn't hurt her much. Just roughed her up a bit."

"Where are they in the room?"

"He's holding her on the seat by the window."

"Weapons?"

"He's carrying a Colt. There'a a shotgun right by him on the floor, and he has her knife in his boot."

"Are you sure that's it?" Slim pushed his gun further into the man's face.

"Hell, yeah, I'm sure. I wouldn't lie to you with a gun staring me in the face."

"That's real good," Slim said softly, pulling the man from the wall and forcing him to the door. "Do we need him for anything else?"

Nathan looked at the man. "Will Strickland come in here if you call him?"

"I don't know. He wants to pay this girl back real bad. I don't think he'll leave her alone."

"Will he come?" Garrett whispered menacingly in the man's ear.

"Yeah, I think I can get him to come."

"You better hope you can get him to come,'cause if you don't, your life ain't worth much." Slim pushed him toward the door, his arm encircling his neck. "I've been known to break a man's neck in less than a second. So if you're thinking of calling out to this Strickland fella, don't."

"All right, all right."

"Call him in here."

The man cleared his throat. "Strickland, I think you better get in here real quick." There was no response. "Strickland, I think you better see this."

Slim pulled the man back from the door as he saw a shadow in the doorway down the hall. "What in hell's the matter with you, Harry? Can't you handle things yourself? You know, this doesn't look good for the second-in-command to have to ask the leader for help."

Slim jerked his muscular forearm against the man's throat. "I don't care what it looks like; you better get in here and take a look at this. This is real trouble."

Slim pulled Harry back from the door. He pushed him onto the floor and changed hats with him. Slim knelt over him, as if he were looking at him. "Don't make a sound, Harry," he whispered. He looked up at Nathan and Garrett. "You two can grab him when he comes in."

Nathan and Garrett stood poised behind the half-open door. They heard Strickland's footsteps in the hallway.

"What is it, Harry?" Strickland was at the door. "If you and Buck are messing around again I swear I'll shoot you both."

Slim put his gun to Harry's crotch, just in case he decided to change his mind. "I'm not fooling with you, Strickland. Come on in here. Buck's dead."

Strickland pushed open the door, seeing the shadows of the two men on the floor. "Are you sure?"

Strickland was now in the room and Garrett and Nathan could see that he had Molly in front of him, a gun to her neck.

"What's the matter with you, Harry? I swear you boys is all falling apart around me." Strickland walked farther into the room, pushing Molly in front of him. Just as he got close to Slim and Harry, Nathan pushed the door shut and Garrett pulled Molly away from Strickland and down to the floor. Strickland looked around wildly and raised his gun, but Nathan and Slim were on him, tackling him to the floor. They disarmed him within seconds, while Slim made sure that Harry didn't try to escape.

"There are more men downstairs," Molly whispered to Garrett.

"We know. Let's hope they're taken care of."

"What do you say we go on down there and make sure those others are out of the way?" Nathan said to Slim.

"What about these two?" Slim motioned to Harry and Strickland.

"Well, we can't just have them lying here bothering Garrett and Miss Molly. I think we need to make sure they won't bother anyone until we can get them to the sheriff."

"Are you kidding, mister? Our sheriff is as worthless as a dry canteen in the desert."

"Well, what do you suggest, Slim?"

"I say we put them out for a while." Slim lifted his gun and smacked Strickland and Harry on their heads. Both were out cold.

"You know, Slim, I like you. I like the way you think."

"Let's get going, mister. I'm in the mood for a little action."

When the men left the room, Garrett turned on the lamp and led Molly to the bed. He sat down next to her, making sure he could keep an eye on the men on the floor. "Are you all right? Did he hurt you?"

"I'm all right. He beat me up a little bit, that's all."

"That's all!" Garrett said angrily, taking the bandana out of his pocket to wipe the blood from Molly's lip. "You're shaking."

"I just saw my life go up in flames. There's nothing left

for me now."

"You can rebuild the Three Sisters."

"I don't have enough money. Besides, it'll never be the same."

"You're a strong woman, Molly. You can do anything you set your mind to."

"It took me and my sisters a long time to get that place to look the way it did. I don't have the energy to do that again."

"I thought you loved that place."

"I did, but I don't know if I can do it anymore. I was getting kind of tired of it, anyway. Duke knows that. That's why he wants me to get myself a man and settle down."

Garrett took Molly's shoulders. "Molly, I have to tell you something."

"What?" Her eyes questioned him like a child's. "What is it?"

"It's Duke. I think he died in the fire."

"Duke? No!" she shook her head violently. She laid her head against Garrett's shoulder and cried. He held her tightly.

"I'm sorry, Molly. I know he meant a lot to you."

"He was like a father since my own father died. He always looked after my sisters and me. He always made sure we were taken care of. I wanted him to give me away at my wedding." She buried her face in Garrett's shoulder. "It's not fair."

"I know, Molly. I know." He held her tightly, stroking her hair.

"I want to go into town."

"Are you sure you want to do that?"

"It's my place. I should be there."

"Okay. I'll take you." Garrett stood up. "Let me check downstairs and make sure everything is all right first."

145

He handed her his gun. "You keep an eye on those two."
Garrett didn't even get to the door before Nathan walked
in.

"Everything's all right. We've got them all."

"What are we going to do with them?"

"Slim said the sheriff here won't do anything about
them. They plan to hold onto them until the territorial
marshal comes through. They can get the reward too."

"Thanks. I'm going to take Molly into town."

Nathan walked to Molly, taking her hand in his. "I'm
sorry about Duke, Molly. I just lost my parents. I know
what it's like to lose someone you love so much."

Molly squeezed Nathan's hand. "Thanks, Nathan.
You're a good person." She looked at Garrett. "Thank
you both for your help."

"It wasn't just us. You have a lot of friends in this
town. Three of your girls came to help, and some of the
men."

"I'll have to be sure to thank them all." Molly walked
down the hallway and down the stairs, looking at the men
who had been responsible for destroying her life. She
walked out of her house and into the road. She turned
back to look at the house. Garrett stood next to her.
"Maybe it's time I moved on. I think I've spent enough
time in this town."

"I thought you loved this house."

"This house was a dream. You can't live a dream." She
started walking defiantly toward town, followed by
Nathan and Garrett. When they reached the crowded
street in front of the Three Sisters, Molly stood among
the other people, watching helplessly as the dying flames
of what had once been her life were now reduced to mere
ashes. People came up and offered their help to Molly to
rebuild the saloon, but she couldn't think about that
now. She just watched as what was left of the building

146

began to crumble and fall to the ground with a loud cracking sound. "I guess it was time," she said softly, tears streaming down her face.

"I'll help you rebuild it, Molly," Garrett said.

Molly looked at Garrett in the flickering flames of the fire, and she touched his face gently. "You are a very nice man."

"I try." Garrett smiled broadly. "I like you, Molly. I want to help you."

"Why? Why do you want to help me?"

"I just told you why. I like you."

"I don't understand that. I've never had a man as a friend before, Garrett. Never."

"Duke was your friend."

"Duke was more like my father."

"You are afraid, aren't you?" Garrett cupped Molly's chin in his hand. "I told you before that I won't hurt you. I care about you. I want to help you."

"Garrett, I don't know what to do. I'm not good at this."

"You don't have to be 'good' at it." Garrett pulled Molly into his arms. "I want to take care of you."

Molly pulled away. "You don't even know me." She strode toward the building that was once her saloon. Her eyes filled with tears. "I have nothing. Nothing."

Garrett walked up behind her and wrapped his arms around her, forcing her to stay within the shelter of his arms. "If you don't want to stay here, I want you to come with me." He lowered his mouth to her ear. "I think I love you, Molly."

Molly slowly turned around in Garrett's arms, her eyes looking up at him, questioningly. "Garrett, don't—"

"Don't what? Don't be honest with you? I was raised to say how I feel about things, Molly. I won't lie to you. I told you that before. I don't know how to make you

147

believe me."

"It's not your fault, it's mine. I've never learned how to trust."

"Then maybe it's time you did." Garrett pulled her head to his chest and held her tightly. "Come with me, Molly. Let me take care of you."

Molly looked up at Garrett and smiled. "It's hard to say no to you, you know that, don't you?"

"I was hoping it would be hard for you to say no. In fact, I was counting on it."

"This doesn't mean we're engaged or anything like that. We'll just take some time and get to know each other. We may even find out we don't like each other very much."

"Whatever you say, Molly." Garrett smiled his irresistible smile.

"If I do decide to go with you, where exactly are we going?"

"Nate and I are heading to New Orleans. We're trying to get his girl back."

"His girl?"

Garrett thought about the details of the story and his part in it and decided to wait before he told Molly all of it. "I'll tell you everything later. But trust me; it will be an adventure. You'll be glad you came."

"Well, now, I never could resist an adventure." She wiped the tears from her face and turned back to look at the remains of the saloon. "New Orleans, huh? I've never been out of Texas, except when we traveled here from the East."

"Then it's about time you did some traveling, don't you think?"

Molly looked at Garrett, a serious look in her eye. "I can't promise you anything right now, Garrett."

"I won't ask for anything right now. Just come with me. See how you feel when it's all over."

Molly shook her head. "All right. I'll come with you. If I like traveling with you, then I'll come back and sell my house. Then we'll talk about us."

Garrett held out his hand. "Sounds fair to me. Let's shake on it."

Molly put her hand in Garrett's and felt the strength radiate from it. She was sad, but she also felt that for the first time in her life she was doing something just for her. For the first time, she was starting to live.

Chapter VI

Anna looked at herself in the mirror and scrunched up her nose. "It isn't me, Roberto. I don't look good with all these frills."

Roberto looked up at the lady who was holding some dresses. "Do you have something simple yet elegant? Something in a dark green or blue. Perhaps even black?"

"Certainly, sir. I am sure we can find something for your wife."

Anna looked at Roberto. "You certainly seem at ease doing this. I would never have thought you'd feel at home in a ladies' dress shop."

"As I've told you many times, there's a lot you don't know about me."

"I'm finding that out all the time." Anna couldn't believe that they had been in New Orleans less than a week and already they had done so much. Roberto had rented a beautiful red-brick house in the city. He had bought a complete new wardrobe, and now they were shopping for clothes for her. Roberto had also given her a simple gold band and had placed it on her finger—in friendship, he had said. When she asked him where he had gotten all of the money for their clothes and the house he just shrugged his shoulders and told her not to worry. "Excuse me while I change," Anna said, glancing at Roberto before she stepped behind the screen. A change had come over him since they had reached New Orleans. She couldn't quite put her finger on it, but something was different.

"Here you are, madam. I will be right out here if you need some assistance," said the saleslady.

Anna stepped behind the screen and wriggled out of the ruffly red dress she had been trying on. She was amused at the thought of a man picking out her clothes for her, but she had learned that it wasn't worth it to argue with Roberto. She had learned the hard way that he was one man you didn't argue with. Besides, she was hoping that if she helped him to get what he was after, he would let her go back to Nathan.

Anna slipped into a deep blue silk dress that was cut off the shoulders, with large cupped sleeves and a tightly gathered waist. It fell in straight lines to the floor. "Could you please fasten this?"

Roberto stood up and waved the woman away, walking behind the screen. He fastened the buttons deftly. "It's perfect."

Anna turned around, startled. "I didn't ask for your help." She blushed involuntarily.

"I know." He backed out from the screen.

Anna walked to the mirror and smiled. She had never seen anything so lovely. "I like it. What do you think, 'Berto?"

"It's more important what you think. Do you want it?"

Anna shrugged. "I'm not used to buying expensive clothes."

"You mean Nathan never bought you anything expensive? That surprises me."

"Forget the dress!" Anna said angrily, walking to the screen and trying her best to unbutton the dress. "Will

151

you help me undo this damned thing?"

Roberto unbuttoned the dress. "I'm sorry, Anna. I shouldn't have said that."

Anna turned around, holding the dress to her. "You're right, you shouldn't have. You have a knack for saying the wrong thing. I'm trying very hard to be your friend, but you keep making it difficult for me. Why do you do that?"

"I don't know. Maybe I'm afraid."

"What are you afraid of?"

"Maybe I'm afraid of getting close."

"But I'm your friend. I thought I'd proven that you can trust me."

"I'm not as stupid as you might think, Anna." Roberto walked away from the screen.

"What does that mean?" Anna followed Roberto out into the room, her dress half falling from her shoulders. "What does that mean?" she repeated, more urgently this time.

"It means that I know you're trying to make me believe that you're my friend, and then you think I'll let you go back to Nathan. Isn't that right?"

Anna walked back to the screen and stripped off the dress, reaching for the worn traveling suit. She pulled on her skirt, ignoring the fact that she stood only in her pantalettes and camisole. "You are a pathetic person. I think the only emotion you know is hatred."

Roberto grabbed Anna, his fingers digging into her shoulders. "Don't you ever say that again!"

Tears stung Anna's eyes, but she tried not to cry. "What do you want from me? Do you want me to tell you that I've forgotten all about Nathan? Do you want me to tell you that new clothes and a fancy house will make everything you've done to us all right? Why don't you hit me? Maybe that will make you feel better."

Roberto eased his hold on Anna. He backed away from

152

the screen. "I'm sorry, I don't believe in hurting women. I don't know what happened."

Anna rubbed her shoulders. "That doesn't make it all right, Roberto. You seem to think that all you have to do is say 'I'm sorry' and that will make everything all right. But that won't work. You've disrupted my life and taken me away from the man I love and the only real home I've ever known."

"Get dressed."

"What?"

"You don't want to hear 'I'm sorry,' so get dressed. You seem to respond better to orders, anyway."

Anna pulled on her blouse and tucked it into her skirt, then pulled on her jacket. She stomped out of the shop and waited outside on the street for Roberto. She was so angry she felt like running away and hiding. But Roberto knew she had no money, and it would be almost impossible for her to find a place to go on her own. She ignored Roberto when he came out of the shop and gently took her elbow. He led her down the street to a small outdoor cafe.

"Are you hungry?"

"No."

"I know better. You're the only woman I know who can eat more than a man."

Anna pulled her arm from Roberto's. "If you're going to continue to insult me, why don't we fight right here?" Anna looked around at the people on the street. "I'm sure the wonderful people of New Orleans would love to hear about our lives."

"That's enough, Anna." Again, Roberto took her arm.

"No, it's not enough." Anna pulled free again, this time stepping backward into the street. "You want to control my life so completely that I can't even think my own thoughts anymore. I hate you, Roberto. I tried so hard to like you, but I can't, not anymore. You have made my life miserable." Anna turned to run across the street, but a carriage came down the street in front of her. Roberto pulled her back, holding her against him.

"You're the most foolish woman I've ever known. I should put you on a raft and send you down the Mississippi."

"Why don't you?"

"I don't know."

"Just take me home. I'm not hungry."

"Let's walk." Roberto took Anna's arm and they walked in silence down the busy city streets.

Although Anna wouldn't admit it to Roberto, she was fascinated by New Orleans. It was unlike any place she had ever seen before. Neat brick houses lined the streets, orange trees filling their courtyards. Wrought iron railings surrounded windows and balconies. Anna smiled at a Negro woman who passed by, a flat basket on her head.

"Ginger cake, madam?" she asked, her white teeth flashing from her dark skin. She was dressed in a loose cotton skirt and blouse and she had a scarf wrapped around her head.

Anna looked at Roberto. "What's ginger cake?"

Roberto smiled. "We'll have one, please."

The woman took the basket from her head and handed Anna a slice of cake. "A big piece for you, madam. You be skinny. Need to fatten you up." She laughed uproariously.

Roberto handed the woman more than enough money. "You best be off, woman. She doesn't like people to insult her."

The Negro woman appraised Anna for a moment. "This one's got a kind face. You take care of her."

"I will." Roberto took Anna's arm. "How's the cake?"

"It's wonderful."

154

"I thought you weren't hungry."

Anna stopped, savoring the flavor of the cake. "You heard the woman; you need to fatten me up."

"Well, then." Roberto guided Anna along to the square. Vendors sat in stalls selling vegetables, fruit, meats, fish, shrimp, and ginger beer.

"I've never seen anything like it."

"You should see it on Sunday. Sunday is a feast day, and this entire square is filled with people and vendors. It's quite a sight."

Anna glanced at the people they passed—Creoles, who were a mixture of French and Spanish blood; Indians; Negroes; and white men. Anna stopped when she saw a beautiful young woman dressed in bright pink and blue walk by. Her skin was almost a light chocolate color and her eyes were large brown ovals. "She's beautiful," Anna exclaimed in wonder.

"She's an octoroon."

"What is that?"

"It's the child of a white man and a quadroon mother. She has one-eighth Negro blood. Years ago, before the war, it was quite the thing for a man to have a quadroon mistress, because they were usually so exotic-looking."

"Not anymore?"

"Since the war, things haven't been quite so frivolous here. Years ago, they actually had quadroon balls, where men of means would go and pick out a mistress. These women were housed and given money in return for their affections. When the war started, most of the men who had mistresses gave them up. After the war, the city had become less Southern in its thinking. People frowned upon things like having quadroon mistresses, so many of the women married men of their own color. Many of them fled north."

"But why did they have to leave at all?"

"Because they were branded, Anna. They weren't quite Negro and they weren't quite white. They weren't accepted by either race."

Anna turned to look in the direction that the girl had walked. "But she's here."

"Some have stayed. Some have gone into business and done well for themselves. Come on." Roberto led Anna down a small alleyway. The distinctive smell of coffee floated through the air. "Would you like some coffee?" Roberto made a wide sweep of his arm toward the open courtyard that had tables situated amid orange trees.

Anna looked at the courtyard. "It's so lovely."

"Would you like to go in?"

"No, I just wanted to see it. Let's walk some more."

They passed more vendors, men selling candied fruits, sweet cakes, and flowers. At the flower vendor, Roberto stopped and bought a single red rose for Anna. "A perfect rose."

Anna smiled and held it to her nose. She breathed in the sweet fragrance. "Thank you. It's lovely."

They walked for a while until they reached the river, then walked along the bank until Roberto stopped. "If you got on a boat and went down this river, it would take you all the way to the ocean," he said absently.

"Have you ever seen the ocean?"

"I have seen enough of the ocean to last me forever." Roberto gazed out over the river, watching as boats traveled by.

"Is that where you were for so long?"

"I was many places," Roberto answered, thinking of all the ports where his ship had stopped and he was not allowed to get off. It was a wonder he had survived those years. If it hadn't been for Richard Thornston, he would probably have died on that stinking ship."

"Are you all right? You've got that look again."

"What look?"

"You look like you want to kill someone. I hope it isn't me."

Roberto looked at Anna, a slight smile appearing on his face. "Why would I want to kill you?"

Anna shrugged. "Why do you want to kill Nathan?"

"I never said I want to kill him."

"You want to make him suffer. He's suffered enough, 'Berto."

"So you tell me." Roberto walked along the bank, kicking at the loose rocks along the edge.

"Why are you so determined to believe that Nathan is bad? Does that make it easier for you to do what you're doing to us?"

"If you expect me to feel guilty, it won't work." Roberto stooped down to pick up a rock. He had a fleeting image of Nathan skipping a rock across a lake, and him begging Nathan to show him how to do it. Was it a memory or was it just wishful thinking? He stood up and skipped the flat rock over the surface of the water. "Five," he said out loud.

"What?"

"The rock skipped five times. Nathan could get it to skip seven, sometimes eight times." He remembered.

Anna gripped Roberto's arm. "You do remember something, then?"

"I don't remember much. Maybe I didn't want to remember anything. Remembering how my life used to be only caused me pain." He looked at Anna. "But I do remember that Nathan showed me how to skip rocks." A slight smile played around the corners of his mouth. "I never left him alone."

"You two did everything together. When Trenton and Aeneva came back from Mexico, they were afraid that Nathan would feel left out because of the new baby. Aeneva said he adored you, and looked after you as if you were his own. He didn't want any of the other Indian children touching you."

"Is that true, or is that a lie to get me to like my brother?"

"Why would I lie to you when the truth is so much more persuasive?"

"I don't know if it's the truth that's persuasive or if it's you."

"I'm not lying. Aeneva and Trenton thought you were both dead and she found solace in talking about you. You two were the brothers I never had, so I loved to listen to all the stories about you two. I even used to go into your rooms and look through your things."

"Why did you do that?"

"It made me feel closer to you both somehow. I wanted so badly to have brothers."

"Lucky for you that we weren't there. If you and Nathan had grown up in the same house, it would have been hard for you to admit your love to each other."

Anna looked at Roberto, waiting for the sarcasm, but it didn't come. He had actually said something kind. "Even when I found out that Nathan was Trenton and Aeneva's son, I felt strange. It didn't seem right somehow."

"And how did he feel about it?"

"He left me. He said he'd fallen in love with another woman. He didn't feel right about us, either."

"What happened?"

"We were in love and we couldn't fight it. I suppose it was inevitable. Aeneva said that sometimes a man and woman are meant to be together, and no matter what happens, nothing will keep them apart."

"My mother and Trenton, did they understand the love you and Nathan have for each other?"

"Yes, I think they understood it better than we did. You do remember that your grandparents, Young Eagle and Little Flower, were raised as brother and sister, and they fell in love and had Aeneva and her brothers."

"Yes, and they were banished from the tribe. What a horrible thing to do to two people who loved each other."

"Yes, but at least they were able to love each other." Anna bent down and looked through the rocks, finding a nice round flat one. She stood up and skipped it over the water, laughing in delight at the circles that appeared from the skipping rock. "Six."

"What?"

"Six skips. Didn't you see them?"

"I think your eyes are going bad, sweet lady, because I only saw that rock skip four times."

Anna gave Roberto a defiant look. "We both know it skipped six times, 'Berto. Shall I try it again?"

Roberto smiled. "Let's make a bet. We each throw three rocks. Total number of skips wins."

"What does the winner get?"

"Whatever they choose."

"I can't think of anything that I want." Anna decided not to mention Nathan; things were going too well at the moment. "I know. If I win, I would like to go to a fancy ball and dance all night. I've only done that one time in my life, and I had a wonderful time."

"That's what you want should you win?"

"Yes. And you?"

"I would want you to be patient with me and try to be my friend, although at times I know it's difficult."

Anna held out her hand. "It's a deal." As soon as they shook, Anna walked around the bank, looking for the best skipping rocks. Garrett had always told her that the flatter they were, the better they'd skip. When she found her three rocks, she waited, impatiently, tapping her boot on the dirt. "You can't put off the inevitable, Roberto."

"I know." Roberto stood up, rocks in hand. "Ladies first."

Anna turned her body and threw her arm sideways, flicking her wrist and flinging the rock lightly over the

159

water. "Six," she said with a smile. She repeated it a second time for six, and the third time, the rock skipped seven times. "I believe that gives me nineteen."

Roberto barely nodded and flung his rock lightly along the water. It died.

"Too bad," Anna said sarcastically, "only three."

Roberto ignored Anna and flung the next rock. It skipped seven times. He took the last rock in his hands and held it, rubbing it between his palms. He flung the rock lightly across the water. A smile spread across his face. He turned to Anna. "I believe that was ten. Ten, seven and three make twenty. I'm the winner."

"I don't think it skipped ten times. I've never seen a rock skip ten times."

"And I thought you were an honest woman, Anna."

"I am honest. I just don't think it skipped ten times."

"Well, I can do it again if you don't believe me." Roberto bent down and picked up another rock. He flung it out across the water. He turned with a smile to Anna. "How many did you count?"

"Nine or ten. I'm not sure."

"Ten. I won, fair and square. So, now you have to be nice to me. You don't have a choice."

"You didn't say I had to be nice to you, you just said I had to be your friend."

"That's true. I'll settle for that."

"I can't believe you skipped a rock ten times across the water twice."

"I obviously had a better teacher than you."

"You said Nathan could only skip it seven or eight times."

"That's all he did in front of me. I saw him skip a rock twelve times on a bet." Roberto laughed. "He bet pa's Appaloosa, and you know how pa loved that horse."

"My God, Trenton would've killed him."

"He would have, except that Nathan won the bet. Easily."

Anna let Roberto take her arm as they walked back toward the city. She didn't want to mention to Roberto that he was beginning to speak of Nathan with greater ease—she was afraid it would put him off. But she was glad that he was starting to dig up old memories, obviously happy memories, of the times he and Nathan had spent together. Perhaps he was beginning to have a change of heart concerning his brother.

Roberto started to hail a carriage, but Anna begged him not to. She loved walking in the city. Roberto bought her some candied fruit as they walked down the streets and looked at the various things. Anna felt like a child. She had always loved to see new places. She had felt the same way the first time she had seen San Francisco, where she had first met Nathan.

"Anna?"

"What?" Anna answered in a distracted tone.

"I asked you if you'd like to take a drive out to the country tomorrow and see some of the plantations. I think you'd enjoy seeing them."

"That would be fine."

"What's the matter?"

"Nothing. I suppose I'm just a little tired."

"I think you've had enough walking for today." Roberto stepped out into the street. An extremely ornate black carriage pulled by two beautifully matched black horses stopped by Roberto. The passenger door opened.

"Can I give you and your wife a ride, monsieur?"

Roberto looked at LeBeau. "No, thank you. We'll find a carriage."

"Why look for a carriage when mine is here and I would be glad to take you anywhere you wish to go?" He looked at Anna. "How are you today, Anna?"

161

"Well, thank you, LeBeau."

"Please, monsieur, it would be my pleasure." LeBeau stepped out of the carriage and offered his arm to Anna. "Careful, that's right." He followed her quickly into the carriage without a backward glance at Roberto.

Roberto climbed into the carriage and shut the door. He was irritated to find LeBeau sitting on the same side of the carriage as Anna. He sat himself down opposite Anna and LeBeau, his distaste quite evident.

"Where are you going?"

"Home," Roberto answered curtly.

LeBeau asked Roberto directions and gave orders to the driver. He looked at Anna. "You seem pale today, my dear. Perhaps our southern weather does not agree with you."

"It's very warm here."

"Is it not also warm in Arizona?"

"It's a different kind of warm," Roberto answered angrily. "Here, the heat clings to you and makes you feel as if you can't breathe. It's heavy. It's not natural."

"You speak as if you have been here before, monsieur."

"I've been to places like it before and I don't like it. Weather like this makes people crazy. Makes them do things they wouldn't normally do."

"Yes, I think that is true. But you will find that you get used to it." He looked at Anna. "Have you been enjoying your stay in our lovely city?"

"Yes, it's really an unusual city."

"Have you been to many cities?"

"No, I've only been to San Francisco, and a few other small towns when I was a little girl."

"Then I must show you around."

"I'll show my wife around, LeBeau."

"Whatever you say, monsieur."

The carriage stopped and Roberto jumped out, holding

162

his hands up to lift Anna down. LeBeau came out after Roberto and stood in front of him, putting his hands on Anna's waist to help her down from the carriage.

"Thank you, LeBeau. It was very kind of you to give us a ride home."

LeBeau took Anna's gloved hand and kissed it. "It is always my pleasure, Anna." His eyes traveled to Roberto's, ignoring the threat in them. "Here is my card, monsieur. If you should need me for anything, do not hesitate."

Roberto locked his eyes with LeBeau's. "I don't think so, LeBeau." He opened the wrought iron gate and guided Anna up the brick stairway to the house, unlocked the door and opened it for Anna. He looked back at the street. LeBeau was still standing next to his carriage, his arms crossed, a strange smile on his face.

"You don't like LeBeau much, do you?"

"I don't trust him."

"Why?"

"I don't like the way he looks at you. He acts as if we're not even married."

"We're not, really, 'Berto." Anna walked into the small sitting room. "This is a lovely house."

"What do you mean we're not really married?"

"I thought we weren't going to get into this again. I said I'd be your friend and I will be."

"But?"

"But you can't expect me ever to be your wife."

"Did I ever say that I was going to let you go back to my brother, Anna? I don't think I said that."

"But I thought—"

"No, you were hoping. You think I'm stupid? You think that if you're nice to me I'll send you back to Nathan?" He looked at Anna, a hardness in his eyes. "I won't send you back to Nathan. You are my wife and you will remain my wife." He stood by the window that overlooked the street. "Why don't you go up and rest? You've had a long day."

Anna picked up the nearest object, a small vase, and threw it at Roberto. "What has made you so full of hate? Tell me, please, so I can try to understand."

Roberto rubbed his shoulder where the vase had hit. "Is there anything else you'd like to throw at me?" He looked around the room. "I'm sure there are heavier objects. Why don't you aim for my head next time?"

"Never mind! Maybe next time I'll try to hit you in your sleep. Maybe I'll be lucky and kill you." Anna stomped out of the room and up the stairs. She went into her room and slammed the door. She lay across the lace bedcover and stared out at the darkening sky. The house Roberto had rented was beautiful, the kind of house any woman would want to live in. Her room was a rose color, with a rose bedspread and a cream lace coverlet. She had a dressing table and chair, a nightstand with pitcher, bowl, towel, washcloth, and soap, and she had a windowseat covered in rose-colored cushions that overlooked the gaslit streets. It was a lovely room, but totally meaningless to her. There was a knock on her door, but she refused to answer it.

Roberto opened the door and stepped in. "Why don't you turn on the lamp?"

"Because I don't want any light. I just want to go to sleep."

Roberto walked over to the night table and turned up the lamp. A rose hue spread over the room. Roberto went to the windowseat and sat down. "What do you want to know about me?"

Anna propped herself up on her elbows. "Where did you go after San Francisco?"

"I was taken on a boat and became a glorified cabin boy. I was really a slave."

"I don't understand."

164

"The captains of a lot of the ships that sail around the Horn and down into South America can't get men to stay on board and do the dirty work. This man pulled me out of the bay, and for that I was to gratefully become his slave. He kept me on that rathole for eight years."

"Why couldn't you get off when the ship was in port?"

"I was always shackled and locked in the captain's cabin or in the hold. My feet didn't touch land for eight years. God, I can remember looking out at the land as we were approaching it. I never stopped dreaming or remembering what it was like. I constantly dreamed up ways to try to escape, but I was never successful."

"Didn't you get sick? My God, no one can stay on a ship for that long!"

"I got sick plenty of times, and I almost died once of some tropical disease."

"Didn't anyone ever try to help you?" Anna sat up.

"Anna, the men on that ship didn't care about me. The only thing I was good for was doing work."

"So, how did you get off?"

"The owner of the ship sailed with us to Mexico. On the way back we were in a storm. He was washed overboard. I saved his life and, eventually, he saved mine. He took me off the ship with him and into his home here in New Orleans."

"Here? Is that why you've come to New Orleans? You want to visit this man?"

"Not exactly." Roberto got up and held out his hand to Anna. "Let's go down to the kitchen. If I'm going to tell you my life story, the least you can do is make me some supper."

Anna set about preparing a light meal, and Roberto poured them each some wine. "I can't believe you were alive all that time on a ship that sailed all around the ocean. It doesn't seem fair. You and your parents and Nathan could've had that time together. Instead, all four

165

of you were robbed of the time you had left."

"I was robbed of a lot, Anna." He held up his wineglass and looked at the rose-colored liquid through the light. The first time he had ever tasted wine was with Caroline. She had taught him how to appreciate its delicate flavor. Up until that time, the only liquor he'd ever drunk was rum or whiskey, and that was on the ship, to help dull the pain. Now he drank only sparingly. As he'd told Anna, he didn't like being out of control.

Roberto looked at Anna. She was different from any woman he'd ever known. Most women he'd known were brassy and cheap, only after his money. Caroline was so innocent and sweet she couldn't even stand up for what she believed in or the man she loved. Anna was different. She was good, but she wasn't innocent; she'd seen something of the world and it had given her a different outlook. She was as loyal as anyone he'd ever seen. She'd die first, rather than accept the fact that she might never see Nathan again. She was beautiful; there was no denying that. LeBeau couldn't keep his eyes from her. And she had more spunk than three women put together; his shoulder attested to that. A part of him was sad, sorry that he had missed growing up with someone like Anna. Perhaps the way he felt about women would be different if he had.

"Why don't you eat? You're staring at me like you don't know me."

"I don't, really. Why don't you tell me about yourself?"

"I thought this was about you."

"I haven't forgotten. I'll tell you, but I would like to know. How did you ever come to be with my family? It's so strange."

"I thought Clare would've filled you in on my background," she replied angrily. She sipped at her wine, giving Roberto a glare over the rim of the glass. "What was Clare to you, anyway?"

Roberto shook his head and laughed. "Do you always ask this many questions? God, you remind me of—"

"Of you, 'Berto? The way you always used to badger Nathan with questions?" Anna ignored Roberto's darkening look and leaned across the table. "Just think, if we'd all grown up together, you and I could have driven Nathan crazy." She laughed, a purely delightful laugh. "That would have been fun, wouldn't it?"

"I have to admit, the thought is appealing. I used to drive Nathan so crazy with my questions that he'd take me out in the country and beat me up so our parents couldn't hear me scream. A lot of times he'd make me eat dirt."

"He made you do that?"

Roberto shrugged. "I deserved it. I caught him and Clare behind her parents' barn and ran home to tell mother and Trenton. He caught up with me and made me promise that I wouldn't tell. Of course I wouldn't do that, so he took a fistful of dirt and pushed it into my mouth. I started choking, but he kept doing it until I promised I wouldn't say anything." Roberto laughed.

"What a horrible thing to do!"

"Actually, I think he was pretty easy on me. I was always spying on him and Clare. I'm surprised he didn't beat me black and blue."

"You do have good memories of him, don't you, 'Berto?"

Roberto met Anna's eyes and he couldn't lie. "Yes, I have good memories. Nathan was a good brother to me. I'm just sorry we lost the last ten years." Roberto sipped at his glass of wine. "So, what about you? How did you come to be with my parents?"

"Do you remember the wagons you saw on the way to California? Aeneva wanted to stop because the people on them had cholera. I was one of those people. My father and I were on our way to San Francisco when our wagon train was hit by the disease. Many of the passengers came down with it, and finally the healthy ones decided to leave us some food and water and go on without us."

"They left you there to die?"

"Yes. But Aeneva came to help us. My father tried to get her to leave, but she wouldn't. She made him drink some of her tea, and it almost killed him because he was so used to whiskey. She threw out his whiskey, and he got so angry I thought he'd spit." Anna smiled at the thought.

"How old were you?"

"Eight or nine, but I was quite grown up. I had become accustomed to traveling from town to town with my father and staying in hotel rooms while he gambled and drank."

"Where was your mother?"

"My mother was Cheyenne. She died when I was very young. I don't remember much about her, except that she was very kind to me."

"What about your father? He was white?"

"Yes, he was Irish, and he could drink like any good Irishman could. He tried to be a good father to me, but he didn't do a very good job. I spent most of my young life taking care of him."

"That's why you have blue eyes—your father."

"Yes, my father. He did an incredibly unselfish thing—he left me with Trenton and Aeneva."

"You don't resent him for that, for just leaving you?"

"I love him dearly for it. He gave me a life of happiness. I would never have known that with him, and he knew it." She smiled, her eyes staring at some unknown point in the room. "I think of him sometimes and wonder if he is all right. I wonder if he's even alive. It scares me to think of him all alone somewhere in a dirty room, drinking himself to death."

"You amaze me. I can't believe you wouldn't hate your father for what he did."

"What did he do, 'Berto? He gave me a better life, with two of the best people I have ever known in my life. Should I hate him for that?"

"I suppose not. I just don't understand how you can be so forgiving."

Anna reached across the table and took Roberto's hand. "There is nothing to forgive, 'Berto, don't you understand that? If I had stayed with my father, God only knows what would have happened to me. He was a kind man when he didn't drink, but he drank almost all the time. He always left me by myself. Even he knew that if I stayed with him something terrible might happen to me."

"I just can't imagine ever wanting to leave my parents."

"That's because you had wonderful parents. If they had treated you badly, you would have wanted to leave them. I just feel bad about one thing."

"What?"

"I wish he had left me a letter. I wish I had something to connect me to him. It's almost as if I never had a real father or mother. It's a strange feeling."

Roberto got a strange look on his face. "Anna, I have something for you."

"What?"

"A letter from your father." Roberto averted his gaze, not wanting to meet Anna's eyes. "I went into my mother's room one night. I lay on her bed, I touched many of her things, I just wanted to be close to her. I looked through her bureau and found a box."

"Yes, Aeneva kept an old wooden box with all of her special things in it. She showed me a necklace that Nathan had made for her and a rock that you had given her. She kept dried flowers in it."

"Flowers that Nate and I picked for her. She also kept

169

some letters in there. There was one for Nate, one for me, and two for you."

"There were two letters for me? You have them?"

"I have all of them."

"You took Nathan's letter? Why? You had no right."

"I had every right. He had some time with my parents. He was the last person to see them alive."

"So you will take whatever his mother wrote to him away from him?"

"She was not his mother."

"She was as much his mother as Trenton was your father."

Roberto didn't reply. "I have your letters."

"Why don't you just tell me what they say? I'm sure you read them."

"I didn't read them. I took them because I thought there would come a time when you would want them."

"How thoughtful of you."

"Please, don't start, Anna. I didn't take your letters out of spite."

"But you took Nathan's out of spite. I will never understand you."

"Do you want the letters?"

Anna stood up. "No, I don't want the letters. Whatever they say, you have taken the meaning from them. You have defiled them." She walked to the back door, took a shawl off the hook, and threw it around her head and shoulders.

"Where are you going?"

"I'm going for a walk."

"You can't go out there by yourself. I'll go with you." Roberto stood up.

"Don't bother. I prefer my own company." Anna slammed the door as she went out.

Roberto shook his head in disgust. He didn't seem ever to do the right thing when it came to Anna. No matter

170

what he did, he always seemed to upset her. He went to his room, to his bureau drawer, and pulled out a large envelope, emptying the contents on the bureau. There was a large amount of cash, some deeds to some property, some keys, and the four letters of which he had spoken. He picked up Nathan's and looked at the envelope. He had been tempted many times to open the letter, but he never had. He knew that what was inside was between his mother and Nathan. He took Anna's two letters and put the rest of the contents back into the envelope and into the drawer. He walked into Anna's room and put the letters on her bed; then he went downstairs and waited. Anna was back within the hour. Roberto was sitting outside on the stairs, getting ready to look for her, when she opened the gate. She started to go past him on the stairs, but he grabbed her hand.

"I'm sorry. I didn't mean to hurt you. I took the letters because I knew you would want to read them."

"And you knew I would never go back home again." She pulled away and went into the house.

"Anna, wait." Roberto closed the door. "I want to talk to you for a minute."

"I'm tired of talking to you. It never gets us anywhere. Goodnight."

Roberto strode to the stairs and grasped Anna's wrist. "I will give you Nathan's letter to keep for him."

Anna started to speak in anger, but she controlled herself. She realized that this was Roberto's way of reaching out to her. "Why would you do that?"

"Because I know it means a lot to you."

"Have you read it, 'Berto?" Anna's eyes searched his, but she thought she already knew the answer.

"No."

"Then you keep the letter. It's safe with you. Goodnight." Anna walked up the stairs and went into her room, closing the door. She didn't lock it this time. For

171

some reason, she felt no compunction to lock herself away from Roberto. She knew he posed no threat to her. She unbuttoned the jacket of her suit and had started to take it off, when she noticed the white on her bed. She sat down and picked up the envelopes, recognizing Aeneva's neat, legible handwriting immediately. She opened the envelope and unfolded the letter. It read:

My dear Anna,

I wanted you to have something after I was gone, something to let you know just how much you have meant to me and Trenton. You have been like a dream come true, our own daughter. You have brought so much joy to our lives that I cannot express the void you have filled for us. When we thought we had no children, you came into our lives. You are a blessed child, a shining star that lights up the entire world. I am just sorry that I cannot live to see you grow into full womanhood. We want only the best for you, my dear Anna, and please know that wherever you go in your life that you have been loved as much as any person could be loved. Goodbye, my daughter. We will see you in Seyan.

Aeneva

Anna held the letter to her chest, sobbing. "I love you, mother. Thank you." She refolded the letter and put it back into the envelope, wiping the tears from her face. She picked up the other letter and looked at the scrawled handwriting in puzzlement, then opened the envelope. The letter read: "To my bonnie lass, Kathleen Anna O'Leary." Anna smiled to herself as she could hear her father speak in his Irish brogue.

I'll be leaving you now, but I couldn't be leaving

you in better or more loving hands. Aeneva and Trenton will take good care of you, I know that. And I don't want you to be giving them any trouble. They are good people and they will love you as you should be loved. You are a dear lass, much better than I ever deserved. I hope that your life turns out to be good for you. I just want you to know that in my own strange way, I do love you, Anna.

I never told you much about my life, but I think it's time you knew some things. Before I married your mother, I was married to another woman. When I met her she was a handsome woman and I do believe she loved me, but after we had our first daughter, your sister Rosie, she was never the same. I don't think she liked it much that I adored Rosie. When Rosie died, there was nothing to keep us together, not even little Megan. Me wife was from a very wealthy and prominent family and they bought me off. They wanted me out of their daughter's life forever. And being the scoundrel I am, I took the money. Megan was just a baby at the time, so I expect she's five years older than you. What I am trying to tell you Anna, is that you have a sister. Her name is Megan O'Leary and the last I knew she lived with her mother in San Francisco. Her mother didn't much like me, so she may have changed her name to her family's name which is Foster. I want you to know this because it's important. Someday you might want to look your sister up. As I recall, she had blue eyes like yours but light hair like her mother's. She cried a lot as a baby. She wasn't strong like you are. Neither of my two daughters was as strong as you are, Anna. You are an amazing child. Aeneva told me that you were special and it makes me sad to think that I couldn't see it until she pointed it out to me. God makes very few special children in this world and you are one of them. I do love you, Anna. You are a gift to all those who know you.

Your loving but sometimes failing father, Patrick Michael O'Leary.

Anna's eyes filled with tears. She felt totally overwhelmed. There were no more doubts. She now knew that her father had loved her, and he had given her the greatest gift of all—he had given her to Aeneva and Trenton. Anna looked at the letter again. She couldn't believe it. She had had two sisters, one who was dead, the other out there somewhere, alive, and living a life of her own. Should she look for her? Would her sister resent her coming into her life? Would she hate her because of what their father had been? Anna's mind whirled. Never in her life had she imagined that anything so wonderful could happen to her. She had a blood sister somewhere in this world. She stood up and ran out of the room, taking the stairs as quickly as she could. She found Roberto in the small sitting room.

"Roberto, you must help me. If you care for me at all, you'll help me."

Roberto stood up and walked over to Anna. "Calm down. Tell me what has you so upset."

"I'm not upset. I'm excited. I just found out that I have a sister somewhere, maybe even in San Francisco. You have to help me find her, 'Berto. You have to."

"You have a sister? Is that what was in one of the letters?"

"Yes, it was in the letter from my father. She's about five years older than I am. Her name is Megan."

"O'Leary?"

"I don't know. She could be married. In fact, if she's twenty-five years old, she probably is married." Anna

174

began pacing the room. "What if she moved? What if she lives in Europe or Mexico or somewhere in the East? I'll never find her."

"I'll see what I can do. Do you know anything about her mother's family?"

"Just that they were a rich and prominent family in San Francisco."

"That's good. People will know what's happened to the family."

"You will help me then?"

"It's the least I can do. I'll start on it tomorrow."

Anna threw her arms around Roberto. "Thank you, 'Berto. I don't even know if she wants to see me, but I have to find out. I have to see for myself whether she wants to talk to me."

Roberto looked into Anna's deep blue eyes; he couldn't imagine anyone not wanting her. "Don't worry, I'm sure she'll be just as happy as you are to find out she has a sister." He lowered his mouth to Anna's, touching his lips lightly on hers. "You are so beautiful." He tightened his arms around her waist.

"'Berto, don't."

"You are my wife, Anna. We are legally married." Roberto kissed Anna again, his mouth savoring the sweetness of her lips. "I want you, Anna. You know that, don't you?"

Anna looked up at Roberto, her hands on his chest. "You frighten me, 'Berto. I never know what you are thinking."

"Does it matter what I'm thinking?"

"Yes, it matters." She laid her head against his chest, enjoying the feel of a man's arms around her. It had been so long since she had been held. She just wanted to feel loved; she wanted to feel safe.

Roberto stroked Anna's long, dark hair. "I can take

care of you. I will never let anything happen to you." He pulled her chin up and looked into her eyes again. He wasn't sure what he saw there, but he knew it wasn't desire. He kissed her on the cheek. He couldn't take advantage of her, not when all she wanted was to be held. "Go to bed. You've had a long day."

"What about you?"

"I'll be up later."

"'Berto, I'm sorry."

"What do you have to be sorry about?"

"I seem to yell so much around you. I'm like a shrew. I don't like myself very much when I'm around you."

"Maybe the problem isn't you. Maybe the problem is me. Go on up to bed, Anna. I'll see you in the morning."

"Goodnight, 'Berto."

Roberto nodded. He watched Anna as she left the room. He imagined her taking off her clothes and wiping the cool washcloth over her soft skin. "Holy Jesus," he said to himself. He walked to the front door and sat outside on the steps. "Cool off, 'Berto. She's not your woman. She belongs to your brother. She doesn't even love you." But even as Roberto said this to himself he knew that Anna was beginning to weaken. She was lonely and she was becoming dependent on him. He knew it was only a matter of time before she gave in to him completely. But somehow, the thought didn't comfort him as he thought it would.

LeBeau stood up and walked from behind his desk, holding out his hand to Roberto. "Well, monsieur, I never expected to see you here, and certainly not this soon."

"I didn't expect to be here. I need your help, LeBeau."

"What is it you need, monsieur?"

"My name is Roberto. I need to find my wife's sister."

"I'm sorry, I do not understand."

"My wife just found out that she has a sister. She doesn't know where she lives. You seem to have many contacts; at least I see them all over town following us."

LeBeau nodded. "Touché. Please continue."

"If I give you what information I have, can you find something out?"

"I will do what I can. I have been known to find people who do not want to be found."

Roberto handed LeBeau a sheet of paper. "As far as we know, she doesn't know about Anna, either. She might not even want to see Anna. They're only half-sisters."

"I understand." LeBeau looked at the paper. "San Francisco. I know the city well and have many contacts there. I can get a telegram off today. If we're lucky, we should hear something in a few days."

Roberto took out his wallet. "How much do you charge?"

LeBeau held up his hand. "You insult me, Roberto. Please, let us see what we find out first; then we will talk money."

"All right." Roberto stood up. "There's something else, LeBeau. Anna is my wife. Don't try to come between us, or you'll regret it."

LeBeau held up his hands. "I have never meant to insult your wife, but we Cajun men cannot help ourselves. It is in our blood."

"Just so you understand me."

"I understand." LeBeau stood up. "Would you and your wife be interested in coming to a ball in your honor? I think you will enjoy it. It's on a beautiful plantation in the country."

Roberto started to say no, but he remembered what

Anna had said about wanting to go to another ball. "All right, LeBeau. Just let us know when it is and we'll be there."

"*Très bien.* And I will inform you if I hear anything from my contacts."

"Thank you." Roberto left LeBeau's house and started down the street. There was something familiar about LeBeau; he had sensed it that first night on the riverboat. It wasn't only that he didn't trust LeBeau, it was that he recognized him, but he couldn't say from where.

Roberto walked to the dress shop and ordered more dresses for Anna, on top of the ones he had ordered the day before. He also had the clerk order shoes and bags to match all the dresses. He picked out two different capes for her, one black, the other a deep blue, both with hoods. He stopped at a jewelry store and picked out an emerald necklace with matching earrings, and a sapphire necklace with matching earrings. He wanted to do something nice for Anna. He was saving his best surprise for last. He hailed a carriage and drove back home; ran into the house and got Anna. She was dressed in a simple yellow dress; a thick yellow ribbon pulled her dark mane of hair back from her shoulders. She looked incredibly lovely, Roberto thought. "Are you ready?"

"Where are we going?"

"I told you we'd take a drive in the country." He took her arm and led her out to the waiting carriage.

Anna was like a child. She leaned forward, looking out both sides of the carriage, not wanting to miss a thing. She smiled as the carriage left the city and went onto a narrow dirt road, bordered by oak, willow and hickory trees. The lush green foliage completely engulfed the sides of the road. It was practically impossible to see through the wall of green and the silky moss that hung from the trees. "I've never seen anything like this,"

Anna exclaimed. "It's so beautiful."

Roberto recalled trying to crawl through the wall of green. He had no fondness for it at all. "There are swamps back there in the trees."

"Swamps?"

"A lot of the land back there is covered in water. All kinds of strange birds and animals live back in there. And there are water snakes."

"Snakes live in the water?" Anna shivered. "At least we can see our snakes crawling on the ground."

"You have to be careful around here. The snakes are deadly. You'll be swimming along and all of a sudden you see it coming at you in the water. It's a terrifying feeling. It doesn't just bite you once; it'll bite you as many times as it can." Roberto involuntarily rubbed his right thigh, thinking of the bites he had suffered from the vicious snake. He'd managed to get to the other side of the swamp and get out, but the poison had already begun to work on him.

"What happened when you were here, 'Berto? My God, it doesn't sound like it was any better here than it was on that ship."

"It was wonderful for a long time, for over a year, but then things went wrong. Maybe it was my fault; maybe I thought I was someone I wasn't." The carriage stopped and Roberto got out, helping Anna down.

Anna held onto Roberto's hand. "Roberto, please talk to me."

"There's nothing to talk about." He looked around. "Here we are. This way." He led Anna to a small pasture where horses grazed peacefully on the green grass.

Anna ran to the fence, stepping up to lean on the top railing. She pointed to a large horse in the far corner of the pasture. "Look at that Appaloosa. He looks like Trenton's; his coloring is even similar."

179

"I know." Roberto stood next to Anna. "I remember how much he loved that horse. We weren't even allowed to go near it. Nate got himself a good beating once for taking him out."

"Trenton beat Nathan?"

"It was for his own good. That horse wouldn't listen to anyone but Trenton. Nate could've gotten himself killed."

"I used to ride him," Anna said softly. "Trenton didn't like me to but I did. The horse didn't seem to mind. Aeneva said he responded better to a gentler touch."

"What do you think of this one?"

"He's beautiful, he has good lines, he looks strong, but it's important that a horse have a good temperament. You never know what a horse is made of until you ride him."

"Do you want to ride him?"

"I'd love to!" Anna looked around. "Who do these horses belong to, anyway?"

"They belong to someone I know. He said we could come out and go for a ride if we wanted to. Are you ready?"

Anna hopped down from the fence and walked with Roberto to the nearby barn and tack room. Anna didn't wait for Roberto. She looked over the saddles and picked one that would suit her, putting it on the ground, then got a blanket, bridle and reins and threw them on the saddle. She looked around by the feed bags and found some sugar cubes to put in her pocket, picked up the saddle and carried it back out to the fence, Roberto following closely behind. She fastened the reins to the bit and climbed over the fence.

"Be careful, Anna," Roberto called from outside the fence.

"I'll be careful." She approached the Appaloosa slowly, making a clucking sound with her tongue. He seemed not the least bit interested in her; he was too busy chomping on the sweet grass. Several other horses in the pasture shied away from her. She reached into her pocket and got a cube of sugar; holding her hand out to the big horse in front of her. "Here, boy, do you want some sugar?"

The horse lifted his head for a moment and then returned to chomping at the grass. Anna stepped closer. The markings on the horse were beautiful, white everywhere except for his black shoes, his spotted black rump, and a black patch around each eye. Anna stood close to the animal, letting him get used to her scent and her voice. "What are you doing this far south, boy? You don't belong here. You belong in the land of my mother's people, where you can run as freely as you want." The horse looked up and regarded Anna. "So, you do know I'm here." Anna held out her hand again. This time the horse was interested; his nostrils flaired and he put his soft muzzle into her hand. He sucked up the sugar cube. "You like that? Here's another." Anna held out her hand again and the horse ate the cube, then pushed at her with his muzzle and snorted. "You're not going to get the rest of the sugar, at least not yet." Anna laughed, reached up and patted his soft nose, rubbing it up and down. "You are so beautiful." She laid her head against his. "If only I could be on your back and we could ride like the wind, back to my home." The horse snorted and Anna laughed. She gave him another sugar cube and ran her hand along his head and neck. She slowly lifted the bridle up to his head. "It's all right. I'm not going to hurt you." She put the bridle over his head and ears and the bit in his mouth. He shook his head, not enjoying the feeling of the bridle but not fighting it. "Good boy." She patted his neck and led the horse over to the fence. He balked slightly when he saw Roberto, but Anna urged him on.

"If it took you that long to get the bridle on, you'll never get the saddle on."

"Who said I was going to use a saddle?" Anna reached through the railing and grabbed the blanket, tossing it over the horse's back. She handed Roberto the reins. "Hold him close to the fence while I climb up." She patted the horse's neck. "It's okay, boy."

"You lack common sense, woman."

"I may lack a lot of things, 'Berto, but one of them isn't the ability to ride a horse." Anna slipped her leg over the horse's wide back until she was sitting firmly. She grabbed a handful of mane until Roberto handed her the reins, then leaned over and patted the horse's neck. "It's all right, boy. I won't hurt you." Anna pulled him to the right and they walked away from the fence. She let him get used to her weight and the feel of her on his back, then pressed her knees into his sides. "Come on, boy, let's see what you can do." The Appaloosa bucked slightly but took off, running across the pasture. Anna held the reins tightly, keeping his head up, but she let him have his lead. He ran like the wind and Anna closed her eyes as she breathed in the feel of freedom, something she hadn't felt in a long time. As they approached the far end of the pasture Anna tried to pull the horse to the left, but he wouldn't turn; he wanted to jump. Anna leaned low against his neck and went with him. The Appaloosa jumped the fence as if it didn't even exist. Anna laughed out loud. "God, you are wonderful." She sat up and patted the horse's neck, slowing him down to a canter, then riding around the outside of the pasture until they reached the barn. Anna walked the big horse to where Roberto was sitting on the fence. "What did you think?"

"Did you have to jump that fence?"

"I didn't have a choice. He wanted to jump it. He's

182

wonderful, isn't he?"

Roberto smiled. "You ride beautifully, Anna. Just like an Indian. You remind me of my mother."

"That's because Aeneva taught me how to ride. I knew a little bit about horses from riding with my father, but Aeneva taught me how to be friends with them. She taught me what freedom there is in riding."

"So you like the Appaloosa?"

Anna leaned against the horse's neck. "He's one of the most magnificent animals I've ever seen. I'm surprised to see one this far south. The Gros Ventres raise them on the Plains and they're often stolen by other Plains tribes because they make such wonderful war horses. But you don't see many white men with them."

"Trenton had one."

"Trenton was more Indian than white."

"This one was probably stolen by some trader or some soldier and sold to someone down here."

"You're sure the man who owns it doesn't mind that I rode him?"

"No, he doesn't mind. Would you like to ride him again?"

"I'd like to ride him every day if I could."

"You can. Because I just gave him to you."

"You? You own him?"

"I bought him for you yesterday. I thought he might make you happy."

Anna slid off the horse's back, climbed to the top of the fence and put her arms around Roberto's neck. "I don't understand you sometimes. You try to be so mean, but you seem to have such a good heart. Thank you." Anna kissed Roberto softly on the cheek, but he held her to him.

"What would it take for me to make you forget Nathan?"

"Don't, 'Berto."

"I want to know."

"Nothing could ever make me forget Nathan. I love him."

"But love can be felt in different ways. Even my mother was able to love my father enough to conceive me, and we know how much she loved Trenton."

"'Berto, don't. You're scaring me."

"Why? Because you know it can happen?"

Anna pulled away from Roberto and climbed down the fence, opened the gate to the corral and led the horse inside. She took the bridle and blanket off, then smacked him on the flank and sent him back into the pasture. Putting the bridle and blanket over her shoulder, she climbed back over the fence, picked up the saddle, and headed back toward the tack room, where she put back the bridle and blanket and hefted the saddle onto the side of one of the stalls.

"I didn't mean to upset you."

Anna caught her breath. "God, you scared me." They were in the back of the tack room, all alone, and Anna was afraid. She looked up at Roberto. He was a darkly handsome man, so unlike Nathan, but there was an air of mystery about him that frightened her. She also didn't like the way he made her feel when he touched her.

"Why are you so afraid of me, Anna? I've never hurt you." He touched her cheek lightly.

"But you have hurt me, Roberto. You've taken me away from my home."

"And away from Nathan?" Roberto stepped nearer, backing Anna into a dark corner of the tack room. "I can make you forget Nathan." He put his hands on the wall on either side of Anna and leaned forward, his body against hers. "You're lonely, Anna. I know you are." Roberto lowered his mouth to Anna's neck, gently following the line of it up to her mouth. He could feel her lips tremble as he pressed his mouth against them, but he could also feel them respond. "Do you want me, Anna?" He whispered softly, his mouth brushing hers, his strong body pressing against hers. He knew what the answer was, but he wanted to hear her say it.

Anna looked at the man in front of her and suddenly felt more frightened of her emotions than she ever had in her life. What had happened to her to make her forget Nathan so easily? Was the love she felt for Nathan not really love at all? Or was it just as simple as wanting to feel Nathan's body against hers, feel his arms around her, remembering what it was like when he made love to her? Was that all she felt for Nathan? She looked at Roberto and knew that she could just as easily feel those same things for him. What kind of a woman did that make her? Perhaps her experience with the captain on the slave ship had affected her more than she wanted to admit. Before she realized it, her legs gave way and she started to fall to the ground, beginning to sob. She didn't understand what was happening to her, and she didn't like it.

Roberto knelt in front of Anna and put her arms around his neck, pulling her against him. "I'm sorry, Anna. Forgive me."

Anna buried her face in Roberto's shoulder, feeling comforted, yet frightened of his presence. "I'm scared, 'Berto."

"Don't be scared. I'll never force you to do anything. I promise you."

"What is happening to me? I always thought I knew what I wanted."

"What do you mean?"

"I grew up with my friend Garrett and I thought I loved him, but then I met Nathan and I fell in love with him. I thought Nathan was my life, would be my life, but

185

then you came along. It was easy to blame you for everything, but I don't think it's your fault. I think it's my fault. I think if I can feel attracted to three different men, there must be something wrong with me." She held onto Roberto as if she were a little girl who was afraid to face something bad she had done.

"Anna," Roberto lifted Anna's chin up, "I want you to listen to me. There's nothing wrong with you. You are a wonderful person. You didn't do anything wrong. If anyone is to blame, it's me."

Anna sat back against the wall, wiping the tears from her face. "I don't understand all of these feelings. How can I care for so many men at one time?"

"Every human being has the ability to love more than one person; it's just that most choose to be with one person. There's nothing unnatural about the way you're feeling. Men feel it all the time. Why do you think young boys have so many girlfriends? It's all right for them, because their fathers encourage it, but it would be frowned upon if a girl were to do it."

"I'm afraid to be around you, 'Berto." Anna could not meet Roberto's piercing gaze.

"If it makes you feel any better, I'm afraid to be around you, too. You bring out feelings in me that I thought were dead."

"What feelings?"

"Feelings of love and protectiveness. Being with you makes me think of my mother and my real father. I know they must've loved each other, or I never would've been born, and I know if that's true, then you can learn to love me."

Anna looked down at the floor. "If you want me to be with you, 'Berto, I will. I can't fight you anymore. I will stay with you forever if that's what you want, but don't ask me to love you, because I don't know if I can do that."

Roberto nodded slightly and stood up. He held out his

hand to Anna and pulled her up. "I haven't forgotten that you're here because I made you come with me. I also know that you have grown fond of me. Let's take our time, Anna. There's no hurry. But I want you to know one thing—if you do decide to come to me, I will never let you go."

Anna looked at the man who stood before her, and nodded her head. Her future, however limited it seemed, was now in her own hands.

Chapter VII

Nathan sat up, sweat dripping down his face and chest. He looked around him at the dark, starry night and the smoldering campfire. He saw the silhouettes of Molly and Garrett lying side by side across the fire from him. He closed his eyes and wiped the sweat from his brow. "God, how I miss you, Anna. Where are you?"

He got up and walked to the edge of their small camp, standing by one of the huge oak trees that sheltered them. The air was stifling; he could hardly breathe. It was different from the kind of heat that was in Arizona. There the weather got hot but it was extremely dry; here it was hot and humid, the air so heavy it felt as if it was weighing your lungs down.

"What's wrong, Nate?"

Nathan smiled to himself. It was uncanny how close he and Garrett had become. It was almost as if the man could read his thoughts. "I'm wondering if I've brought you two here for nothing. Anna might not even be here. She could be anywhere."

"Let's take it a step at a time. We'll be in New Orleans tomorrow, and we can start checking when we get there."

"Jesus, Garrett, I don't know anyone in New Orleans."

"This doesn't sound like you, Nate. When I first met you, you weren't afraid of anyone, not even Franklin Driscoll. Why are you so afraid to try to find Anna?"

"Because I'm afraid of what I'll find. We've been apart for almost four months now. She's legally Roberto's wife, remember?"

"Hell, I don't know what I'm going to do with you. Are we actually talking about the same woman here? This is the woman who grew up with me and promised to marry me, but when she saw you for the first time, she fell in love with you."

"You just proved my point. She's been away from me and she's had to depend on Roberto. Maybe she's fallen in love with him. Maybe she wants to stay with him."

"Maybe so, but you'll never know unless you find out, will you? Of course, as soon as the sun comes up we could just turn tail and go back to Arizona. I'm sure Clare would be real glad to see your face."

"How did I ever hook up with you, anyway?"

Garrett put his hand on Nathan's shoulder. "Listen, Nate, do you remember when I was down and out in California and Driscoll was ready to take my land from me? I felt humiliated, but you came to me and gave me a loan and got me back on my feet again. You even asked me to marry Anna." He laughed. "Maybe that would've solved all of our problems."

"Sure, and I could marry Molly."

Garrett looked across the dark camp at Molly. "She's something special, isn't she?"

"Yeah, she is."

"If something were to happen to her I don't think I'd give up on her so easily as you're willing to give up on Annie."

"I've been thinking a lot about my pa. I don't know how he was able to accept the fact that Aeneva fell in love with another man and had his child. I don't know if I could do that."

"Sure you could. You're just getting antsy because nothing's happening right now. As soon as we get into the city and get ourselves set up, you'll feel much better. Besides, Chin's contact should be able to tell you more."

"Thanks, Garrett. You're right, it's not like me to have these feelings of doubt, but something's eating at me. I have a gut feeling that something is wrong."

"Just wait until tomorrow. We'll find out then." He slapped Nathan on the shoulder. "I'm going back to bed now. Goodnight."

"Goodnight." Nathan stared out into the darkness beyond, hearing sounds he'd never heard before in the trees around them. He hated this place. He just wanted to find Anna and go home. But he knew it wouldn't be that easy. Unlike Garrett, he felt there was a bond between Anna and Roberto, and he was afraid he might not be able to break it.

Nathan looked at himself in the mirror and shook his head. As many times as he had seen himself in a suit, he couldn't quite get used to it. It made him look too civilized. After he'd opened an account at the bank, he'd given money to Garrett for him and Molly to buy clothes and to get a room at a good hotel. He would check in later after he had bought himself some clothes and, more importantly, had seen Chin's contact. He bought three more suits, some shirts, boots, gloves and a hat. It was important that he fit in.

Once out on the street, Nathan took out the card Chin had given him and decided to walk. New Orleans reminded him of San Francisco, with its quaint brick houses and narrow streets. It was laid out much the same way. The area by the water was also much the same, with the dirty little taverns, whores, beggars, thieves and murderers. His memories of San Francisco were not pleasant.

Nathan walked for quite a while until he reached his destination. He opened the wrought iron gate and went up the stairs, knocked on the door and was greeted by a butler. Nathan had no card to give the man, but he gave him Chin's name instead and was shown inside seconds later.

He followed the small black man into a large wooden office filled with books and maps. A huge globe sat on the floor and maps dotted the walls. "Can I get you something, monsieur? Café, something to eat, perhaps?"

"No, thank you."

"Monsieur will be with you in a few moments." The man closed the doors to the office.

Nathan got up and studied the maps on the wall. "Ship routes," he said to himself, tracing the routes with his finger. He spun the globe around to the United States, looking for California, Arizona and Louisiana.

"It is a long distance, no?"

Nathan turned, quickly appraising the man who had just entered the room. "I didn't hear you come in. I was interested in your maps and the globe."

"Geography is my love. Every map you see on the wall, I have been there. It is rather like a hobby with me."

"Some hobby." Nathan shook his head in wonder. "Sorry, my name is Nathan Hawkins. I'm Chin's friend." Nathan extended his hand.

"Yes, I know. My name is LeBeau." LeBeau shook Nathan's hand. "Now tell me, what is it I can do for you?"

"I'm trying to find my brother and a woman. I believe Chin gave you their descriptions."

"Yes, he did." LeBeau regarded the man in front of him. He was tall and lean, with light hair and light eyes, straight, even teeth, and a smooth manner that belied his

191

toughness. LeBeau knew by the man's handshake that he was not one to be taken lightly. "If you do not mind my asking, what are you to Chin? Are you a business acquaintance?"

"Actually, I do mind you asking," Nathan replied curtly. "My relationship with Chin is no business of yours. I came here on business. If you can't help me, I'll go elsewhere."

LeBeau nodded. "No, that will not be necessary. Please, sit down." LeBeau walked behind his desk and sat down, unlocking one of the drawers and taking out a sheet of paper. "Your brother and the woman have been seen in the city—several times, in fact."

"Where? Do you know where they are staying?"

"No, not yet, but I will. I have two men waiting to follow them the next time they come into the city."

"You mean to tell me you spotted them more than once and you lost them?"

"No one is perfect, monsieur, not even LeBeau."

"Where have they been seen?"

"I have the places written down here. Perhaps you will have better luck than I. Do you wish me to continue?"

"Yes. I want them found."

"Yes, of course. There is also a matter of money, Monsieur. I have spent—"

"Look, LeBeau." Nathan leaned forward, his eyes narrowing. "Don't play games with me. You haven't spent any time or you'd know where they are. Or maybe you do know where they are and you just don't want to tell me now because you think you'll get more money out of me. Either way, I'll find them, and I'll be back for you." Nathan stood up. "I think you should remember something, LeBeau. I am like a son to Chin. If he finds out that you have double-crossed me, you'll be sorry you were ever born."

LeBeau nodded, a satisfied look on his face. "You

know, I think I like you, Nathan. I like a man who does not believe LeBeau so easily."

"What in hell are you talking about?"

"Sit down. I was just testing you. We Cajuns are very distrusting of people. I had to make sure of you, that is all. I like Chin; he helped me out once. I would not like to see his honor betrayed."

"In that we are in agreement. Now, can you tell me anything about my brother?"

"May I ask one thing? The woman. She is in love with you, yes?"

Nathan's eyes lit up. "You've seen her?"

"Yes, we were on a riverboat together. Your brother was very angry that we were talking and he finally went to his cabin. Anna and I talked for quite some time. She is a beautiful flower." LeBeau laughed. "A smart one, too."

"How did she seem around him?"

"Let me put it this way, my friend: She did not seem like a woman in love. I even said this to her."

"Did she look all right? He hasn't hurt her?"

"No, she looks well. I saw her just last week.

"Does she seem to want to stay with him?"

"Does she have any choice?" LeBeau got up and walked around the room, straightening the maps that hung on the walls. "I believe she has resigned herself to her situation, but I do not think she loves this man, no."

"Do you know where they live?"

"Yes, I know."

Nathan stood up. "Tell me, LeBeau."

"I cannot do that, my friend." He held up his hand as Nathan stepped closer. "You can kill me if you wish, but that will do you no good. I have my orders from Chin."

"Chin? What does he have to do with it?"

"He told me that you might react this way, and he said that I must make you slow down and think. How did he say? 'The babbling brook will still flow to the sea but, unlike the rushing river, it will not ruin everything in its path.' Do you understand?"

"Christ, I should've known." Nathan walked to the window. He tried to calm himself. "It sounds like Chin. He's afraid I'll run off half-cocked and kill my brother."

"Is that not what you were planning to do just a few moments ago, my friend?"

A quizzical expression spread over Nathan's face. "Are you Cajuns related to the Chinese?"

LeBeau burst into laughter. "Yes, I do like you. You have good wit. That is important."

"Don't play games with me, LeBeau. What about my brother?"

"He is staying here in the city with Anna. But you cannot get into the house."

"Why not?"

"He has men watching the house. I think perhaps, he is expecting you."

"So, Anna is a prisoner."

"They go out frequently, but always together. I do not think she even knows about the men who watch her."

"Can you get a message to her from me?"

"I must warn you, Nathan, your brother does not like me. He thinks I have designs on his wife."

"Do you?"

"Of course I do, but I would not be a good Cajun if I did not try to pursue a beautiful woman. Alas, she would have nothing to do with me outside of friendship. I think she finds me quite humorous."

"So you can get close to her."

"I have a better idea, a brilliant idea actually. In two weeks, friends of mine are throwing a party for your brother and Anna. I will make sure that you are invited."

"Two weeks? I don't know if I can wait two weeks."

"You must. If your brother finds out that you are here, he will take Anna and leave immediately. Where

194

are you staying?"

"I haven't found a hotel yet, but I'm planning to stay here."

"No, that will not do. We must get you out of the city."

"Where?"

LeBeau drummed his fingers on the desk. "It is too perfect. I will arrange it so that you stay with the people who are throwing the party for Anna and your brother."

"Who are they?"

"Richard Thornston and his daughter Caroline."

"Thornston? He's the man Roberto saved, isn't he?"

"Yes, he is the man."

"Chin says that Thornston helped him out. He says that Thornston is well-regarded in this city; maybe—"

"Hold on, my friend. There are a few things you must know about our Mr. Thornston."

"He did help Roberto, didn't he?"

"Yes, that much is true. In fact he took him into his own home and came to think of him as a son. He taught him how to run the plantation and taught him how to keep the financial records. He also taught him about his shipping business. All went well for a time, until Roberto met Caroline."

"Thornston's daughter?"

"Yes, and the apple of his eye. There is something that you must understand. Things are different here in the South. People have lived here for hundreds of years with the belief that if they have white skin they are better than anyone who has brown or black skin."

"But you said he grew to care for Roberto."

"He did, in his own way. But when he saw how Roberto and Caroline felt about each other, that was something else. He was grateful to your brother for saving his life; he gave him shelter, clothing, food, money and an education, but he would not give him his daughter."

"I can understand a man being protective of his daughter."

"It was not just protectiveness, my friend. Trust me. I have grown up with these kinds of feelings all my life."

"Did Caroline love Roberto?"

"Yes, she loved him very much. So much, in fact, that she wanted to run off with him and get married. But Roberto wouldn't do it. He didn't want to go behind Thornston's back after everything he had done for him."

"So what happened?"

"Caroline did what any woman who is desperate and in love will do. She gave herself to Roberto and he couldn't resist. She found herself pregnant. She was elated, but she was never able to tell Roberto. Her father read her diary. He publicly accused Roberto of raping his daughter, and when your brother didn't confess, he had him beaten until he was unconscious. Your brother screamed for Caroline, but she did nothing to help him. He was dragged to the swamp and thrown in. I suppose you could thank Thornston for that. He could've killed the boy but instead he threw him where he knew he'd be found and taken care of by people."

"People in a swamp?"

"Yes, they live there. It is said they are dangerous."

"But they helped Roberto?"

"Yes. They took care of him and nursed him back to health. Then one day, he just took off. That is when he went west, I suppose."

"So that's why he's here. He wants to get revenge on Thornston. Do you think he'll try to see Caroline?"

"I do not think so. Your brother is a very proud man. He feels he was betrayed by her. The sad thing is, he doesn't even know he has a son."

"A son? I have a nephew?" Nathan couldn't contain a smile.

"Yes, my friend, you have a handsome nephew who

looks every bit like his father."

"Which must drive his grandfather crazy."

"Thornston wants no reminders of your brother. Caroline almost died having the baby, but she did it. She loved your brother that much."

"And he doesn't even know."

"That is why we must plan this carefully. If I can get you into Thornston's estate and you can gain Caroline's trust, perhaps you two can come up with a plan. The night of the party, your brother will see her, and he will not be able to stay away from her."

"It sounds too easy, LeBeau. Roberto is not so easily fooled."

LeBeau twirled his moustache. "Perhaps you are right, but between now and then we most certainly can come up with a plan that will get you back with Anna, and get your brother to meet his son."

"It's almost as if you care for my brother, LeBeau."

"I have thought many times about his story. I, myself, did not have a good life as a boy, but at least I knew that I was loved. Once your brother was taken from your parents, love ceased to exist for him, at least until he met Caroline. Then, again, it was snatched away from him. I feel sorry that any man should have to endure such pain. I do not believe your brother to be a cruel man, Nathan."

"I don't think he is either, LeBeau." Nathan stood up and walked to the globe, spinning it around in its wooden frame. How many times had Roberto sailed across the great oceans of the world, shackled and treated like a slave? How many times had he almost died? And when he finally found love again, how cruelly it was taken from him. Tears filled his eyes, tears not of sadness, but of anger. Quickly, he brushed them from his face.

"Do not be ashamed, my friend. We Cajuns, we cry all the time. I cannot imagine what it must feel like to find your brother after all these years and then find out what

197

he has been through. Let that guide you instead of the anger you have for him. He does not mean to hurt you; he just does not know how not to hurt."

"I love him. I want to help him."

"In time, my friend. In time. Now you must be patient."

Nathan nodded. "Would it be possible for you to get two other people into Thornston's house? I'm traveling with a woman and a man, close friends of mine."

"Does Anna know either one of them?"

"She knows the man quite well. They grew up together. He came along to help me find her."

"And the woman?"

"His woman, LeBeau, and she can more than take care of herself."

"Ah, what a shame. Well, I will see what I can do. I will introduce you as a business associate from San Francisco. You cannot use your last name, because your brother is using it."

"Use Randall, Steven Randall. I've used it before."

"Good. And your friend?"

"His name is Garrett McReynolds and his woman's name is Molly. But why don't we call them Mr. and Mrs. Reynolds, just to simplify things?"

"But of course. And what business shall I say you are in?"

"Well, we don't have to lie. Tell him I'm a wealthy rancher and I'm interested in using his ships to take my cattle to Baja California and Mexico. That should do for a start."

"Good. Money always interests Richard Thornston."

"You never told me, LeBeau—just how did you find out all of this about Roberto and Caroline?"

"Oh, did I forget to tell you? Caroline and I are engaged to be married."

"What? But you said—"

LeBeau waved his hands in a flourish. "I know what I said, but that doesn't matter anymore. It was merely a contract. Thornston wanted a husband for his daughter and a father for the child, and I wanted more money and more land. I admit it, I am a cad. The truth is, I like Caroline. I don't love her, but I like her. We have talked many times and she told me what happened. I couldn't believe her father would do anything so heartless, but I am not surprised. I still plan to get my money from Thornston."

"How?"

"When we make our engagement public, which we will do at the party, he will pay me one hundred thousand dollars."

"But why you? You don't exactly come from pure bloodlines."

LeBeau raised his eyebrows. "Be careful, my friend. We Cajuns are proud people."

"I didn't mean it the way it sounded. I'm part Indian myself. I just mean, the way Thornston feels about dark-skinned people, I'm surprised he'd let you marry his daughter."

"Well, as you see, my skin is no darker than yours. But you are right, Richard Thornston wouldn't normally let his daughter marry a Cajun. But this isn't a normal circumstance. He's getting scared. He wants a father for his bastard grandson. I'm sorry, I did not mean to insult your nephew. I get angry when I speak of Richard Thornston."

"There must be another reason."

"Why do you say that?"

"You're not stupid, LeBeau."

"As it happens, you are right. I have money and some power, but I also happen to own the most respectable bordello in the city."

"A whorehouse?"

"Curious. That is exactly what Anna said."

"Yes, she would."

"Anyway, Thornston has come there for many years. About a year ago, he hurt one of my girls badly. She almost died. I got him out of there and no one ever found out, but he knows that I can talk at any time. And I will. I want him to pay."

"You hate him."

"I hate what he stands for, and I hate what he's done to people like your brother."

"He reminds me of a man I knew once. What that man did to Anna . . ." Nathan stopped himself. "When will you let me know about Thornston?"

"I will go out there as soon as you leave. I do not think it will be a problem. Thornston is anxious to have Caroline mix with people of her race and station."

Nathan gave a lopsided grin. "Wait until he sees Anna and Roberto."

"I cannot wait. The best part of it is that there will be nothing he can do unless he wants to embarrass himself. Yes, it will be a night to remember."

Nathan walked to LeBeau, extending his hand again. "Thanks, LeBeau. I should've known Chin would never let me down."

"Chin is a good man. We are both the wiser for having known him."

"I may be wiser, but I don't think I'm much more patient. Thanks again."

"I will be in touch, my friend."

Anna leaned against the fence, sticking her arm through to feed sugar to the Appaloosa, now named Wind. She didn't feel like riding today. She had felt strange since the few days before, when she and Roberto had almost become intimate. The thought still frightened her. Since then, she had stayed in her room, feigning illness. Roberto threatened to bring a doctor if she didn't go for a ride in the carriage today.

"Aren't you going to ride him?"

"No." She patted Wind's soft muzzle and tried to ignore Roberto.

"You can play sick for as long as you like, Anna, but I'm still not going to go away."

Anna climbed to the top railing, leaning her face against Wind's. She missed Nathan more than she had ever missed anyone in her life. It was more than what they had experienced physically together; it was also the intimacy of their talks, the way they were able to say anything to each other without holding back. She closed her eyes, remembering how Nathan had held onto her when she was so sick from the opium, vomiting hour after hour, and still he was beside her in the morning. He had loved her unconditionally. She remembered him as he lay dying, his face flushed and sweating, his hair matted against his head, his already lean body grown thin from the sickness. She didn't think she could feel any worse fear than she had at that moment, knowing she might lose him forever. But she felt it again now. She didn't know if she could live without ever seeing Nathan again.

"You're going to make yourself sick if you keep on like this, Anna."

Anna turned and looked at Roberto with angry resignation. "What do you want me to do, Roberto? Do you want me to lie down on the ground and spread my legs for you? Would that make you feel better? You'd like to have your brother's woman, wouldn't you? Is that the only way you'd feel like a real man?"

Roberto lashed out before he could stop himself. He struck Anna across the face, knocking her from the fence to the ground. She crumbled in a heap, but when Roberto tried to help her she pushed him away. "I didn't mean it, Anna. God, I didn't mean it."

Anna stood up, holding the side of her face. "You never mean it, Roberto. You always make excuses for yourself. Maybe you could get away with it when you were eleven years old, but you can't get away with it now. You were always so used to getting your way with Nathan that you just can't accept the fact that you were the one who almost got you both killed. Nathan almost died trying to save you, and all you can do is harbor this terrible hatred for him. Maybe that's the only way you can live with yourself." Anna walked past the carriage and down the road.

"Anna, wait. You can't walk back into town." Roberto ordered the carriage driver to follow as he walked after Anna. "I don't know what to say. I've never hit a woman in my life." He put his hands on Anna's shoulders. "Please, stop." Anna stopped. "I am afraid. You've shown me emotions I thought were dead and buried. I've felt everything with you—anger, jealousy, confusion, love, and even trust. You have taught me about friendship. That is something I never thought I would know again." Roberto shook his head. "Let's walk. It's time I told you some things about me."

Roberto continued the story he had started to tell Anna earlier. He told her everything, including the love he had felt for Caroline and the hero-worship he had felt for her father, Richard Thornston. "I loved Caroline more than I thought it was possible to love anyone, and when she betrayed me, I felt as if my heart had been cut out of me. I suppose in a way it had been. When her father beat me, I suppose I thought I deserved it. I just couldn't believe—I still can't—that she didn't love me. Since then, I haven't felt any real emotion but hatred."

"'Berto," Anna put her arms around Roberto's waist, hugging him to her. "If only you had told me this before.

You could have saved us both a lot of trouble."

"I know. But I suppose I wanted to hurt you, too, Anna. I didn't want you to love my brother."

"Do you still feel that way?" She looked up at him.

"I don't know how I feel. I'm still confused. I know now that Nate tried to help me, but I just wish he had come looking for me. I dream about it every day. I was sure my big brother would rescue me from that stinking ship."

"How could he, 'Berto? He thought you were dead. My God, if he had known you were alive, he wouldn't have stopped until he found you. You must believe that."

"Nate was always everything to me. That's why I didn't want him to die when he was sick. I told myself I wanted him to die but when I saw him lying there so helpless, calling out for me, I couldn't stand it. I wanted him to live."

"So, what do we do now?"

"Am I going to let you go back to Nathan? Isn't that what you really want to know?"

"Is it so much to ask?"

"I suppose not." Roberto turned away and continued walking down the tree-lined road.

"Why are we here in New Orleans, Roberto? You haven't told me that yet."

"I want to pay back Richard Thornston for what he did to me." Roberto stopped and looked at Anna. His dark eyes looked deadly. "He almost beat me to death and then he threw me in a swamp to die. It's a miracle I didn't die, Anna. He doesn't deserve to live. People shouldn't treat people like that."

"Roberto, you can't kill him. If he's as important as you say, you'll go to jail for the rest of your life."

"It would be worth it."

"No, it wouldn't. No man is worth that." She grabbed onto his shirt. "Listen to me, 'Berto. We have enough money. We can leave here and find a home somewhere, maybe in the East. I'll stay with you. I'll be a real wife to you. We can have children together."

Roberto stared at Anna, his eyes filling with tears. He took her hands and brought them to his mouth, kissing each one gently and then holding them against his chest. "You are the kindest person I have ever known. You remind me so much of my mother it makes my heart ache." He stopped, embarrassed by his sudden display of emotion, and stared off at the trees behind Anna. "I could never let you do that. Yesterday I could have let you, but not today."

Anna reached up and wiped the single tear that streaked its way down Roberto's cheek. "Then let me help you in some other way. There must be another way to hurt Thornston. You know his business. Things couldn't have changed that much." Anna stopped, a smile covering her face. "There's the best way of all, 'Berto. I can't believe you haven't thought of it."

"What?"

"Caroline."

"Caroline doesn't love me. She never did."

"I can find that out. Get me introduced to her. I will find out if she's married and, if she's not, why. Everything you told me about her father tells me that she had no choice in the matter, 'Berto. He may have threatened her."

"It's possible, I suppose."

"Of course it's possible. Can you get me an introduction?"

"No, but I know who can."

"LeBeau."

"Yes, LeBeau. He would be the perfect one. And what do we do if she's married?"

"You kidnap her."

"Just like that?"

"You didn't have much trouble doing that with me."

"God, it would drive him crazy. You're right, it is a better plan."

"'Berto." Anna took his hand. "I am so sorry you have suffered so much. But I want you to understand something. Your parents loved you more than anything in the world, except for Nathan. And Nathan died inside when he thought you were dead. Did you see his face light up when he saw that you were actually alive? He loves you so much. You must let all of those past feelings go. It's time to get on with your life."

"It won't be easy for me, Anna."

"I didn't say it would be easy, but I'll be there to help you."

"Why? Why would you want to help me after everything I've done to you?"

"Because I know that underneath your anger there is good. I could see it when Cain hurt me. You couldn't stand it."

"I can't believe I just hit you. I've never hit a woman before."

"You did it out of anger; I understand that. But you must promise me that you won't try to hurt Richard Thornston. Promise me."

"I promise you." Roberto lifted Anna's left hand. "You can take the ring off now. I'll take you back to Nathan as soon as this is all over."

Anna folded her hand into a fist. "This ring was given to me in friendship and I will always wear it in friendship."

"There's something else, Anna, that we have to talk about . . ."

"What?"

"About what happened in the tack room. That wasn't fake for me. I really wanted to make love to you. In fact, I think part of me does love you. I'm sorry if I forced

205

myself on you."

"You didn't force yourself on me, 'Berto. I wanted you, too. That's why I've been so confused. It didn't make any sense to me that I could love Nathan as much as I do and still want to be with you."

"I told you before, there's nothing bad about that. Everyone has those feelings at one time or another."

"I know that now, thanks to you. I also know that if I weren't going back to Nathan, I could stay with you and I could be happy. You're a good person, 'Berto."

Roberto took Anna's face in his hands and kissed her deeply, savoring the sweetness of the lips that he would never again taste. "Thank you, dear Anna. Thank you."

"What do you think?"

"It is up to you, my friend. She is your woman. I can either get her into Thornston's or keep her out. I do think it is quite fascinating, however, that your brother should suddenly be letting her go off by herself."

"What do you think it means?" Nathan couldn't suppress the anxious tone in his voice.

"It could mean that they have fallen in love and she is willing to help him, or it could mean that he trusts her and she wants to help him."

"Which do you think it is?"

"Come, my friend, you know your woman better than I."

"You said she seemed uncomfortable around him. Why would she suddenly trust him?"

"I don't know, but we will not find out unless you make a decision."

"I don't suppose we have anything to lose if we let her meet Caroline. But then we can't stay out there."

"Of course you can. It is an enormous estate. I can take her out there today, and if Caroline wishes to see her again, you just make sure that you and your friends are out of the way."

"I suppose it could work. Hell, the names. She'll recognize the names. When she first met me I was using the name Steven Randall, and my friend's full name is McReynolds. I'll have to come up with something else." Nathan walked around the room for a bit thinking. "What about you, LeBeau, why don't you give us some good French names to use."

LeBeau nodded his head. "No, that will not work. Caroline and her father both speak French."

"Tell them we don't speak French but our grandparents came from here and we wanted to see what it was like. Tell them anything you want."

"All right. Your friends will be Monsieur and Madame Rondieux, first names Henri and Danielle. And you, my friend, must have a good name, something like . . . I have it. Etienne Fortier. Romantic, no?"

"It wasn't exactly what I had in mind—"

"But you will take it. Thornston will think you are French aristocrats." LeBeau walked to his desk and wrote on a piece of paper. "Here are the names in case you forget."

"I think I can remember, LeBeau."

"Take them anyway. We don't want any mistakes."

"All right. So, we'll expect you tomorrow?"

"Yes, if all goes well today, I will send my carriage for you tomorrow. And if I find out anything about Anna and Roberto, I will let you know."

"I don't suppose you could tell her that I love her?"

"I do not think that would look too good. She has a very possessive husband."

Nathan nodded. "All right. I'll see you tomorrow."

"Tomorrow, my friend."

*　　　*　　　*

Anna looked anxiously out of the carriage. She didn't know what to expect of Caroline Thornston, but she hoped that the woman had truly loved Roberto. She and Roberto had been through a lot together. There had been times when she had wanted to run away, times when she thought she hated him, but now that she knew the truth, she wanted only to help him. He deserved that, at least.

"You seem very pensive today, Anna."

"I'm sorry, LeBeau. I'm not very good company."

"There is nothing to be sorry about. May I ask you something?"

"Of course."

"Why did you request this meeting with Miss Thornston?"

Anna rubbed her gloved hands together. She and Roberto had already been over this; LeBeau must not know that Roberto had any connection to the Thornstons. "My husband has heard of the Thornstons and he thought it would be good for me to get out. He says that Caroline Thornston is my age. He wants me to be around women of my own age."

"And just how did he find all of this out in so short a time?"

Anna cocked an eyebrow and looked at LeBeau. "My husband is not without money, either, LeBeau, and as you well know, money will buy anything, especially information."

"You see, I was right about you from the beginning. You would have made a wonderful harlot." LeBeau rolled his eyes. "I cannot think of the money you would have made for us. Such fire and spunk! Men pay highly for these things, you know."

Anna slapped LeBeau playfully on the knee. "There is a Cheyenne expression that my great-grandmother used to use about a friend of hers. Let's see if I can translate it. 'The cock walks around strutting, his chest full of air, but

208

once the air is knocked out of him, he is nothing but a skinny little bird.' Do you understand?"

"All too well, I'm afraid. This friend of your great-grandmother's, what was he like?"

"He was French," Anna said dryly, trying to hide a smile.

LeBeau laughed uproariously. "I like you very much, Anna. I think we could be great friends, even if you will not consider working for me."

"I think we're already friends."

"If we are friends, then why is it you lie to me, eh?"

"What are you talking about?"

"I know you do not love your husband. Why do you stay with the man? Is he forcing you in some way to be with him?"

"LeBeau, my husband is not forcing me to do anything. I am with him because I want to be with him." Anna was telling the truth. She did want to be with Roberto now, because she wanted to help him.

"But you do not love him. I knew that on the boat."

"No, I don't love him."

"*Sacré bleu,* woman! Why do you stay with him?"

"I told you before—"

"Do not lie to me, Anna. I can help you. You love someone else, yes?"

Anna met LeBeau's eyes. "Yes, I love someone else. I love my husband's brother. We were going to be married, but . . ." She stopped, realizing she had already said too much. Roberto was counting on her. He had to be able to trust her. "It doesn't matter now, LeBeau. Are we close to Rolling Oaks yet?"

LeBeau saw that Anna had put up a wall and there was no way he could break through it now. "Yes, we are almost there."

"What can I expect of Caroline Thornston? What kind of woman is she?"

"Caroline is a very kind person, a delicate person. She is in fragile health. I think it will do her good to be around someone like you."

"You sound like you know her well."

"I should. I am engaged to be married to her." LeBeau watched as his words hit Anna. Perhaps now she would give some clue as to why she wanted to meet Caroline Thornston.

"You are engaged to Caroline Thornston? But I thought . . ."

"What did you think, my dear? Did you think that I am a man who would never settle for one woman? That is probably true, but Caroline is different. She is a sweet little creature who needs a man to take care of her. It also does not hurt that her father is one of the richest men in the city."

"LeBeau, you can't do this!"

"I can't do what, my dear?" LeBeau looked out of the carriage, deliberately ignoring Anna. "Well, here we are. Lovely, isn't it? I can assure you, you will never see anything like this again. This is one of the most unique and beautiful plantations in the South."

The carriage stopped and the door was opened by a footman. LeBeau stepped out and the footman helped Anna.

"Thank you," she said softly, staring in wide-eyed wonder at her surroundings. There were rolling hills of grass everywhere, dotted with flowers of every kind and color. A grove of oaks surrounded the property and created a find arch along the driveway. Orange trees, magnolias, and hickory trees were planted in various places, and flowers of numerous smells and vibrant colors dotted the property. A tiny cherub played a horn of water in a fountain in an adjoining garden. The house itself was brick set off by four white columns in the front. There was a gallery that ran the length of the house on all four sides. Chairs and tables were set out on the lawns.

"It is beautiful, eh?"

"Yes. I've never seen anything like it."

"Wait until you see the inside. It has no less than ten bedrooms, two sitting rooms upstairs, a large sitting room downstairs, a library, a music room, a large dining room with a cookhouse off to the side, a game room, and a garden room. It really is quite something."

"Yes, I can see that."

LeBeau led Anna up the brick steps. The footman knocked on the door and a tall, handsome black man with snow-white hair opened it. He was dressed all in black, except for a white shirt and white gloves. He smiled when he saw LeBeau.

"Good afternoon, Monsieur LeBeau. We've missed you around here." He bowed to Anna. "Good afternoon, Madame."

"Good afternoon."

"Samuel, this is Madame Hawkins. She has come to visit with Mademoiselle Caroline."

"Yes, she is expecting you both. Please, follow me."

LeBeau leaned down to Anna. "All of the servants are taught to be very formal. Look at the paintings on the entry hall. They have all been done by European painters. Some were even painted for royalty, but Thornton managed to buy them."

Anna stared in wide-eyed wonder at the enormous entryway lined with gold-framed paintings. Most of the paintings were of the countryside, but some were of children dancing or playing.

"My father bought those in Europe because he said they reminded him of me before I became so sickly. Hello, I'm Caroline Thornston."

Anna curtsied and held out her hand. "I'm Anna Hawkins. I'm very pleased to meet you."

"You are a friend of LeBeau's?"

"Well, actually—" Anna didn't know what to say.

"This is the lovely young woman I met on the riverboat. Her husband will be tied up with business for another week in Baton Rouge, so I thought it would be a good idea for her to meet you. You are giving the party in her honor."

"Oh, how wonderful," Caroline said happily. "I can't believe I'm actually talking to someone my own age."

"Aren't there people your own age around here?"

Caroline looked at LeBeau. "My father doesn't think it is wise for me to be out in public, as I am so sickly. He is afraid I could catch any germ there is. I think he is silly, but he will have it no other way."

Anna regarded the woman who stood in front of her. LeBeau said she was Anna's age, so that meant she was twenty years old, yet she looked years younger. Her skin was so pale it was almost translucent, and her eyes were such a light shade of blue that it almost seemed as if she had no color in them at all. Her hair was thin, and so white that it almost blended in with her skin. She was very small and thin, and, indeed, she did appear to be extremely frail. Caroline Thornston was not at all what Anna expected her to be. Could this be the woman that Roberto had almost gotten himself killed for? There was something very strange about her. It was almost as if she wasn't there; it was almost as if she were a ghost.

"Mrs. Hawkins, did you hear me?"

"Oh, I'm sorry. I was just so entranced with the paintings."

Caroline smiled half-heartedly. "You don't have to apologize. I'm used to people staring at me. I am not exactly the picture of good health."

Anna grabbed Caroline's hand. "I am so sorry. I didn't mean to be rude. I think you're lovely in a way that I could never be."

"And what way is that?"

"You remind me of a delicate flower that needs constant nurturing and water. I am more like a cactus. I can sometimes bloom and be pretty, but most of the time I can make it no matter what."

"I think that you sell yourself short, Mrs. Hawkins. You are an extremely beautiful woman."

"Pardon me, I hate to interrupt this, but I must be going. I would like to say hello to my lovely fiancée." LeBeau kissed Caroline on the cheek. "Mrs. Hawkins is right. You are a delicate little flower." He turned to Anna. "I will send the carriage for you in the afternoon. Will that be satisfactory?"

"Yes, thank you, LeBeau."

"Goodbye, LeBeau. Thank you for bringing Mrs. Hawkins to me." Caroline watched LeBeau leave, and smiled. "LeBeau is a good man. He will make a good husband." She took Anna's hand. "Come. I took the liberty of having lunch served in the garden room. It is my favorite room in the house."

Anna followed Caroline down the entryway and past a long wooden staircase. There were many doors, and Anna tried to peek in each one, but the doors were kept shut, to keep down the dust, Caroline said.

"Here we are." Caroline led Anna into a huge, bright room, that had windows on all sides and plants and flowers of every species planted outside the windows. White wicker furniture was all around the room, with pillows covered in bright floral patterns. "Please, sit down over here. This is my favorite place. We can look out onto the lawns and see everything, and we don't even have to move."

Anna smiled. Caroline was different. There was something quite girlish about her, but something very strange. She couldn't describe it, but it was almost as if Caroline was someplace else.

Anna sat down opposite Caroline, with a table between

213

them. The table was covered with silver trays filled with finger sandwiches, sliced fruit, fruit tortes, and there was a large pitcher of mint iced tea. "This is lovely. It reminds me of a tea party."

"Yes. Only I never had tea parties when I was little. Father was always afraid I might catch a cold from the other little girls. What about you, Anna? I bet you had lots of tea parties."

"I never had a tea party, Caroline." Anna decided to take a chance. "My mother died when I was quite young and I traveled around with my father. He drank and gambled and I usually stayed alone in our wagon or in a hotel room if we could afford one. I couldn't even imagine what a tea party was back then."

"I am so sorry. Here I was feeling sorry for myself and you—"

"Don't feel sorry for me, Caroline. Things turned out for the best. My father met some wonderful people and left me with them. I stayed with them and they became my parents. I don't think I could have loved them any more if they had been my real parents."

"Loved?"

"They died a few months ago. There's an empty space inside me without them."

"Yes, I know." Caroline poured the tea and handed Anna a glass. "I know my father does the best he can for me, but he isn't my mother. She was a dear person." Her face clouded over. "She was dark like you." Caroline stopped, realizing that she was rambling. "Anyway, what's done is done." She handed the tray of sandwiches to Anna. "Please, help yourself. Our cook has outdone herself. If she sees we haven't eaten, I'll never hear the end of it."

Anna put some sandwiches and fresh fruit on her plate. She looked past Caroline, out the window. There

214

was a large man talking to a Negro gardener. "Who is that?"

"That's my father. He's probably telling Jedediah that the flowers are planted crooked. He can always find something wrong around here."

"Do you ever go outside, Caroline? I would think the fresh air would be good for you."

"Sometimes I venture out, but mostly I'm content to stay inside. There's nothing of interest for me outside."

Anna nibbled on her sandwiches and watched Richard Thornston. He was a big, burly man, and she could tell by the way he used his hands, that he was a man of many words. Trenton always said that if a man couldn't say in just a few words what was meant to be said, then it must not be very important. She smiled at the thought and how aptly it pertained to Thornston.

"What is it, Anna? You're smiling."

"I just thought of something my father used to say. I hadn't thought of it in a long time. So, what do you do for fun?"

"Well, I read, I play the piano, and I play chess with my father."

"Do you ever ride?"

"Horses?" Caroline's clear eyes became animated for the first time. "I've never ridden a horse in my life."

"I could teach you."

"No, I couldn't. What if I fell? I could break an arm or a leg."

Anna touched Caroline's hand. "Caroline, why are you so afraid? The outside world is not so frightening. It can be very exciting if you let it be."

"I don't know, Anna."

"We don't have to ride right now. We could start with a walk. You'll be surprised how good you'll feel when you're done."

215

"But my father and my doctors won't allow it."

"Just what do your doctors say?"

"They say I am infirm and I should be especially careful to stay away from things that could cause me harm."

"That's the entire world, Caroline!" Anna was surprised by her own vehemence, yet she couldn't believe that this poor young woman had been so totally controlled by her father, and made to believe that she would die if she ventured outside. Anna looked at Caroline again. She looked as if she were dying already. "I'm sorry, Caroline, I don't have a right to say that. I don't even know you."

"It's all right. I must look a fright to you. You come from the West, where women are strong and healthy and work hard all day. I must seem like a pampered little girl to you."

"No, you don't seem pampered; you seem like a prisoner. How do you feel, Caroline?"

"I don't know. I've always felt this way."

"Always?" Anna knew that Caroline hadn't felt this way when Roberto was here. She had been ready to run off with him.

Caroline stared out the window, to some unknown point. "No, there was a time when I went outside every day. I walked and I ran and I laughed and I even loved. But that was so long ago." Caroline withdrew suddenly, looking paler than before.

Anna looked out to the gardens. Thornston was still outside. She didn't want him to interfere. She looked at Caroline. This poor girl needed a friend more than anything else in the world. "Caroline, forgive me if I've judged you harshly. It's one of my worst faults. I'm a very impatient person. I want everyone in the world to be happy."

Caroline's pale eyes brightened. "There's nothing wrong with wanting people to be happy, Anna. I've just never had a friend who cared." Caroline stood up, gently smoothing the creases in her dress. "I think I'd like to go for that walk now."

"Are you sure? I don't want to push you."

"You're not pushing me. I'd like to show you around. We have horses, you know. Would you like to see them?"

"I'd love to see them."

"You like to ride very much, don't you?"

"Yes. My mother was Indian. She taught me many things about this world, but the most important thing she taught me is that freedom comes from within. She and I would get on our horses and we would ride for hours. I can remember looking over at her and seeing her laugh. She gave me so much." Anna's eyes filled with tears as she thought of Aeneva.

"You were very lucky, Anna."

"I know. She and my father were the most honorable people I have ever known. They took me in as their own and they loved me as their own." She thought of Aeneva's words to her. "They were a gift to me and to this world."

"What a lovely thing to say. I wish I had known them."

"I wish you had, too." How different things might have been if Roberto had married Caroline and come home, Anna thought. How much joy he would have given his parents. How different Caroline's life might have been.

Caroline led Anna out of the garden room and outside to the gallery that over looked the gardens, encountering the wide-eyed stares of the servants. As they walked down the stairs, Caroline turned to Anna. "Do you think

217

I'll need my shawl?"

Anna was shocked. It was so stifling hot outside, she could think of nothing but stripping off her skirt and blouse and jumping into a pond. "I don't think so, Caroline. It's really quite warm."

"I suppose you're right. Well, what do you want to see first?"

"It doesn't matter. It's all so lovely. What's your favorite place?"

"I don't know. I told you I really don't go out much. I suppose the gardens are pretty . . ." Caroline trailed off, thinking of the special place she and Roberto had had, far under the willows. It was cool there, and they would lie on their backs and look up through the veiled greenery at the sky above. They had made their plans there. They had talked of marriage and children. Caroline started to shake.

"Caroline, what's wrong?"

"Nothing, nothing's wrong. I want to go back inside now."

"All right, come on."

"I feel sick, Anna. I think I'm going to faint."

"No you're not, Caroline. You're going to be fine."

"No really, I feel so faint."

Anna had had enough. She took Caroline's arms. "Caroline, you are sick, but not in the body. You've let your father convince you that you are an invalid. The only thing that's wrong with you is that you haven't had any fresh air or freedom in years. Why do you let him do this to you, Caroline?"

"I don't know. I—"

"Caroline! Caroline! My God, what are you doing out in this heat, child?" Richard Thornston came running across the lawn. He glared at Anna, his face contorted in rage. "And just who the hell are you to be taking my little

218

girl out in this blazing sun?"

"My name is Anna Hawkins, Mr. Thornston, and the last time I looked, your daughter was not a little girl." Anna ignored Thornston and turned to Caroline. "I'm sorry this happened, Caroline, but you're fine. LeBeau knows where I am if you wish to see me again." She returned Thornston's disdainful look. "Do you have a carriage that can take me to town, Mr. Thornston?"

"Just who are you, Mrs. Hawkins?" He stepped toward Anna, towering over her. He grabbed her arm, squeezing it tightly. "What gives you the right to come onto my estate and make my daughter think she is normal?"

Anna pulled her arm free. "She *is* normal, Mr. Thornston, but for some reason you and she refuse to believe it. Good-bye Caroline." Anna stomped across the manicured lawns and into the driveway, waiting for a carriage. She turned to look at Thornston and Caroline. He had picked her up in his arms and was carrying her into the house. Anna shook her head in disgust.

"The carriage be here soon, madame."

Anna didn't hear the footman who had walked up behind her. "Oh, thank you."

He followed Anna's eyes. "The master, he dotes on his daughter. He don't take kindly to people treating her like she was anything but a fragile little girl."

"What's your name?"

The man looked around, lest he be caught talking to a white woman in such a familiar way. "My name is Lawrence. My mother said it was an intelligent name."

"I'm pleased to meet you, Lawrence." Anna held out her hand, but Lawrence lowered his head. "I thought you were supposed to be intelligent, Lawrence. If that's so, why won't you shake hands with me?"

"You're not from around here, madame. If you was, you'd know that I could get a beating for even looking at

219

you the wrong way."

"The slave days are over, Lawrence. You don't have to do what he tells you to do."

"I do if I want to eat."

"Well, if you won't shake hands with me, you can at least call me by my name. It's Anna."

"Pleased to meet you, Miss Anna. You sure are different from the women around here. What were you thinking, taking the master's daughter out of the house like that? I haven't seen him that mad in a long time." A slight smile appeared at the corners of his mouth.

"I was thinking I'd take her for a walk. I don't see anything so strange about that."

"The master, he never allows Miss Caroline out." Lawrence looked behind them. "I hope he don't get real angry at you, Miss Anna. He can be mighty fierce when he wants to be."

"Don't worry, Lawrence." Anna touched Lawrence's arm, but quickly took her hand away, "I can take care of myself."

"Yes, ma'am."

"How long have you been here, Lawrence?"

"I've been here all my life, Miss Anna. Someday I'm gonna leave. I don't fancy to staying and working for Mr. Thornston anymore. He gets crazier every day."

"Do you remember a young man who was here about two years ago? His name was Roberto?"

Lawrence's face brightened. "I knew Roberto real good. He was always nice to me and my family. It was a terrible thing that happened to him, but he should never have set his eyes on Miss Caroline."

"Did Caroline love him, Lawrence?"

"I can't say for sure . . ."

"Please, Lawrence, it's very important."

"Well, from everything I heard, Miss Caroline loved

that boy with all her heart. She liked to die when he left. She almost did die after she had the . . ." Lawrence stopped when he heard the door to the big house open and slam shut. Richard Thornston came stomping down the stairs. Lawrence immediately turned his eyes straight forward.

"I want to talk to you."

"Are you speaking to me, Mr. Thornston?"

"You know damn well I'm speaking to you."

Anna ambled away, looking around at the flowers. "You really should watch your language in front of the servants, Mr. Thornston."

Thornston grabbed Anna's shoulders and started shaking her. "What the hell were you doing in my house, upsetting my daughter?"

"Let go of me," Anna said slowly, her eyes never leaving Thornston's. She had been bullied by men too many times; she wasn't afraid anymore. "If you don't let me go, Thornston, I'll have to let LeBeau know how you've treated me. I don't think he'll like it."

Thornston released his hold on Anna. "What do you want? Is it money? Land? What?"

Anna shook her head. "I don't want anything from you except the truth."

Thornston suddenly looked very pale. "What does that mean?"

"You'll find out soon enough."

"You'll get nothing from me except this—get off my land and stay off. If I find you here again I'll—"

"You'll what—have me beaten and thrown into the swamp?" Anna looked at Thornston derisively. "I've met men like you before, Thornston, and you're all the same. You're no better than those 'gators in the swamp whose bellies drag on the ground when they walk. The only difference is, I think they have a conscience." Anna

221

walked away. "Don't bother with the carriage. I'll find my own way back to town."

Anna walked off down the road, acting as if she were on a carefree summer walk, when, in fact, she had no idea how Richard Thornston would react. For all she knew, he could shoot her in the back. But she didn't think he would; for some reason, he valued LeBeau and didn't want to make LeBeau angry. She shook her head and smiled, thinking how glad she was that she wasn't a frightened little mouse like Caroline. Her initial anger at Caroline for not sticking up for her, and falling into her father's waiting arms, had subsided. Now all she felt was pity for the woman. She would never understand how Roberto could have fallen in love with such a woman.

"Ouch," she said, lifting up one foot and hopping on the other. She hated the narrow dress boots with all the buttons up the front. Her feet would never be the same. If she had to walk all the way into town in these boots, she would have blisters as big as cactus apples. She stopped and unhooked the laces from the buttons and trudged along her way. She stopped when she heard something in the trees. What if it was Thornston? His property extended for another two miles at least. He could kill her, dispose of the body, and no one would ever find out.

"Psst. It's me, Miss Anna. Over here."

Anna followed the sound of Lawrence's voice into the trees and smiled with relief when she saw his face. "I'm glad to see you. I thought for sure it was Thornston and he was going to kill me."

"I have to say, Miss Anna, I've never seen anybody stand up to the master that way, especially not a woman."

Anna shrugged. "I may have gone a bit too far." She leaned against Lawrence and loosened her boots some more. "Sorry, Lawrence. I know I'm not supposed to touch you, but I can't stand these damned boots. By the way, we never formally met." She held out her hand. "I'm real happy to know you, Lawrence."

This time Lawrence took Anna's hand in a firm handshake. "Happy to know you too, Miss Anna. You wasn't planning to walk all the way back into town in them shoes, was you?"

"I wasn't planning to walk back to Thornston's and ask him if I could borrow a carriage."

"I sees what you mean. I know a shortcut through the woods. We go by some swamps, but I know them real well. If you stay real close to me, you'll be fine."

"What about Thornston? Won't he know you're missing?"

Lawrence waved his hand impatiently. "He's so put upon by Miss Caroline that he won't notice nothing for a coupla hours."

"How long would it take if I walked on the road?"

"About two hours."

"Oh, God."

"I can get you to the edge of the city in less than an hour. Once you're in the city you can hail a carriage."

"I'll follow you, Lawrence."

They walked through a thick forest of willow, oak and cypress trees, always reaching through the ever-present hanging moss. It was like a hideous shroud that covered the trees. Anna smacked at the bugs that attacked her face, neck and arms, and stumbled numerous times in the soft, boggy ground. There were strange noises from animals she had never even heard of, and always she looked around to make sure there were no alligators following her. She didn't want to complain, but she had to admit to herself that this was not a pleasant experience. In fact, it was almost frightening.

"Are you all right, Miss Anna? Look at me, just walking along and not even checking to see if you're all right."

223

Anna slapped her neck. "I'm all right, Lawrence. Are there alligators around here?"

Lawrence looked serious. "We grow alligators so big around here they've been known to carry off women and children."

"Women and children?" Anna looked around her, slapping again at her neck and face. "Maybe it would be easier if I went back to the road and found my own way."

Lawrence laughed loudly, bending over, resting his hands on his knees. "I'm sorry, Miss Anna. I was playing a little joke on you."

"You don't have alligators?"

"Oh, we have alligators all right, but they don't come this far away from the swamp. Not usually, that is."

"Stop it, Lawrence. I thought you were my friend."

"I am your friend, Miss Anna, but I can't resist a little joke now and again. Are you sure you're all right?"

"Yes, I'm all right. I'm just not used to this kind of heat."

"It's not hot where you come from?"

"It's very hot where I come from, but it's very dry. The wind blows off the desert and you can feel it against your face. The sky is as clear and as blue as anything you've ever seen, and the mountains look as if they were painted on the horizon."

"That sounds real pretty. I'd like to see your land someday. Maybe I can leave this place and come see you."

"I live on a ranch in Arizona. We raise cattle and horses. I think you'd like it. But you do have to watch out for one thing."

"What's that?"

"The rattlesnakes."

"Yeah, I heard of them before. They be like our water snakes."

"No, they're much worse than your water snakes. Our snakes have been known to eat a full-grown horse. They've also been known to fly off rocks and land on people's heads. It's the most amazing thing I've ever seen."

"A flying snake? I've never heard of that." Lawrence regarded Anna for a moment. He nodded his head. "You're a-fooling with me, aren't you, Miss Anna?"

"What do you think, Lawrence?" She smiled. "Yes, I'm fooling with you. Just don't tell me any more stories about alligators."

"Let's go, Miss Anna. Just follow me."

Anna followed Lawrence deeper into the forest of green. She tried to concentrate on the fact that she would be home soon. She looked around her and had a strange feeling that someone was looking at her. She touched Lawrence's shoulder. "Is there someone in the trees? I feel like we're being watched."

"We are being watched."

"Thornston?"

"No, it's the swamp people. They just want to make sure no one like Thornston is coming into their territory. They know who I am. My aunt and uncle live in there."

"In the swamp?"

"Yes, ma'am. They live off the land. They trap 'gator and catfish and they grow some vegetables. They have their own religion. But I mostly stay away from them. They be good people, but we're real different."

Anna looked into the trees, but could see nothing; yet she knew without a doubt that she was being watched. "Do they mind if I'm here?"

"They do not mind as long as you're with me. See in there?" Lawrence pointed to a narrow trail that led into the trees. "Way in there is where Thornston's men took Roberto. My aunt and uncle found him and took care of

225

him. They fixed special medicines for him to get rid of the poison from the water snake. They are good people."

Anna stared into the green darkness. She couldn't imagine what kind of existence a person could have in a swamp, a place where there was no sunlight and no dry earth. She shivered. "Can we go now?"

"Yes, ma'am."

It took twenty more minutes before they reached the edge of the forest. Anna was drenched in sweat and her hair was tangled and hanging in her face. Her dress was dirty and torn and her boots, the boots she so disliked, were covered in mud. "Oh, dear, I'm a mess. No one will give me a ride looking like this."

"I'll walk you to your home, Miss Anna. Don't worry."

"I can't let you do that, Lawrence. You've done enough already." She was thinking about Roberto. He might not want Lawrence to know that he was alive. "I'll be fine."

"I don't like leaving you alone, Miss Anna. There are some bad people in the city. You'd be better off to stay here and wait for Mr. LeBeau's carriage. He should be here soon."

"I suppose you're right." Anna pulled the skirt of her dress around her legs and sat down on the bank by the road, her back against a tree. Lawrence sat next to her.

"Why are you so interested in Roberto, ma'am? If you don't mind my asking."

Anna had to make a decision. Could she trust Lawrence? "Do you think Roberto was guilty of what Thornston accused him of?"

"Makes no never-mind to me. No man deserves to be beat like that and then thrown away like trash."

"Do you think he was guilty, Lawrence?"

"No, I don't, Miss Anna. I came to know Roberto real

226

good. He was a good, fair man. I don't think he woulda hurt Miss Caroline like that. Besides, Miss Caroline was crazy about him. She woulda run off with him if she could."

"Why didn't she help Roberto that day?"

"She was afraid to stand up to her father. You saw what happened with you today. I still can't believe she had the nerve to have the baby."

Anna turned to Lawrence, trying to contain her shock. "What baby?"

"Roberto's baby, of course. He never knew about it; the master wouldn't let him know. He was afraid that if Roberto found out Miss Caroline was having a baby, he would do anything to get her away from Rolling Oaks."

"Her father let her have the baby?"

"He didn't have a choice. She was too far along to do anything about it. She almost died giving birth, but she was determined."

"My God," Anna said. Perhaps she had underestimated Caroline. "She still has the baby?"

"Yes, ma'am. That's one of the reasons she won't leave the house. She's afraid something will happen to him. I guess she's just like her daddy."

"He? A boy? Do you know his name?"

Lawrence laughed and slapped his knee. "The master, he swears his name is Richard, but Miss Caroline named him Robert Nathan Thornston. A real pretty name, I think."

"My God!" Anna couldn't believe it. Not only did Roberto have a son, but he was named after him and Nathan. That meant he must have talked to Caroline about Nathan, even after everything that had happened to him.

"Will you answer my question now, Miss Anna? Why are you so interested in Roberto?"

Anna had already made her decision. "I am married to Roberto."

Lawrence's eyes widened. "You be Roberto's wife? No wonder you're so interested in what happened. Well, this sure is going to liven things up around here."

"You don't know the half of it," Anna replied dryly. "I'm going to need your help, Lawrence. Can I count on you? I'll make sure you get paid well."

"I don't care about the money, Miss Anna. It's been a real pleasure just meeting you. You brought some real excitement into my life this day."

"I'm still going to pay you."

"What is it you want me to do?"

"I'm going to try to come out here again, with LeBeau's help. I just want to know I have a friend here in case I need one."

"I am your friend, Miss Anna. You can count on it."

"Thank you, Lawrence. And thank you for letting me know about the 'gators."

Lawrence smiled. "A carriage is coming. Should be around the bend in a few seconds."

"I don't hear anything." Anna stood up. She soon heard the clacking sound of carriage wheels on the dirt road. It was uncanny and almost eerie that Lawrence had heard the wheels when she'd heard nothing. "How did you hear the carriage?"

"It's a gift." Lawrence slid down the bank and held out his arms, helping Anna down to the road. He stood in the road, waving the carriage to a stop.

LeBeau leaned out the side. "What's going on here?" When he saw Anna he opened the door and jumped down, striding over to her. "What has happened to you? Thornston didn't hurt you, did he?"

Anna thought it was interesting that it didn't even occur to LeBeau to accuse Lawrence. He obviously knew

Thornston well. "I don't think I'm one of Richard Thornston's favorite people."

LeBeau's nostrils flared in anger. "I will strangle the life out of the fat pig! He has had it coming to him for a long time."

"It's all right, LeBeau. Lawrence got me safely to the road. Instead of being angry with Thornston, why don't you give Lawrence something for his trouble."

"I told you before, Miss Anna, I don't want nothing from you."

"Don't argue with the lady, Lawrence. She is much too stubborn." LeBeau reached into his vest pocket and brought out his wallet. He handed Lawrence some bills. "Thank you, Lawrence. Again, you have proven to be a friend."

"This ain't necessary, Mister LeBeau."

"But it is. You don't belong here, Lawrence. You're much too smart. Save your money and get out. Are you ready, Anna?"

"Yes." She turned to Lawrence and impulsively gave him a hug. "Thank you. I hope I can return the favor someday."

"It was my pleasure, Miss Anna." Lawrence stepped back up into the forest and was gone.

Once in the carriage, Anna related the events of the day to LeBeau, omitting any details about Roberto. "So, I don't think I'll be invited back."

"Do not worry. If you want to go back to Rolling Oaks, I will take you there. Richard Thornston would not dare to say no to me." He took a handkerchief out of his breast pocket and wiped the dirt from Anna's face. "To think you had to walk through that abominable forest. It makes me cringe to think of it."

Anna took the handkerchief from LeBeau and wiped her face. "I'm fine, LeBeau. Lawrence was wonderful. He made me laugh all the way."

"Still, it is not right. I cannot believe that Thornston treated you so badly. And all because you took Caroline outside for a walk." He shook his head angrily. "I should have warned you not to interfere."

"Don't you take her out, LeBeau?"

"No, never. We always visit at Rolling Oaks. We spend our time in the music room or the garden room. Thornston would never let me take her out of the house, although they both pretend that she is making plans to go out."

"Why would you even consider marrying her? You don't love her."

"I told you, she has the kind of money that I admire."

"But you have money. Surely, you don't need to marry Caroline Thornston to make more."

"Perhaps not, but I would like it. I would like nothing better than to be the son-in-law of Richard Thornston, and then be in the position to make the man give everything over to me."

"Why do you hate him so, LeBeau?"

"I hate him for many reasons, my dear. He is a man who is easy to hate." LeBeau regained his composure. "So, did you find out what you wanted to know?"

"I wanted to meet Caroline, and I did. She's such a strange person. I don't think there is anything wrong with her. Her father has her convinced that she's ill and infirm."

"She has herself convinced as well. They are a sad pair, are they not?" LeBeau looked out the window. "Well, here we are. I do not think your husband will be too happy to see you looking the way you do. He will probably want to kill Thornston with his bare hands. Tell him I will be glad to help."

"I'm fine, LeBeau, really. Please let me know if it's

possible to meet with Caroline again."

"Yes, I will get word to you tomorrow, my dear." LeBeau got out of the carriage and lifted Anna down. "You are sure he did not hurt you?"

"No, he just blustered about. I said a few things I shouldn't have and he grabbed me, that's all. Go, LeBeau. I'll let myself in."

"Good-bye, Anna."

Ann opened the gate and walked up the stairs, leaned on the door and slipped off her muddy shoes. She opened the door and Roberto was standing in front of her. "'Berto! You startled me." She saw his eyes take in her appearance, and his face immediately grew angry.

"Did Thornston hurt you?"

"We had words."

"Did he hurt you?"

"I'm fine, 'Berto. He didn't hurt me." She walked into the small sitting room, sat down, and dropped her boots on the floor. Her white stockings were completely brown from the mud that had soaked through her boots. She rubbed her feet. "Oh, God, that feels good! My feet are killing me."

"Do you want to tell me why your feet are killing you?"

"It's a long story, 'Berto, and all I want to do is sit in a hot bath for about an hour. I don't suppose you'd heat the water and fill the tub for me?"

"I would if you'd tell me the truth."

"I met Caroline."

Roberto's eyes softened. "How is she? Is she all right? Did she look well? Is she still as beautiful?"

Anna looked down. She couldn't bear to tell Roberto that the woman he had loved was a frightened little girl who was as pale and wan-looking as someone who had been kept in a prison for years. What could she tell him?

Perhaps she had always looked like that and Roberto had loved her that way.

"Anna? What is it?"

"I'm sorry, I'm just tired. I walked a long way in those stupid shoes."

"What about Caroline?"

"Caroline doesn't leave the house. In fact, that's why Thornston and I got in the fight."

"What do you mean, she doesn't leave the house?"

"I talked her into going for a walk outside, and as soon as her father saw her she fell apart. She started to cry and she fell into his arms and fainted. He accused me of trying to hurt his daughter."

Roberto's head dropped. "And she didn't try to defend you? It was the same with me."

Anna touched Roberto's cheek. "I don't think she knows how to defend anyone, 'Berto. She's so afraid of her father she'll do anything so that he won't be angry with her."

"She's a coward."

"It's not her fault. If she is a coward, he taught her how to be that way."

"I don't have to ask if she spoke of me. She probably doesn't even remember my name."

"She remembers your name, 'Berto, and I'm convinced she still loves you."

Hope flickered in Roberto's eyes. "How can you be sure?"

"'Berto"—Anna took Roberto's hand firmly in hers—"you have a son. Caroline gave birth to him after you left. She almost died giving birth to him, but she wanted to have him."

"Who told you this, LeBeau?"

"No. Lawrence, a man who works there."

"Yes, I remember Lawrence."

"He said that Thornston didn't want her to have the baby, but she refused to have anything done about it. She threatened to kill herself if she wasn't allowed to have her baby."

"A son? Are you sure it's mine?"

"Lawrence says it looks just like you. And there's something else, 'Berto."

"What?"

"The child's name is Robert Nathan."

Roberto lowered his head. "Robert Nathan. She named him after me and Nathan."

"She obviously still loves you, 'Berto. Why else would she have your son and name him after you and your brother?"

"I don't know. It doesn't make any sense."

"It makes perfect sense. She's never been able to control her own life. This was the first time she could control something without her father telling her what to do."

"I can't believe he let her keep the baby, especially if he's got dark skin."

"Lawrence thinks that's why she's not allowed to go out. Thornston doesn't want anyone to know about the baby. Maybe they struck a deal—he'd let her keep the baby if she wouldn't let anyone know she has it."

"I can't believe it, Anna. I have a son!"

Anna smiled and nodded her head. Roberto looked just like a small boy. "What do you want to do?"

"I don't know. I hadn't counted on this. I don't want my son anywhere near that man."

"You wouldn't take him away from Caroline, would you?"

"If I had to."

Anna saw the look in Roberto's eyes, and she knew that he meant what he said. She had seen the same look when he told her she had to go away with him. "'Berto, don't do anything crazy. Let's find out a little bit more first. Caroline isn't married, and from the way she talked, I think she still loves you."

"Did she talk about me?"

"In a way. She talked about a time when she was happy and in love. Her face lit up when she spoke of it. 'Berto, listen to me. LeBeau says he can get me back on Rolling Oaks. I think he's holding something over Thornston's head."

"I don't want you back there alone. It's too dangerous."

"We don't have a choice. I can make sure LeBeau stays with me. He wanted to kill Thornston for touching me."

"It's the first time I agree with him on something."

"There's something else. LeBeau is engaged to Caroline."

Roberto shook his head. "I should have known LeBeau would be involved in this somehow."

"It's not what you think. He doesn't love Caroline. He hates Thornston as much as you do. Something happened between them."

"So he's using Caroline to get back at her father?"

"Isn't that what you were going to do?"

"Does LeBeau care for her at all?"

"I think they're friends. There seems to be a genuine affection between them. He doesn't want to see her hurt." Anna leaned forward, pressing Roberto's arm. "LeBeau can help us, 'Berto. I don't think we have any other choice."

"Did you see my son?"

"No, she didn't even speak of him to me, but I think if I spend more time with her she might tell me the truth."

"She also might let her father do something to hurt you. I don't like it, Anna."

"Roberto, this is the woman you loved with all your

heart. She can't have changed all that much. I know there's good in her. She's just so afraid."

"I still don't want you out there alone with Thornston. You don't know how dangerous he can be, Anna. You don't know."

"If LeBeau stays with me, will you let me go? I want to help you." Anna stomped her foot angrily. "And don't give me that look. You think the only reason I want to help you is so that I can go back to Nathan. That's not true, 'Berto, and if you don't know that by now, then we are wasting our time."

"I know, Anna. You are the best friend I've ever had." He took her in his arms. "I want to see my son."

"Then let me go back out there with LeBeau. He'll make sure nothing happens to me; I know it."

Roberto finally assented. "All right. But I swear by all that's holy, if Thornston lays a hand on you, I'll kill him."

Chapter VIII

Nathan wrung his hands as they rode in the carriage to Rolling Oaks. He didn't like what LeBeau had told him. It was just like Anna to get herself in trouble, and from everything LeBeau had told him about Thornston, he was just the man to give it to her.

"Relax, my friend. Everything will be fine."

"How can everything be fine when Garrett and Molly and I are going to be staying at Rolling Oaks and Anna is going to be visiting there? We're bound to run into each other."

"Why must you avoid Anna?"

"Because if she sees me she'll tell Roberto and he'll take her away."

"I do not think so. He has changed toward her; he has softened."

"In what way?" Nathan asked anxiously.

"He feels differently about her now. I think he trusts her."

"But that doesn't change anything between me and my brother. For some reason he has it in for me, and he wants to use Anna to get back at me."

"I think his mind is on other matters now. He knows about his son."

"How? Did Anna see the boy?"

"No, the man who helped her, Lawrence, told her all about Roberto."

"Do you think he'll try to get the boy?"

"Wouldn't you, if you knew a man like Richard Thornston was going to raise him?"

"No, I can't take the chance, LeBeau."

"What about taking Anna while she's at Rolling Oaks?" Garrett asked.

"Yes, that would be easy," Molly added. "She'd probably leave in a second."

"No," Nathan said firmly.

"Why not? This is your chance, Nate. Take her and get out of this godforsaken place."

"If you two want to go, don't let me stop you, but I'm going to stay."

"Do you want to tell me what in hell's got into you, Nate? Just a while ago you would've done anything to get Anna and get back home."

"A while ago I didn't know everything that had happened to Roberto. He's still my brother, Garrett. I'm not leaving here until I get a chance to talk to him."

"Do you actually think he'll talk to you? I think you're fooling yourself, pal."

"Maybe, but I have to try. He needs my help, whether he knows it or not. Thornston almost killed him once, when he finds out Roberto is still alive, he'll do everything possible to try to kill him again. I want to be around to make sure that doesn't happen."

"Yes, I would agree with you, my friend. I know Thornston. When he finds out Roberto is alive he will kill him and probably try to kill Anna as well."

"Then do you want to explain to me, Mr. LeBeau, why the hell you've planned a party for them? You hoping they'll get killed in front of a lot of people?"

LeBeau twirled his moustache and smiled. "Would

237

you think of selling this beautiful woman to me, monsieur? I could make a lot of money with this one in my parlor."

Molly laughed uproariously. "You mean to tell me you run a whorehouse? Well, I'll be damned!"

"What is so strange about that? It is a fine establishment, clean, elegant, and with the finest girls in the city."

"So was mine," Molly said playfully.

LeBeau cocked an eyebrow. "You were the proprietor of a—"

"Yes, you could call it that."

"Fine place it was, until it got burned down." Garrett put his arm protectively around Molly's shoulders. "Molly wasn't one of the girls, LeBeau; she just ran the place. So don't get any ideas."

"I would not think of it."

"I hate to interrupt, but we need to go over some things," Nathan said. "Molly, Anna doesn't know you, so when she's meeting with Caroline I want you to try to get close to her. See what you can find out. Make sure she's all right."

"I'll do the best I can, Nathan, but I doubt she'll talk to me."

"Just stay close to her. Thornston wouldn't think of harming her with you around."

"This is the road that leads to the house. Look there." LeBeau pointed to the bank that Anna and Lawrence had been sitting on just days earlier. "This is where Lawrence brought Anna out. If you go too far in there, there are the swamps. It is not pleasant." He turned to Nathan. "That is where Thornston had his men take your brother after he was beaten. It is a wonder he did not die."

Nathan stared off into the dense green forest and tried to comprehend what Roberto had been through. His life had been taken from him when he was just eleven years

238

old and, when he thought he had it back, Thornston took it away from him again. No wonder Roberto was filled with so much hatred.

"We are almost to the driveway. Listen, my friend. I think it would be wise of you to become friends with Caroline. She is dying for attention."

"You're engaged to her, for Christ's sake!"

"It is only a marriage of convenience. We are both aware of that. Besides, the marriage may never occur, if your brother has anything to say about it. But that is beside the point. Become her friend and perhaps you can find out how she really feels about her father and if she still loves Roberto. It might make things easier for all of us. Ah, here we are." LeBeau looked at the people in the carriage. "Good luck, my friends, you will need it."

Richard Thornston smiled graciously at the people who sat at his dinner table. He found the men rather effeminate, not the kind of men he pictured coming from the West at all, and the woman was much too strong and brassy for him. Why had he let LeBeau talk him into this, anyway? Maybe it was not the company at all; maybe it was the woman who had been at the estate earlier in the week. She had almost ruined everything for him. It had taken him two days to get Caroline calmed down after she left, and now she was talking about having the woman visit again. Who the hell was this Anna Hawkins?

"Don't you think so, daddy?"

"I'm sorry, dear, I didn't hear you. What did you say?"

"I said that the women in the South seem to have it much easier than the women in the West."

"Well, that all depends on where you're from in the South. I'm sure there are lots of people who wouldn't say they have it easy."

239

"You mean like the Negroes?" Molly asked, a cutting tone to her voice.

"We don't force our Negroes to stay here, Madame Rondieux. They stay here of their own free will."

"But isn't that because they are uneducated and no one will hire them for jobs other than what they've done as slaves for over a hundred years?"

Thornston slammed his wineglass down on the table. "Pardon me, madame, but if you are insinuating—"

"I don't think Danielle is insinuating anything, Richard. May I call you Richard?" Nathan tried to control the hatred that was just boiling below the surface.

"Yes, of course."

"She was just making a statement, and she probably drank too much of your good wine at dinner."

"I—" Molly started to reply, but a kick from Garrett under the table make her stop.

"I must apologize for my wife, Richard. She never has been able to drink wine." Garrett's eyes penetrated Molly's. "Have you, dear?"

Molly forced herself to smile at Thornston. "I must admit that is the truth, Mr. Thornston. My father always said I should stay away from wine if I wanted to carry on a conversation. I do hope I haven't offended you. You have been so kind to us."

Thornston picked up his glass and tilted it toward Molly. "No harm done, madame. I must admit, being from the South, I've had to defend myself so many times on the issue of slavery that I get a bit defensive."

"Oh, let's do change the subject," Caroline said lightly, as if nothing had happened. "I think I'll have Hester serve the dessert and coffee in the sitting room. What do you think, daddy?"

"Whatever you think, dear. Actually, I think I'd like a cigar before I have my dessert. Would you men care to join me?"

"I think I'll pass on the cigar, but I wouldn't mind some brandy, if it wouldn't be too much trouble," Nathan said.

"I'll have the same," Garrett added.

"We'll, if it won't offend you gents, I'll just light up." Thornston waited for the cigar case to be brought out. "Why don't you go ahead, Caroline. We'll be in soon."

"All right. Why don't you follow me, madame."

Molly followed Caroline into the large sitting room, all the while shaking her head. She had never seen such extravagance in her entire life. How could two people need all these things and a huge house too, Molly thought.

"Here we are." Caroline opened the door. "We keep all of the doors shut to keep down the dust. We have so many things, we'd be dusting all of the time if we didn't."

"Yes, I bet you would," Molly muttered, wondering who "we" was. She was sure it wasn't Caroline and her father. The sitting room was like a hotel lobby, except that it had expensive brocade furniture, velvet drapes, delicate little carved tables, and paintings all over the wall. Porcelain figurines dotted the mantel over the fireplace, and a massive crystal chandelier dominated the room.

"What do you think? Is it different from the places you're used to?"

"Oh, it's different all right. We live much more simply."

"I suppose we must seem excessive in our tastes, but it's a lifestyle that should be preserved."

"You don't really believe that, do you?" Molly knew she was stepping into hot water again, but she couldn't control herself.

"The South has a tradition to maintain."

"I'm sure those people who live in the little cabins by your stables feel the same way."

"You're angry." Caroline went to Molly. "Please don't be angry. I'm not angry with you."

"It doesn't matter." Molly walked around the room, trying to keep her temper in check, all the while staring at Caroline in disbelief. She was the strangest person she had ever met. It was almost as if she had no real thoughts of her own. She reminded Molly of a puppet.

"You're staring at me because I'm pale."

"No, I was just thinking of a puppet I once had."

"It's all right," Caroline continued, as if she had not heard Molly. "Anna stared at me, too."

"Anna?" Molly held her breath. "Is she a friend of yours?"

"She was, but I drove her away. She tried to help me."

"What did she do?"

"She took me for a walk. She said it wouldn't hurt me. She said the fresh air would do me good."

God bless Anna, Molly thought to herself. "Have you known Anna long?"

"No, I only just met her. LeBeau introduced us. He thought we would get along."

"And did you?"

"Yes, I liked her very much. Oh, she is so beautiful. She looks so alive. And she doesn't seem to be afraid of anything. I admire her."

"Then why don't you invite her back? It sounds like she is the kind of friend you should have. Besides, I'd like to meet her."

Caroline's eyes brightened. "We could have a tea party."

"Sure, if that's what you'd like."

"Daddy doesn't like her."

"Why not?"

"He thinks she's trying to hurt me."

"Why, because she wanted to take you for a walk?"

Caroline rubbed her head. "I don't know, it's all so

242

confusing. I know he doesn't want her out here again."

"It seems to me your father dotes on you. I think you should invite this Anna out here, if that's what you want to do. I don't think your father will object if it's what you want. You're a grown woman, Caroline. You should have some say in your own life."

"I think tomorrow I will have LeBeau bring her out here. Then the three of us can get to know each other."

Molly smiled at Caroline. She just hoped Anna was prepared for this.

Anna stood at the window, looking out on the lamp-lit street. An occasional buggy or carriage clacked by, but it was mostly quiet. She looked down at the small garden, where two men stood in front of the house. She wasn't supposed to know that Roberto had hired guards, but she'd seen them following whenever they walked through town. There was a light tap on the door; she grabbed her robe from the bed, slipped it on, and opened the door.

"'Berto? Are you all right?"

"Can I come in? I need to talk."

"Of course. I'll turn up the lamp."

"No, don't. Let's sit over by the window."

Anna followed Roberto to the windowseat. She saw his face outlined in the light from the street, and could see that he was troubled. "What is it?"

"I don't know." His voice was quiet, almost pensive. "I don't know what to do about my son. It wouldn't be right to take him from his mother. That's all I can think about. My father almost kept me from my mother. My life would have been so different without her."

"Do you ever regret that your father didn't take you?"

"Never."

"Even with everything you've been through?"

"I couldn't have made it through everything without

243

the love of my mother and Trenton. I knew that no matter what, they loved me."

"Why didn't you try to write them when you finally got off the ship in New Orleans?"

"I was weak and sick, and Thornston and Caroline took care of me. By the time I was well, I had fallen in love with Caroline. Even though she was away at school, I knew I wanted her to be my wife. So I thought if I devoted all my time to learning Thornston's business, I could make him approve of me. I thought I could win his approval. I was hoping that I could take Caroline home to meet my family and that she would be my wife by then."

"You had even forgiven Nathan then, hadn't you?"

"How do you know?"

"Your son's middle name. The only way Caroline would've known that is if you had talked about Nathan."

"I suppose I began to realize, or at least hope, that Nathan wasn't to blame for what happened to me. All I know is that I missed my brother."

"But that all changed when Thornston had you beaten. When you made it out of that swamp alive, you decided that everyone was going to pay for anything they had ever done to hurt you, including your brother."

"Especially my brother. I wasn't sure what I was going to do, but when I got to Arizona and met up with Clare, I got angry. She made it sound as if Nathan had had it easy all of those years. And he had you."

"That sounds like Clare."

"Don't blame her, Anna. She was so in love with Nathan—"

"Don't try to defend her to me, Roberto. I'll have plenty to say to her when I get back. Anyway, what about Caroline?"

"I'll just have to wait and see what you can find out. I'd like to be able to meet with her and talk to her. Then I would know for sure."

244

"I can try and arrange it."

"No. It's too dangerous."

"Then Lawrence can help us. I'll talk to him."

Roberto laughed. "Does Lawrence still talk a lot?"

"Yes. I like him. He's our friend."

"All right, see what he thinks. But please be careful." Roberto took Anna in his arms and held her. "One thing hasn't changed, Anna. My feelings for you are just as strong as they were before."

"I think you give me too much credit. You're forgetting about all the times I screamed and yelled and threw things at you." She touched his face gently. "I'll never forget the times you helped me. I think I knew the night Cain—hurt me, that we were going to be friends."

"Those Bender men sure did take a fancy to you, didn't they?"

"That's not funny."

"I know it's not, but sometimes you don't seem to know when to keep your mouth shut. Don't make the same mistake with Thornston again. If he sees you with Caroline, act sweet and nice and don't argue with him. Do you understand me?"

"Yes."

"Promise me, Anna."

"I promise." Anna decided it was time to push her luck. What did she have to lose? "'Berto?"

"What?"

"When this is all over, will you talk to Nathan?"

"Anna, don't."

"Please, listen to me. You two love each other. You're brothers. You can get through this. I couldn't stand it if you both lived the rest of your lives apart. Aeneva and Trenton wouldn't want it that way."

Roberto shook his head in disgust. "Why do you always have to bring my parents into it?"

245 -

"Because I know how much you loved and respected them. You know I'm right, don't you?"

"I didn't say that." He looked out the window, staring at the street lamp. "All right, I'll talk with Nathan. But I'm not promising anything."

"Oh, thank you!" Anna hugged Roberto fiercely. "I think this was meant to happen, you know."

"What?"

"All of this. Maybe it was Aeneva's way of getting us all together again."

"Don't be crazy."

"I'm not being crazy. You know how strongly she felt about Seyan and the afterlife. She's probably looking down on us right now."

"It's possible, I suppose, but I never much believed in that stuff."

"Liar."

"I didn't. I've had to make my own way in this world for the last ten years."

"Then why is it that when your brother was dying, you fixed him a medicine just like the one your mother used to make? You believe, 'Berto, maybe more strongly than any of us."

Roberto stood up. "I shouldn't try to argue with you. It's a losing battle." He pulled Anna into his arms and hugged her tightly. "Thank you, little sister."

Tears filled Anna's eyes as she watched Roberto walk out of the room. She had finally broken through his wall. Not only were they friends, but he had just called her 'little sister,' something she hadn't thought Roberto would ever do. She lay down on her bed. Although she had been away from Nathan for a long time, it had been worth it, because she had gotten to know Roberto. If only she could help Nathan and Roberto to get to know each other again.

*   *   *

"Are you all right? You look as nervous as a pig without mud," Molly said to Nathan.

"I'm fine," Nathan replied curtly, pacing back and forth in front of the window in his bedroom. "She should be here soon, don't you think?"

"She'll be here, Nate. Just relax." Garrett joined him at the window. "There's nothing you can do right now. Molly will keep an eye on her."

"Yeah, I know. Jesus, I haven't seen her in almost five months. I'm going crazy just thinking about her."

Molly put her arm around Nathan's waist. "It'll all be over soon, Nathan."

"I hope so."

"Listen, I'm going to go on down now."

"I'll walk you out."

Nathan turned from the window. "Thank you both. You've been good friends. Anna is going to like you, Molly."

Molly and Garrett walked out of Nathan's room. Molly took Garrett's hand, looked up at him, and smiled. "I think I'm getting real used to you, cowboy."

"Yeah, well I'm getting real used to you too, lady." Garrett started to kiss Molly, but she pulled him down the hallway to their room, pulled him inside and shut the door. "That's much better." She put her arms around his neck and kissed him passionately.

"What was that for?"

"I just feel lucky, I guess. Nathan and Anna have been separated for so long, Roberto is in love with a crazy woman who has his son, and LeBeau is in love with all women. I'm glad we met."

"So am I. Now what about that other subject we were discussing a while back?"

Molly put her head against Garrett's chest and shut her eyes. He had been so patient with her. All he wanted was to marry her and love her, but she wasn't sure if she was ready. She wasn't sure if she could ever be ready. They had been together for over two months now, but they hadn't really been together. They had slept side by side on the ground and they shared the same bed in the hotel and here, but still Molly wasn't ready to let Garrett love her completely. She couldn't even tell him why. "Try to be patient with me for a while longer, Garrett. I know it's not fair, but I need some time. Please."

"How can I say no to that face?" Garrett kissed Molly on the nose. "We'll talk about it later. I want you to do something for me."

"Anything."

"Be careful. You already made Thornston angry at dinner last night. If he sees you and Anna with Caroline, there's no telling what he'll do."

"Then why don't you and Nathan keep him busy? Ask him to take you into the woods. Tell him you want to ride or hunt or something. Use your imagination, Garrett."

"I'm serious, Molly. I've seen what people like Thornston can do to women."

"You're talking about Anna, aren't you?"

Garrett nodded. He walked across the room, recalling all the times he and Anna had run or ridden together as children, the times they played under their favorite tree, the times they swam in the river, the times they played at love. She was his first love, his friend, and he missed her.

"Garrett? Did you love Anna?"

Garrett nodded. It didn't embarrass him to admit it, and he knew Molly well enough to know that it wouldn't threaten her. "I loved her enough to want to marry her at one time. But she met Nathan and they fell in love, and that's the way it should be."

"There's more to it than that."

"We grew up together, Molly. We did everything together. God, the first time I saw her my heart almost broke. She was the skinniest, shyest, sweetest little thing I'd ever seen, with the biggest deep blue eyes in the

248

world. I was hooked the first time I saw her laugh. Her mother used to say she lit up the world with her smile. She was right."

"You're lucky."

"Why?"

"I never had a friend like that. I can't wait to meet her."

"You are something, you know that?" Garrett kissed Molly lightly on the lips. "Look after Anna. If anything happened to her now, I don't know what Nate would do."

"Don't worry, everything will be all right. I better go."

"I better keep Nate company, or he's likely to forget himself and carry Anna away with him."

"It would surely be the easiest thing to do, wouldn't it?"

"Yeah, but that's not Nathan Hawkins. He's too loyal. Roberto is his brother and he's not about to give up on him yet. Let's go."

Molly left Garrett in the upstairs hallway. She walked down the ornate staircase and waited in the smaller sitting room for Caroline. She fidgeted with her dress. She hated dresses and slips and fancy boots and things. There was nothing as practical as a pair of pants, a shirt, and a good pair of boots.

"Oh, you're here."

"Hello, Caroline. You look lovely today," Molly lied. She couldn't for the life of her figure out why someone so pale would wear such pale, washed-out colors. It was as if she was trying to make herself look even sicker than she was.

"Thank you. This is one of daddy's favorites." She smoothed out the skirt of the dress. She held a lace handkerchief in her small, delicate hands, and used it to dab at her face. "Anna should be here soon. I really think you'll like her."

"I'm sure I will. Your father didn't mind that you

asked her back out here?"

"He wasn't very happy about it, but I said that you would stay with me and that LeBeau would probably be around."

Molly nodded. She hated this room. It was overwhelming and ostentatious, filled with tiny porcelain knickknacks and gold filigree tables. But the worst thing about the room was the enormous painting of Richard Thornston holding Caroline by the hand that hung over the fireplace. It would have been a quaint painting if Caroline had been a little girl, but she looked the same as she did now. It gave her a strange feeling.

"Do you like the painting?"

"It's interesting."

"My father loves paintings of children, and he realized just last summer that he and I had never had our portrait painted together. He hired an artist to come here all the way from New York. It was really very tiring, posing for him all day."

"I'm sure it was," Molly answered dryly, thinking of the painting of the rather overweight naked lady lounging on her side in all her glory, that had hung over the bar in the Three Sisters. One cowboy said that the woman in the painting could be all three sisters put together and more. She smiled at the thought.

"There you go smiling again. Why ever do you do that?"

"I don't know. My mind just starts racing and I start thinking of things that amuse me." Molly looked out at the driveway. A carriage stopped. "I think your friend is here."

"Oh, dear. You're sure I look all right?"

"You look fine. What did you have planned?"

"Well, I thought we'd have lunch in the garden room and then . . . I don't know. I suppose we could take a tour of the house. I'm not used to receiving many guests."

"What would you like to do, Caroline?"

"I don't know, but I know what Anna would like to do."

"What?"

"She'd like to see the horses."

"You didn't tell me you had horses. I'd like to see them too, if you don't mind."

"Honestly, do all you women from the West like horses? I, personally, think they are filthy animals."

Molly bit her tongue. It wouldn't do any good to say anything that might upset Caroline. She looked out the window again. The carriage was gone.

"Miss Caroline, you have a guest."

"Oh, thank you, Emily." Caroline rushed to the door of the sitting room holding out her hands. "Anna, it was so lovely of you to come."

"Thank you for having me, Caroline."

Molly turned from the window and her eyes locked with Anna's. Garrett was right—Anna was a beautiful woman. She was tall and thin, but not delicate by any means. She had dark skin with black hair, and round blue eyes that stood out in her narrow face. She smiled at Molly and Molly smiled back.

"Anna, I want you to meet Danielle Rondieux. She and her husband Henri are visiting here from California. Perhaps you know them?"

Anna gave Caroline a sideward glance. "California is a large state, Caroline." Anna moved forward and took Molly's hand. "I'm very pleased to meet you."

"And I, you."

"You're French?"

Molly hated this part of it. Already, she didn't want to lie to Anna. "Both my family and my husband's are from France originally, but we were both born in California."

"Danielle is a beautiful name."

"Thank you."

"Well, now that you both have met, why don't we go have lunch? Just follow me."

Anna and Molly trailed behind Caroline, who swayed down the hall, waving her hanky in front of her. Anna looked at Molly.

"Have you ever been in the garden room?" She whispered.

"Unfortunately."

Anna smiled. "A person could die from the heat in there. But she seems to love it."

"She's very strange. I've never met anyone like her."

"Neither have I."

"Here we are. Danielle, you sit right here next to Anna. I'll sit on this side so I can serve you both." Caroline hovered over the two women until they were sitting down, then poured them each a glass of mint iced tea.

Molly looked at Anna. "So, Anna, Caroline tells me that you're married. Where is your husband?"

"He's in Baton Rouge on business."

"What type of business is he in?" Molly could see the look of panic come over Anna's face. "Oh, it really doesn't matter. I tend to ramble when I'm hot." What an idiot you are, Molly. Don't make Anna feel uncomfortable, she thought.

"It is quite warm in here, Caroline. Isn't there someplace outside where we could have lunch?"

Caroline smiled strangely. "Are you trying to get me in trouble again, Anna?"

"No, I was merely suggesting—"

"Lunch is already here, Anna. We couldn't possibly take it outside."

Molly looked at Anna, cocking an eyebrow. "Well, I, for one, agree with Anna. It's so hot in this room you could cook an egg on the floor."

Anna laughed. "If it's all right with you, Caroline, why don't we eat lunch and then go outside?"

252

"What a good idea," Molly quickly added.

"Oh, all right, if you both insist. I was taught very early on to respect the wishes of my guests. But if I get in trouble, I'll have to blame you two."

"How old are you, Caroline?" Anna asked in an irritated tone.

"I'm twenty years old. Why?"

"Why aren't you married?"

Caroline, quite suddenly, looked totally nonplussed. "I suppose because I never loved anyone enough to get married."

"Why don't you do something for yourself, something just for you?"

"Like what?"

"Like take a carriage ride into the city and go shopping," Molly said.

"Or go to the theatre or the opera."

"Or go to a party with a man. Haven't you ever had any boyfriends, Caroline?"

Caroline stood up and walked to the window, staring out. "Why are you both attacking me like this? I thought you were my friends."

"We are your friends," Anna said, joining Caroline by the window. "Caroline, listen to me. Look at me, please." Anna spoke to her as if she was speaking to a small child. "If you came to visit me in my house and I never left, I never went outside, wouldn't that bother you? Wouldn't you wonder why I felt I had to stay in my house all the time? Caroline, you're young and attractive, and I don't understand why you keep yourself locked up in this house as if you're a prisoner."

"Because I *am* a prisoner!" Caroline exclaimed.

Molly walked over to the women. "What do you mean, Caroline?"

"Nothing. I didn't mean anything by it. I'm just tired. I've had a long day. Maybe this wasn't such a good idea."

253

Caroline was quickly slipping away from Anna and Molly and they had to find a way to make her stay.

"I'm sorry, Caroline, I didn't mean to upset you. I told you I was an impatient person."

"Just like I have a big mouth," Molly joined in. "Why don't we eat lunch?"

"Yes, that sounds like a good idea. Let's all sit down."

Caroline seemed placated. She served Anna and Molly their finger sandwiches and fruit, which seemed to be Caroline's lunch of choice, but served nothing for herself. She seemed content to watch the other two women eat.

"Would it be possible to get a glass of water?" Anna asked.

"Yes, of course. You don't like the tea?"

"The tea is wonderful, but I would like a glass of water. If you could tell me where the kitchen is—"

Caroline jumped up. "No, no, I'll find Emily. I'm sure she's around somewhere. She can get the water. Do you want anything, Danielle?"

"No, thank you, Caroline." Molly watched until Caroline was out of the room. She put her plate down. "Well, I've finally met a woman who has a bigger mouth than I do."

Anna laughed. "I can't seem to control myself around her. I just want to take her by the shoulders and shake some sense into her."

"Have you noticed she doesn't eat?"

Anna glanced at Caroline's empty plate. "I've only been around her two times, but both times she didn't eat anything."

"She doesn't eat at any of the meals. There's something wrong with her."

"Have you ever heard of laudanum? If you take enough of it, it makes you not care about anything."

"Now that you mention it, I did know a girl once who

254

tried to kill herself with that. All it did was knock her out for over a day. Why would Caroline be taking it?"

"She might not know she's taking it. Someone could be putting it in her food or her tea." They both looked at the tea and began to laugh. "I don't think it's in our tea. But it could be easily done. I know."

Molly had the good sense not to ask Anna how she knew. She figured Anna would tell her if she wanted her to know. "Do you suppose her father is doing it to her?"

"He would be the person most likely to do it. I don't know what you know about him, or if he's a friend of yours, so I don't want to say anything against him—"

"Wait. Let's get something straight. LeBeau arranged for us to stay here because he thought we'd enjoy it. As far as Richard Thornston is concerned, I'd like to see him forced to work in the fields on his plantation for the rest of his life."

"That's pretty much how I feel about him. For some reason, he doesn't want his daughter out of his sight."

"It's kind of eerie. I could never imagine my father doing that to me."

"Nor could I. My father respected what I had to say and he always had time to listen. God, I miss him." She looked at Molly. "How long have I known you? One hour? I feel like I've known you all my life. I've never had a womanfriend before."

"It's a new experience for me, too."

"Here's your water." Caroline came rushing into the room with a tall glass of water on a silver tray. "I couldn't find Emily anywhere, and I had to walk all the way to the cookhouse."

"Not all the way?" Molly said in a mocking tone that only Anna understood. "You know, Caroline, Anna and I would love to see your room. Wouldn't we, Anna?"

Anna looked at Molly with a puzzled expression. "Yes, we'd love to."

"Oh, would you, really? My room is my favorite room in the whole house." She clapped her hands together. "Well, if you're all finished here. I can take you right now."

Anna drank her water and put down the glass. "I'm finished."

"So am I," said Molly. "Lead the way." Molly remembered suddenly that Nathan and Garrett were still upstairs. There was nothing she could do about it now except talk loudly and hope that they didn't walk around the halls.

As it turned out, Caroline's room was on the other side of the house from the guest rooms. She and her father had one entire wing. Caroline opened the door of her room with a flourish and held out her arm. "Here we are. I call it my playroom."

Anna and Molly went into the huge room. The walls were painted white and the room smelled strongly of flowers. A large four-poster bed in the middle of the room was draped with rich lace curtains that could be pulled to ensure privacy, and the bed was covered in the same lace material. A long window seat ran the length of one entire wall and looked out over the east side of the estate, toward the forest and the swamps beyond. Delicate floral vases filled with white flowers were placed all around the room. The room was as pale and lifeless as Caroline.

"Oh"—Caroline breathed deeply—"don't you just love that smell?" She walked over to one vase and lifted it to her nose. "Jasmine. They bloom at night. Can you imagine? Don't you think that's downright audacious of a flower to bloom at night?"

Anna felt dizzy. The smell in the room was almost overbearing. "What's that other smell, Caroline?"

"It's tuberose. Isn't it heavenly?"

"It's heavenly, all right," Molly said, walking to the window. The only time she had smelled a tuberose was at

256

her aunt's funeral. She would never forget the smell as long as she lived. "May I open this window?" Molly waved her hand in front of her nose. "I think the flowers are a little strong for me."

Anna leaned against the door, her head swirling. "Yes, do you mind?"

Caroline ran to the window. She stood in front of it so Molly couldn't open it. "No, you can't open the window. I'll lose the smell of the flowers. They'll die."

Anna closed her eyes. "I have to get out of here." She ran out of the room and down the hall, gulping in fresh air, glad to be free of that stifling atmosphere.

"Are you all right?" Molly followed Anna. "Come on, let's go outside. I think Caroline is too busy dreaming about her flowers to notice that we're even missing."

They started toward the staircase, but Anna stopped. "Did you hear that?"

"What?"

"It sounded like a baby crying." Anna walked toward the sound. She walked back down the hall past Caroline's room and turned the corner. There was a door at the end. "Don't you hear it?"

"You must have good ears. I haven't heard anything."

Anna put her ear against the door listening, then turned the knob and opened the door. There was a wooden staircase that led up to another story. The sound of a baby crying was very clear. "Don't tell me you can't hear that, Danielle."

"I'll be damned!" Molly cocked her ear toward the sound. "You want to take a look?"

"We're probably already in trouble as it is. Let's go." Anna went inside and Molly closed the door behind them. Anna walked carefully up the wooden stairs, trying to step to the side, rather than the middle, to avoid making creaking sounds. There was a small hallway at the top of the stairs, with a door on either end. They walked toward the sound of the crying baby and Anna put her ear against the door. She couldn't hear anything but the baby. "I think the baby is in there alone." She opened the door, but Molly caught her arm.

"Be careful, Anna."

Anna walked into the room. It was brightly lit, with white and blue flowered wallpaper, a large rocking horse in the corner, a bassinet against one wall, a bed by the window, and a rocking chair by the bed. "Someone sleeps in here with the baby."

"Probably a maid."

"I don't think it's a maid's baby." Anna walked to the bassinet and looked in. A small, dark-haired, dark-skinned baby of about eight months screamed at the world in all his fury. He was hungry and he wanted everyone to know it. Anna reached into the bassinet and picked him up. His blue sleeping gown was entangled in his chubby little legs. "There, there, it's all right. Are you tired of being alone? Did you want some company?"

"He's a cute little thing, isn't he?" Molly reached over and rubbed the baby's cheek. "He sure seems to like you."

"He just wanted some attention." Anna stared at the baby in her arms and melted. He was a beautiful baby— he looked just like his father and grandmother. He was almost her nephew. "How are you today, Robert Nathan?" Anna froze as soon as the words were out.

"How did you know his name, Anna?"

"LeBeau told me Caroline had a child. He even told me his name." Anna couldn't believe her blunder. Danielle was sweet, but she was staying at Caroline's house. Anna wasn't sure yet if she could be completely trusted.

"Why the hell does she keep him all the way up here?" Molly hated this cat-and-mouse game she and Anna were playing. They knew the truth, but neither one of them could say anything.

"LeBeau says it would disgrace her father if anyone knew she had a child out of wedlock." Anna shook her head. "I can't for the life of me imagine Caroline taking care of anything. She can barely take care of herself." Anna patted the baby on the back.

"God, this is a strange place. It's almost like they've locked the baby away. If you want my opinion, the wrong person is locked up here. It ought to be Caroline."

"Damn! We forgot to check her room for the laudanum."

"Hell, who needs laudanum to get drugged when you've got so damned many flowers in your room?"

Anna laughed loudly. "I like you, Danielle. You don't hold anything back."

"Do me a favor," Molly said in a conspiratorial tone. "Call me Molly." At Anna's puzzled expression she quickly added. "It's my middle name. It was the name of my mother's best friend. My real friends call me Molly." If she only knew, thought Molly.

"I like it. It fits you much better than Danielle." Anna turned toward the door. "There's someone coming."

"God, woman, you have ears like a bat." Molly walked to the door and listened. "You're right. Someone's coming up the stairs. You better put the baby down. We can say we just wandered in here by accident."

Anna hurried to the bassinet and placed Robert carefully on his back, smiling when he wouldn't let go of her finger. "I don't want to leave him."

"We've got company."

The door opened. "Oh, my, you ladies ain't supposed to be up here." It was one of the maids.

Anna and Molly exchanged relieved looks. "We heard a baby crying and came up to make sure everything was all right. I held him to settle him down a bit. He's a lovely child."

"Yes, he's a good boy." The woman walked over to the

259

bassinet and picked up the baby. "I'm his wet nurse." she placed the baby at her breast and sat down in the rocking chair. "I'm not supposed to leave him alone, ever. If the master finds out that I left this room, I'll get the beating of my life. You ladies won't say nothing, will you?"

Anna looked at the woman. "What's your name?"

"My name is Marie."

"We won't say anything, Marie." Anna knelt down by the rocking chair. "Is this Caroline's baby, Marie?"

Marie's dark eyes looked from Anna to Marie. "I ain't allowed to say nothing to nobody. I'm just supposed to take care of this little thing."

Molly walked across the room. "We're not going to get you in trouble, Marie. We just can't believe that Caroline could have a baby. She doesn't seem capable of taking care of one."

"She ain't; that's why I's with him all the time. Miss Caroline was real good with this little fella when he first came into the world. She wouldn't let nobody touch him. She was so proud of him. She almost died giving him birth, you know. I don't think a mother coulda loved a baby more than Miss Caroline loved Master Robert."

"What happened, Marie? What happened to make Caroline like she is now?"

Marie shook her head, smiling and cooing at the baby in her arms. "She just went sort of crazy. She was always frail and weak, never in the best of health, but a coupla of months after the birthing, she wouldn't get outta bed. She was tired all the time, and she didn't seem to care nothing 'bout Master Robert. I'd bring him in to her, and she wouldn't even care. She didn't want him around. She wanted him moved from the second story to up here. She said his crying was keeping her awake at night."

"Who is the father of the child, Marie?" Anna asked, knowing full well who the father was.

"Oh, I can't say nothing 'bout that."

Anna gently touched Marie's knee. "Do you remember Roberto, Marie? Were you here when he was in love with Caroline?"

Marie's eyes turned to the tiny baby. "Yes, ma'am, I was here."

"Please tell me what happened. It's very important that I know."

"Why?" Marie suddenly looked unsure of herself. "You trying to hurt Miss Caroline?"

"No, I'm not trying to hurt Caroline. I was a good friend of Roberto's, and I'm trying to find out if Caroline ever really loved him at all."

"Yes, ma'am, she loved him; she was crazy about him. She woulda run away with him if the master hadn't found out about them. I think that's part of why Miss Caroline got so sick. She got her poor heart broke."

"We'd better go, Anna." Molly's hand was on Anna's shoulder. "Caroline's bound to notice we're not around, sooner or later."

Anna nodded and stood up. "Can I hold the baby one more time?" She took the baby from Marie and held him to her breast, kissing him softly on the top of his head. "Good-bye, Robert Nathan. I'll be back." She gave the baby back to Marie. "Thank you, Marie. We won't tell anyone we were here."

Anna followed Molly out of the room and down the staircase. They were about to open the door to the second floor when they heard voices.

"I told you I didn't want her back in this house!" Richard Thornston said angrily. "Why do you persist in pushing me, Caroline?"

"I'm sorry, daddy. I thought it would be nice to have a friend."

"And that other one. I don't trust her either. The two of them are probably planning something right now."

Anna and Molly stared at each other with wide eyes.

261

"Do you think so, daddy? I think they like me."

"They don't like you, Caroline. They're just pretending to be your friends."

"But why would they do that?"

"I've told you before, people will do anything to get at me. I'm a rich and powerful man. I've made many enemies along the way."

"I think you're wrong about them, daddy. They're different from any women I've ever known."

"Of course they're different. They're heathens from the West. Hell, I wouldn't be surprised if they'd slept with Indians."

Anna covered her mouth to keep from laughing.

"What is it?" Molly whispered.

"I'll tell you another time. Do you think we should go back up? If they come in here and find us, there's no telling what he'll do."

"What do you suppose is in that other room?"

"I don't know. But let's get out of here. I've seen him when he gets mad."

They quickly ran back up the stairs and turned to the right, to the door at the other end of the hallway. Anna tried the doorknob.

"It's locked."

"Let me see." Molly knelt down and looked through the keyhole. "Do you have some kind of hairpin?"

Anna reached into the knot of her hair and pulled out one of the pins. "Here."

Molly stuck it in the keyhole and moved it around. "These locks are tough to get open. It may take me a while."

Anna turned. "We don't have very long. They're coming up."

Molly worked hurriedly at the lock and managed to get it unlocked. They opened the door and stepped inside the room, just before Thornston and Caroline got to the top of the stairs.

"Jesus Christ, Marie, is that all you ever do, is feed that brat?" They heard Thornston say before he shut the door.

"Whew," Molly sighed, leaning against the door. She looked around. "What is this place?"

Anna stepped forward. "If I didn't know better, I'd swear it was a museum."

The room was filled with every kind of children's toy imaginable, from stuffed animals and dolls to wooden soldiers and rocking horses. Cabinets filled with dolls lined the walls. They were all dressed in costumes from different parts of the world. There were blocks and trains and books. Every toy a child could think of having. A large painted screen in the corner depicted a little girl playing in a field of flowers.

"Anna, come look at this." Molly was standing in front of one of the doll cabinets.

Anna walked over and looked into the cabinet. "What is it?"

"Just look."

Anna looked at the dolls. They were all made of white porcelain painted with pale blue eyes, pale hair, and very little coloring to their lips. Their hair hung straight and colorless around their shoulders. Although they were all dressed in different dresses, each one of the dolls had the same face. "I don't believe this. They're Caroline."

"And so are they." Molly pointed to the next two cabinets. "I've never seen anything like this in my life."

"Richard Thornston actually had a dollmaker make up all of these dolls to look like his daughter? This must've cost him a fortune."

"He can afford it. These are strange people, Annie." Molly hesitated, realizing that 'Annie' was Garrett's nickname for Anna.

"Why did you call me that?"

263

Molly shrugged her shoulders. "It just seems to fit you. You look like an Annie, like I look like a Molly."

"There was only one person who ever used to call me that," Anna said, as she walked around the strange room. "My father used to call me that once in a while, but my friend used to call me that all the time." She shook her head, crossing her arms in front of her. "I miss him."

"Was he a good friend?"

Anna turned. "He was the best. If I'd had any sense at all I would've married him, and then I wouldn't be here." She looked at Molly. "Never mind what I'm saying, I'm just rambling. This room, this house, these people make me feel very strange."

"It's all right. I understand."

"What does your husband think of it here?"

"He doesn't like it much, either." Molly couldn't stand it. "Annie—" She pulled Anna's arm. "My god, someone's coming."

Anna looked around the room. She grabbed Molly's arm and pulled her behind the screen. They stood close together, trying to be as quiet as possible.

The door opened and Richard Thornston stormed in. "Goddamn niggers, can't trust 'em with the time of day. I knew they were sneaking into this room." He shut the door behind him and his footsteps reverberated loudly on the wooden floor. He walked to the doll cabinets and stood in front of them, looking at each doll. "Hello, my lovelies. How are you today?"

Anna held onto Molly's arm and looked at her. She could see by the look in her eyes that Molly was as frightened as she was.

"I've missed you, you know. I just haven't had the time for a visit. Caroline hasn't been herself lately. I'm afraid we're going to lose her soon. She's not the same girl she used to be." He took out some keys and opened the middle cabinet, taking out a doll that was dressed in a pale dress. "You look especially lovely today. I'd take you out for a walk, but we have people here, snoopy people who might talk. As soon as they're gone, I'll take you out. The weather is just fine for a walk under the oaks." He stroked her hair and held her to his face. "It's been so long, but I promise I'll be back soon." He put the doll back in the case and locked it. "Well, I must be going. I wouldn't want our guests to wonder where I've gone. You be good girls. Remember, daddy loves you." Thornston walked across the room and opened and shut the door, locking it from the outside.

Anna and Molly stood in complete silence for minutes before either one of them dared to move. Anna peeked around the screen to make sure Thornston was gone.

"He's gone."

Anna and Molly walked to the doll cabinets. "I guess the doll collection isn't Caroline's."

"No, I'd say it definitely belongs to him. Did you hear the way he was talking to those things?" Molly shook her head. "That man is definitely not normal."

Anna looked out the window. "My God, it's getting dark! I'd better be getting back to town. My husband will worry."

"I thought you said he was in Baton Rouge."

"Still, I should be getting home. I don't want to be here any longer than I have to." Anna smiled. "As much as I've enjoyed meeting you, I really should go."

"Now, let's see if we can get out of this damned place." Molly walked to the door and knelt down. "Anna, I don't think you want to hear this."

"What?"

"The lock works only one way. I can't unlock it from this side."

"No," Anna said in disgust, walking over to the window. "It looks like this is our only way out." She flipped over the lock and pushed at the window, but it wouldn't budge. "Would you help me push this thing?"

Molly stood next to Anna and together the two of them pushed as hard as they could. The window wouldn't budge. Molly slowly nodded her head. "Well, Annie, it looks like our adventure isn't quite over."

Anna went over to the rocking horse and sat down. "There should be something around here that we can pry it loose with."

"The hell with it. We'll just wait until it's almost dark and then we'll break the damned thing. I always was a good climber." She looked at Anna, one eyebrow arched. "You're not afraid of heights, I hope."

"I've never been afraid of heights. It's just that I've never been real good at climbing in these kind of shoes." She lifted her skirt to reveal the button-down boots with the heel.

Molly pulled up her skirt and looked at her shoes, exactly like Anna's except for the color. "Well, girl, I reckon we're going to have to put our brains together and come up with something good."

Anna sat sideways on the rocking horse, rocking back and forth. "We could yell for Marie, but we don't know who's in there with her. Do you know what the outside of the house is like? I have no idea what room is underneath us."

"We could try to break the door. Of course the entire house will probably hear us."

"I just hope Thornston doesn't decide to visit his dolls anytime soon." Anna rubbed her face, suddenly feeling very tired. If she didn't show up soon, LeBeau would tell Roberto and he would be out here looking for her. "Why can't we just scream for help and say we got lost? We could say we found the room and became enchanted with the dolls and we couldn't get back out."

"Anna, you don't actually think Thornston will believe that? He'll know we were in here while he was

266

playing dolls, and I don't think he'll take kindly to it. Just relax. It'll be dark soon. Then we have some climbing to do." Molly looked out the window and tried to figure the best way over the roof. They would have a long step from the window to the rooftop, and from there, they would actually have to hang onto the roof to climb down to the next story. She tried to lean out to see. "I don't know how we're going to do this."

Anna joined Molly at the window. She looked out, and a smile brightened her face. She put her arm around Molly's shoulders. "I can't say when I've had this much fun. If we get out of this alive, we'll have to do this again sometime."

"Don't count on it."

"Is there anything we can use for rope? Maybe we can tie something from the windowsill and use it to hang onto."

"I like the way you think, girl."

They looked around the room but found nothing. They stood side by side, next to the thick velvet curtains, the heavy rope pulls hanging down by their sides. They were both playing with the pulls when they looked at each other. "Right in front of us," Anna muttered, grabbing her rope as hard as she could.

It took two hard yanks before the pulls and heavy curtains fell to the floor.

"These are perfect." Anna ripped her pull from the curtain.

"If we can tie these together, it should easily get us down to the second story."

"Let's just pray that it's not Thornston's room."

"Well, if it is, we'll just have to hang on until we can get to our side of the house. Oh, my God," Molly muttered in disgust. "I just remembered that all of the rooms have balconies. If we get stuck on Thornston's balcony, we're doomed."

"We don't have any other choice. We'll just have to hope he's downstairs."

They tied the ends of the rope together and then pulled from opposite ends to make sure the knots were tight. The windowsill was flush to the wall with nothing for them to tie the rope to.

"What about the rocking horse?" Anna asked. The rocking horse was carved from one solid piece of heavy wood, probably pine, and it was extremely sturdy. Anna shoved it over to the window. "We can tie it to the horse. The horse may move but it won't fit out the window. I think it's our only choice."

"And you don't think Thornston is going to know we were up here?"

"He can't prove it. Maybe you can sneak up tomorrow and clean it up."

"What about the broken window?"

"We clean up the room, try to put everything back into place, including the curtains, and leave the window. He can't prove anything, and it's better than letting him think we were in here listening to him talk to his dolls."

"We can talk about that later. It's almost dark. I think we'd better get that rope tied around the horse." Once they had tied the rope to the horse and pulled at it as hard as they could, they made sure there was no possible way the horse could fit out the window. "Well, I guess that's it."

"Let's try the window once more. If we don't break the glass, all we have to do is fix the curtains." Anna looked around the room once more. She removed a piece of the metal train track and stuck it all around the window, hitting it with the palm of her hand.

"You're wasting your time."

Anna ignored Molly as she chipped paint away from all around the window frame. She put down the metal and pushed at the top of the frame. It moved. "Do you want

268

to help me?" Together the women managed to get the window up far enough for them to crawl through. "Okay, who's first?"

"It doesn't matter to me. We're both going to die anyway."

"I'll go." Anna dropped the rope out the window and straddled the sill. She took a deep breath and took hold of the rope, using her feet to keep her from sliding too quickly. Her boots slipped against the brick and she swung out slightly, banging against the side of the house. She looked down and saw part of a balcony. The rope fell just to the side of the railing.

"Are you all right?" Molly tried to whisper but her voice carried in the stillness of the night.

"Yes," Anna responded, working her way down the rope. Her arms were getting tired, but she forced herself to keep going. She was nearing the edge of the balcony when she heard voices. She stopped.

"I don't know where they could have gone. They just disappeared."

"They could not just disappear, Caroline. I do not think you understand the gravity of the situation. If my friend discovers that his wife is missing, he will get very angry."

A sigh of relief spread through Anna. It was LeBeau. Somehow, she had to get his attention. She couldn't think of any way other than climbing onto the balcony and trying to get him to see her. She edged her way to the railing and grabbed it, letting go of the rope, then climbed over the railing and walked toward the glass doors. Caroline was fluttering around the room, but LeBeau was standing close to the doors.

"LeBeau," Anna whispered. LeBeau looked around for moment, then looked back at Caroline. "LeBeau." He looked out toward the balcony, walked to the doors and stopped, wide-eyed with shock when he saw Anna. "*Sacré bleu!* I thought you were dead in the swamp somewhere."

"I need your help. Can you come out here without her?"

LeBeau nodded and went inside. "I am going onto the balcony for a cigar, my dear. You don't mind, do you?"

"I detest those horrible things. I don't know why you smoke them, LeBeau."

"Alas, it is my only vice. I shall close the doors so the smoke does not drift into your room." LeBeau went onto the balcony and walked over to Anna, who was standing in the corner. "Just what are you doing here?" He took a cigar and lit it while he was listening to Anna.

"Not now. Molly is up there waiting to come down."

"Molly?" LeBeau asked in surprise.

"I mean Danielle. Can you hold me and make sure I don't fall off the railing, so I can tell her to come down?"

LeBeau shook his head. "I am now very glad you are not my woman. I do not think I could live through one day with you."

Anna climbed onto the railing as LeBeau eagerly held her hips. She couldn't see Molly because of the overhang from the third story, so she grabbed the rope and pulled herself up a little way. "Molly, you can come down now."

"It's about time," she heard Molly reply anxiously.

Anna shinnied back down the rope and stepped onto the railing, jumping down into LeBeau's arms. "Thank you."

"Now, do you want to tell me where you have been?"

"Molly and I had a visit with Caroline's baby today."

"*Merde!* Do you know how dangerous that was? No one is supposed to know about that child but me."

"Well, we went exploring. We also found something else."

LeBeau waved his hands. "I do not want to know."

"There's another room up there and it's filled with dolls, all painted to look like Caroline. Thornston came

270

up there while we were still there. While we hid, he visited with the dolls."

LeBeau waved his hands. "I do not wish to hear this."

"He talked to the dolls, LeBeau. He told them he was sorry he had not been to visit them for so long."

"Holy Jesus!" Molly groaned, swinging herself onto the railing and into LeBeau's arms. "I hope I never live to see another adventure like that one."

"LeBeau? Are you done with that nasty thing yet? I want to go downstairs," Caroline called from inside.

"You two stay here and do not move or I swear I will shoot you myself!" LeBeau walked to the glass doors, chewing on his cigar and blowing smoke into Caroline's room. "Why don't you go ahead, my dear. I just want to finish my cigar and enjoy this lovely evening. I'll be down soon."

"Well, you hurry."

"Yes." LeBeau watched until Caroline left the room and he shut the glass doors. He ground out his cigar on the railing and threw it into the shrubbery below. "So, you two were in places where you should not have been, eh?" He stepped close to Molly. "Do you know that your husband and your friend are frantic with worry?" He looked at Anna. "And do you know that your husband will kill me if anything happens to you?" He threw his hands up in the air. "What am I to do with you?"

"Well, you could always put us to work in your brothel," Molly said teasingly.

"You cannot be serious. You two would scare all of the men away!"

Anna couldn't contain her laughter anymore. She put her arm through LeBeau's. "It's all right now, LeBeau. We're safe and there's nothing to worry about."

"What about Richard Thornston? You don't think he's going to know you two were sneaking around his house?"

"We were hoping you could help us with that."

"What?" LeBeau extricated himself from Anna. "I think I have helped you all enough." His eyes moved to Molly. "I think you'd better go calm your husband and friend down now, Danielle, before there is trouble."

Molly nodded. "Is Thornston up here?"

"He is downstairs. You should have no trouble getting to the other side of the house. I will talk to you later." He waited until Molly was gone, then turned to Anna. "If Roberto is on his way here, it could be dangerous for him. Do you understand what I mean?"

"All right, I'll go. LeBeau—"

"Where are you, LeBeau?" Richard Thornston walked into Caroline's room. His face wore a strange expression when he saw Anna. "So, there you are, Mrs. Hawkins. We were worried about you. Where were you?"

Anna shrugged her shoulders. "Mrs. Rondieux and I took a walk around the grounds, and I guess we lost track of the time."

LeBeau stood in front of Anna. "I was just telling her I should take her home now. Her husband will worry."

"Why would he worry if he's in Baton Rouge?" He moved toward Anna. "I think you should stay here for a few days, Mrs. Hawkins. I think, perhaps, I judged you too harshly."

"I don't understand, Mr. Thornston. I didn't think you wanted me around your daughter."

"That was before today. Today I saw a different side of her. She was more like the Caroline I used to know. I think you and Mrs. Rondieux are good for her." He took Anna's hand in his. "Please, would you consider staying on for a while? We could send LeBeau to get some of your things."

"No, that is impossible. What if her husband comes home and finds her gone? He will be crazy with worry."

"I would love to stay, Mr. Thornston," Anna replied.

She recalled Thornston's angry words to Caroline not long before. She knew that Richard Thornston hadn't had a change of heart toward her, but if it gave her more time she would take it. She had to find out about Caroline. It was the least she could do for Roberto.

"Good, good." Thornston looked at Anna. "You're a little taller than my Caroline, but perhaps you could fit into something of Mrs. Rondieux's until we can send for some of your things. I'll put you in the room next to hers."

"Thank you."

"Would you like me to show you the room?"

"I can do that, Richard," LeBeau replied. "You go on ahead."

"Very well. We will be in the main sitting room."

LeBeau and Anna followed Thornston out the door. They walked down the hallway to the rooms on the other side of the grand staircase. LeBeau opened the door to Anna's room and dragged her inside, slamming the door behind him. He turned up the lamp on the wall, making the room glow with light. "What are you thinking of, woman? This man is dangerous. He hasn't forgiven you. He is only biding his time until he can get you alone and kill you."

"You are too melodramatic, LeBeau. He knows you and I are friends. He won't hurt me."

LeBeau grabbed Anna's shoulders, digging his fingers into them. "I was there the day Roberto was beaten," he said slowly.

Anna stared at him. "You were there?"

"Yes. Thornston enjoyed beating Roberto. You should have seen the look in his eyes, Anna. He relished inflicting pain; it gave him great pleasure."

"You were there and you didn't help him? Why? Why, LeBeau?"

"Because I could not help him. I had plans of my own

273

that could not be interfered with." He let go of Anna and shook his head. "When I found out he had been taken into the swamps, I told Lawrence to tell his people."

"So you did help him?"

"I did what I could, but it was not enough. No man deserves to be beaten like Roberto was."

"Why do you hate Thornston so much, LeBeau? What did he do to you?"

"It is a long story, one I cannot go into now." He looked around the room. "Well, if you are going to stay here for a few days, I should give you this." LeBeau reached into his breast pocket and gave Anna a pearl-handled derringer. "Keep it under your pillow. I don't trust Thornston. And keep your door locked at night."

"Thank you, LeBeau. You have been a good friend."

"Do not ask me why. I knew that first night I looked at you on the riverboat that you were going to be trouble."

Anna smiled. "You did not."

"I did, but I also knew that I would not be able to help myself. Well, I should get back to town and try to calm your husband. He will probably shoot me for allowing you to stay out here."

"I'll write him a note." Anna went to the desk by the window and sat down. She pushed up the top and found cream-colored paper, a pen and an inkwell. She dipped the pen into the inkwell and wrote,

Dear Roberto,

Please do not be angry with me, but I had to stay. I found out some very strange things today about Caroline and her father. I need to find out more. I saw your son today. He is beautiful. He looks like you and your mother. He is being well cared-for and he's quite charming. Please, do not come out here. I don't want anything to happen to you, 'Berto. I care for you and I want you to trust me. Please. LeBeau will come for some of my things. Don't blame LeBeau; I talked him into letting me stay. It's the only way I can find out more about Caroline and Thornston. I will see you in a few days. It will be over soon, 'Berto. Hang onto the fact that you have a beautiful son.

Anna.

She folded the note and put it into an envelope. "Give this to Roberto. He won't shoot you."

"Easy for you to say. You do not have to face him like I do."

"Thank you, LeBeau." Anna hugged him. "Will I see you tomorrow?"

"But of course. I have to bring out your things. I do not like this, Anna. Things are getting too complicated."

"What things?"

LeBeau thought of Nathan and closed his eyes. What would Roberto do if he found out his brother was here in the same house with his wife? What would Anna do when she found out everyone had lied to her? He didn't like this business of lies. But perhaps it would all work out for the best, especially if they managed to bring Richard Thornston down. "Nothing. I am just tired. I will see you tomorrow." He kissed Anna on the cheek and left.

Anna watched LeBeau as he walked out of the room. She had a strange feeling that LeBeau knew more than he was saying. She just hoped that LeBeau remained their friend. The way things were going, they would need him.

Chapter IX

Anna looked at herself in the mirror. She had to admit that she didn't look very impressive. Her dress was wrinkled and dirty from their climb out the window, and her hair had fallen out of its knot. She took out the pins and brushed it, letting it fall in thick waves over her shoulder. She then pulled it back up and twisted it into a knot on her head. Small strands of hair fell down her neck. "Well, it will have to do." She thought of asking Molly for another dress, but decided against it. She didn't really care about that right now; she was more interested in Richard Thornston and his daughter. She went to the washbowl and washed her face and hands, feeling better.

She took the gun LeBeau had given her and put it under her pillow, then decided against that. If one of the maids came in to turn down the bed, she might find it. She lifted the mattress and put the gun there. She went downstairs, excited about coming so close to the truth. She wanted more than anything to help Roberto, and more than that, she wanted to be with Nathan again. She turned right at the bottom of the stairs and saw Marie.

"Hello, Marie."

"Madame." Marie curtsied, acting as if they had never met. She was obviously quite afraid that Thornston would find out that Anna and Molly had been in the baby's room.

Anna decided not to pursue it. She heard voices coming from the sitting room. Laughter emanated from it. It was Caroline, actually laughing! Anna reached the doorway and stopped, looking at the people in the room. Her heart was beating in her ears and she felt as if her legs would give out from underneath her. Garrett and Molly were talking to Richard Thornston as if they had known one another for years, and Caroline was sitting next to Nathan. Nathan! She couldn't believe it. He was dressed in a charcoal gray suit and his hair was cut shorter than usual; he looked more handsome than she had thought possible. Caroline's laughter was genuine, as Nathan said something to her. She was enjoying his company.

"Ah, Mrs. Hawkins, you're here. Please come in. I'd like you to meet our guests." Richard Thornston walked across the room and took Anna's arm, acting as if she was an honored guest. He walked her over to Garrett and Molly. "Henri and Danielle Rondieux, Anna Hawkins."

Anna looked at Garrett, trying to control the anger building inside her. Garrett, of all people, had not tried to talk to her, had not tried to tell her what was going on. She felt totally deceived. "Nice name," she said curtly. She looked at Molly. "And what should I call you, Danielle or Molly?"

Molly reached out for Anna's arm, but she turned away, walking toward Nathan and Caroline. Nathan was standing, waiting for the showdown. "This is Etienne Fortier. Anna Hawkins."

Anna stared at Nathan, her eyes starting to fill with tears. "It's nice to meet you, Mr. Fortier. How long have you been in New Orleans?"

"We've been here a few weeks."

"A few weeks? I'm surprised we haven't run into each other."

"Yes, so am I."

Caroline put her arm through Nathan's. "Monsieur Fortier has been telling me all about the West, Anna. It sounds so exciting. I think I'd like to take a visit out there sometime." She looked up at Nathan adoringly.

"Oh, I'm sure you'd love it, Caroline. But you have to remember to watch out for the snakes." Anna walked to Richard Thornston. "So, Mr. Thornston, it seems as if you and I are the only ones without dinner partners."

"We can remedy that, Mrs. Hawkins. You will sit by me tonight. Why don't we go into the dining room? I've got a hefty appetite tonight."

Anna walked with Richard Thornston into the dining room and allowed him to seat her. "You'll sit here on my right, Mrs. Hawkins. Caroline, why don't we have Etienne sit on my left, you sit on his left, Henri, you sit on Mrs. Hawkins' right, and your wife can sit next to you." Thornston surveyed the table. "Too bad LeBeau had to leave. The table would've looked better with an even number of guests."

"It's lovely, daddy. Don't you think so, Etienne?"

"Yes," Nathan responded, looking across the table at Anna. He couldn't believe he was finally with her. He could tell by the fire in her eyes that she was angry with him. This was the Anna he knew. Tiny wisps of dark hair fell around her face and neck, framing it perfectly so that her blue eyes stood out like dark moons. He had gotten lost in those eyes before. She looked thinner, but she looked well. It didn't appear that Roberto had hurt her in any way. Nathan decided it was time to begin the skirmish. "So, Mrs. Hawkins, where is your husband? I can't believe a man would leave a beautiful woman like you alone."

Anna's eyes narrowed. "My husband is in Baton Rouge on business. He should be back any day."

"What does your husband do?"

"He's in banking," she responded curtly. "And what is it you do, Mr. Fortier?"

"I'm in the cattle business."

"And you, Mr. Rondieux?" Anna glared at Garrett, kicking his ankle underneath the table.

"Ouch," Garrett responded, looking at the people around him. "Pardon me, it's those nasty bites. They just don't seem to let a fella alone." Garrett looked at Anna. "I'm in the cattle business also. You should come out West and see our ranch sometime."

"I'm from the West."

"Well, you and your husband will have to make it a point of coming to visit us sometime."

"Yes, you look like you'd be able to sit a horse with ease," Nathan said from across the table.

"I can ride." Anna looked at Caroline. "But if you want to teach someone, you should teach Caroline. She's scared to death of horses."

"Is that so, Caroline? Well, then, I'll just have to teach you myself." Nathan smiled at Anna.

"Emily! Where's our dinner?" Thornston screamed. "A man could starve to death before he gets served around here!"

Within minutes, four servants had emerged from the kitchen with platters of food—roast chicken, sweet potatos, blackeye peas, corn, green beans, biscuits, gravy, and sweet potato soup. While the servants milled about serving the guests, Richard Thornston rambled on about the scarcity of good food and the prices he had to pay to obtain it. He talked about his shipping empire and the fact that his ships traveled around the world and took supplies, materials, and books to places that had never had access to such things before.

"What about the hands who work on your ship, Richard? How old are they usually?" Nathan asked.

"They range in age from fourteen to forty. We have

279

men who love the sea and will stay on it no matter what. We have others who are sick their first day out."

"How long are your cabin boys usually on the ship?"

"Why are you so interested?"

Nathan shrugged. "One of the boys who works for me has a romantic notion of the sea. He wants to become a cabin boy on a large ship that sails around the world. I just want him to know what he's getting into."

"It's a hard life, especially for the young ones. They have to do the dirty work, the work the older, more experienced deck hands don't want to do. They get pushed around a lot and they get lonely because they don't have anyone to talk to. It's not a good life for a boy."

"Have you ever known any boys who've done it for long?" Nathan persisted.

"Yes, I knew one. He was a good boy. He worked hard. He even saved my live in a storm. I tried to help him out when we came to shore. I even got him a job, but he proved to be ungrateful. He was a liar and a thief. I suppose it was all those years spent on the ship."

Nathan clenched his jaw. He downed his glass of wine and poured another, looking at Anna. She was staring at him strangely. Did she know about Roberto's past? Did Roberto trust her enough to tell her? He couldn't tell.

"So, tell me, where did you two ladies walk today?" Thornston looked at Anna and Molly.

Anna leaned forward, looking down the table past Garrett to Molly. She saw Molly was at a loss for words; she didn't know what, if anything, Molly had told Thornston. "We walked around the estate. It's really lovely."

"I just wondered where you walked, because none of my gardeners saw you."

"Well, we—"

"We went into the woods," Anna interrupted Molly. "It was really quite frightening. The ground was very soft and there were huge bugs everywhere." Anna decided to play the role for Thornston. "I swear there was an alligator running after us, wasn't there, Danielle?"

"Yes, a huge alligator. I know it was going to eat us."

"Now, now, ladies, I think you let your imaginations run away with you. The 'gators don't eat people, but they have been known to wander around a bit. I suggest you stay on the grounds of the estate next time. Leave the forests to the 'gators and snakes."

Anna breathed a sigh of relief. Thornston seemed placated. In fact, he seemed to be geniunely enjoying her company this evening. She couldn't figure him out.

"Anna is full of little surprises. I bet she is a handful. I feel sorry for that husband of hers." Caroline giggled.

"My husband likes a woman with spirit, Caroline. It brings excitement to his life." She looked at Nathan.

"I bet it does," Nathan muttered. "I bet he can hardly stand to have you out of his sight."

"As a matter of fact, he's quite willing to share me with other people. He's not possessive. He likes to see me have friends. Whatever I do makes him happy."

"You are lucky," Caroline said, waving her lace fan in front of her cheeks, "but I would rather my husband be jealous. That way I know he cares."

"How can you equate jealousy with love, Caroline? They are two different emotions."

"Much like love and hate, wouldn't you say?" Nathan sipped at his wine. "Let's say you start out hating someone, but the more you're with them, you learn to love them. Your hate turns into love. Does that make sense to you, Mrs. Hawkins?"

"Perfect sense, Mr. Fortier." Anna lifted her glass to Nathan and downed the contents. She was growing tired of the games. "If you don't mind, Mr. Thornston, I'd like to take a little walk around the gardens before we have dessert."

Thornston leaned forward. "Didn't get enough of a walk today, eh?" He laughed.

"I promise I'll stay in the gardens. Excuse me." She stood up.

"If you don't mind, I think I'll join Mrs. Hawkins," Garrett said. "Do you want to join me, dear?"

"No, you go ahead," Molly said. "I'm sure you and Mrs. Hawkins can find something to talk about."

Anna walked out the front of the house, down the gallery stairs and around the corner by the fountain. She crossed her arms in front of her, tapping her foot on the ground. Garrett stopped behind her. "Well?" she said angrily.

"Well, what?"

Anna punched Garrett in the chest. "You're insufferable. You haven't changed a bit. You three are in Richard Thornston's house, you're in New Orleans for Godknows how long, and none of you tries to get in touch with me. Why, Garrett?"

"I think it's up to Nathan to tell you that."

She looked toward the house. "I think Nathan's too busy right now."

"Didn't you just give a lecture about jealousy?"

"Oh, shut up!" She walked around the fountain, stooping to pick up little stones.

"I don't think they'll skip very well in there."

"Leave me alone."

"Anna"—Garrett put his hands on her shoulders—"I'm your friend. That will never change."

"Then why didn't you tell me you were here?"

"What would it have changed? Would you have gone to Nathan?"

"Of course I would have."

"Annie, this is me, remember?" Garrett tilted Anna's face up in the torchlight. "You never could lie to me."

Anna leaned forward and wrapped her arms around

Garrett. She closed her eyes and laid her head on his chest. He felt just as good as he always had. That hadn't changed. There was a certain comfort she could find in his arms that she couldn't find in anyone else's. "You'll always be a part of me, Garrett. You know that, don't you?"

"Just like you'll always be a part of me. I guess we're like old baggage that you can't bear to part with; you always want to take it with you."

Anna began to cry suddenly; her brave front dissolved while in Garrett's arms. She knew he wouldn't make fun of her; he wouldn't ask her to be strong; he wouldn't demand that she be his lover; he would only want her to be herself.

"It's all right, Annie. You go ahead and cry." Garrett rubbed Anna's back, holding her tightly. "Remember the first time I held you like this?"

"No," Anna replied softly, still holding on to her friend.

"Some of the girls at school made fun of your dress; it was a red dress, I think. They said you looked like a skinny old Indian squaw. Well, after you proceeded to beat the tar out of all three of them, I found you under the oaks by the stream. You were crying your eyes out. I asked you what was wrong and you couldn't talk. You just kept crying. I couldn't stand to see you so upset, so I did what any gallant twelve-year-old would do; I took you in my arms and held you while you cried."

Anna stood back, wiping the tears from her cheeks. "You did that a lot of times as I recall. I was more trouble than I was worth."

"Never. Life would've been dull without you."

"Aeneva made that red dress. She had to burn the one she found me in because of the cholera. I was so proud of that dress. When those girls made fun of me, it was as if they were making fun of Aeneva, and I couldn't stand it. I

283

couldn't stand the thought that someone would hurt someone I love."

"I feel the same way." Garrett took Anna's hands in his. "Has Roberto hurt you?"

"No!" Anna answered quickly. "He's done nothing to hurt me. He's a good man, Garrett."

"You can leave him right now. We can leave this place tonight. You'll never have to see him again."

"I can't do that."

"Why, Annie?"

"I just can't."

"Explain it to me."

"He needs my help, and I won't leave him until I make sure that he is all right."

"Even though you might hurt Nathan in the process?"

"Nathan looks fine."

"Stop being so childish; it doesn't become you."

Anna gave Garrett an angry look. "What do you want from me? I was taken against my will, I've been away from my home and the man I love for almost five months, and—"

"And what? If you've missed Nathan so much, why aren't you in his arms right now?"

"I told you why. Roberto needs my help." She shook her head in frustration. "I don't expect you to understand, Garrett. I know it seems strange, but I've gotten to know 'Berto. He's been through so much, and I want more than anything for him and Nathan to be close again. But I can't risk anything right now. If he thinks I've gone back to Nathan he'll never trust me again. He has to know that I'm on his side."

"Why you? Why did you have to be in the middle of this?"

"Because it was meant to be."

"What does that mean?"

"It means that Aeneva wanted it this way. She led

284

Roberto back home, knowing that somehow we would all be together again."

"That's nonsense."

"You think it's nonsense; I don't." She kicked at the rocks on the ground. "So, tell me about Molly."

"I hear you two had quite a time today."

"Yes, we sure did. I have to admit, I haven't had that much fun in a long time. She's wonderful, Garrett."

"I know." He stood up and went to Anna. "I'm going to ask her to marry me, Annie."

"Garrett." Anna reached up and lovingly touched Garrett's cheek. "You don't need my permission."

"I know I don't need your permission. I just wanted to be the one to tell you."

"I'm happy for you. I truly am. Since I can't have you, I'm glad Molly will."

"You could've had me anytime, and you know it."

"It's strange, isn't it?"

"What?"

"How things turn out sometimes. Do you ever wonder how things would've turned out if we had gotten married?"

"All the time."

"It would have been easier on all of us."

"It wouldn't have been easy on me; I can tell you that."

"That's not fair."

"It was meant to be, you know. You and Nate belong together. That's the way it's supposed to be."

"And when did you and Nathan become such fast friends?"

"When he told me what happened to you."

"Thank you for coming, Garrett. I feel better already, knowing that you're here."

"What about Nathan?"

"I don't know. I'm confused. I don't like seeing him

285

with Caroline, either."

"Jealous?"

"It has nothing to do with jealousy. She's very strange, Garrett. Ask Molly."

"I know, she told me. Don't worry about Nate, he can take care of himself. I think he's just trying to cozy up to her to find out what he can."

"About what?"

"About his brother. He cares too, Annie."

"You two gonna stand out here all night?" Molly walked up to Garrett and Anna. "Well, I'm glad the truth finally came out. I was about to bust a gut today, girl. I wanted to tell you the truth so badly, I could almost spit."

"It's all right, Molly. You did what you had to do."

"So did you."

"What do you mean?"

"Your husband in Baton Rouge? That's a good one."

Anna kicked at the ground again. "I couldn't let Thornston know that Roberto's here."

"Well, he won't know from us." Molly put her arm through Garrett's. "They're expecting us inside now. Miss Caroline is ready to serve dessert. She seems to have her sights set on Nathan."

"I just told Anna that Nate can take care of himself." Garrett offered his arms to Anna and Molly. "Let's go inside."

They went into the sitting room, where Caroline was fussing over Nathan and Thornston was sipping brandy.

"Well, there you are. I thought we were going to lose you again, Mrs. Hawkins."

"No, I was just enjoying the garden and the smell of that jasmine. We don't have anything like that out West."

"That's my favorite flower," Caroline said. "I love flowers. I have them all over my room."

Anna and Molly exchanged puzzled glances. Didn't Caroline remember that she had shown them her room just that afternoon?

"Would you like some coffee, Anna?"

"Yes, please."

"Anything in it?"

"Cream and sugar," Nathan responded without realizing it. He froze, his eyes locking with Anna's. "You look like the kind of woman who would take cream and sugar in her coffee."

"What a lucky guess, Mr. Fortier." Anna graciously accepted the coffee.

"What about you, Danielle?"

"Please. Black."

"Well, Etienne, you haven't told us. Is there a woman in your life?" Richard Thornston asked while swirling the brandy around in his glass.

"Yes, there is a woman in my life."

"Are you serious about her?" Caroline seemed disappointed.

"Yes, I'm very serious about her." Nathan stared at Anna over the rim of his coffee cup. "As soon as I get back to Arizona, I'm going to marry her."

"Well, tell us about her," urged Thornston. "What's her name?"

Nathan set his coffee cup down on the saucer. "Her name is Kathleen O'Leary. She is beautiful, she is strong, she is sometimes too willful, but she is generous of heart and spirit. I can't imagine loving anyone more than I love her." His eyes willed Anna's to meet his and to understand the depth of feeling that was in them.

Anna met Nathan's eyes. She wanted more than anything to be with him. She wanted him to hold her, to kiss her, to talk to her. She just wanted to be with him and stop playing these silly games. She didn't think she had ever loved him more than she did right now. His words had touched her deeply. "She sounds like a lucky woman," Anna said softly, trying to control her tremulous voice.

"No, on the contrary. I'm the lucky one."

"Well, congratulations, Etienne. You will have to bring your wife back here for a visit sometime. We'd love to meet her."

"Thank you."

Garrett stood up, taking Molly's arm. "Well, we're going to head up to bed now. It's been a long day."

"But—" Molly started to protest, but she put her cup down. "Yes, it has been a long day. I'll leave a nightgown on your bed for you, Anna."

"Thank you."

"Goodnight."

Anna sat quietly, watching as Caroline fussed over Nathan, acting as if she'd never heard that he loved another woman. Anna tried to carry on a conversation with Richard Thornston, but she decided she couldn't do it. She couldn't stay in the same room with Nathan and watch him with another woman. It had been too long without him, and she wanted to be alone with him. She stood up. "Thank you for the lovely dinner. I'm feeling rather tired myself. If you don't mind, I'm going to go on up to bed."

Richard Thornston stood up. "Why don't I walk you. I'm sure Caroline and Etienne have things they'd like to talk about."

Anna nodded, glancing once more at Nathan as she walked out of the room. Maybe she should go back to Roberto, she thought. Maybe it would be easier than staying in this place, so close to Nathan and yet as far apart as they had ever been.

"You're very quiet this evening, Mrs. Hawkins. Is there anything wrong?"

"No, I'm just a bit tired, I suppose. All this fresh air."

"I'd think you'd be used to fresh air, what with you being a woman from the West."

"The air is different here."

"Yes, it is. Some people say it makes a person crazy." He held out his arm as they reached the staircase. "You best take my arm. These stairs are quite tiresome."

"Thank you." Anna took Thornston's arm, totally confused by his demeanor. She decided to take a chance. "Mr. Thornston, what exactly is wrong with Caroline?"

Thornston stopped for a moment, then continued walking up the staircase. "Caroline lost her mother when she was just a young girl. They were very close. They were almost like sisters. She never quite recovered from that loss. I've taken her to several doctors. They say she suffers from something called 'melancholia.' It means she's sad all the time and we don't know quite what to do about it."

"I'm so sorry. I didn't realize."

They reached the top of the staircase and Thornston stopped. "That's why I overreacted when I saw the two of you outside the other day. It frightened me. The last time Caroline was outside by herself she found a pair of gardener's shears and tried to stab herself with them."

"Oh, God."

"So, you see, I'm very protective of her. You might think that a bit strange, but I love her and I'm doing what I think is best for her."

Anna couldn't believe this was the same man who earlier in the day was talking to a cabinet full of dolls. But who knew why he acted as he did? Perhaps Caroline had driven him wild with anxiety and fear. "Is there anything I can do, Mr. Thornston?"

"Actually, I've been thinking on it, and I suppose it wouldn't hurt if Caroline went outside tomorrow. Perhaps you and Mr. Rondieux could take her on a little walk around the grounds. I think the fresh air would do her good."

"If you think it would be all right."

"I don't see how she could do herself any harm if she's with you two." Thornston walked Anna to her room and stopped. "I'm glad you'll be staying with us, Mrs. Hawkins. I'm looking forward to getting to know you better."

"Please, call me Anna."

Thornston nodded. "All right Anna. Sleep well."

"Goodnight." Anna opened the door and walked inside. Molly was sitting on the bed. "What are you doing here?"

"I hate to bring up a bad subject, but have you forgotten anything?"

"What?"

"The doll room, remember?"

"My God, I forgot all about it." Anna shook her head. "Molly, we have to get that room back the way it was. He just started talking to me. If he suspects that I was in that room . . ."

Molly nodded. "Say no more. I have our key right here." She held a hairpin in her hand. "Shall we?" She regarded Anna for a moment. "Wait a minute. I think it would be a good idea if you took off your shoes. Might be a bit loud at night."

Anna hastily undid her shoes and slipped them off. "What about Garrett?"

"I told him we were going to catch up on some girl talk."

Anna opened the door and looked out. No one was there. She and Molly hurried down the hallway and out to the open staircase. They looked down to make sure no one was coming up, and then hurried across the landing to the other hallway. They had started down when they heard a noise.

"What room is that?"

290

"I don't know. I think it's Thornston's study or something," Molly replied. "Let's get closer to see what he's doing."

They walked slowly up to the door, which was slightly ajar. Molly peeked around. Thornston was going through some papers on his desk, a crystal decanter and glass on the desk next to him, his head down. Molly quickly walked by the door. Anna looked inside, made sure Thornston wasn't looking, then moved across the doorway. They ran quietly down the hall, their stocking feet making no noise on the wooden floors. When they reached the doorway at the end of the hall, Molly turned the handle and opened it just a bit. There was a slight creak. They both looked down the hall toward Thornston's study and decided not to wait to see if he would come out, then squeezed through the opening, shut the door, and climbed the stairs. Anna went to Robert's door and put her head against it. It was quiet, and she waved Molly to the other room.

Molly knelt down and this time opened the lock in seconds. "Practice," she whispered to Anna, a sly grin on her face.

"Will it lock if we shut it?"

"Only if someone comes along and locks it like Thornston did."

"All right." They went inside and shut the door. "There's no lamp in here," Anna said. She walked to the window, carefully avoiding the toys on the floor. The moonlight shone through the window and provided them with enough light to see. "The moon will have to do." The rocking horse was pulled up against the window where their weight had pulled it off the floor. Anna set it on the floor and pulled the rope up from the side of the house, shutting the window. "These knots are impossible to untie."

"They better not be." Molly worked on the ones that

tied the ropes together, while Anna worked on untying the rope from the horse. Molly managed to untie her ropes and then helped Anna. When they finished untying the knots, Molly picked up the panels of velvet curtains. "Good God, these things are heavy. Just how in the hell are we going to get these things up there?"

"I don't know. There must be something to stand on."

"If you're going to tell me to get on that damned rocking horse—"

"No, it's not high enough. What about the windowsill?"

"What about it?"

"I'll do it." Anna grabbed the sides of the window frame and pulled herself up to the windowsill. She was able to reach the top of the window. "Hand me that pole."

Molly held the heavy brass pole up to Anna. "Just how are you going to get that thing up there?"

"Maybe if you helped me, I could do it."

"I should've known the first time I laid eyes on you, you were trouble."

"Come on, Molly, he might come up here tonight."

Molly handed one end of the pole to Anna while she stepped onto the rocking horse. Anna braced the horse with her foot until Molly stepped onto the windowsill. She grabbed hold next to Anna, then took the middle of the pole and raised it. "All right, now we have to get it in that little holder."

"No, first we have to slip the curtains on."

"Oh, wonderful. This has to be as difficult as possible."

"I'll get them and hand them up to you." Anna climbed down from the windowsill and picked up the heavy curtains, feeding them to Molly, while Molly pushed them onto the pole. When the curtains were on, Anna climbed back up onto the sill and took the other end of the pole. "All right, let's push it up." They stretched as far as they could, pushing the thick, heavy pole into its holder. "We've done it."

"Thank God," said Molly.

Anna stepped down from the sill, ready to pull the rocking horse away, when she saw the rope pulls. "Don't get down yet, Molly. We forgot the pulls."

"Of course, we did. Anything else we've forgotten?"

Anna draped the ropes over her shoulder and climbed back up on the sill. "How do these go? Do you remember?"

"You expect me to know about these things?"

"Let's just tie them at each end of the pole."

"And if that's not how they go?"

"Do you actually think Thornston is going to notice the curtains when he comes to visit this room? He'll be visiting with his friends over there. Let's just tie the things on and get out of here." They quickly tied the ropes on the ends of the pole and again, reached up and pushed the pole back into place. They smoothed the curtains as much as they could before climbing down from the sill. "I wish I could see what they look like."

"God, Anna, we don't have time for that. Maybe we can come back up here tomorrow and check. Right now, we've got to get out of here."

"Wait, where's that piece of metal I used to unjam the window?"

"It's right here," Molly said, picking up the metal track and putting it back where it belonged.

Anna dragged the rocking horse back to its place and looked around. "I hope we didn't leave anything too obvious."

"As you said, the man will have better things to do. Come on."

Molly opened the door and looked out. There wasn't a sound. Molly quickly relocked the door and they hurried down the stairs.

Molly opened the door to the second floor and looked out. The hallway was clear and the door to Thornston's study was only slightly ajar. Molly walked out and Anna followed, closing the door behind her. As they got closer to Thornston's study, they could hear voices.

"He's just dreamy, isn't he, daddy?"

"Yes, he is, Caroline."

"Did I do good tonight?"

"Yes, you were a good girl."

"I won't be punished?" Caroline sounded like a little girl.

"As long as you take your medicine and do as I tell you, I won't punish you."

"Thank you, daddy."

Anna glanced at Molly, an incredulous look on her face. Molly shook her head in disgust. They inched closer to the study, staying close to the wall.

"What about LeBeau, daddy?"

"What about him?"

"Will he be upset if he knows I'm seeing another man?"

Thornston laughed derisively. "Don't flatter yourself, Caroline. LeBeau is in this for the money."

"But LeBeau is a friend. He is even willing to marry me and take care of Robert."

"Caroline, we have to talk about the baby."

"What, daddy?"

"I think it's time we found a home for him."

"But he has a home here, with me."

"You hardly give that boy the time of day. You're not a fit mother, Caroline. You really should be thinking about him. He can't stay locked up in that room for the rest of his life."

"But you promised, daddy."

"I said you could keep him here until you were on your feet and feeling better. That time has come. Now, I've

294

taken it upon myself to look into this matter. I know a couple. They're quite wealthy, and they can't have children. They'll pay a sizeable amount to have a child of their own."

"I don't care about the money. He's my son."

"He's also the son of that half-breed."

"Don't talk about Roberto that way. He was the most wonderful man I've ever known in my life."

"But that's over now. You have more important things to think about."

"I know. I think Etienne likes me."

"Make sure he likes you."

Molly looked through the crack and, before she could say a word, she took Anna's hand, pulling her behind her as she ran past the study. They looked back once, and then turned the corner, coming out to the landing above the staircase. Stopping only to see if anyone was on the stairs, they quickly ran past the staircase and into the hallway on the other side of the house. Once in front of Anna's room, Molly opened the door and they ran in. Molly looked out once more before shutting the door.

"Well, I think I've had my share of excitement for the day. You sure do manage to get yourself into trouble, girl."

Anna walked across the room and threw herself across the bed, resting her chin in her hands. "As I recall, you were just as anxious to get a look at the room. You probably would've looked around the corner of the screen if I hadn't held onto you."

Molly sat down on the bed. "How long have I know you—one day? I've had more trouble today than I have in my entire life."

Anna shoved Molly. "Why don't you tell the truth? You loved every bit of it. You're just like I am, Molly. You can't resist temptation."

Molly shrugged. "Maybe." She crinkled her nose.

"Did you hear the way Caroline was talking? It didn't make any sense. I'd watch out for her if I were you, Anna."

"Why me?"

"Because if she finds out you're the woman Nathan is in love with, there's no telling what she'll do."

"Caroline wouldn't hurt anyone. She's harmless."

"I wouldn't be so sure. And Thornston, he treats her horribly. I don't trust either one of them."

"Neither do I."

Molly rubbed her stomach. "God, I'm starving. What I wouldn't give for a thick steak."

"And fried potatoes."

"And a good glass of beer."

Anna hit Molly on the arm and laughed. "I'm so glad I met you, Molly."

"It doesn't bother you that I'm with Garrett? We're not even married, you know."

"Who am I to judge? I'm married to my lover's brother, I've been in love with my best friend and my lover at the same time, and I was kept captive on a slave ship. I wouldn't say I've had the kind of life that most church-going people would aspire to."

"You didn't answer my question."

"I love Garrett; I always will. He'll always be a part of me. But I love Nathan in a different way. I want to spend the rest of my life with Nathan. I want to have his children. So, if I can't have Garrett, I'm glad you do."

"Good, because it wouldn't have mattered, anyway." Molly laughed again. "Anna, I'm serious about Caroline. She's a strange one. She's talking about marrying Nathan and she's only known him one day. Can you imagine?"

"Yes. I fell in love with Nathan the first time I looked at him. I think he knew it, too."

"Just be careful."

"You're beginning to sound like my mother, Molly."

"Just think of me as a big sister." Molly stood up. "I'd better get to my room or Garrett is going to start asking questions. If he finds out that we were in that room again, he'll kill us both."

"Just remind him of all the things he and I used to do that we weren't supposed to do."

"Anna."

"What?"

"I truly am sorry for lying to you today. I didn't want to. I knew before I even met you that I was going to like you. I figured any woman who could have two men like Nathan and Garrett in love with her, must be someone very special."

"There's nothing to be sorry about. Besides, look at all the fun we had." Anna stood up. "Thank you, Molly. Now get back to Garrett. I'll see you tomorrow."

"Lock the door."

"I will. Goodnight." Anna locked the door after Molly left, and turned out the lamp. Moonlight filled the room, casting an iridescent glow. She quickly stripped off her clothes and put on the nightgown that Molly had given her. She took the pins out of her hair and shook it free. She ran her fingers through it until it fell around her shoulders. She turned down the covers and lay on the bed, reaching under the mattress to make sure the derringer was still in place, feeling the cold metal when she touched the gun. She lay on the bed, breathing deeply. It was hot and humid, and it felt as if there was no air at all in the room. She got up and walked to the double glass doors that led to the balcony. As soon as she opened them, the overpowering smell of jasmine filled the room. She walked out on the balcony and leaned on the railing. A slight breeze blew the thin satin nightgown around her and she closed her eyes and breathed deeply.

"I'd almost forgotten how beautiful you really are."

Anna gasped in alarm and turned to look into the

shadows of the balcony. "Nathan?"

Nathan stepped out of the shadows and into the moonlight. "You look like a dream." He touched her cheek, brushing back strands of hair that the breeze blew into her face. "You smell wonderful."

"It's the jasmine," Anna said unconvincingly, closing her eyes and rubbing her cheek against Nathan's hand.

"I don't think so." Nathan put his finger on Anna's lips, brushing it gently across them and tracing the line of her jaw and neck. He put his hand behind her head and pulled her close.

"You shouldn't be here."

"Where should I be?"

"Caroline is very interested in you."

"Caroline's not my type. Too frail."

"It's dangerous."

"When has that ever stopped us?" He moved forward, pressing his body against hers, his mouth touching hers lightly, enticingly. "I've missed you, Anna."

Anna put her hands on Nathan's chest, her mouth seeking his in the moonlight. "I've missed you, too." She pressed her mouth against his, eager to accept his kisses. "Oh, God," she sighed, pulling away.

"What's the matter?"

"We can't do this."

"I love you, Anna. I want to marry you."

"Nathan, listen to me. If Caroline finds out that you've been with me, there's no telling what she'll do."

"Are you afraid of Caroline?"

"I'm afraid she might hurt Roberto's son."

Nathan tensed up, dropping his arms from Anna. "How is my dear brother, anyway?"

"He needs our help. You don't know what he's been through."

"I know it all, Anna. That still didn't give him the right to take you away from me."

"I agree, but that's over now. He just wants to get his son. He doesn't want to hurt you or me anymore."

"I wouldn't be so sure of that if I were you. How do you suppose he would react if he found us together?"

Anna pulled completely away. She knew the answer to that question: Roberto would never trust her again. "I've earned his trust, Nathan. I can't lose it now."

"You've earned his trust? Shouldn't it be the other way around?"

"You don't understand."

"Explain it to me."

"He's been alone since he was eleven years old, cut off from everyone and everything he ever loved. At least you had Chin; Roberto had no one. He was locked up on a ship, a virtual slave for eight years. Then he saved Richard Thornston's life."

"I know all about it. He came here, worked with Thornston, and fell in love with Caroline."

"And because he fell in love with Caroline, Thornston wanted him out of his daughter's life."

"It can't be that simple, Anna. Thornston seems more than willing to let Caroline lavish her affections on me. Roberto and I aren't that different."

Anna shook her head. "I can't believe you just said that. You do know where we are, don't you, Nathan? This is the South, the place where white people discriminate against people with dark skin, even people like Roberto. You and Roberto aren't alike. The only two things you have in common are your parents and your love for each other."

"And you."

"Nathan, listen to me. He's your brother. How many times have you told me you'd give anything to have him back? Well, now is your chance. He needs your help. He's been hurt so badly. When he thought he'd found love again, it was taken from him. Thornston didn't even give him a chance to defend himself, and Caroline didn't defend him either. She agreed that Roberto had raped her. After Thornston had beaten him, his men threw him in the swamp to die."

"What do you want me to do, Anna? Do you want me to go to Roberto and tell him that I forgive him for almost ruining my life and yours? What if I'd never found you? That's what scares me. I almost think you would've stayed with him."

Anna grabbed Nathan's arms. "That's not true. I just want to help him."

"What about me, Anna? Have you thought about me? Have you ever once wondered what I thought when I woke up and Clare told me that you had run off and married my brother?" He shook his head. "I still can't believe you're married to him."

"I didn't have a choice, Nathan. He told me he'd kill you if I didn't marry him."

"I'm sure you could've found a way to get out of it."

"He had the medicine."

"What are you talking about?" Nathan's voice rose in anger. "Why are you making excuses for him?"

"I'm not making excuses for him. I'm trying to explain to you why I left." She closed her eyes and took a deep breath. "I knew the only thing that could save you was Aeneva's medicine, but I couldn't find it. So I went to her scaffolding because I thought that's where you might have put it. Roberto had already been there. He had the medicine. He told me if I wanted to save you, I had to marry him."

"That's crazy."

"I'm not making this up."

"Why would he want you to marry him?"

"To hurt you."

"But why? What did I do to him?"

"It's what he thinks, or thought you did to him. He

300

can't remember that night in San Francisco. All he knew was that he was suddenly alone. Then there was hope for him when he saved Thornston, but after Thornston treated him so badly there was no hope left for him. The only thing he had left was home. He went back to Arizona."

"Why didn't he come back to the ranch? I don't understand."

"He went to see Clare. He wanted to find out what had happened to you and he knew Clare would know."

"And Clare told him everything except that I had been gone for ten years. He probably thinks I was at the ranch all this time." Nathan shook his head. "That sounds like Clare."

"He knows what really happened, because I told him. He remembered the cockfight and you fighting with Driscoll, but he doesn't remember anything after that."

"So he knows I was gone? Did you tell him everything?"

"Yes, I told him that you blamed yourself for his supposed death."

"What did he say?"

"He didn't believe me."

"God, this is crazy. We've both been through so much, yet we're against each other."

Anna took Nathan's hand. "That's why I want to help him, Nathan. I want to help you both."

Nathan put his arms around Anna. "I want to help him, Anna. He's my brother. But I don't want to lose you again."

"You'll never lose me, Nathan." Anna pressed her mouth against Nathan's. "I love you. I'll never stop loving you."

Nathan swept Anna into his arms and carried her to the bed. He put her down and stood over her, his silhouette outlined by the moonlight. He took off his

301

shirt and lay on the bed next to Anna, touching her face. "You are so beautiful." He kissed her passionately, his body hard against hers.

Anna put her arms around his neck. "I've missed you so much. I never thought I could be so lonely."

"At least you had Roberto," Nathan said teasingly, kissing her neck.

"That's not funny, Nathan." Anna pushed him away.

"I was only teasing you."

"Then why did you say it?"

Nathan sat up. "Jesus, we can't be around each other five minutes without fighting. Maybe we don't belong together."

"Maybe you're right. Maybe you'd be better off with someone like Caroline. I'm sure she'd love to do anything you tell her to do."

"At least she'd listen."

"I'm not a pet that you bark orders to, Nathan." Anna stood up. "Maybe you should leave."

"If I leave now, I won't be back."

"We can't seem to get along, so maybe that's best. Maybe you're right." Anna walked back out to the balcony, shaking in spite of the heat.

"You're being childish, Anna."

"And you're not? You want me to forget everything that Roberto has been through, and just ride away with you?"

Nathan grabbed Anna. "Why not? We deserve to be happy. I love you; isn't that enough?"

"What about your brother? Can you really be happy knowing you didn't help him?"

"He kidnapped you, for Christ's sake! Why do you keep forgetting that?"

"I haven't forgotten it."

"Then what is it?" Nathan looked at Anna in the moonlight. "Is there something else between you and

Roberto? Have you fallen in love with him?"

Anna pulled away. "Of course I haven't fallen in love with him. Can't I have a genuine affection for a man without being in love with him?"

"You tell me."

"You're being cruel, and I don't deserve it." Anna held onto the railing. She felt the tears well up in her eyes. Why did it have to be this way between them?

"You're right. You don't deserve it." Nathan's voice softened. "I know that you loved Garrett as a friend and I know that you probably feel the same way about my brother. Still, he's been with you for five months. I haven't."

"But you have been with me." Anna put her arms around his waist. "Whenever I was scared, or lonely, or I felt like I wouldn't make it, you were there with me."

"You can't expect me to forget what Roberto's done, Anna. I can't do it."

"I don't expect you to forget anything. I'm just asking you to remember that he's your brother and he needs your help." She looked up at him. "What would Aeneva and Trenton want you to do? What did Trenton do when he was faced with helping Roberto's father?"

Nathan shook his head. "I'm not my father, Anna. I never will be."

"But you're as good a man as he was."

"I don't know if I am or not."

"Then why did you come here?"

"Why do you think I came here? I came here for you."

"If that's true, you could've gotten me away from Roberto anytime. Instead, you waited. Why?"

"Because it was safer this way."

"I don't believe you."

"What do you want from me?" Nathan walked to the corner of the balcony and looked out over the estate. "I couldn't help Roberto ten years ago; what makes you think I can help him now?"

Anna walked to him. "On the outside, Roberto is a man, but on the inside he is still just an eleven-year-old boy who needs his family."

"You really believe that?"

"I know it. He tries to hate you but he can't. Every once in a while he'll slip and start talking about you."

"What does he say?"

"I was skipping a stone one day, and he bet me he could skip one farther than I could."

"And of course you bet him."

"Of course."

"Who won?"

"He did. He said he had the best teacher there was. You. He said you could skip a stone farther than anyone he'd ever seen."

"So, he does remember some things."

"He remembers a lot, even though he tries to act as if it doesn't mean anything. He says he caught you and Clare out behind her father's barn and that you chased him all the way home and beat him up."

"I did." Nathan nodded, smiling. "He was always around when I didn't want him to be, but he was tough. Did he tell you about the time he got beaten up by some boys who called him and his family a bunch of half-breeds?"

"No, he didn't say anything about it."

"He was about eight and I was fourteen. I saw him on the way home from school, sitting by the oaks. He was a mess, all dirty and bloody. I cleaned him up and asked him what happened. He wouldn't tell me. I kept bothering him until he finally told me, and then he started to cry. I put my arm around him and told him it didn't matter what people said about him; it was what he thought that mattered." Nathan looked at Anna, a gentle look on his face. "Do you know what he said? He said he didn't care what people said about him, but he didn't want anybody talking about his parents and brother that way. I'll never forget that."

"What happened to the boys who beat him up?"

"What makes you think anything happened to them?"

"I know you, Nathan."

Nathan shrugged. "It was a strange thing. Somehow they managed to get themselves locked up in an outhouse overnight."

"Were they all right in the morning?"

"They were fine. Didn't smell too good, but they were fine. And they never touched 'Berto again."

"Nathan—" Anna turned at the sound of a knock on the door. "Who could that be?"

"Shut the doors and go on in. I'll wait out here."

Anna closed the glass doors and walked across the room, unlocking the door and opening it slightly. "Who is it?"

"It's me, Anna. I must talk to you." Caroline pushed open the door and walked in, slamming the door behind her. She turned up the wall lamp. "Have you seen Etienne?"

Anna looked at Caroline; her mood had changed radically again. "Why would I see Etienne? I don't even know him."

Caroline walked across the room, her pale eyes narrowed. "Don't give me that. I saw the way he looked at you."

"What are you talking about, Caroline? You're crazy."

"Don't you ever say that!" Caroline came at Anna, hitting her furiously.

Anna held up her hands and grabbed a handful of Caroline's hair. "Stop it, Caroline. I want you to settle down right now."

Caroline looked around the room. "He's been here; I

305

can tell."

"Caroline, you hardly know the man. Why are you acting like this?"

"I'm in love with him!" She knocked Anna's hand away. "He's going to be my husband."

Anna glanced at the balcony, wondering if Nathan could hear Caroline's ravings. "I think you should relax, Caroline. You're upset for no reason."

"Don't you think I know the kind of woman you are? I see the way LeBeau looks at you, and Etienne, and even Henri. You're bad, Anna. I knew it from the first time I laid eyes on you."

"What do you want me to do, Caroline? Do you want me to leave?"

"I think that would be best."

"I have a question to ask you first." Anna walked closer to Caroline, not letting the girl intimidate her. "Did you ever love Roberto?"

Caroline's eyes looked suddenly dazed. "What do you know about Roberto?"

"I know that he loved you very much and you let him suffer because of it."

"How do you know about us?"

"I know everything about you, Caroline, and I don't like you very much." Anna regarded Caroline with a quizzical expression. "At first I thought you were crazy; now I'm beginning to wonder. Maybe you just pretend to be crazy so you can do anything you want."

"I think you're the one who's crazy."

"We'll see."

"My father is one of the most influential men in the South. He can make your life miserable."

"Is that supposed to frighten me?"

"You'd be stupid not to be afraid of Richard Thornston."

"Listen to me, Caroline. Neither you nor your father

306

scare me. As a matter of fact, I'm rather looking forward to what's going to happen."

"What are you talking about?"

"You'll just have to wait and see, won't you?" Anna walked to the door and held it open. "Unless you plan to kick me out tonight, please leave my room. Now."

Caroline's eyes narrowed in a deadly gaze. "You're going to regret this, Anna. You'll be sorry you crossed me."

"I was right, wasn't I, Caroline? You aren't crazy at all."

Caroline stomped out of the room. Anna slammed the door behind her.

Nathan opened the balcony doors and came inside. "Are you sure you should have done that?"

"Done what? I stood up to her. I'll be damned if I'll let her intimidate me. I had a feeling she wasn't as frail as she led everyone to believe. But what I can't figure out is why she acts like she does."

"I think you're right; she's too unpredictable. Stay away from her, Anna." He put his hands on her shoulders. "In fact, I think it would be best if you went back to town."

"I'm not going back to town. I'm close to something here; I can feel it."

"What are you talking about?"

"There's something strange going on in this house."

"Caroline has a child out of wedlock and they're trying to keep him hidden, that's all."

"No, Nathan, it's more than that. I can feel it."

"Leave it alone, Anna."

"What am I supposed to do?"

"Nothing."

"Nothing? You expect me to stay in this house and do nothing?"

"If you do stay in this house, I'll deal with Caroline."

"I will not stay here and watch you play games with Caroline."

"You don't have a choice. Either you keep quiet and keep your nose out of things, or I'll tell Caroline I don't want you here. She'll listen to me."

"You wouldn't do that."

"Don't push me, Anna. You're more important to me than anything in this world. If I have to get you out of this house to keep you safe, I'll do it."

"Don't bother. I'll go back to Roberto."

"Don't play games with me."

"It seems as if you're the one who's playing the games, Nathan. If you want to be with Caroline, go ahead. But you won't stop me. I'll find out what's going on around here." She turned the doorknob. "I think you should go now."

"You can't be serious."

"I am serious. Until we straighten this thing out, I think it would be best if you leave now." Anna stood by the half-open door.

Nathan walked to the door. He regarded Anna a moment, then put his hand on the door and slammed it shut. "No, Anna, not this time. It's been too long." He pinned her against the wall, his mouth touching hers.

Anna turned her head. "Nathan, don't."

"I want you, Anna." Nathan kissed Anna's throat and neck. "Are you going to tell me you don't want me as much as I want you?" He leaned his body against hers, pressing her against the cold wall. His mouth moved urgently on hers, while his fingers unbuttoned the nightgown.

"Nathan," Anna said breathlessly.

"What, Anna? Do you want me to stop?" His mouth covered hers.

Anna turned her head, putting her hands on Nathan's chest. "I'm confused."

"Why?"

"I don't know."

"Is it Roberto?"

"No, I just—"

Nathan put his fingers over Anna's mouth. "You are my wife, Anna, no matter what that paper of Roberto's says. You are my love." His hands went to her face. "I love you," he said gently. He pushed the nightgown from Anne's shoulders until it fell to the floor. His hands ran from her shoulders down her arms. He caressed her breasts and ran his fingers gently down her stomach and thighs.

"I've missed you so much, Nathan. I love you."

Nathan leaned against Anna, pressing her naked body against the wall, his mouth seeking hers again. Her hands went around his neck and their bodies molded to each other. Nathan lifted Anna in his arms and carried her to the bed. He stood over her, taking off his pants and boots. The smell of night-blooming jasmine wafted through the room and the warm night breeze rustled the curtains against the balcony doors.

Nathan climbed onto the bed next to Anna. "I want you so much," he whispered, his mouth seeking and then finding hers in the moonlight. His hands touched her young body in ways he had never done before, and her soft moans of pleasure drove him wild. His passion rose and with it, his desire to possess Anna in every way possible. Gently, he spread her legs apart. He looked down at her in the soft moonlight, and his desire was all-consuming. Anna opened herself to Nathan and he gave himself to her completely, holding onto her, plunging himself into her softness.

"Nathan," Anna whispered, her mouth devouring his with deep, passionate kisses. "Oh, Nathan," she moaned, digging her nails into his back, "I can't wait any longer."

Nathan responded to the urgency in Anna's voice, and

his love-making because furious. Their bodies moved against each other in a rhythmic dance of passion until their desire exploded in a final burst of loving. Anna cried out; Nathan covered her mouth with his, kissing her until their bodies were spent. "My God, Anna," Nathan whispered, rolling to the side, his arm encircling her. "I could die a happy man right now."

Anna laid her head on Nathan's chest, her arm across his stomach. "I don't think I've ever felt so fulfilled or frightened in my life."

"Why frightened?"

"It's scary to feel so strongly about another person."

"Don't be frightened, Anna. I love you. You're the world to me. My love for you knows no bounds."

Anna smiled. "Whether it's true or not, it sounds beautiful."

"It's true. I want to marry you as soon as this mess is over, and I want to have children with you. Beautiful little girls and strong little boys."

"Just how many girls and boys did you plan on having?"

"As many as we can." Nathan tilted Anna's face up to his, kissing her gently. "All I know is that I love you and I don't ever want to lose you again."

"This will all be over soon. Then we can go home."

"Home. I never thought I'd miss it so much."

"You've got some decisions to make, you know."

He kissed Anna again. "I've made the only decision I want to make."

"You have to decide what you're going to do about Roberto."

"I don't want to talk about him right now."

"But Nathan—"

"No, dammit! Why does he always have to enter into our conversation?"

Anna sat up. "Because he's your brother."

"And that's all?" Nathan stood up, quickly pulling on his pants.

"What are you talking about?"

"Why don't you tell me? You can't seem to get my brother out of your mind, not even after we make love."

"Nathan, don't do this."

Nathan grabbed his shirt and boots. "You know, Anna, tonight was incredible. I never thought I could feel that way about anyone."

Anna got off the bed and picked up her nightgown, slipping it on. "I feel the same way about you, Nathan. Don't you know that? I gave myself to you tonight completely. Doesn't that prove something?"

"It proves that we make incredible love together. Past that, I'm not sure." Nathan walked to the door.

"Nathan, please. I love you. Don't go like this."

Nathan looked at Anna. He gently brushed her cheek with his hand. "We need to sort a lot of things out, Anna. Goodnight."

Anna closed the door. She leaned against it, her eyes filling with tears. "I love you, Nathan. I do love you."

Chapter X

Roberto slammed his fist down on the table. "How could you let her stay out there, LeBeau? I trusted you!"

"Roberto, you know as well as I how stubborn your wife is. She could not be persuaded to leave."

"It's too dangerous for her out there alone."

"She's not alone."

"What do you mean?"

"I suppose you will find out anyway." LeBeau walked over to the desk and poured himself a drink. "Your brother is at Rolling Oaks."

"Nathan is here?"

"Yes, he has been here for weeks."

"And you've known it?"

"Yes, I have known." LeBeau downed his drink. "I am ready now."

"Ready for what?"

"I am ready to die." LeBeau looked at Roberto. "You are planning to kill me, aren't you?"

Roberto walked to the desk and poured himself a drink. He downed it and poured himself another, as well as refilling LeBeau's glass. "Relax, LeBeau, I'm not going to kill you."

"I would not blame you if you did. You entrusted your

wife's safety to me."

"There's nothing we can do about that now. You're right about one thing—if Anna makes up her mind to do something, she does it."

LeBeau lifted his drink to Roberto and then downed it. "What are you planning to do?"

"There isn't anything I can do. Nathan will take Anna and go home."

"No, I don't think so. Your brother is planning to stay here for a while."

"Why?"

"He wants to help you."

"I don't need his help."

"Why is there so much bitterness between you two? You are brothers—that bond can never be broken."

"I don't know my brother anymore."

"He doesn't know you either; yet he is here, is he not?"

Roberto turned to LeBeau. "What do you know of Caroline and her father, LeBeau?"

"He is a ruthless bastard who thinks nothing of hurting other people." LeBeau poured himself another drink. "Thornston took my mother for his mistress when I was just a small boy. My mother was Spanish, very beautiful. Thornston gave her many presents and bought us a fine little house in the city. But one day he thought she was carrying on with another man. And he killed her. He came to our house, went into my mother's room, and stabbed her. I was ten years old. I found her."

Roberto looked at LeBeau. "I'm sorry, LeBeau. It seems I'm not the only one Thornston has hurt." He poured them both another drink. "You know all about me, don't you?"

LeBeau nodded. "Thornston hired me to try to find you."

313

"So, he knows I'm here?"

"No, I didn't tell him anything about you."

"Why?"

"I was there the day you were beaten, Roberto. I saw what he did to you."

"You were there? I don't remember seeing you." He shrugged his shoulders. "But I don't remember much of anything about that day."

"How do you feel about Caroline's part in that?"

"I blamed her for a long time, but Anna seems to think she still loves me, or at least she did."

"Anna is a good person. She sees the best in people."

"What are you saying?"

"Caroline is not as innocent as she appears. I hate to do this to you, Roberto. But you should know the truth about Caroline."

"What is the truth, LeBeau?"

"Caroline is not the woman she used to be. She doesn't seem to be able to feel anymore. Oh, I think she cared for you; she may even have loved you in her own way, but it was icing on the cake for her that you were a half-breed. The only thing that would have made it better would have been if you were one of her father's Negroes."

"You're not serious?"

"I am deadly serious. When I decided that I would get Thornston for what he did to my mother, I thought the best way to do it would be to get to know him and his family. When I first met Caroline, I liked her. I felt sorry for her, actually. She seemed so sad, so lost. We became friends. She told me about you and how much she had loved you. She then told me she had your son out of wedlock because it was all she had left of you."

"But you don't believe that's true."

"I know it's not true. She had the baby to make her father crazy. She knew what it would do to him, not only if she had a child out of wedlock, but also if the father of

314

that child had dark skin. She was right. Richard Thornston went crazy. He came into my place one night and hurt one of my girls. He almost killed her."

"And that's how you were able to get so close to him. He didn't dare turn you away, because you knew the truth about him and his daughter."

LeBeau raised an eyebrow. "It was perfect. We also went into some business ventures together."

"What business ventures?"

"I used his capital and a little of my own to build a school for the Negroes around here."

Roberto smiled. "He obviously doesn't know."

"No need to upset him needlessly." LeBeau smiled for the first time. "It does have a rather nice touch to it, don't you think?"

"What about his shipping business? Is it still solvent?

"I am afraid that in the next year or so, Mr. Thornston will find that he is no longer in the shipping business."

"What have you done, LeBeau?"

"He has been selling shares of the company off little by little and I have been buying them all up, under assumed names, of course." He looked at Roberto, a devilish grin appearing. "You wouldn't like to go into the shipping business, would you, Roberto?"

"I can't think of any business I'd rather go into right now, but Thornston isn't stupid. I know him. He'll still maintain fifty-one percent ownership."

"Twenty-five percent belongs to Caroline."

"That's why you wanted to marry her."

"If we can get that controlling interest, in writing, we will own the business and Thornston will be out."

"What about his other business ventures? What about the plantation?"

"The plantation can barely subsist on the crops it grows. The only reason it is as successful as it appears is because he puts so much of the shipping money into it.

He has been very foolish. He spends too much time thinking about other things and not worrying about business."

Roberto walked around the room. "Two years ago he owned a hotel and he had invested in a bank. What about those?"

"I am on the bank board and hold more stock than Thornston, as well as more influence. Most of those men come to my place, if you understand what I mean. And the hotel; he sold that earlier this year."

"To you, I presume?"

"Who else?"

"LeBeau, if you're interested in having me as a partner in the shipping business, I'll write you a check right now. I want to make it legal."

"I trust you, my friend. You see, you and I have a bond. We were both almost destroyed by Richard Thornston."

"I want to make it legal."

"Tomorrow will be soon enough. But there is the problem of the other stock."

Roberto nodded, squinting his eyes. "I think maybe it's time for the return of Roberto Hawkins."

"Yes. I was going to introduce you and Anna at the party in a week, but perhaps now would be better."

"You were going to take us to that party without telling us about Thornston?"

LeBeau shrugged. "That was before I got to know your beautiful wife, and before I realized that perhaps you and I and your brother should work together."

"Yes, my brother. Just what is he doing at Rolling Oaks?"

"He is there to make sure Anna is safe."

"That's what I thought."

"He is also there because he wants to help you. He knows the truth about Thornston."

"You told him?"

"He needed to be told. He did not understand why his own brother would hate him so."

"It'll be strange to see Nathan. I wonder how he'll feel about me, especially after what I did. I took the woman he loves away from him."

"But she still loves him, and that is what matters, is it not? Your brother is a smart man, my friend. He will not let a thing like a woman come between you two."

"Don't be so sure of that. Anna is not just any woman."

"I know that; believe me, I know that, but she would be the first one to tell him that you two must work together."

"How was Caroline toward Anna?"

"I wasn't there long enough to see, but I know Caroline. She is as unpredictable as a mountain lion. She cannot be trusted. That is why I think it is time for you to go to Rolling Oaks."

Roberto held the glass in his hand and downed the contents. "I'd never forgive myself if anything happened to Anna because of me."

"There is also your son to think of."

"Have you seen him?"

"Yes, I have seen him. He is kept in a room at the top of the house. Caroline rarely goes to see him, and he is not allowed out of that room. She keeps him locked up like a pet."

Roberto clenched his jaw. "Come by here in the morning with the partnership papers and I'll give you the check. Then we'll go to Rolling Oaks. It's time Richard and Caroline Thornston faced up to what they've done."

Caroline looked at herself in the mirror. She smiled, a strange, unearthly smile. She straightened the lavender bow that she had tied in her hair. It matched the bow that was tied around her tiny waist. Her dress was a white cotton with lavender flowers and lavender trim. She pulled the rounded neckline down over her shoulders but grimaced. Her shoulders were much too boney. She covered her shoulders back up and touched her face. Her skin was so lovely, she thought, pale and untouched, not like Anna's. Anna's skin was dark and evil-looking. She smiled again. She was much prettier than Anna. There was nothing for her to worry about. She looked around her room and took a deep breath. She loved the smell of the tuberoses and the jasmine; it almost made her dizzy. She was feeling rather strange today, very angry and upset, and it was all because of Anna. Well, she would just have to do something about the woman.

She left her room and started downstairs but stopped, deciding to check in on Robert. After all, she hadn't seen him since yesterday. She hurried down the hall and up the little stairway that led to Robert's room. Marie was holding the baby at her shoulder, patting him on the back.

"Mornin', Miss Caroline. Did you want to hold Master Robert?"

"Heavens, no," Caroline snapped. "Can't you see that I'm dressed up, Marie? Honestly, sometimes I think you don't use that small brain of yours."

"Yes, ma'am."

"I want you to be sure to keep him quiet for the next few days. We have very important guests in the house, and I don't want them being disturbed. Do you understand me, Marie?"

"Yes'm."

"Good. Now make sure he stays quiet." Caroline left the room and hurried down the stairs, shutting the door behind her. She was afraid she would miss Etienne at breakfast. She practically skipped down the stairs and ran

318

across the entryway to the dining room. Garrett and Molly were the only ones there. "Where is Etienne?"

"He went for a morning ride," Garrett said.

"You know us Western people, Caroline; we have to have our fresh air."

Caroline attempted a smile. She walked to the sideboard and grabbed a plate, serving herself some eggs and a roll and sat down. "Where is your friend?"

"We told you, he's riding."

"I mean Anna."

"I thought she was your friend, Caroline. After all, you were the one who invited her here," Molly said. "She's taking a morning ride." Molly couldn't contain the glee she felt.

"She's riding with Etienne?"

"I imagine they've run into each other. They left about the same time."

Caroline slammed her fork down on the table. "I knew it. I knew she was that kind of woman." She stood up and paced around the dining room. "I knew I couldn't trust her."

"She's just going for a ride, Caroline. Why are you getting so upset?"

"You're very foolish, Danielle. She's out there with Etienne right now, and I know they're not riding. They are probably lying somewhere together like animals."

Garrett had had enough. He stood up. "I don't think you'd better say things you might regret later." He looked at Molly. "Are you finished?"

"Yes. I couldn't eat another bite." Molly stopped and looked at Caroline. "I should warn you, Caroline. Etienne can't stand jealous woman. They make him sick. Have a good breakfast."

Caroline ran to the sideboard and opened a door on the bottom. She took out a blue bottle and took a sip, closing her eyes and letting the liquid go into her body. She took

319

another large sip, put the cork back in, and put the bottle back in the sideboard. She took a deep breath, feeling much better now. The laudanum always made her feel better. Now she would be in a better mood when Etienne returned. It wouldn't do for her husband-to-be to see her in a jealous rage. She smoothed her dress and sat down to wait.

Anna sat under the oak tree, chewing on a piece of grass. A slight breeze blew, but it did nothing to relieve the oppressive heat. Already, she was wet from sweating. She couldn't understand how people lived in this climate.

She thought about the night before. Nathan had made her feel more passionate than she ever thought was possible. It had been a wonderful experience, and the only thing that had ruined it was when she started talking about Roberto. Perhaps he was right; maybe she should just stay out of things and let Nathan sort them out. After all, he was Roberto's brother. She smiled as she imagined the two of them together. It would have made Aeneva and Trenton so happy to see them together.

"Why are you smiling?"

Anna jumped. Nathan was standing behind her. "Do you always have to sneak up on me like that? Where did you come from?"

"I saw you go riding this morning. I saw you take the horse back and walk down here, and I decided to follow you. I told you I'd keep an eye on you."

"Caroline is not going to do anything to me out here. She never even goes outside."

"Thornston has men all over. You could very easily have an accident."

"You worry too much." She looked up at him, dressed in his gray riding pants and white shirt. He didn't look right in those clothes. "Shouldn't you be with Caroline?

She'll be wondering where you are."

"Let her wonder." Nathan sat down next to Anna, pulling at a piece of grass and sticking it into his mouth. "I miss the ranch. I've gotten used to the desert."

"It's beautiful, and I feel so at peace there. I feel uncomfortable here. I don't like it."

"It's strange weather."

"It's always wet. I suppose that's why everything is so green." She pointed to the forest on her right. "Way back in there is the swamp. That's where Thornston's men took Roberto. He beat him half to death and then left him there to die."

"How did he get out?"

"Some people who live in there, 'swamp people' they call them, took him out of the swamp and took care of him. He stayed with them until he got well."

"No wonder he's so angry."

"He doesn't need to be angry at the whole world."

"I suppose you told him that?"

"Of course I did. He has to let go of that hate, or he'll never have a normal life."

"Are you sure you didn't spend more time with Chin? That sounds like something he'd say."

"It also sounds like something your parents would say."

"I wish they had lived to see Roberto. It would have made them so happy."

"They were happy enough to have you back."

"I still wonder if I did enough to help them. If I had used mother's medicines, maybe I could've helped them."

"It wasn't meant to be, Nathan."

"I don't believe that. That's like giving up."

"It's not like giving up. You did everything you could."

"But you managed to save me."

"Roberto saved you."

"But you remembered about mother's medicine. Why didn't I?"

"Nathan, don't do this to yourself. You couldn't have known. You probably didn't spend as much time with her as I did. I saw the medicines she used to help people when they had high fevers. How could you have known that?"

"I don't know. I just wish I had done something more."

"Stop it." She put her arms around him. "It's all right. I miss them too."

"I suppose we should be getting back." He smiled at Anna. "I wouldn't want Caroline to get jealous."

"No, we wouldn't want that." Anna touched his face and kissed him gently. "You are the love of my life, Nathan."

"What's wrong?"

"Nothing's wrong. I just want you to know that. If something should ever happen to me, I want you to know that I've loved you with all my heart. I want you to know it like Aeneva and Trenton knew it about each other."

Nathan took Anna in his arms. "Nothing is going to happen to you. I will make sure of that." He kissed her deeply, savoring the sweetness of her mouth. "So, you want to have my children?"

"Yes, I want to have your children. But I want to marry you first."

"You're already married, remember?"

"When this is all over and Roberto gives me my divorce—"

"You're sure he'll give you a divorce?"

"Of course he will."

"What are you two talking about?" Caroline came from behind the trees. "What is this about divorce?"

Nathan stood up. "Nothing that would interest you,

Caroline. What are you doing out this early in the morning?"

Anna stood up, brushing off her skirt. "What are you doing out at all?"

Caroline smiled weakly. "I was looking for you, Etienne, but I heard you were with Anna."

"I was taking a ride and we ran into each other."

"Way over here? The riding trail is back that way."

"I'd better get back." Anna cast Nathan a warning look. "It was nice talking with you, Etienne."

"Yes, it was a pleasure." Nathan watched Anna walk away.

"She's a beautiful woman," Caroline said, "in an outdoorsey kind of way."

"Yes, she's very beautiful."

"She is married, Etienne. You do realize that, don't you?"

Nathan looked at Caroline. "What about you, Caroline? Aren't you engaged?"

Caroline smiled demurely. "It is an engagement of convenience that can be called off at any time." Caroline looked up at Nathan. "And what about your engagement, Etienne? Is it one of convenience or love?"

Nathan looked at the pale woman in front of him and was tempted to walk away from her. She held no interest for him whatsoever, except that she was the answer to all of Roberto's problems. "The woman I am engaged to is beautiful and charming, but she knows little of the kind of life you have."

"Is she poor?"

"No, she's not poor, but she hasn't had the advantages that you've had."

"Well, then, I guess I was lucky to be born into a rich family, wasn't I?" Caroline put her arm through Nathan's. "Shall we go back to the house now? You haven't even eaten breakfast."

Nathan nodded and walked back up the hill with Caroline. "I want to get my horse."

"Leave him. I'll send the stableboy after him."

"I'm not used to doing that, Caroline. I don't have servants where I'm from."

"You should, you know, a man like you."

Nathan was getting increasingly irritated. He couldn't bear to be around this woman much longer. "You go on back to the house and I'll get the horse," he said finally.

"You're in love with her, aren't you?"

Nathan turned around angrily. "There's something you should know about me, Caroline. I don't like women who cling and whine. Anna is a beautiful woman and I like her very much, but she is a married woman. That does mean something to me, even if it doesn't to you."

"I'm sorry, Etienne. I didn't mean to offend you." Caroline held onto Nathan's arm.

Nathan took his arm away from Caroline. "I'll see you back at the house, Caroline. If you would like to go for a walk later today, I'd be glad to take you."

Caroline watched Nathan as he strode up the hill, his long legs covering the distance quickly. She frowned. Things were not going the way she had planned. She didn't want to marry LeBeau. He was nice enough, but he was not the kind of man a woman wanted to wake up next to every morning. Etienne was the kind of man a woman could spend the rest of her life with. But there was a problem with Anna. She would have to do something about that now. She didn't trust the woman, and it was time to put an end to her constant interference.

Anna ran up the stairs to her room. She wanted to clean up before breakfast. The one dress she had was quickly getting dirty. She opened the door to her room and found her trunk sitting on the floor. Various dresses

324

were lying across her bed. "These are beautiful," she said to herself as she quickly looked through them, selecting a deep blue silk and holding it up to herself. "I wonder where these came from." She looked through the trunk and saw her other clothes and shoes. LeBeau had been here, but where had the dresses come from? She slipped out of her soiled dress and washed up, making sure she was clean and fresh, brushing her hair and pulling it back with a blue ribbon. She stepped into the dress and buttoned it up the front, tying the ribbon on the bodice, putting on clean stockings and the shiny black button shoes. She took a cursory look at herself in the mirror, smiled, and raced downstairs, wanting to catch LeBeau before he left. She hurried into the dining room, expecting to find everyone, but the room was empty.

"Can I help you, ma'am?"

"Oh, yes, Emily. Has everyone finished breakfast?"

"Yes, ma'am. But if you're still hungry, I can get you something."

"No, thank you. Is Monsieur LeBeau here?"

"Yes, he is in the main sitting room."

Anna picked up the hem of her skirt and hurried to the sitting room. She stopped at the doorway. LeBeau was standing by the fireplace; Garrett and Molly were sitting on a couch; and Roberto was standing by the window. She didn't see Nathan and Caroline enter the house just after she crossed the hallway. "Roberto!" she exclaimed loudly, crossing the room. She looked up at him, her eyes questioning, her voice low. "What are you doing here? You know how Thornston feels about you."

"I'm happy to see you too, darling." Roberto swept Anna into his arms and kissed her deeply. "I've missed you."

Anna looked at Roberto. "What are you doing?"

"Never mind, but I think it would be wise for you to act like you're glad to see me." Roberto saw Nathan and

Caroline at the doorway. He kissed Anna, holding her close to him. "Do you like the dress?"

Anna's face brightened. "It's beautiful. You didn't have to buy me new clothes."

"I wanted to. You deserve them." He looked at Nathan across the room. "You know how I feel about you."

Anna followed Roberto's gaze and turned, disentangling herself from Roberto's arms, seeing the look on Nathan's face. She had spent so much time convincing him that there was nothing between her and Roberto, and now she was in his arms. Before she could say anything, LeBeau crossed the room, obviously distressed by the situation.

"Well, if you love-birds could stop for a moment, perhaps we could make some introductions. Everyone, this is my friend, Roberto Hawkins." LeBeau walked to Garrett and Molly. "Roberto, this is Henri and Danielle Rondieux." Garrett and Molly stood up. Roberto walked over to Garrett, holding out his hand.

"Pleased to meet you, Henri," he said with a note of cynicism. He and Garrett were almost the same age, and although they hadn't seen each other in over ten years, Roberto still recognized Garrett's boyish face. "You look very familiar to me."

"You never know, we might've met someplace." Garrett's eyes acknowledged Roberto's. "This is my wife, Danielle."

Molly extended her hand and grasped Roberto's firmly, a smile broadening her face. "It's nice to meet you, Mr. Hawkins."

"It's my pleasure, Mrs. Rondieux," Roberto replied, and he meant it. There was an open and honest look about Molly's face that Roberto immediately responded to. He felt as if she were already his friend. "Have you been to the South before?"

"No, never. I'm just here on business with my husband and Etienne."

"Etienne?"

LeBeau walked to Nathan and Caroline. "This is Etienne Fortier. And this is Caroline Thornston."

Roberto walked to his brother. Neither extended their hands. They stood, almost the same height, but completely different. One dark, one light, one haunted and angry, the other ready and willing to forgive. Roberto's black eyes stared into Nathan's blue ones. Hesitantly, Roberto held out his hand; Nathan took it. It was as if there was an ocean between them, a great dark barrier that could never be crossed. "Etienne," Roberto said.

"We almost thought you didn't exist, Mr. Hawkins. Why any man would leave a beautiful woman like that alone is beyond me." Nathan's grasp tightened.

Again, LeBeau intervened, seeing the awkward moment between the two brothers. "Miss Caroline Thornston," he said, standing next to Caroline.

Roberto released Nathan's hand and looked at Caroline. Her face was almost completely white. "Are you all right, ma'am? You look as though you've seen a ghost." Roberto held Caroline in his gaze, overpowering her with his eyes.

"I don't believe this," Caroline stammered, backing up to the door. "You're dead."

Roberto raised his eyebrows. "Are you speaking about me, madame? As far as I can tell, and I'm sure my wife can attest to this, I am very much alive."

Caroline looked past Roberto to Anna. "No, she can't be your wife. Not her."

Roberto looked innocently at Anna. "Is there something wrong?"

"She can't be your wife. You promised."

"What is it that you say I promised?"

Caroline stepped closer to Roberto, lowering her voice.

327

"You said that you would love no other woman but me. Don't you remember?"

"You must be thinking of another man, because I have never loved you." He turned to look at Anna, holding out his hand. Anna walked across the room and took it. "This is the only woman I love." He turned to everyone. "If you'll excuse us, my wife and I have a lot of catching up to do."

Anna looked at Nathan as she walked out of the room with Roberto, but she didn't say anything. She could see how angry he was, and she didn't blame him. But she would have to talk to him later.

Roberto took Anna's arm, and they walked up the staircase to her room. "You rubbed it in just a little, didn't you?" Anna opened the door. "Nathan is furious."

"It has to look real. That's the only way we'll catch Caroline in a mistake. She's upset already."

"Will you please tell me what you're doing here."

"As soon as you tell me how it is with Nathan."

"That's none of your business," Anna snapped.

"It isn't going well, is it? I didn't think so."

"Does that make you happy?"

"Do you want my honest answer?"

"No," Anna replied, walking to the windows. "We haven't said two civil words to each other. We've argued every time we've spoken. Something has changed."

Roberto walked up behind Anna, putting his hands on her shoulders. "Of course something has changed. He's seen that you're desired by another man, and he doesn't like it."

Anna turned, her expression furious. "That's not funny."

"It wasn't meant to be. It's true."

"We've been through this before, Roberto. I love Nathan."

328

"I know you say you love Nathan, but I see how you look at me."

"I was happy to see you, that's all. Don't do this. You promised me you wouldn't do this."

"I know, and I'll keep my promise. That doesn't mean that I can't show my affection for you. I'm not going to hide my feelings for you, Anna. No person has ever cared for me the way you have. Ever." He put his hand on her face.

"Don't confuse love with affection. I love Nathan and I feel affection for you."

"Whatever you say." Roberto sat down on the bed. "So, you like the clothes?"

"You shouldn't have spent so much money."

"I wanted to. Did you open that box?"

"What box?"

"There's a box at the bottom of your trunk."

Anna walked to the trunk and rummaged through her clothes. She brought out a velvet-covered box and opened it. Inside was a piece of rolled paper tied with a ribbon. Anna untied the ribbon and unrolled the paper. Tears filled her eyes. She looked up at Roberto. "You didn't have to do this. I trust you."

"Yes, I did have to do it. No one has ever believed in me as you have, Anna. It's the least I can do for you." Roberto took the paper from her hands and read it. He shrugged his shoulders. "Besides, it's just a piece of paper that shows we were married."

"It's an act of good faith. It shows you mean what you say."

"If I were smart I would hold onto it and you."

Anna shook her head. "I don't think I'll ever understand you."

Roberto stood up, taking Anna in his arms. "There's no need to understand me." He kissed her deeply, enjoying the feel of her mouth and her body against his.

The door opened, but Roberto didn't pull away from Anna. He had an idea who it was.

"Let her go, 'Berto."

Roberto slowly let go of Anna. "Why should I, brother? As I recall, she's my wife, not yours."

"You selfish bastard," Nathan seethed. "I thought there was some heart in you; Anna had me convinced of it. I should've known better."

"That's right, just like I should've known that my own brother wouldn't try to save my life. His own life was more important."

Anna stepped between them. "Stop it, both of you! This isn't the time or place for this."

"There is no better time as far as I'm concerned," Nathan replied.

"It doesn't matter, Anna; you tried, but my brother and I will never see eye-to-eye. Maybe the problem is you."

"You are a heartless bastard, aren't you? You come back and don't even see our parents before they die, you sit around and cook up some wild scheme with Clare, you blackmail Anna for medicine so she can save my life, and then you make her marry you. And now you're blaming her."

"I'm not blaming her, brother; I'm just saying that she'll always be between us. You see, I love her, too."

Nathan's eyes grew cold. "She's mine and you know it."

"But she's been with me for the last five months, hasn't she?"

"Stop it!" Anna screamed. "I am not a piece of baggage to be argued over. You two act as if I don't even have a mind of my own. The way you're both acting now, I don't want either one of you!" Anna stomped out, slamming the door behind her.

Nathan walked to the door. "This isn't over, 'Berto."

"I'll be here, Nathan, right here in Anna's room. You can think about that at night while you're lying alone in your bed."

Nathan wanted to smash his brother in the face, but he held himself in check. He looked at Roberto once more and walked out. He went downstairs to look for Anna, but he couldn't find her anywhere. He found Molly and Garrett walking outside.

"Have you seen Anna?"

"No. Why?"

"She got a little upset. Roberto and I had a little argument."

Molly shook her head. "Grown men acting like schoolboys. I'll bet Garrett didn't even act this childish when he and Anna were kids. I'll look for her. You stay here." She put her hand on Nathan's arm. "And try not to fight with your brother. Anna cares for him."

"I know."

"She doesn't deserve that, Nathan. If you're not careful, you're going to lose her. You don't strike me as the jealous type."

"I'm not, usually."

"Then don't start now. She's crazy about you, it's obvious, but she also cares for Roberto, and she wants to help him. You are the big brother, after all." Molly kissed Garrett on the cheek and left.

Nathan ran his fingers through his hair. "How can I get so crazy over something?"

"You mean Roberto?"

"Yeah. He makes me so damned mad I want to strangle him. The thought that he's been with Anna for all these months and—"

"Stop it, Nate. Molly's right; that doesn't sound like you."

"I know, that's what scares me. I haven't been myself in a long time. Things are different between Anna and me. We don't seem to be getting along very well."

"There are not many women who would run off and marry a complete stranger in order to get medicine for the man they love. Or have you forgotten that already?"

"I'd only say this to you, Garrett, but I think I'm scared."

"Scared of what?"

"I feel like I'm losing Anna."

"You won't lose her, Nate. She loves you."

"I think she loves Roberto too."

"Then she has to decide who she loves more. She's done it before."

Nathan slapped Garrett on the shoulder. "Sorry, you're the wrong person to be saying this to."

"It's all right, Nate. That's what friends are for. Now, just let Molly calm Anna down. It'll be all right. We've got more important things on our mind right now."

"Yeah, like why in hell did LeBeau let Roberto come out here? When Thornston gets back from town, he'll go crazy."

"Let's find LeBeau and see what's going on."

Anna walked along the path that Lawrence had shown her the day Thornston attacked her. It was all so strange. Nathan was here and she loved him; there was no doubt about that. But there was Roberto. He did have a strange effect on her; perhaps, if she was honest with herself, she was attracted to him. A sound in the bushes made her jump, and she looked through the thick green of the trees, but couldn't see. She walked back along the path. She heard footsteps in the foliage, and thought of the swamp people. What if they found her? What would they do to her? She ran as fast as she could, right into Lawrence.

"Whoa, Miss Anna!"

"I'm sorry, Lawrence. I thought I heard someone following me. It was probably my imagination."

"Maybe, or maybe someone *is* following you." He took Anna's arm and walked her back along the path to the grounds of the estate. "I don't think you should be going anywhere by yourself, Miss Anna."

"Why?"

"Because I think the master and Miss Caroline are out to hurt you."

"But why?"

"You know too much. They don't like that." Lawrence looked around, taking Anna closer to the house. "Miss Caroline doesn't like you. I've seen what she's like when she doesn't like someone. She can be very hurtful."

"What are you saying, Lawrence?"

"She's dangerous, Miss Anna, and I think you should leave Rolling Oaks."

"I'll be all right, Lawrence. My husband is here."

"Roberto is here? I haven't seen him."

"He came this morning. I'm sure he'll be pleased to see you."

"Not as pleased as I will to see the look on the master's face when he sees Roberto." Lawrence whistled. "What a sight that will be!"

Anna shook her head. "I'm not sure I understand what's going on around here."

"There's nothing to understand, Miss Anna. Mr. Thornston and Miss Caroline are almost at the end. They've abused people for too long. They can't keep getting away with it."

"Lawrence, you're not going to do anything stupid."

"Never you mind; you just stay close to the house. It's too dangerous for you to be off by yourself."

"Thank you, Lawrence." Anna started to walk to the house, but stopped to say something to Lawrence. He was gone. She saw his back as he ran into the forest. Was he going to the swamp people?

"You all right?" Molly walked up to Anna. "Had yourself quite an eventful day, haven't you?"

"It's good to see a friendly face."

"Nathan's not a friendly face?"

"I didn't say that. Look, if you've come here to lecture me, forget it. I'm not in the mood."

Molly held up her hands. "No lectures, I promise. Let's go for a walk."

Anna looked back the way Lawrence had gone. "We should probably stay close to the estate. Why don't we go into the gardens?"

They walked along a stone path and over a bridge. There was a stone bench set under an old oak. Flowers bloomed everywhere, made to look wild, but obviously grown with much care. "God, this is the most beautiful place I've ever seen. Everything is perfect."

"Except the people who live here."

"Yes, Caroline looked a mite peaked at the sight of Roberto."

"I looked peaked at the sight of him. I can't believe he's out here. Thornston will probably shoot him on sight."

"I don't know. I thought you looked rather happy to see him."

"I thought you weren't going to lecture me."

"It wasn't a lecture; it was merely an observation. You were glad to see him, weren't you?"

"Yes." Anna walked over to a gardenia and plucked one from the bush. She breathed in the delicate fragrance. "I think Caroline is rubbing off on me, Molly. I'm acting like a schoolgirl who's smitten with two different boys."

"Don't feel bad. The boys aren't acting much better. I can see why you like Roberto. He has a nice face."

"He does, doesn't he? He also has a good heart, Molly.

334

If only I could make Nathan see that."

"I don't think it's up to you, Anna. Both of them are so damned stubborn when it comes to you, they won't agree to anything you say. They're going to have to figure it out on their own."

"I'm beginning to think there's something wrong with me, Molly." She twirled the gardenia around in her fingers.

"Why, because you have feelings for both men?"

Anna turned to Molly, an earnest expression on her face. "Just last year I was in love with Garrett, and then Nathan, and then I wasn't sure. Is that normal?"

"How old are you, Anna?"

"Almost twenty. In December."

"And how many men had you loved in your life?"

"Besides my real father and Trenton?"

"Besides them."

"Garrett, Nathan and Roberto."

"You grew up with Garrett and your feelings for him will always be strong, but you were able to see that they weren't the kind of feelings you had for Nathan. And now there's Roberto. He's a very attractive man, and you've seen a side of him that no one else has seen, a gentle side. So now your feelings for him are confused with what you thought you felt for Nathan."

"What do you mean 'felt'?"

"You're growing up, Annie. You're changing every day. You've been through a lot in the last two years, and it's changed you. And it should. You wouldn't be human if it didn't."

"But what about my feelings for Nathan?"

"You tell me."

Anna dropped the flower onto the ground. "I can't imagine life without him. He is so good and gentle. I love him."

"But?"

335

"But we fight so much now."

"That's because you have more to fight about. There may have been a time Nathan was a little unsure of your feelings for Garrett, but I don't think he ever truly felt threatened. It's different with Roberto. Roberto is his brother, the brother he hasn't seen in over ten years, the brother who came out of nowhere and took you away from him. He doesn't know him. He doesn't really know what he's capable of, and he doesn't really know your true feelings for Roberto."

"*I* don't know my true feelings for Roberto."

"Do you love him? Do you want to spend the rest of your life with him? Do you want to have his children?"

Anna stood up and walked over to the bridge. She leaned over and watched the water in the stream trickle by. "Maybe all of this would have been eliminated if I had grown up with Nathan and Roberto. Then they would really have been my brothers."

"You didn't answer my question about Roberto. How deeply do you care for him, Anna?"

"I guess I care more deeply than I realized. When I saw him today, I was so happy. I want the best for him. I want him to have his son, and I want him to be loved."

"By whom? You?"

"I didn't say that. I just want him to be happy, Molly. I care about him so much. Yes, I'm attracted to him, but it doesn't mean I love him."

"It sounds to me like you've figured it out on your own."

"I just hope Nathan will understand. I can't leave Roberto right now."

"He'll understand if you make him."

"God, I look at you and I wonder what Garrett ever saw in me. You're so wise. You're so different from me."

"Oh, Annie." Molly put her arms around Anna and hugged her. "You are so silly. Garrett loves me because

I'm so much like you. Even I can see that."

Anna held onto Molly, tears streaming down her face. She missed a woman in her life. She hadn't had Aeneva long enough. Molly was the closest thing to a friend and sister she had ever had. "Thank you, Molly."

Molly stroked Anna's hair. She was like the younger sisters she wished she had had. Her sisters had been so ashamed of what she had done for a living that both of them had run off to live with relatives in the East. Molly hadn't seen either of them in years. Duke was the only person who had known the truth. It had broken her heart when they left. She could never imagine Anna being ashamed of her. She would be the kind of sister who would love her no matter what. Somehow, God had brought them together, knowing that they needed each other. She looked at Anna, wiping the tears from her face. "Besides Garrett, you are the best thing that's happened to me. I never thought I'd have a friend like you."

"I know. I was just thinking the same thing."

"Well, before we get too emotional, do you suppose we ought to get back to the house and see what's happening? I imagine Caroline has had some time to digest the fact that Roberto is back in her life. I wonder how she'll take it?"

"Depends which Caroline we see."

Molly laughed. "God, that's the truth. That girl puts on more faces than a clown in the circus."

"Shall we?" Anna smiled and she and Molly headed back up to the house.

Caroline sipped at the laudanum. She took another sip and put the bottle away, waiting anxiously for Roberto to come to her room. She had sent Emily to find him. Her hands began to shake at the thought of him, and she reached again for the laudanum bottle. One more sip wouldn't hurt. She had started drinking it when she was pregnant. It helped her to deal with everything her father had done to her and to Roberto. It had also helped to give her the strength to face her father and defy him. She had loved the look on his face when she presented him with a dark-skinned grandson.

She closed her eyes. She had refused to nurse the baby and a wet nurse had been brought in, but her breasts had been heavy with milk and the pain was excruciating. The laudanum had helped with the pain. The doctor had said a little would help her to sleep, and would calm her nerves. A lot seemed to make her crazy. She had built up an immunity to it, because she needed more and more to help her relax. Once she had started taking it she couldn't stop, but she knew that without it, she would have died. The laudanum had helped to dull her mind to everything that Richard Thornston had done to her.

She thought about Roberto again. She remembered the touch of his hands on her body, the way his mouth had sought hers so eagerly in the night. She remembered the way they had clung to each other the first time they made love. A shiver ran through her. No man could ever make her feel that way again. A knock on the door made her jump. She stood up and smoothed her hair and dress. Calmly, she opened the door. Roberto was standing there, dressed in black and looking dangerous. His eyes looked through hers as they had always done. His hair was longer and curled slightly at the neck; she longed to reach up and run her fingers through it. It had been over a year since she'd seen him, yet he still had the same effect on her. It was as if he had never left.

"Hello, Caroline."

"Hello, Roberto. Come in." She watched him as he walked across the room. He seemed taller, more confident, and he looked so handsome in his new

338

clothes. He wasn't the young, love-smitten boy she had once known.

"What did you want to see me about?" Roberto walked through the bedroom to the sitting room. He knew the room well.

"I had to see you alone. It's been so long."

"It hasn't been that long," Roberto said coldly. "Your room hasn't changed at all."

"Roberto." Caroline walked up to him, reaching up to touch his face. "You've gotten even more handsome. I didn't think it was possible."

Roberto removed Caroline's hand and surveyed her with a calculating eye. "You don't look good, Caroline. I don't think you get enough sun, or is it that you listen to your father too much?"

"Don't be cruel, Roberto."

"Why not? As I recall, you and your father were very cruel to me. Or doesn't that matter to you?"

"Of course it matters to me. I was out of my mind with worry when I found out what daddy had done to you."

"You saw what he did, Caroline. You were there. Why didn't you try to stop him?"

"I couldn't."

"Why not, Caroline? You had the perfect opportunity, right there in front of everyone, to say that your father was lying."

"He threatened me, Roberto. He said if I interfered he would arrange it so that no man would ever love me again. He said he would make sure I was scarred for life."

Roberto shook his head. "He wouldn't do that. I was with your father for almost two years. He loved you; he did everything for you."

"You don't know him like I do. He's an evil man."

"God, Caroline! I don't know who's more of a liar, you or your father."

"I'm not lying, Roberto. I loved you, you know that."

"Did you try to search for me?"

"I didn't know where he had taken you."

"Everyone saw where I was taken. Jesus, Caroline, do you think I'm that stupid?"

"He locked me up for a long time, and he drugged me." Caroline crossed her arms in front of herself, trying to remain calm. "By the time I knew you were gone, it was too late."

"What did you do then?"

"Nothing. I couldn't eat and I couldn't sleep. I wanted to kill myself." She looked at Roberto with her pale eyes. "Don't you remember the times we were together, 'Berto? They were so wonderful. No man has ever touched me since you. No man ever will."

"Not even Etienne Fortier?"

"I would leave with you in a second if you would have me."

"I'm a married man, Caroline. Have you forgotten that?"

"What is it about that woman? What do you all see in her?"

"I see something you can't begin to understand."

"What? What is it?"

"Selflessness. She would do anything to help me, even if it meant hurting herself. I certainly can't say the same thing about you, can I?"

Caroline crumbled. She hadn't expected this from Roberto. She had expected his anger but not his cruelty. She sat down on the couch, her shoulders slumping. "I can't defend myself to you, Roberto. Think what you will. But I did love you. I loved you more than anything on this earth."

Roberto softened. This was the Caroline he remembered, the soft, fragile, lovely Caroline. He sat down next to her. "Do you have something else to tell me, Caroline?" He asked in a much gentler tone.

Caroline looked at Roberto, her eyes filling with tears. She leaned her head against his shoulder. "Before you left, I suspected that I was pregnant, but I wasn't sure. I had never been around a pregnant woman before. After you were gone, I kept getting sick. Every morning. I thought I was dying. Then one morning I saw that my stomach was getting bigger. I knew then I was going to have your child."

Roberto pulled Caroline to him. "What did your father say?"

"You know him. He was enraged. He threatened to make me give the baby up for adoption. I told him I would kill myself if he made me do that. So he locked me in my room and I stayed there for eight months. But I had our son. I named him Robert Nathan, after you and your brother. You always used to talk about your brother."

"I know." Roberto stroked Caroline's fine hair. "Where is he, Caroline? Where is my son?"

Caroline looked up at Roberto, her eyes wide. "Don't hate me, Roberto."

"Why should I hate you?"

"I gave him up for adoption."

Roberto stiffened. "When?"

"Daddy took him this morning." She closed her eyes suddenly feeling quite tired. "I can't think anymore."

"Caroline, where did your father take him?"

"I don't know. He said he had a nice young couple who couldn't have children. It's for the best, Roberto. I wasn't a good mother to him. I wasn't fit to be his mother."

"I don't believe that, Caroline." He looked at her eyes, noticing the blank look in them. "What are you taking, Caroline?"

"What do you mean?"

"You aren't yourself. Are you drinking or taking some kind of medicine?"

Caroline closed her eyes. "Yes, I need some more medicine. It helps me to think clearly. It's under my nightstand."

Roberto leaned Caroline back against the couch and walked back into the bedroom, looked underneath the nightstand and found numerous bottles. He took one out and uncorked it, then took it into the other room. He knelt in front of Caroline. "Caroline." He ran his hand along her face. "Caroline?"

Caroline opened her eyes. "Oh, you brought my medicine." She reached for the bottle, but Roberto kept it from her grasp.

"How much of this are you taking a day?"

"I don't know."

"Concentrate. This is important. How often do you take this?"

Caroline's brows knit together in confusion. "I don't know. I take it in the morning if I don't feel well or if I'm in a bad mood. I took some before you came, because I was nervous. Sometimes I'll take it at night to help me sleep."

"You take it all day long, don't you?"

"I have to, Roberto. Otherwise I couldn't face myself."

Roberto put the bottle down and took Caroline's face in his hands. "Let me help you, Caroline. I know you're not a bad person."

"You always saw the good in me, didn't you, 'Berto?" Caroline smiled and closed her eyes. "I remember when we made love under the oaks; do you remember that? No one has ever made me feel as loved as you have."

Roberto stood up. "Come on, Caroline," he said, helping her to her feet, "I want you to take a nap."

"Are you leaving?"

"No, I'll be here. I need to talk to your father when he returns. I want to find out where my son is. Come on, lean against me." Roberto walked Caroline into her bedroom and helped her onto her bed. She grasped his hand.

"You can't talk to daddy; he'll kill you."

"I don't work for him anymore, Caroline. He can't take me out and have me beaten."

"You don't know him like I do, Berto. He's mean and cruel. He'll do anything to get what he wants." Caroline closed her eyes.

Roberto stroked her forehead until she fell asleep. He looked at the pale, thin woman lying on the bed and couldn't believe this was the Caroline he had been so in love with. Where had her spirit gone? In spite of her frail state, she had always had spirit.

He went to the nightstand and took out the bottles of laudanum. He walked to the balcony and uncorked them all, pouring the contents into the bushes below, then took the bottles and left the room. Emily was coming up the stairs as he was going down. He smiled. Emily had always been kind to him. "How are you, Emily?"

"I am well, Mr. Robert." She had always called him Robert. "I am so glad to see that you are all right."

"I need your help, Emily."

"Anything for you, Mr. Robert."

Roberto pulled her up the stairs. "How long has Caroline been on this stuff?" He held up the blue bottles.

"Since before the baby was born, I guess. Now, she can't live without it. It's made her a horrible person to be around. Why, I've seen her throw a knife at cook because the ham wasn't just right."

"Do you know where there are any more bottles of this?"

"Sure I do; it's all around the house."

"All right. I want you to collect all the bottles and pour them out."

"Yessir, it'll be my pleasure."

343

"Thank you, Emily."

"It's all right, Mr. Robert. You know I always felt bad about what happened to you. I'm glad to see you're fine."

"Yes, I'm fine."

"Will Miss Caroline act crazy or somethin'?"

"I don't know. We'll just have to see."

"If the master finds out, he'll be real upset. He likes her taking that stuff. It keeps her from arguing with him too much." Emily straightened out her apron. "'Course, I expect the master will try and kill you anyway, so I won't worry."

Roberto laughed and gave Emily a hug. "You haven't changed a bit. There's one more thing. What do you know about my son?"

Emily's eyes got large and round. "What would I know about your son?"

"Emily, I know that you know everything that goes on around this place. I know about my son and I want him. I want to take him with me, and if Caroline is well enough, I want to take her too."

Emily looked around to make sure no one was listening. "Well, I just happened to hear the master say to Miss Caroline that he found a couple in Baton Rouge who want the baby. But I know that's a lie."

"How?"

"I heard the master talking, and he said he found a couple in the city. Can you imagine, giving his own grandbaby away to people who live in the same city?"

"And what might their name be?"

"Granville. They live on a plantation called Sara Bella. Are you aiming to go after him?"

"No, I have some things to finish here first. But I'll get him, Emily. Don't you worry."

"But what if they take him away someplace? You'll never see him again."

"I'll get my son."

"I hope so, Mr. Robert."

"I'll be in Caroline's room if you need me. Thank you, Emily." Roberto walked back to Caroline's room, thinking about what to do. He thought about sending Lawrence after Thornston, but the more he thought about it, the more he realized it was a bad idea. No white man would give up a child to a black man. Either he'd have to go himself, or he'd have to send someone he really trusted. But who could he trust with his son's safekeeping? He knew the answer to the question. But would he be willing to do it? He looked at Caroline, sleeping peacefully. He left the room and went downstairs, found Emily and told her to keep an eye on Caroline for a little while. He went out to the stables, knowing full well he'd find Nathan there. Nathan glanced at him when he approached, but otherwise, he ignored him. Roberto went up to him, placing his hand on his brother's arm. "I need your help, Nate. You're the only one I can trust."

Nathan studied Roberto for a moment. He answered without hesitation. "What can I do?"

"I just found out that Thornston took Robert to a couple here in New Orleans. He's selling him to them. I need you to go after Thornston and bring my son back." He looked at his brother. "This isn't a game on my part. It's not a trick so I can be alone with Anna."

"I believe you."

"You always make things so easy. I've always hated that about you." Roberto shook his head.

"Would you rather I say no?"

A slight smile touched Roberto's lips. "Not this time. I need to be here when Caroline wakes up. I'll explain later, but I have to get her signature on some papers. If I don't, I'll lose Robert and everything else I've worked for."

"I said I'd do it, didn't I? Just tell me where I go and

who the people are. I think I'll take LeBeau with me. He might have a little more of a persuasive effect on Thornston."

"Good idea."

"What's the name of the couple?"

"Granville. They live on a plantation called Sara Bella. I'm sure LeBeau has heard of it."

Nathan nodded and began to saddle up two horses. "You know this doesn't change anything between us, don't you?" He looked at Roberto. "You still have to answer for what you did to Anna and me."

Roberto's gaze was unwavering. "I know that. I won't run away this time."

"You're entrusting me with your son; I am entrusting you with Anna. Look out for her, 'Berto."

"I will, Nate." Roberto turned to go, but stopped. "Thank you. I don't know if I would have been as forgiving as you."

"I never said I forgave you. Anyway, Robert's my nephew. Do you think I'd ever let a nephew of mine be raised on a plantation?"

Roberto nodded. "You are like your father. He forgave my father and even raised me as his own. I think you would do the same for me, even after all that's happened between us."

"Of course I would, and so would you." Nathan stepped forward, his face just inches away from Roberto's. "You need to get something straight, little brother. Trenton wasn't just my father; he was your father too. He was the one who was around when you wet your pants, got sick, cried, or got into trouble. He loved you so much, 'Berto. If there is one thing you can believe, it's that."

"I guess we have a lot of catching up to do."

"Yeah, I guess we do. Why don't you go find LeBeau

346

and send him down here. Thornston's got a few hours start on us."

"I'll see you when you get back, *hoovehe*." Roberto was stunned; the word had come out of nowhere. It was a Cheyenne word meaning "brother." He remembered a time when Aeneva had caught them fighting and had told them the story of her grandfather, Stalking Horse, and his friend, Jean. They had started out as enemies, but had become friends when Jean saved Stalking Horse from a grizzly bear. He had carried Stalking Horse for three days, pulling him on a travois. When Stalking Horse had recovered, he made Jean his blood brother. It was a surprise to everyone, because Jean was a white man and Stalking Horse was Cheyenne. One light, one dark.

Nathan stopped. He had not heard the word since he was a boy in the Cheyenne camp. He, too, knew the story about Stalking Horse and Jean. He knew what it meant that Roberto had used that word. He nodded, knowing that each of them had taken a step on the road toward friendship.

Richard Thornston smiled smugly, standing by the window of his favorite room, looking out on the grounds of the estate. He watched as Etienne and LeBeau rode out to look for the baby. If they only knew that the baby was nowhere near Baton Rouge. He was with some people who would keep him safe and hidden, out of the way, in case he needed him. That child was his ace in the hole.

He walked to the cabinets that held his dolls, unlocked one of the cabinets and took out a doll dressed in black. "This really isn't a good color on you, you know. It makes your skin look much too pale." He rubbed her porcelain cheeks with his pudgy finger. "It won't be long now. Soon it will all be over, and we will be alone again."

He brought the doll up to his mouth and kissed it one the cheek. "I will be back soon, my lovely."

He put the doll back in the case and locked it up; then he went back to the window to wait. It would be dark soon, and he could finally finish what he had started a long time ago.

Chapter XI

Anna read the note and crumpled it up. Why would Lawrence want to see her right now? It was dark. She had almost decided against it, except that she thought of the way Lawrence had helped her. She decided to go. If he needed help, then she needed to go.

She took out one of the cloaks Roberto had brought for her and put it on. Roberto had been with Caroline the entire day. She didn't want to worry him. Nathan and LeBeau were on some mysterious errand, so she couldn't ask either one of them for help. And Garrett and Molly had gone to the city to see a play. She started to write Nathan a note, but decided not to. She would probably be back before long. There was no need to worry him. She was on her own.

She walked down the stairs and out of the house, hurrying across the grounds, past the ice house, past the neat rows of cabins, to the stables. The torches from the driveway barely lit the way. She thought of the times Lawrence had warned her to be careful. But what was there to worry about? Thornston was gone and Caroline was in her room with Roberto. No one was going to hurt her.

She waited around the stables, pulling the cloak

around her. It was an unseasonably cool night, or perhaps she just thought it was cool because she was scared.

"Miss Anna?" Lawrence's voice came out of the blackness behind the stables.

Anna peered into the darkness. "Lawrence? Are you all right?"

"You got to be careful, Miss Anna. The master, he . . ." There was a loud groan and then a thud. It sounded as if Lawrence had fallen against the stable wall.

Anna hurried behind the stable. Lawrence was lying on his side. "Lawrence, what's the matter? What happened to you?"

"I have this terrible pain in my side, Miss Anna. The master, he do it to me."

"Has he hurt you in some way?" Anna lifted Lawrence's hand away. "I don't see anything, Lawrence."

"He did it, Miss Anna. He's one of them."

"I don't know what you're talking about, Lawrence."

"He practices that evil magic. He has a doll, dressed in my clothes, and he's stuck it with pins. He's trying to kill me."

"Lawrence, let me get you into the house. You need help." Anna put her arm under Lawrence to try to lift him up.

"No, I won't go in that house. That house is evil! Don't make me go, Miss Anna."

Anna took her arm away. Lawrence was genuinely frightened of something. But what? "What do you mean, the house is evil?"

"The master, he's a practitioner of evil. He puts spells on people. He even put a spell on his own daughter."

"Caroline?"

"He make her give up her baby. He make her do anything he wants."

"I don't understand what you're saying, Lawrence. If

350

you'll just let me get you into the house, I'm sure I can help you. Mr. Thornston isn't even here. He's in Baton Rouge. He was gone before I left for my ride."

"He's here, Miss Anna. He never went to Baton Rouge."

"Of course he did. He hasn't been around all day."

"He's here."

A chill went through Anna. "Have you seen him, Lawrence? Are you sure?"

"I ain't seen him, but he's here. I know it. I feel it."

"Does he know Roberto is here?"

"I don't know, Miss Anna. All I know is he's hell-bent on killing you."

"Me? Why?"

"I don't know, ma'am, I just had to warn you." Lawrence cried out in pain, leaning over.

"Lawrence, is there anything I can do?"

Lawrence reached out to Anna. "Can you get me into the swamp? My people will take care of me. They knows what to do."

Anna's heart raced at the thought of going into the swamp at night. She wanted to go back and get Roberto or Garrett. "Let me get someone to help us."

"Please, Miss Anna, don't go back to the house. I'm begging you. The master, he's there." He tried to stand up, but fell. "It be all right, ma'am. I'll get there on my own."

Anna put her arms around Lawrence and helped to lift him up. "I'll get you to your people, Lawrence. Just tell me the way."

Anna wrapped one of her arms around Lawrence's waist and draped his arm around her shoulders. She held onto his hand. "It's all right. Just hang onto me."

"I have a lantern right over here, Miss Anna." They walked past the stables. Anna bent over and picked up the faintly glowing lantern, handing it to Lawrence.

"Hold it in front if you can, Lawrence. Do we head for the path?"

"Yes'm. I'll tell you where to go from there."

They walked the same path that Lawrence had taken Anna on the day Thornston had attacked her. During the day she had found it lovely and interesting; at night she found it frightening. She heard sounds she had never heard before, and she steeled herself against the terror that threatened to overcome her.

"It's all right, Miss Anna. Them's just owls. We won't be stepping on no 'gators at night."

"I hope not, Lawrence." Anna stared ahead of her into the darkness, the faint light of the lantern providing little to lead their way. Branches and moss brushed their faces, and Anna shivered, certain that all manner of creatures had found a new home in her hair. She had never been in such a dark, strange place before. Their footsteps made a sucking sound as they plodded their way through the sand.

"Stop here, Miss Anna. We have to go over this way."

Anna looked in front of them. "How do you know where you're going? I can't see a thing."

"I just know, that's all. Keep going this way." Lawrence stopped, screaming out in pain and bending over. Anna tried to hold him up, but she couldn't and he fell to the ground.

"Oh, God, Lawrence, don't stop. I don't know where to go."

Lawrence moaned. "We're far enough. They'll find us."

"Who will find us?" Then she realized—the swamp people would find them. She sat on the wet ground, cradling Lawrence's head in her lap. She took off her cloak and covered him with it. "Just hang on, Lawrence. Please." Anna looked around her. Her heart beat furiously at every sound. The wetness of the swamp seemed to seep into her bones.

"Boy?"

Anna jumped at the sound of the voice. It was a man's voice, soft and strange-sounding. "We're over here. Please help us." Anna looked around her, but could see nothing. She rocked back and forth, trying to be brave, but she felt as if she would faint.

"What you be doin' here, woman?" The voice came out of the darkness.

Anna looked around her. "I can't see you."

"Answer me."

"Lawrence wanted me to bring him here. He said his people would help him."

"Why would he be goin' to a white woman for help?"

"I'm his friend," Anna said simply. She squinted her eyes and looked around her. "You've seen me before; I know you have. You watched us the day Lawrence led me through the forest."

Lawrence moaned and opened his eyes. "Where are we, Miss Anna?"

"It be all right, boy." The rich voice came out of the darkness and moved forward. A tall, thin black man with white hair came into view. He was holding a long curved stick. He knelt down next to Lawrence. "Tell me 'bout it, boy."

"The master, he hurt me real bad, Cy."

"He be foolin' with the magic?"

"Yes."

Cy looked up at Anna for the first time. "It be good of you to bring the boy here. I will lead you back."

"Will he be all right?"

Cy looked at Lawrence. "This be bad magic that the man play with, but we have magic that is stronger. Can you help me lift me up?"

"Of course." Anna quickly slipped on her cloak.

Cy stood up and took one of Lawrence's arms, while

Anna took the other. "Hold onto him. Keep your head low."

Anna nodded silently, mesmerized by the tall, elegant man who seemed to be able to see in the dark. They walked farther into the cypress trees, the low-hanging branches and leaves brushing against their faces. There was a loud screech and Anna jumped.

"Do not be afraid, woman. It only be a bird."

Anna couldn't believe she was here. She was scared to death, and there was no one she knew who could help her, but quite suddenly, she was intrigued by this man who could see in the dark, and the place where he lived.

"Stop here." Cy knelt down and reached for something. "Give me your hand. You'll be steppin' onto a raft. Step carefully now, that's right. Hold onto the boy. Good. Now we almost be there."

The sound of the raft going over the water at night was eerie and strange, unlike anything Anna had ever experienced. Her eyes still had not become accustomed to the darkness of the swamp, yet the old man seemed to see as if it were day. He used the long pole to stick into the ground and push them across the water. Anna could see the vague outlines of cypress trees bent in strange, human-like poses, but could see nothing else. The raft stopped and Cy jumped off onto the bank. He tied the raft to a branch and helped Anna and Lawrence step onto the bank.

"This way." Cy led them up an embankment and through some more trees.

Anna squinted her eyes, sure she could see some kind of light. Suddenly, they were in a small clearing, and light from the window of a small cabin shone on them. Smoke from a fire filled the night air. "This is your home?"

"This be my home." He took Lawrence. "Go in, woman. It be all right."

Anna followed Cy's orders. She opened the door of the

354

rickety cabin and covered her nose at the smell as she walked inside. It was unlike anything she had ever smelled before. A mixture of pungent, flower-like aromas mixed with an overwhelming spicey odor filled the cabin. She stood to one side as Cy brought Lawrence into the cabin and laid him on a bed. A large black woman sat on a chair, stirring a pot. She glanced up at Anna, but otherwise didn't seem to care that she was there.

Anna looked around. The cabin was one large room. It had a bed against one wall, a rough table and four chairs in the middle of the room, some shelves built on another wall, and a fireplace for cooking. There was a window on both sides of the cabin and the floor was hardened mud.

"Sit down, woman." The woman spoke for the first time. She didn't look up.

"Thank you." Anna walked to a chair and sat down, watching the woman. She sat over the pot and threw parts of different plants into it. She spoke words of a language Anna had never heard before.

"Do you want tea?"

"No, that's all right."

The woman stood up and walked to the table. She looked at Anna, her large round eyes taking in every detail. "What kind of blood do you have in you, woman?"

"I don't understand." Anna clutched her cloak to her.

The woman touched Anna's cheek. "Your skin, it is not white, it is not black. What blood runs in your veins?"

"I am part white, part Indian," Anna said proudly.

"I thought as much." She walked to the cupboard and took down a cup, then went back to the fire and picked up a kettle, pouring some of the contents into the cup. She opened a jar of honey that sat on the table, and poured some in, handing the cup to Anna. "Drink this."

Hesitantly, Anna took the cup, but she didn't drink. "I am not poisoning you, woman. This will warm you. It also keeps the bad spirits from entering into your body."

Anna held the cup to her lips. It smelled strange, but she drank. She had been around Aeneva long enough to know that many things that helped you didn't always taste good. She didn't realize how cold she had been until the warm liquid went into her body. The sweetness of the honey made the tea taste good. "It's very good. Thank you."

"Do not be thankin' me. I should be thankin' you. You bring the boy to us."

Lawrence moaned and Cyrus bent over him, wiping his head with a cloth. "Is all right, boy. You be safe now."

"What's the matter with him?" Anna looked at the woman.

"Do you believe in magic, girl?"

"I suppose I do. My mother's people believed many strange things."

"Did they believe that they could control someone if they had a piece of him?"

"Yes, they thought it could take his power away. Bad medicine, they called it."

The woman nodded. "Yes, very bad medicine. I come from an island where we practice things such as this. We try to use it to help people, but there are those who would use it for evil purposes."

"Thornston? But how would he know about this?"

"He has believed it for a long time. Ever since his daughter died."

Anna set the cup down. "His daughter? His daughter is at the house right now."

The woman walked over to the pot and dipped a cup in it, handing it to Cyrus. "Make him drink." She pressed Lawrence's stomach. He moaned and rolled to his side. "It be all right, boy. You be safe now."

"Is that all you can do for him?"

"It be enough for now. I will help him."

"But what about Thornston? What if he keeps trying to hurt Lawrence?"

"I will take care of the man."

Ann didn't dare doubt the woman's word. "Did Thornston have two daughters?"

"He have one daughter, and her name be Caroline." The woman took another cup and prepared tea for herself as she had done for Anna. She sat down at the table.

"But Caroline is alive. She is there, at the house."

The woman sipped at the tea and regarded Anna over the rim of the cup. "That woman not be the man's daughter."

"Who is she?"

"She be his wife."

Anna stared in disbelief. "That's not possible. She's so young."

"I know what I say, girl. She be his wife. His daughter Caroline died when she was nine years old."

Anna watched as Cyrus forced Lawrence to drink from the cup. She couldn't believe what the woman had just told her.

"You think maybe I be crazy, eh? You think this old woman has lost her mind?" The woman laughed. "I work at the house when Caroline was born. I bring her into the world, I wet-nurse her, I take care of her. I love her like she one of my own."

"Who gave birth to Caroline?"

"Ah, her mother was a sweet thing. Her name was Lilith and she was gentle and kind. She died when she gave birth to Caroline."

"What happened to her, to Caroline?"

"She got lost in the swamps. Her body was never found. Probably a 'gator got her."

Anna shivered. She held onto the cup, wrapping her

357

hands around its warmth. "Then who is this person, this girl who is supposed to be Caroline?"

"The man love his wife very much. When she die, he almost go crazy. But he take to lovin' his daughter. She was the light of his life. When she die, he almost lose his mind. He start drinking and delving into the magic. He start to find out about the black side of magic. He travel to some islands and when he come back, he have her with him. She was very young at the time but he says she be his wife. Then one day he wake up and say she be his daughter Caroline. He say she come back to him."

Anna covered her mouth with her hand. She had never heard anything so disgusting in her life. Thornston had married a young girl and then decided to make her his daughter. No wonder Caroline was so strange. There was no telling what she had been through. Anna looked at the woman. "Why does he want to kill me?"

"He thinks you are evil."

"Why? What have I done to him?"

"It is what you stand for that scares him."

"Tell me, please."

The woman held out her hand. "Come here to me, girl. Sit down." She took Anna's hand and ran her hand over the palm. "I see many things here. You are a good person with a big heart." Her dark eyes drilled into Anna's. "He do not like it when he cannot control someone. He be afraid you take the girl from him."

"How do you know so much about Thornston?"

"I have my ways, girl." She reached out and took a strand of Anna's hair. She looked at her a moment, then reached for a knife, holding the knife close to Anna's face. Anna didn't move. "I take a strand of your hair." She cut the hair and put it in her lap. She looked at the cloak, cutting a piece of the material. "I take some of your clothes." The woman looked at Anna. "You not be afraid of me, girl. Why?"

"I don't know."

"Have you seen the magic before?"

"No. My mother was a Cheyenne healer. She mixed many medicines together from many different plants. I saw her heal people who were dying. I never knew everything she did, but I trusted her. She had a pure heart."

"Ah, so you get your pure heart from your mother."

"She wasn't my blood mother. She raised me and loved me like a mother."

"Does not matter. She show you the purity of the heart." She stood up, her large mass moving slowly to the cupboard. She dropped the hair and material in a jar. "I will make protection for you against the man. His magic be powerful. You need something to help you." Anna watched in awe as the woman mixed many different kinds of ingredients in the jar along with the hair and cloth. The woman seemed to have hundreds of jars, and Anna was reminded of Aeneva and her baskets. When the woman was through mixing, she said some words and closed her eyes. Then she sang a strange, haunting chant. She reached into the jar and took the piece of cloth from Anna's cloak and poured the contents of the jar in it. Then she tied it with a thin strip of rawhide and tied this to another longer piece of rawhide. She put it around Anna's neck. "There, you leave that on. It protect you."

"Did Lawrence have this on?"

The woman looked over at Lawrence, who was now sleeping comfortably. Cyrus was sitting silently next to him, his eyes closed. "The boy say he do not believe in our magic, so he not wear one of these."

"But he came here."

"Yes, he come here." She smiled at Anna for the first time. "So, what you be wanting to do? You want to stay here until tomorrow, or you want Cyrus to take you

359

back tonight?"

Anna thought of going through the swamp again and the thought terrified her, but she knew she had to go back. She had no choice. "I have to go back." She looked at Cyrus. "I don't want to disturb Cyrus."

"You not be disturbing me, girl." Cyrus's eyes popped open as if they had never been shut. "I will take you back."

"Remember, girl, you have a pure heart," said the woman. "The man really cannot hurt you."

Impulsively, Anna reached out and hugged the woman. "Thank you. I don't even know your name."

"It do not matter. Go and be safe now. Thank you for bringing the boy to us."

Anna nodded and followed Cyrus out of the old shack. She stepped onto the raft and looked at the outline of the shack as they pulled away. The faint glow of the firelight shone through the windows. It was a strange experience, Anna thought, but not unpleasant. She felt safer, somehow.

They reached the other shore and Cyrus took Anna's hand. "Hold onto me, girl."

Anna grasped Cyrus's hand tightly, like a small girl holding onto her father's hand. She couldn't see a thing in the swamp, and the sounds and smells still assaulted her senses, but she was no longer afraid. She let Cyrus guide her through the swamp until finally they were in the trees by the estate. Cyrus stopped.

"You be all right now?"

"Yes, thank you."

"Thank you for bringin' the boy to us."

"Are you related to him, Cyrus?"

"He be my nephew."

Anna was quiet. Timidly, she touched Cyrus's hand. "He is a good boy. Tell him I hope to see him before I go."

"I tell him."

"Cyrus," Anna started slowly, "you took care of a young man almost two years ago. Thornston had left him in the swamp to die. Do you remember him?"

"I remember. He was dyin'. He had no will to live. His heart was broken."

"He's back here now, Cyrus."

"I know."

"You know everything. Do you know if he will be safe?"

"I cannot tell you that, girl. I do not know the future." Cyrus put his hand on Anna's shoulder. "Do not be afraid, girl."

"Thank you, Cyrus. Good-bye." Anna watched as the old man disappeared into the blackness of the forest. She looked out on the grounds of the estate; no one was around. She ran as quickly as she could across the grass, holding her cloak around her. She ran around the side by the cookhouse. It was quiet. She walked through the cookhouse and in the door that led to the dining room. She walked through the darkened room into the entryway, and up to her room, and shut the door. She stripped off her clothes and put on her traveling outfit, tucking the medicine bag the woman had made for her into her blouse. She didn't know if it had any powers or not, but she was willing to believe it did. She got a hairpin from her nightstand and then quickly left the room, heading for the room upstairs. She knew the answer to Thornston lay somewhere in that room.

She closed the door to the stairway behind her, hurried up the stairs, and knelt on the floor in front of the door. She stuck the pin in the lock, but she didn't have to do anything because the door was already unlocked. She opened it and walked inside. There was a lamp sitting on the windowsill, a faint glimmer of light coming from it to brighten the room, but no one was there. She shut the door and walked to the cabinets full of dolls, staring at them. What was it about them? They all looked like Caroline, but what else? She pressed her face against the glass. Their lifeless pale eyes stared out at her through the glass. She moved from one cabinet to the next. She noticed that one of the dolls was missing, but which one? She looked at their clothing. She saw the lavender flowered dress that Caroline had worn that day. Was it possible that these dolls had had clothes made for them out of the same material as Caroline's dresses? She went back to the empty space. Which doll was missing?

"You lookin' for this?" Anna turned around, frightened by the sound of Thornston's voice. He was holding the missing doll, which was dressed all in black. He walked steadily toward her, holding the doll out in front of him. "This is what you were looking for, wasn't it?" He reached out and grabbed Anna's arm, yanking her toward him. "I told you I didn't like you. You didn't believe me."

"What do you want?"

"What do you think I want?" He held the doll to her face. "I want you dead."

"I haven't done anything to you."

"You came into my home and tried to turn my daughter against me. That's reason enough."

"I haven't tried to turn her against you. She loves you."

"She pretends to love me, but I know better. She's no better than the whore I bought her from." He grabbed Anna's other arm. "You do know she's not my daughter, don't you?" He shook Anna. "Don't you?"

"Yes."

"Then you also know that she has to die."

"Why? She hasn't done anything."

"She has betrayed me. She's my wife and she went with another man. She even had the man's bastard."

Anna tried to back away, but Thornston held onto her.

362

"Don't try anything, or I'll snap your neck." He put his hand at Anna's throat. "I think you better come with me." Thornston pulled Anna to the cabinets, pushing one aside. He pressed on an area of the wall, and a door opened. "Magic, isn't it?" He pushed Anna forward and shut the door, walked back across the room, locked the door, then shut it. He walked back to the wall and pressed on it, waiting for it to open, and looked at Anna. "There's nothing to be afraid of." He stopped inside and pulled the door closed. He led Anna up a dark staircase to a small attic room. Candles flickered everywhere, and against a wall, there was a kind of alter. Flowers, food, clothing and numerous artifacts lay around the alter, built of wood and rocks. Thornston pushed Anna down in front of the alter. "It's time you learned something of my religion, girl."

Anna looked up at Thornston. A madness had come into his eyes. He looked at her but didn't see her. Anna looked around and for the first time saw the painting of Caroline on top of the alter. Or was it Caroline? Unconsciously, she started to grab at the small medicine bag under the blouse, but forced her hand away. "Who is the girl downstairs that you call Caroline?"

Thornston took the doll dressed in black and smoothed out its dress, placing it on top of the alter. "She's a girl I found on the island of Haiti. Her father was a white plantation owner, her mother an octoroon."

Anna suddenly remembered Caroline's comment about her mother being dark like Anna. It hadn't made sense at the time. Now it did.

"She should have had darker skin, but she was born with the palest of skins. I knew her mother from visiting the island when my ship stopped there. The mother couldn't take care of her, so I bought her and made her my wife."

"Why? Why such a young girl?"

"Thirteen is not all that young. Many women are married and have children at that age." He walked around the room, staring at Anna. "She was not a suitable wife in the ways that count, so I made her my daughter."

"You can't just make someone your daughter, especially after they've been your wife."

"I can do anything I please. This is my plantation. These are my people. They stay because they are loyal to me."

"They stay because they're scared, and because they have nowhere else to go."

"You know nothing of our life in the South. You think you have all the answers?" He walked close to Anna. "I know who your husband is, Mrs. Hawkins."

Anna's fears suddenly intensified. "I don't believe you."

"I've had you followed since you came off the riverboat."

"That's impossible."

"Is it? Who was with you the entire time?"

Anna shook her head. LeBeau. LeBeau was her friend. He had proved it many times over. He couldn't possibly be working with Thornston. But he had warned her many times to be careful, and he was a strange person. And right now he was with Nathan. It had all been set up.

"I can see from the look on your face that you believe me."

"Why would LeBeau work for you?"

"LeBeau and I have many common interests. You do know that he is Cajun?"

"Yes. What does that have to do with anything?"

"The Cajuns are strange people. They believe strongly in my magic. In fact, it was LeBeau who got me into this. He is a practitioner."

"I don't believe you."

"Believe what you will; it doesn't matter to me. Just rest assured that your lover will not come back to you."

"What do you know about us?"

"Everything. I know that you were all raised by the same people, and that you are in love with the older brother but married to the half-breed. Why you married him, I don't know, but I don't care. All I know is it has worked out well for me. Roberto will think that his brother killed you in a murderous rage, and he will go crazy. He will be vulnerable. Then he will be mine."

"Why do any of us matter to you?"

"You matter because you have interfered in my life."

"What about Caroline?"

"Caroline is under my control. I will deal with her later."

"But why did you try to make Caroline into your wife and then your daughter?"

Thornston shrugged his shoulders indifferently. "When I first saw her, she reminded me so much of my dear Lilith. I thought she could replace her. But no one could replace Lilith. Then I thought I could make her into my darling Caroline, and it worked until the half-breed came here."

"He saved your life."

"Yes, and just so I can have the pleasure of killing him." He picked up a bottle from the alter and walked over to Anna, holding it to her lips. "Drink."

Anna looked at the blue bottle. Panic seized her. She stood up and ran to the door, trying to open it, screaming as loudly as she could.

"You don't think I would leave the door unlocked, do you? You must think I am a very stupid man, Anna." Thornston laughed. "Oh, please scream all you want. No one will hear you way up here. No one even knows about this room."

Anna turned, her back against the door. Thornston

365

approached, the blue bottle held in his hand. "Why do you think you can fight me, eh?" He took a handful of her hair and yanked her head back, pressing the bottle to her mouth. Anna locked her lips together, refusing to let Thornston put the drug in her body. She knew that it was laudanum, and she knew laudanum was opium. She had almost given herself up to opium once before; she couldn't do it again. Again, Thornston yanked her hair, forcing her head back. He put the bottle to her mouth and poured. It dripped down the sides of her mouth. Thornston forced her head back so far that she had trouble breathing. She opened her mouth and gasped for air and the liquid went down her throat. She coughed, but Thornston held her mouth shut, forcing her to swallow. He did it again, forcing more the liquid down her throat. "Good. Soon you won't fight me at all."

Anna felt the drug course through her body. She felt herself relax in spite of her resolve not to. Her mind raced. She remembered the feeling of complete calm and relaxation that came from the opium. Somewhere in her numb mind there was panic, but she couldn't force herself to react. She stumbled against Thornston, her legs giving out beneath her. Thornston held her against him and dragged her over to the altar.

"Do you feel better now?" He lifted her face up. "Of course you do." He picked up a necklace of flowers and placed it around her neck. "You really are very lovely. It is a shame you must die."

Anna tried to focus, vaguely aware of the pungent smell of the flowers. She squinted and watched as Thornston did something by the altar. She saw a glimmer in the candlelight. Thornston held up a knife and turned to Anna, an evil smile covering his face. Somewhere in her drugged mind, Anna recalled the black woman. She reached up and touched the medicine bag that was under her blouse, and closed her eyes. She could do nothing but think of the "purity of the heart" and hope that the woman was right.

Caroline opened her eyes. Her head ached and she felt sick to her stomach. She looked around the dimly lit room. Roberto was sitting next to her.

"What are you doing here?"

"I need your help, Caroline."

Caroline sat up. "Why?"

Roberto leaned forward and took Caroline's hand. "If you ever loved me at all, you'll help me."

Caroline smiled, the color coming to her cheeks. "I loved you, 'Berto. More than I've ever loved anyone in my life. You treated me like a lady. You never made me do things I didn't want to do."

"You are a lady, Caroline."

Caroline pulled her hand away. "You don't know the truth. You wouldn't say those things if you knew the truth."

"What truth? Your father is a ruthless man who has directed your every move. I understand why you didn't help me that day, and I forgive you."

"You don't understand, 'Berto."

"Then tell me."

Caroline's eyes welled up with tears and her lips quivered. "I did love you. You made me feel so special, so loved. But when he found out about us, I knew there was nothing I could do to help you."

"I understand, Caroline. I know your father controlled you."

"No, you don't understand." Caroline reached out and touched Roberto's face. "You are so good; I think that's what he hated most about you. He could never understand a truly good person."

"Caroline, you're not making sense. Your father has

367

some good in him. He took me in, cared for me, treated me like a son."

"Why do you think he did that, 'Berto?"

"He did it because he cared about me. He felt he owed me something for saving his life."

"He never felt he owed you anything. He intended to use you from the moment he brought you into this house." She touched his cheek. "But he found out you were too good."

Roberto sat up straight. "What are you talking about?"

"Have you ever heard of 'voodoo'?"

Roberto stood up. "Those strange meetings that the workers had in the orange grove?"

"You do remember. Yes, many of them believe that you can control another human being through voodoo. It is considered to be very powerful."

"How do you know so much about it?"

"I came from an island where it is practiced. My father was a wealthy plantation owner who practiced voodoo. I was conceived when my mother was brought to one of their ceremonies. She was just fifteen and forced to be taken against her will. It was considered an honor."

Roberto was confused. "Thornston met your mother on an island?"

"No, not Thornston. My father." Caroline's pale eyes finally seemed to have some life in them. "Thornston is not my father, 'Berto. He is my husband."

Roberto sat down slowly in the chair. "You are Thornston's wife?"

"Yes."

"For how long?"

"Since I was thirteen years old. He bought me from my mother because he said I looked like his dead daughter. The only way my mother would let me leave is if I was married. She tried to do what she thought was best for me."

"His daughter's name was Caroline."

"Yes."

"You've been with this man for seven years? You lived with him as his wife?"

Caroline hesitated, not wanting to hurt Roberto, but she knew she had to tell him the truth. She owed him that, at least. "He tried to make me his wife, but I failed."

"What do you mean, you failed? That's crazy! How can a thirteen-year-old girl be expected to—"

"It's all right, 'Berto. In some cultures, wives are taken at a very early age and expected to bear children."

"Is that what he wanted you to do?"

"Yes, but I couldn't have children." She smiled, her eyes twinkling. "At least that's what he told me. He told me that I was a failure as a wife. He said he would sell me to someone else. But he was the failure, because I was able to have a child. Your son."

"No wonder he acted like he did when he found out. I was in love with a married woman." He shook his head. "Why didn't you tell me, Caroline?"

"Because I never felt like his wife. I felt closer to you than I ever did to him."

"Were you really going to run away with me?"

"Yes, I wanted to spend the rest of my life with you. After I had spent time with you, I realized what it was like to be loved. I knew he had never loved me; he never even cared for me."

"Why did he suddenly decide to pass you off as his daughter? Didn't people question him?"

"He never told anyone he married me. He told everyone that I was his daughter. Only the people who worked on the plantation knew the truth. No one outside the plantation knew his daughter had died. I was the same age as his daughter, and I looked very much like her. For a while he treated me like a daughter. He taught me

369

things, gave me anything I wanted, and never demanded that I act like a wife to him again. And then I began to get ill."

"The laudanum?"

"No, it was before that. He began taking me to his ceremonies. He even made me participate in them. I couldn't stand it. I couldn't stand myself. When I told him I wouldn't go anymore, he started giving me things."

"What things?"

"It was usually some kind of drink. It always made me feel sick. I began finding things in my room—amulets, necklaces, bones of different animals. He started practicing his magic on me." She closed her eyes for a moment, then opened them.

Roberto took Caroline's hand. "I'm sorry."

"Don't be sorry, Roberto. You brought goodness to my life. He hated that."

"When did you start taking the laudanum?"

"He started giving it to me when you were here. Even when he had that stroke, he still managed to persuade one of the maids to make sure I got some in my tea every day. He didn't want me falling in love with you."

"But it didn't work."

"No, I guess I was so in love that nothing would've affected me. But by the time he found out about us, he knew he had me. I loved you, but I needed the laudanum. I did anything he wanted me to. I even stood by as he almost beat you to death."

"But why keep you drugged after I was gone? There was no threat then."

"I had defied him by having the baby, and he wasn't about to let me get away with that. He uses me sometimes in his ceremonies."

"What ceremonies?"

"He has dolls, all painted to look like his daughter. He uses them to experiment." Caroline sighed. "I know it sounds strange, Roberto, but it's true. He takes a piece of my clothing or a dress that I've worn before and puts it on the doll. Then he does things to the doll and I feel it."

"Caroline—"

"It's true. If he sticks a pin in the doll's arm, I have a pain in my arm. If he squeezes its head, I get a bad headache. It's horrible, and sometimes I'm afraid he won't stop."

"Caroline, you can't be hurt by something like that. It's not possible."

"It is possible. I know."

"But if you don't believe it, it won't happen. Do you understand me?"

Caroline looked at Roberto, a frightened expression on her face. "How do you know?"

"Do you remember me telling you that my mother was a Cheyenne healer? When she was a young girl, she was a warrior. Warriors were taught from a young age that if something precious of theirs was taken away, they would become weak. My mother saw many young warriors die on the battlefield after their shields or lances were taken away from then. My mother didn't understand that. She believed that no man could take her strength away just by taking her shield or weapon. She knew her strength came from within."

Caroline's eyes were filled with tears. "Do you believe that?"

"Yes, I do. I couldn't have made it on that ship for eight years if I didn't."

"What do I do?"

"You start fighting back, Caroline. LeBeau and I want you to sign some papers. Between the three of us, we'll own Thornston Shipping."

Caroline smiled. "I'll sign anything if it'll mean getting him out of my life."

"Good. There's something else."

371

Caroline nodded. "Robert. You want to take him with you. I won't fight you, Roberto. I haven't been a fit mother."

"I just want to see him, Caroline."

"But I told you—"

"It's all right. My brother and LeBeau are going after him." Roberto stopped. "Etienne is really my brother, Nathan."

"I know. I've known from the beginning. Thornston made me pretend to act like a crazy person, unable to think or do anything for myself. If I didn't listen to him, he'd use the dolls."

"Tell me what he knows."

"He's had you followed from the moment you arrived here. I tried to warn you, but he punished me."

"How long has he known about me?"

"He didn't know for sure you were alive until you came here. He had someone following your every move, someone close to you."

"LeBeau," Roberto muttered. He had felt it at the beginning, but he didn't want to believe it.

"Yes, LeBeau. He's in business with my father."

Roberto thought about what LeBeau had told him the night before, and decided to keep quiet. LeBeau may have started out working for Thornston, but now he was working against him, although Caroline thought otherwise. But what about Nathan? He had no ties to him. "LeBeau is with Nathan right now. They went to get the baby."

"LeBeau won't hurt your brother. He's not like my father."

"When will Thornston be back?"

"He is back."

"Your father is here?" His mind raced.

"He never left."

Roberto's mind raced. "Why is he here, Caroline?"

Caroline put her hands on her head, closing her eyes. "He's going to kill her, 'Berto. He wants to get back at you by killing everyone who's close to you."

Roberto jumped to his feet. "Where is he?"

"I don't know."

"Where is he, Caroline?" Roberto grabbed Caroline's shoulders. "We are talking about my brother and my wife. Do you understand? And what about my son? Is he crazy enough to kill my son?"

"No, I don't think he'd hurt the baby." Caroline's hands began to shake uncontrollably. "I need some of the medicine, 'Berto. Just a little, please."

"No, dammit! Think, Caroline. Where could he have gone?"

"You're angry with me."

Roberto forced himself to calm down. "I'm not angry with you, Caroline. I need to find Thornston."

Caroline thought for a moment. "He disappears sometimes. He has a room upstairs he goes to—"

"Where? Where is it?"

"It's at the end of the hallway. There's a door. You climb the stairs. The room is to the right."

Roberto headed for the door. "Stay here, Caroline. I'll be back."

Roberto ran to the other side of the house, searching for Anna. Her room was empty. He went downstairs, but couldn't find her. He quickly climbed the stairs and went into Thornston's secret room. The door was unlocked and he went inside. The room was empty. He walked around, looking at all the toys, then walked to the cabinets and saw the dolls, painted to look like Caroline. One cabinet was pulled out from the wall and he looked behind it. There was nothing. Where the hell was he? There were no other doors in the room.

"Hello, Mr. Robert."

Roberto walked to the door, lowering his head, unable

to see in the dim light. "Cyrus? Is that you?"

"It's me, boy. You be lookin' good."

Roberto reached out and hugged the tall old man. "What are you doing here, Cyrus? I thought you never left the swamp."

"I leave when it is important. I see the girl tonight. She bring my boy to me."

"You saw Anna? You saw my wife?"

"Yes. She be in great danger, boy. The man, he have strong magic. It be evil. He want to kill her." Cyrus looked toward the cabinets. "I came here to stop him."

"Do you know where he is, Cyrus?"

Cyrus looked across the room, to the cabinets. "He used to have a room at the top of the house."

"Where? There aren't any doors."

Cyrus lifted his long pole and pointed to the cabinet that was pulled away from the wall. "Behind there."

Roberto walked back to the cabinet and looked. He felt all around. "I don't feel anything."

"It be there. I know, I used to work in this place. I used to see him go in there."

Roberto knelt down and felt along the edge of the floor. He felt a slight ridge in the wood. He pressed against it and the wood creaked; he felt along the ridge until it went upwards. He had found the door. He pressed against it and the door opened. "Here it is," he whispered. "Stay here, Cyrus. If something happens, get help." Roberto almost fell on the first step as he climbed upward. He put his hands on the walls and felt his way along. When he reached the top, the door was locked. He listened for sounds from inside, but there were none. He threw his weight against the door but it didn't budge. He did it two more times and the door burst open. Roberto walked into the room, covering his nose at the overpowering smell of flowers and spices. The room was illuminated by candles that were set all around the floor. He walked to the altar, appalled at the sight of something so bizarre. He saw the doll painted like Caroline, dressed in black and lying on the altar, a pin stuck in its head. He shuddered as he looked at it. He looked around and saw a laudanum bottle on the floor. Anna had been here; he could feel it. He raced down the stairs. Cyrus was still waiting for him.

"What is it, boy?"

"He has her, Cyrus. You must think. Where would he go with her? Do they still have those meetings in the orange grove?"

Cyrus thought for a moment. "There be a place, but it be a bad place. Only the practitioners of evil go there."

"You have to tell me where it is, Cyrus. Please."

"I will show you where it is, boy. But first we must pray so that the evil does not penetrate our souls."

Chapter XII

Nathan looked at LeBeau. They stood outside the gates to the Granville plantation. "Did you know about this?"

"Why would I know about this? I am your friend, no?"

Nathan grabbed LeBeau's shirt. "I thought you were a friend to all of us, but now I'm beginning to wonder."

"Why would you wonder such a thing, eh?"

"Because the woman in there said she had seen you before with Thornston."

LeBeau looked acutely uncomfortable. "I told you before, I have pretended to be Thornston's friend and business partner. There is nothing unusual about that."

"Then why did the woman say she recognized you, unless you'd been with Thornston when he was talking about the adoption?"

"I do not know." LeBeau pushed Nathan's hand away. "What is it you want from me? I got you into Thornston's house. I found out about your brother for you. I have done everything you asked."

"Yes, it's almost been too easy."

"I admit I was working for Thornston at the beginning. I was hired to find your brother and I told Thornston when he arrived in New Orleans. But when I got to know

Anna, I realized that she was innocent, and I realized too, that your brother was innocent. I did not want him to suffer for anything I did."

"Why is it I don't believe you, LeBeau?"

"Believe me or not, it does not matter. But Anna and your brother are still at Rolling Oaks. And tonight is a full moon."

"What is that supposed to mean?"

"It means it is the perfect time for Thornston to sacrifice someone."

"Sacrifice? What do you mean sacrifice?" He grabbed LeBeau and threw him up against the gate, his forearm shoved underneath his throat. "You've been lying to us all along, haven't you? You aren't even a friend of Chin's."

"I didn't lie about Chin. He helped me once and I owed him for that."

"But you didn't owe him enough, did you?"

"I told you about your brother."

"It's what you didn't tell me that scares me, LeBeau." Nathan pressed his arm into LeBeau's throat. "Talk, you son of a bitch, or I'll kill you right here."

LeBeau nodded as he gasped for air. "All right. I did not lie about hating Thornston. He murdered my mother and I swore I would get back at him for that. I gambled and I saved money and then I invested. I knew how Thornston felt about whores; he couldn't resist them. So I opened an exclusive house. I knew all about him because of my mother, and I knew he would slip and hurt someone. And he did. After he beat the girl so badly, he began to pay me for my silence. He also offered me Caroline's hand in marriage when she was old enough. Thornston readily agreed to all of this. What he did not know was that with the money he gave me, I was buying up stock from his company. I had gotten to the point where I owned over forty percent, but I needed more to

377

take the company from him. I knew the only way was to marry Caroline. But then your brother came here, and I figured he could do it easier than I. I knew how she felt about him."

"What's Roberto doing?"

"He's getting Caroline to sign her shares over to us."

"Us?"

"Yes, your brother and I are now partners in Thornston Shipping."

Nathan took his arm away. "So you haven't betrayed Roberto, at least."

"I haven't betrayed any of you, Nathan." He straightened his jacket. "I admit that at the beginning I had no concern for any of you. I don't know if you can understand this, but my hatred for Thornston was so deep that I did not want anything to get in the way."

Nathan thought back to Franklin Driscoll. It wasn't that long ago that he had finally put an end to the misery Driscoll had put them through. Roberto had endured the misery for much longer. "I understand better than you think, LeBeau. Now tell me about this sacrifice."

"There are many people here in New Orleans who are different. Many have strange ways about them. Some practice a religion called voodoo. It can be used for good or it can be used for evil. If a true practitioner believes in it, it is said he can do anything."

"What does this have to do with Thornston?"

"Thornston is a practitioner, but he uses the magic in an evil way. He learned it on the island of Haiti. He learned the evil kind of magic there, the kind that controls and hurts people. The religion also believes in sacrifice, usually animal but sometimes human."

"You aren't serious?"

"I am very serious, my friend. I have seen it myself."

"You've seen a human sacrificed?"

"When I was a young boy, I followed my mother. She

was obsessed with it. She would sing chants and dance around in a circle with other men and women until they dropped to the ground in exhaustion. They would even lie with each other, there, in the open, in front of other people." LeBeau's eyes stared straight ahead. "I remember shaking with fright the first time I saw it. I couldn't believe it was my mother. But I became fascinated by it. I would follow her whenever she would go. There was always a voodoo doctor or priestess who presided over everyone else. The priestess or the doctor would chant and sing, and then the people would start to dance. They drank wine, some men danced with snakes around their necks, and the women were dressed in thin, brightly colored skirts and blouses. They would lift their skirts up and show their bare legs while they danced. The men went wild. They would wrap themselves around the women and sway back and forth." LeBeau walked away from the gate, heading down the long, tree-lined drive. Nathan got the horses and followed. "I had been following her for over a year, when I finally saw a sacrifice. I had seen them kill cocks and other small animals, but this time there was a young girl. They brought her out to the middle of the circle. She didn't fight; it was as if she were drugged. She stood there while the people danced around her. Then the doctor took her and he danced with her, putting his body against hers. She did not resist. When the dance was over, he led her to a pole where she was tied with her hands up high. Again, the people started to dance and sing and the music went faster and faster until they all closed around her. Then it was silent. The people moved away and the girl hung limply at the pole. She had been stabbed in the heart, and the blood dripped down over her white dress. The doctor put his hands in the blood and rubbed it on his face and mouth. Everyone did the same thing, including my mother. It was the first time I ever saw Richard

Thornston. He took my mother and lay with her on the ground, in front of everyone. There were like two animals. I lost my innocence that night."

"I'm sorry, LeBeau. But what does this have to do with Anna?"

"Thornston wants to kill her to get back at Roberto, but there is another reason."

"What?"

"He felt threatened by her the first time he saw her. He knew she was stronger than he and could destroy him."

"What are you talking about?"

"Anna is pure of heart. You, of all people, should know that. It is said if one is truly pure of heart then they cannot be destroyed. He recognized that in her and it frightened him. He thinks if he kills her he will be safe."

"Jesus, I don't believe this. What about Roberto? Does he know about this?"

"I said nothing to him. I thought we would all be there to protect Anna. For that, I am sorry; I did not set you up. I want Thornston as badly as you and your brother do. Maybe even more."

"Then we have to get back." Nathan mounted his horse, waiting for LeBeau. "What about Caroline? Will she try to hurt Anna?"

"I do not think so. Roberto has been with her today. If anyone can get through to her it will be your brother."

"Does she know about her father?"

"She knows. Unfortunately, she knows too much."

"I hope we're not too late."

"We cannot be late, my friend. The group will gather tonight. Once they are together, nothing will stop them."

Nathan glanced at LeBeau as they rode. He couldn't believe this was happening. "Please, mother, look after Anna until I get to her. If it's true that they can't hurt the pure of heart, then she must be saved." He knew that people might think it strange that he prayed to his mother, but he believed in her power still. He knew if anyone could help Anna, it would be Aeneva.

Garrett and Molly were climbing up the stairs to their room when they heard a horrible scream. It was coming from Caroline's room. They ran to the room, and Garrett opened the door. Caroline was lying on the bed, her hands pressed to her head, her legs curled up to her chest.

Garrett tried to hold her still. "Caroline, what's the matter?"

"He's hurting me again. Please, help me."

Molly sat down on the bed. "Get me a wet cloth, Garrett." She reached down and took Caroline's hands from her head, beginning to massage her temples. "It's all right, Caroline. Just relax. We'll try to help you."

"You can't help me. He's trying to kill me."

Garrett handed Molly the cloth and she put it on Caroline's forehead. "Who is trying to kill you?"

"My father. My father is trying to kill me. He hates me."

"Your father isn't even here, Caroline. I think you just have a headache."

Caroline stared at Molly with wide eyes. "Please, I know I haven't been the nicest person, but I need your help. My father has a room on the third floor."

"Yes, I know where it is," said Molly.

"There is a door behind the doll cabinets that leads to another secret room. You must go up there and get the doll."

Garrett looked at Molly. "What doll, Caroline?"

"There will be a doll that looks like me, and something will be wrong with its head. Please, you must do this." She screamed loudly, the sound piercing the silent night.

"Do it, Garrett."

"Molly—"

"Listen to me. Go to the end of this hall. There's a door. It leads to some stairs. The room on the right at the top is the room Caroline is talking about." She took a pin out of her hair. "If it's locked you can use this to get in."

"You don't actually believe this, do you?"

"I'm not sure what I believe, but Anna and I saw him acting very strange in that room. Please, Garrett, hurry."

Molly dipped the cloth in water and rubbed Caroline's face and neck. "It's all right, Caroline. He'll be back soon."

"He's going to kill Anna," Caroline mumbled.

"What did you say?" Molly held Caroline still. "What did you just say, Caroline?"

Caroline tried to focus on Molly. "My father is going to kill Anna tonight. He is going to sacrifice her. It was either me or her."

"My God!" Molly said, not doubting a word that Caroline said. "Why is your father trying to hurt you, Caroline?"

"He always does this to me. He does it to make me understand that I am under his power. He doesn't want me to ever defy him again."

"Here it is," Garrett said breathlessly, handing the doll to Molly.

"She's right. Look at the pin." Molly shook Caroline. "Here's the doll, Caroline. What should I do?"

Caroline stopped. "Take the pin out carefully, please. Very slowly."

Molly nodded, guiding the pin out as slowly as she could. She tried to ignore Caroline's screams as she gently pulled the pin out. When the pin was in Molly's hand, Caroline's screams stopped. Emily ran into the room, a frightened look on her face.

"What's wrong with Miss Caroline?" She looked at the doll. "He's doing it again. The man is evil."

"You know about this, Emily?" Molly stood up,

holding the doll in her hand.

"Yes, we all know about him. We just try to stay out of his way and pray that he don't get angry at us. We have our own religion, too. See." She pulled a little bag out from underneath her blouse. "This is to protect me from the evil."

"Where is he, Emily?" Garrett asked.

"I don't know."

"I know where he is," Caroline said. She tried to sit up. Garrett helped her. "Emily, go to my father's room and bring me a piece of his clothing or jewelry, and some hair from his hairbrush." She looked at Molly and Garrett. "This has gone on far too long. There's a clearing on the other side of the plantation. You have to walk past the orange grove and the workers' cabins. You'll have to walk through a burned-out hickory grove, but when you come out, you'll see the clearing. It's completely surrounded by trees and bushes. It's where they hold their ceremonies."

"Who?"

"My father and people like him. Anna will be there. I don't have time to explain now."

Garrett stood up, taking Molly's hand. "Thank you, Caroline."

"Don't thank me. I'm just sorry any of this ever happened. Go into my father's study down the hall. You'll find pistols and ammunition in there. You might need them. Good luck." Caroline watched as Molly and Garrett left the room. She rubbed her head and closed her eyes. She had taken too much from this man; it was time he was stopped. She climbed out of bed and pulled on a skirt, blouse, boots and a cloak.

"What are you doing out of bed, Miss Caroline?"

"Did you bring me the things, Emily?"

Emily nodded and handed the items to Caroline. There were strands of hair, a ring and a square of material from

383

an oft-worn jacket. "I know what you're planning to do, Miss Caroline."

"Then don't try to stop me, Emily. For once, I want to do the right thing."

"I won't try to stop you. I'll have someone guide you. It's dangerous in the swamp at night."

"Thank you, Emily." Caroline felt strong. It was a feeling she hadn't experienced since she was a small girl taking care of her mother. Ever since her mother had died and Thornston had taken over her life, she had become weak-willed and cowardly. No more. She followed Emily to the cabins and one of the workers led her into the swamp. She wasn't afraid. She followed the man in the eerie blackness and, for the first time for as long as she could remember, she felt alive. When she stepped off the raft and approached the shack, she knew she was doing the right thing. The door opened before she knocked. She looked at the large black woman who stood before her. "Do you know who I am?"

The woman stood aside. "I know who you be."

Caroline reached into the pocket of her cloak and handed the items to the woman. "Then you must use these to stop my father. Right now he could be killing an innocent woman."

The woman took the items. "I have been waiting for you. The time has come." The woman walked across the room and opened a basket, taking out a cloth doll. She quickly pinned the material to the doll, wrapped the hair around its neck, and tied the ring on a string around its waist. "I think this will do." She looked at the pale girl who stood unafraid in front of her. "Do you wish to go back now, girl?"

"No, I'll stay until it's finished."

Anna heard the sounds of music and laughter. She

opened her eyes. She was lying on a mat in the middle of what seemed like a field. She tried to lift her head, but it was too heavy. She shivered and realized for the first time that she had very little on. She looked down at herself. She was barefoot and she was wearing only a thin, white dress. It felt as if she had nothing on. She watched as the people around her danced and sang. It seemed as if their bodies had no bones, as if they moved in liquid motion. Men and women stood next to each other, grinding their bodies against each other, frantic in their movements, and all the time drums beat a rhythm that encouraged the dancers to go faster and faster. Anna shut her eyes. Why couldn't she think? What was the matter? She felt a hand on her arm and opened her eyes. She recognized Richard Thornston immediately, and felt a stab of fear. He pulled her to her feet and held her in front of him as he said some words. Then he dragged her to a pole where he tied her, hands above her head, her waist and ankles lashed to the pole.

Thornston ran his hand along Anna's face and neck. His fingers traced the lace of her bodice. "Perhaps I should take you instead of killing you, eh?"

Anna looked at the man and was reminded of Franklin Driscoll. "I'd rather be dead," she mumbled.

Thornston smiled, pressing his wet lips to Anna's. "You will be dead, my sweet. Have no fear of that."

Nathan and LeBeau crawled through the bushes.

"Be quiet. They have guards with knives. They would think nothing of killing you."

"How do we get in there?"

"Just wait. Let's get close enough to see what is happening."

They crawled to the edge of the clearing. The screams and moans of the dancers could be heard for a long distance, yet no one ever dared bother these people. No one ever tampered with evil. Nathan stopped when he felt LeBeau's arm go out in front of him. They were able to see into the clearing. People moved and gyrated to a drumbeat, their bodies entwined.

"There is Thornston," LeBeau whispered. "By the pole."

Nathan looked at Thornston, but his eyes searched for Anna. He couldn't see her anywhere. He watched Thornston as he walked behind a group of people and then walked back, holding something in front of him. Nathan realized with a sudden shock, that it was someone, not something. Thornston was holding Anna. "God, there she is!"

"Yes, I see her."

Nathan watched as Thornston tied Anna to the pole and ran his hands over her body. "I can't take this, LeBeau. I've got to go in there."

"If you go in there now, you will be killed before you reach the fire. Be patient, my friend. I know about these things. They will not do anything to her for a while. They will dance and drink some more of their wine."

"When do we go in? I can't just watch."

"When they drink some more and begin to dance, we will circle around to where Anna is. Take heart, my friend. She is still alive."

"How do we get her out?"

"We do not get Anna, we get Thornston. Once we have him, they will let her go."

"Are you sure?"

"I am sure. They believe that he is some kind of priest. We will show them otherwise. Come, let us get to the other side."

Roberto grabbed the man from behind, cutting off his

air and hitting him with the butt end of his own knife. The man dropped to the ground. "All right, Cyrus."

Cyrus came out of the trees. "That way, boy. The ceremonies are always on that side."

Roberto followed Cyrus through the trees and into the bushes. They could see into the clearing from where they stood. Roberto searched frantically for Anna. "God," he said softly. Thornston was tying her to a pole. He felt sick to his stomach as he watched Thornston touch her. He also felt intense hatred.

"Be calm, boy. Control your anger. If you want to help the girl, you must think clearly."

"How do we get her out, Cyrus?"

"You must get to the man and kill him. They will not do anything to you or the girl if you kill him. They will see he is powerless."

"Just how do I get down there without being seen?"

"You will know when the time is right. Be patient. The girl is strong and she is good. She will not die."

Roberto looked over at the wise face of the old man next to him and he believed him. He took a deep breath and stood still, waiting.

"Someone is coming," Cyrus whispered. "Be careful."

Roberto backed up against the tree, the knife raised. He steeled himself for another guard, but instead, he saw Nathan. He pulled him over by the tree. "Christ, I almost killed you."

Nathan looked at Roberto. "I'm glad you didn't."

"I'm glad you're all right." He looked past Nathan to LeBeau. "So, you didn't completely betray us."

LeBeau shrugged his shoulders. "I suppose I am not a complete scoundrel, but do not let that get around. I will lose my good name."

"You should be quiet," Cyrus said, coming out of the trees. "We need to be ready. Look, they are forming a circle."

387

Nathan put his hand on Roberto's arm. "Well, I guess there's no time like the present."

"I'm sorry, brother. I don't blame you if you kill me after this is over."

"Let's just make sure we make it out alive, so I can kill you. Come on."

"I will come too," LeBeau said quietly. He drew the pistol from his vest. "I have not shot someone in a long time."

The three men crawled through the bushes until they were behind Anna. They could see the dancers and Thornston as he stood next to Anna. Thornston yelled something in a strange language, and drew a knife from his belt. He held it to the fire, the silver reflecting the firelight. He turned to Anna.

"It is time, my lovely. We cannot have people like you around. You threaten us. You demean us." He held the knife up for all to see.

Nathan and Roberto started into the clearing just as Thornston screamed. It was an excruciating sound. He bent over, holding his chest, gasping for air. The people in the circle closed in on him, frightened. Cyrus pushed past Nathan and Roberto and walked into the clearing, his crooked pole held high beside him, his white hair startling in the firelight.

"Leave him," he commanded, and the people backed away. He stared at the people around him. "Look at him, this man you choose to give so much power to." Thornston fell to the ground, rolling from side to side, screaming for help. "Why is it he is not powerful enough to help himself, eh?" Cyrus reached under his shirt and pulled out a medicine bag. "Do you all see this?" The group backed farther away. "This is medicine made to fight your medicine." He looked at Thornston writhing on the ground. "We can see who has the stronger medicine." He motioned Nathan and Roberto forward.

They cut Anna loose and Nathan carried her out of the clearing while Cyrus stood still. LeBeau stood beside him, his pistol cocked. "I know many of you people, and I am ashamed that you would believe such nonsense. And to believe a man such as this one." Cyrus shook his head. He looked from one face to the next. "I have seen you all, and I will remember your faces. If I hear of anything like this happening again, you will end up like this man, writhing on the ground in pain. Look at him, and remember him well. Go now." The people hurried away, looking much like guilty children. Cyrus walked back to the others. "Take her to the main house. I will come there. I will bring my woman."

"What about Thornston?" Roberto asked.

"Leave him," Cyrus said. "We will come back for the body tomorrow."

The three men exchanged looks, but none of them questioned Cyrus. It was understood that Thornston got what he deserved, however he got it.

Roberto reached out and touched the old man's arm. "Thank you, old friend."

"There is no need for thanks."

"I will go with you, Cyrus," LeBeau said, gently taking Cyrus's arm.

Cyrus nodded and they headed toward the forest and the swamp beyond.

Nathan covered Anna with his jacket and picked her up in his arms. He walked toward the house.

"I can help," Roberto offered.

"I don't need your help, 'Berto. I can carry her myself."

Roberto was silent. He didn't blame Nathan for feeling the way he did. In fact, he didn't expect him to ever speak to him again.

Garrett and Molly ran toward Nathan. "My God, is she all right?"

"I don't know. I'm going to take her back to the house."

"He didn't do anything to her, did he?" Molly asked hesitantly.

"I don't know, Molly. She's drugged, but I don't know what else he did."

"How did you know to come here?" Roberto asked.

"Caroline told us."

"Caroline?"

"Yes, we had just gotten home. We heard Caroline scream and we ran to her room. She told us that her father was trying to kill her, and then she had us get a doll."

"I saw it."

"When we took the pin out of the doll her pain stopped. I've never seen anything like it."

"This is all strange to me. I'll be glad to get the hell out of here," Garrett said.

Nathan hurried to the house, accompanied by his friends and brother. Emily followed them upstairs, explaining what Caroline had done. Nathan laid Anna on the bed, covering her with the bedspread. He quickly got a cloth from the nightstand and dipped it in the bowl. Gently, he wiped her face.

"I can do that, Nathan," Molly offered.

"No, I've been through this with her before. I want to be here when she wakes up." Nathan sat down on the bed next to Anna.

Molly took Emily's arm. "Why don't we go downstairs and get some coffee? I think we're going to need it."

"Nate." Garrett touched Nathan's shoulder. "She'll be all right. She's strong."

Nathan stared at Anna. How much more would they have to go through before they could be together? "If something happens to her—"

"Nothing will happen to her."

Roberto looked at Garrett and walked out of the room. He couldn't take seeing Anna so helpless, and his brother in such pain. All of this was because he had wanted to make Nathan suffer for some supposed wrong. What was wrong with him? He walked to the staircase and sat down. He wasn't sure he could live with himself if Anna died.

"Roberto!" Caroline ran up the stairs, followed by a large black woman, Cyrus, and LeBeau. "Where is Anna?"

Roberto stood up. "She's in her room." Roberto smiled as the large black woman approached him. "Hello, Madam."

Madam nodded. "You are still handsome, boy. You look well, but tired." She looked down the hall. "Why are you not with your woman?"

"It's a long story, Madam," Roberto said, taking her arm and helping her up the last few stairs, "and not one I am proud of. But she is with my brother. They love each other."

Madam walked into the room and up to Anna's bed. She looked at Nathan. "You are the brother?"

Nathan glanced back at Roberto. "Yes. Can you help her?"

"I think I can help her." Madam felt Anna's head. She opened one of her eyes and stared at it. "I have seen it before. It is a drug that these people use, but they mix it with another plant. It can put people into a sleep from which they will never awaken." Madam looked at Nathan's expression. "Do not worry, boy. She be strong, this one." She turned to Roberto. "Tell Cyrus I be needin' my basket. Bring up hot water. It would be best if all of you leave."

"No," Nathan said emphatically.

Roberto walked up to Madam. "Let him stay, Madam."

"It will not be easy for you."

"I don't care. I just want to be here."

Madam nodded. "Take the rag and wipe her down. Make sure you try to cool her body down."

Nathan did as he was told. Madam walked to Roberto. "You stay, boy. I may need your help."

Roberto glanced at Nathan. "No, I think it's best if I go."

"I say to stay here. I may be needin' you. Put your troubles with him aside. Think of the woman."

Roberto nodded. He turned to tell Cyrus to get madam's basket but the old man suddenly appeared with the basket. He was quickly followed by LeBeau, Molly, and Caroline. All but Emily were carrying hot water. Cyrus handed the basket to Madam.

Madam surveyed the group and shook her head. "This be a sad-lookin' bunch. I say I need some hot water, not a whole tub. It be a good thing you keep the fire burning in the cookhouse." She looked at Molly. "You, you come here."

Molly walked to Madam. "What do you want me to do?"

"I want you to take that big pot and put it on this table."

Molly did as she was told. Madam opened her basket and poured various plants into the steaming water. "You keep stirring," she said to Molly, handing her a stick from her basket. She went through at least ten jars, emptying the contents into the water. While Molly stirred, Madam made up another medicine bag for Anna and tied it around her neck.

"Do you need me to take it to the cookhouse? It's stopped boiling."

"No, we don't have time for that." She looked at the tray Emily was carrying. "Give me one of those cups. The rest of you leave the girl in peace. She will never get well with all of you standing around like buzzards." She looked at Caroline. "You did good tonight, girl. Do not

392

be feelin' badly about the man. He was an evil thing."

Madam reached into her basket and took out many candles. "Place these around the bed in a circle and then light them," she said to Molly and Roberto. "You, brother, hold her up for me."

Nathan sat behind Anna on the bed, letting her rest against him. Madam sat on a chair on the other side of the bed. She waited until the candles were lit, and then she moved her hand along Anna's body, from head to foot. While she did this, she closed her eyes and chanted. When she was through she took the cup and dipped it into the water. She brought the cup close to Anna's lips. "It be time to wake up, girl. You must drink."

Nathan held Anna against him, his hand under her chin. He felt her move her head slightly. "Anna," he said softly.

"Be still, brother. She must concentrate on only one thing now." Madam held the cup to Anna's lips. "Drink, girl. It make you well." Anna sipped at the hot liquid, coughing as it went down her throat. "That be good, girl." Madam forced Anna to finish the entire cup, and then nodded to Nathan to let her lie down. "My work is done. It be up to her now."

Nathan looked up at the strange woman, not knowing what to think. He'd never seen anyone like her, or had he?

"Why you lookin' at me like that, boy?"

"You remind me of someone."

Madam smiled broadly, her first display of emotion. "And who might that be?"

"My mother. She was an Indian. She knew a lot about healing. When I was a boy, I used to think she was strange, but I never doubted her ability to help people."

"So, you think I be like her, do you?"

"Yes. You helped my brother, didn't you?"

"It's true, I helped your brother. He was almost dead."

She glanced at Roberto, who was still standing by the door. "But he live because he have such goodness in him. Be good for you to remember that."

Nathan glanced at Roberto. "I've always known that about him. It seems he's the one who doesn't know it."

"I will leave you now."

"Thank you, Madam."

"Do not be thankin' me. She is a good girl." Madam left the room, followed by Molly.

Roberto glanced at Nathan and then started to leave. "Wait, 'Berto."

Roberto stopped. "We can talk later. Stay with Anna."

Nathan stood up and walked over to his brother. "I know we have a lot to sort out, but I want to say one thing. I love you, 'Berto. I never thought of you as anything less than my real brother. When I thought you were dead, I wanted to die too. I went crazy. I didn't even go back home for ten years because I thought mother and father would blame me. Whatever you think about me, I want you to know that I'm glad you're alive. I'm glad to have my brother back. I just hope that someday we can get to know each other again."

Roberto looked at his brother. His brother. Nathan and he would always have that bond; no one or nothing could ever break that. Nathan had always accepted him and loved him for the person he was, and he was still willing to do that. Roberto reached out and put his arms tightly around Nathan. "I'm sorry, Nate; I never meant to hurt you or Anna."

Nathan patted Roberto's back. "I know, 'Berto. It's all right."

Roberto looked at Nathan. "No, it's not all right. Just like it wasn't all right that I ran away from you that day in Chinatown and got us both into trouble. It's time I grew up. I'll pay you back somehow; I swear it."

"You don't have to pay me back. I just want you to

be happy."

Roberto looked at Anna. "I want the same for you. If Anna doesn't—"

"Don't say it; don't even think it."

Roberto nodded. "I'll be outside if you need me."

Nathan nodded. He walked back to the bed and lay next to Anna. He wiped the sweat from her face and covered her. He closed his eyes. Why did it always seem like they had to wait? Why couldn't they just get on with their lives? He forced himself to relax and be patient. Anna would be all right. She had to be.

Roberto was sitting at the top of the stairs when Caroline walked up to him and handed him a steaming cup of coffee. "Drink this; it'll help."

"Thanks." Roberto sipped at the steaming liquid. He looked at Caroline. "You look better than I've ever seen you look."

Caroline sat down next to him. "I feel better than I've felt in a long time. I feel human again."

"Thank you for what you did for Anna tonight."

"It was the least I could do. She suffered needlessly because of Thornston and me."

"It wasn't your fault, Caroline."

"It was a crime of omission, 'Berto. I was too scared to do anything or to say anything to anyone."

"But you weren't afraid tonight."

"That's because you helped me." She kissed him on the cheek. "You were always good for me, you know."

"Richard Thornston didn't think so."

"It doesn't matter what he thinks now, does it? How would you feel about getting to know each other again?"

Roberto put down the cup. "I don't know how long I could live here. This place has too many bad memories."

"But what about Thornston Shipping? You and

LeBeau are the owners now."

"Thornston is dead. You don't have to sign over your stock."

"I know that. I want you to have it. I think you'd be good at running the business."

"What about us, Caroline? Do you think there's anything left to salvage?"

"We'll never know unless we try, will we?"

"I guess not."

"And there is something else. Would you like to meet your son?"

"My God, my son! Do you know where he is?"

"Yes, LeBeau remembered a place father kept in town. He's pretty sure Marie and the baby are there. Would you like to go see him?"

"I'd like nothing better." Roberto stood up, taking Caroline's hands. "You are beautiful, you know."

"You've always made me feel that way." She kissed him softly. "Let's go."

"No promises, Caroline."

"No promises, 'Berto. Let's just give ourselves a chance."

They walked hand in hand down the elegant staircase, only to be met at the bottom by LeBeau. He had a serious expression on his face. "Am I to assume that the engagement is off?" He said with a straight face.

Caroline laughed. "It was never really on, was it, LeBeau?"

"I suppose not." He put his hand over his heart. "Do you know how it pains me that I will not be living here?"

"You're welcome to come anytime. You are like family."

"I should hope so." He stepped forward and kissed Caroline on both cheeks. "I am happy for you, Caroline. It is good to see you like this."

"Thank you, LeBeau."

He looked at Roberto. "And you, my friend, I have some news for you."

"What?"

"I made some inquiries about your wife's sister."

"And?"

"It seems she was sent to live with relatives in the East when her mother died."

"That's it?"

"I am not a magician." LeBeau shook his head. "But it so happens there is more."

"Do I have to beg?"

"That would be nice." LeBeau held up his hands in defeat. "Forgive my mood. I'm not used to feeling this happy."

"LeBeau!"

"Ah, it seems the relatives who took the child in did not want her. She was given to another family with children who raised her as their own. The family came west to settle down, and that is all I know. For now, that is."

"You are amazing, LeBeau. I'll pay you whatever it takes, but please find out what you can. It would be wonderful to be able to tell Anna we've found her sister."

"I promise you, my friend, I will keep looking until I find Anna's sister. Even if it takes years." LeBeau could tell by the look in Roberto's eyes that he was very much in love with Anna. "She has a good friend in you. Or is it husband?"

"Leave him alone, LeBeau. It's all turned out, hasn't it?"

"Yes, it's all turned out. Well, I think I will partake of some of your fine wine, Caroline. I know death is not usually an occasion to celebrate, but in this case . . ." LeBeau wandered off, still talking to himself.

Caroline turned to Roberto. "You're in love with her, aren't you?" There was no malice in her voice.

"She taught me how to love again, Caroline. I want to give something back to her."

Caroline took Roberto's arm and led him toward the door. "You have, Roberto. What greater gift could a person ask for than a friend like you for life?" She smiled. "Come, let's go see our son."

Garrett held Molly in his arms. They lay on the bed, fully clothed. "Are you all right?"

Molly raised her head. "Me? I'm fine. It's Anna I'm worried about."

"You've been through quite a lot yourself. You haven't talked about the fire since we left."

"There's nothing to talk about."

"You don't miss it?"

"Not anymore. I miss Duke, but I don't miss the town. My life was tied up with that saloon." She ran her hand over Garrett's chest. "I have a new life now."

"Have you ever seen California?"

"No. I hear it's big and beautiful."

"It is. There's land as far as the eye can see. My ranch sits in a little valley. I have mountains behind me and the ocean in front of me."

"It sounds wonderful."

"The ranch house could use a woman's touch, though."

Molly leaned on Garrett's chest. "Are you asking me to marry you?"

"Yeah, I guess I am. If you'll have me."

"I'll have you, Garrett McReynolds, in every way that counts." Molly kissed Garrett passionately. "I love you."

"I've been waiting for you to say that." Garrett kissed Molly, pulling her on top of him. He pushed her thick blond hair back from her face and looked into her dark eyes. "I love you, Molly."

Molly kissed Garrett softly and laid her head on his chest. "I don't think I've ever been so happy in my life. Thank you, Garrett. You've made everything seem possible."

Nathan jerked awake, looking at Anna. She was still asleep. He sat up, rubbing his face.

"It seems we've been here before," Anna said softly.

Nathan turned. "You're awake. God!" He pulled Anna to him. "How do you feel?"

"A little tired and hungry, but not bad. I'm not even sure I remember everything that happened."

"It doesn't matter. The only thing that matters is that you're well." Nathan had a strange feeling as he looked at Anna; it was almost as if she had been cured, as he had. It was almost as if Sun Dancer's medicine kept on working, even through other people. He took Anna's hands and kissed them. "I love you, and I want to marry you as soon as you're well."

"I think I have to get a divorce first."

"Well, then, get the divorce and we'll get married as soon as we can."

"I can't believe it. You and I will actually be getting married. Anna O'Leary Hawkins. I like the sound of that."

"You'd better, because you're going to have it a long time." Nathan lay on the bed next to Anna, taking her in his arms. "The last time we were together I told you that my future was with you. I meant it."

Anna closed her eyes. She felt as if she were dreaming. "Are you sure? You want to be with me forever?"

Nathan sat up, a strange look on his face. "I don't know; forever is a long time." Anna hit him and he laughed, grabbing her hands and pulling them up to his chest. "I can't imagine ever wanting another woman as much as I want you. Do you believe that?"

"Yes, because that's the way I feel about you."

"And 'Berto? Have you sorted out your feelings for him?"

"Yes. He's your brother and I love him. I really came to know him these last few months and, no matter what you say, I'm glad it happened. Maybe now we can all be a family." She put her face next to Nathan's. "But you are the man I love and want more than anything in the world. I love you, Nathan. God, how I love you."

Nathan took Anna in his arms and held her to him, knowing that this had been well worth the wait. Perhaps all that they had been through had brought them closer together. Their life and their love was beginning right now.